MIRIANIC OCEAN

N

W   E

S

0   300   600

MILES

PINQUICKLE'S FOLLY

PINQUICKLE'S FOLLY

DEMONWARS SAGA:
THE BUCCANEERS

R.A. SALVATORE

SAGA PRESS

LONDON SYDNEY **NEW YORK** TORONTO NEW DELHI

SAGA PRESS
AN IMPRINT OF SIMON & SCHUSTER, LLC

1230 AVENUE OF THE AMERICAS, NEW YORK, NEW YORK 10020

First Saga Press hardcover edition April 2024

SAGA PRESS and colophon are trademarks of Simon & Schuster, LLC

Simon & Schuster: Celebrating 100 Years of Publishing in 2024

For information about special discounts for bulk purchases, please contact Simon & Schuster Special Sales at 1-866-506-1949 or business@simonandschuster.com.

The Simon & Schuster Speakers Bureau can bring authors to your live event. For more information or to book an event, contact the Simon & Schuster Speakers Bureau at 1-866-248-3049 or visit our website at www.simonspeakers.com.

Interior design by Hope Herr-Cardillo

Manufactured in the United States of America

1   3   5   7   9   10   8   6   4   2

Library of Congress Cataloging-in-Publication Data is available.

ISBN 978-1-9821-7544-3
ISBN 978-1-9821-7546-7 (ebook)

To Diane, to our kids, to our family.

To my friends.

*To those who read these books and walk this
road of adventure beside me.*

ONE

SEA TO SHINING SEA

God's Year 870

(Kueyi Xiuitl)

Eleven years ago, the golden-skinned people with faces marked so distinctly swept across the lands, devouring towns and even the great cities of Honce-the-Bear. They are undeniably beautiful to behold, their skin golden, their facial markings so striking and unlike anything we have ever seen in humans. I have heard whispers, Father Abbot, of a monkey—mandrill, it is called—similarly marked, but I warn now, as before, that these are not animals, not monkeys, not monsters. These Xoconai are men and women, individuals of varying temperament, intelligence, and humor.

When they came in conquest, they were led by a demon dactyl, this creature they called Scathmizzane and worshipped as a god. Even those Xoconai of compassion and mercy thought they were waging a war of goodness, a war to bring the light of Scathmizzane to these lands, our lands. We must never forget that, for to do so is to underestimate these adversaries, and to do so will eliminate perhaps our best chance to turn this tide against the Xoconai.

When they were stopped on that faraway mountain plateau, when their god-figure and its dragon were destroyed, when their crystal of focusing power was taken from them and aimed at their great golden city, only then did we see the truth of the individuals among our enemies. Thus, the war ended in a truce and a pledge of cooperation and cohabitation, human-to-human, and I reiterate now, and argue always, that it was entered in good faith by we of Honce and the Xoconai alike. Two women, a young witch of a distant land and the greatest general of the Xoconai army, found a different way, a better way, a way of peace and hope.

I implore you never to forget that truth.

However, as we have bitterly witnessed, within the hierarchy of the Xoconai many were not pleased with the outcome and the failure of their war. We saw the turn after only three years, when those who were not Xoconai, those who did not wear the facial colors, were once more called sidhe—goblins, lesser than humans, monsters.

Since that time, the Xoconai, most particularly the augurs of Scathmizzane, have worked insidiously to erase all that was Honce-the-Bear. It is God's Year 870 by the reckoning of the Abellican calendar, but no, that too is unacceptable to these zealots, who have once again taken the lead of the Xoconai who now reside among us. We are in Kueyi Xiuitl, Year Eight of Mayorqua Tonoloya, the Golden Empire from Sea to Sea. Yes, Father Abbot, this is a war, albeit a quieter one, town by town, facilitated with fake elections and altered rules and laws, all working against the identity of Honce and the people of Honce. Now, to speak the God's Year, to count the calendar through nearly nine centuries, is greatly discouraged and, in some towns, expressly forbidden.

We are no more Honce-the-Bear. We are Mayorqua Tonoloya, and the year is numbered as eight, as if the eight and a half centuries before did not exist! As if our St. Abelle did not exist!

Darkness is falling all around we humans who do not wear the bright-colored markings of Xoconai in the skin of our faces.

I journey the lands now, and hope to soon return to St.-Mere-Abelle. When last I was there, a half year ago, we observed the tenth anniversary of the battle fought outside those abbey walls, the greatest defeat of the Xoconai invaders. On that day, our adversaries learned that they cannot conquer this abbey. We are too strong, our walls too thick, our magic too deadly and concentrated. They know this still, I am convinced, and I do not expect them to ever go against the might of St.-Mere-Abelle again.

Within those walls, the monks of our sacred order can and should feel safe, for they are. But as I venture about the lands, I see the darkness, my beloved Father Abbot, and I fear that we are safe, but within a prison.

We are no longer considered human to many of the Xoconai. We are sidhe, goblins, and they treat us not as equals, but as servants, even slaves.

My task in this latest journey was to determine what changed in the third year of the truce. And now I have found my answer: gold, Father Abbot. It is as simple and as complicated as that. Gold. The Xoconai have found gold in the south, down the coast past the kingdom of Behren. Gold is their power, their conduit to their god, the source of their magic. Yes, they were willing to share this land in the spirit of the truce until they found the most precious treasure of all. Now we are sidhe, not human. Now there is no Honce, just Quixi, or Eastern, Tonoloya, a part of Mayorqua Tonoloya. Now there is no truce, no sharing. They will reduce us, bit by bit, to servitude, and all in service to their empire, to helping feed their augurs the gold they crave to reincarnate their demon dactyl god, Scathmizzane.

The gold flows up the coast and through the port of Entel, and with the promise of this treasure, I fear the Xoconai will never relinquish their grip on the land of Honce-the-Bear or the people, our people, who live here.

But we must not give up hope. Tuolonatl, who rules Palmaris, remains an ally and has sent word to the west to bridle the augurs.

She would see the truce that she negotiated restored in full. She hasn't the numbers, but her light shines brightly, Father Abbot, and I pray that she will bring many Xoconai of compassion and reason to her side and to our cause.

By the pen of Brother Thaddius Roncourt
Your servant in Abelle, from the city of Palmaris
This Fourth Day of Progos, Second Month of God's Year 870

CHAPTER 1

THE WHISPERING SWELLS

The two figures moved slowly along the uneven and rough stone stairway that ran up the side of the high hill. Although winter was on in full, the vernal equinox still several weeks away, the sky was cloudless and the air comfortably warm. The smaller of the pair, a young woman named Quauh, her Xoconai face coloring beaming in the brilliant sunlight, hopped lightly from stone to stone, moving as if she had too much energy within her lithe frame to maintain such a casual pace.

The other, an old man, kept moving slowly and steadily. He had seen nine full decades of life, and making this climb at all for one of his age was quite a remarkable feat. But he kept going, his breathing steady, calmly lifting one foot before the other, using the rope line strung down on the side of the eight-foot-wide trail for support.

The Basin Overlook was quite deserted this day, with most of the people in prayer in the many golden-domed temples through the Tonoloya Basin.

"Come, Lahtli Ayot," Quauh said when she went over the

last step, only a short rising path before her to the highest point of the Basin Overlook. She glanced back to make sure her old uncle, or lahtli, was moving well, then verily ran up the last expanse to the circular clearing, which offered a full view of the great homeland of the Xoconai. She closed her amber-colored eyes and took a deep breath when she entered that circle, basking in the smells of the desert flowers carried on a strong and warm wind from the northeast this day. She was only a few hundred feet above sea level, she knew, but still, in this low basin, the view . . . ah, the view.

To the west, she saw the distant sea, some eight miles away, the far horizon indistinct and hazy from the ocean mist layer that was so common this time of the year, as winter surrendered to spring. She let her gaze linger there, for always and ever was Quauh called to the great ocean. Eventually, she turned a slow circuit to the right, to the hills in the northwest that formed the northern barrier of the basin, a similar distance from her as the sea. She turned her gaze to the greater mountains lining the east, smaller ones nearby, but moving back more than a hundred miles to high peaks that were still capped in snow. She finished her circuit, turning to the southwest and the haze, and a line of hills that completed the basin wall.

Every view proved beautiful and distinct, showing several large cities within these mountain barriers, clusters of shining golden domes and decorated minarets, and thicker bell or horn towers.

This was Tonoloya, the land of the Xoconai, some thirty thousand square miles of oceanfront, deserts high and low, with a palisade of mountain peaks protecting it on every side that was not the sea—and on the sea, the Xoconai feared no enemy.

When she completed her panorama view, Quauh turned back to the rise, smiling widely to see her uncle plodding along. He wasn't even breathing heavily—the man had mastered the art of pacing himself. Quauh had seen many people much younger than Ayot grab at their sides and gasp for breath as they tried to climb the stairs, or the S-shaped trails that intersected them several times for those who preferred a more leisurely climb.

For the first time, it seemed, since they had begun the climb, old Ayot looked up at her.

Even with the cloudless sky, the sun beaming upon him, his facial colors seemed so dim to Quauh, reminding her that he was so very old and likely had so little time left. She remembered when his nose was brilliantly red, given to blue at its base, and with white wings spreading out to his cheeks. Colors that shone with the inner life and light of a mundunugu warrior. But now that nose was dull, more ruddy than red, and the other colorings might have been gray mud on the face of a sidhe goblin instead of the brilliant facial colorings of a proud Xoconai.

"Ah, Quauh," he said as he approached, and he drew out her name distinctly with each syllable: *Coo-wow*.

He always did that. That was the old and formal way to speak her name, instead of the fast *Coo-ah* she heard more often from her peers.

"This may be my last climb to this place of the spirit," Ayot said.

He always said that, Quauh told herself, but she did wince at his tone, for this time, she found that she believed him, and that made her sad.

He walked up beside her, closed his eyes, and inhaled deeply. "All of Tonoloya in one breath," he said, keeping his eyes closed and seeming very much at peace.

"There is no better place in the world," she replied.

"Where else has Quauh been in the world?"

"South," she protested.

Ayot opened his eyes and chortled. "Barely out of Tonoloya proper. Barely beyond the basin wall."

"Why would one ever wish to leave?"

Now Ayot openly laughed, though it was more of a wheeze, and one that led to some phlegmy coughing.

"You have changed your mind, then?" he asked eventually.

"I know not, Lahtli."

"Because you are scared."

"I am not scared."

"Terrified," he taunted. "And why wouldn't you be? It is a choice that will forever change your life, of course."

She wanted to deny his observations, but she knew that he was seeing right through her. She had been offered a great compliment and a commission—a full commission!—in the Tonoloya Armada. She would be assigned as first mate on a ship for a bit, but within a couple of years would almost certainly be given her own ship to captain!

"It is three thousand miles to the other ocean," Ayot said. "The sidhe call it the Mirianic, I am told, but you will know it as

Tauilueyatl. Do you think it will be as pretty as Laktliueyatl?" He nodded to the west as he asked, to Laktliueyatl, the Sunset Sea.

He had used those names of the oceans purposely, she knew, to emphasize the great distance between them. Sunrise Sea and Sunset Sea, the seas that bordered the fledgling Xoconai empire of Mayorqua Tonoloya after their glorious conquests of the sidhe goblins in the east. The prophecy had been fulfilled, for now the sun rose over one ocean to shine on the empire, and set beyond a different ocean, shining still, unto the last, onto Tonoloya.

"I have heard that the waters are darker in the east," Ayot said after a long silence, he and his grandniece simply taking in the views and the wonderful aromas of the desert flowers. "And colder."

"Are you trying to talk me out of leaving?"

"Hardly!" the old man said, coughing and wheezing with laughter again. "Nay, child, you must go. What is left for you here?"

"My family."

He shrugged. "Here you will serve on a warship that will never see war. Or on a fishing boat—perhaps you will even be given one to captain, eventually. But look at what is before you in the east, my lovely niece. You, Quauh, will almost surely become the youngest captain in the Tonoloya Armada in memory—and I have a very long memory. This honor offered you will bring pride and glory to your father and mother, and opportunities that you will never know if you stay here in the quiet west."

"I will miss them so terribly," she admitted. "I will miss this place—I will miss you!—so terribly. My heart will ache."

"With the golden mirrors, it is only a month's journey," Ayot reminded.

"The magic of the mirrors is reserved. The augurs will use them to bring me to the east, indeed, as that is official military business. But to come back?"

"You will be Captain Quauh of the Tonoloya Armada."

"The magic of the golden mirrors is for the augurs and to move the armies. And for the very important leaders."

"Captain Quauh only to start," said Ayot. "Commander Quauh soon enough. Admiral Quauh, in time. Within a decade, I predict."

She giggled. "You predict it because you are my lahtli, who loves me," she whispered to him.

"No," he quickly answered. "I do love you, but I do not lie to you. You have a gift, girl. No one hears the sea beneath their feet like Quauh. The rolls and the swells talk to you. They tell you of the storms. They warn you of reefs, they show you a place of becalming long before you foolishly enter the dead wind and dead current waters."

She snorted dismissively.

"Yes, you doubt me because you do not understand what others hear from the whispering swells!" Ayot told her. "It comes so easily to you, whether it is the water, the wind, the color of the sky, or all three. Or perhaps in the movements of the fish or the great whales, or the squawks of the various birds. As it is so easy for you, done without conscious thought even, you assume that it is easy for others. But there you are wrong, my dear girl. What you have is a precious gift, and it is so very rare. Why else do you think the commanders of the armada have made this offer to you?"

"Because so few want to go to the far east, where it is thick with ugly sidhe who wish us harm. And fewer still wish to sail in the cold waters of the Mirianic, with its fierce storms and sea monsters, and lanes full of the red 'n' black sails of the buccaneers."

"Bah!" Ayot snorted, seeming more full of energy than since he had begun the climb. "Nonsense! Every fighting sailor wants to go there, for that is where reputation, rank, glory, and gold are to be made," he told her. "You know this to be true. As you know that you have a gift, a great sense of the sea, any sea. My dear, dear Quauh, you are going. You cannot decline this great honor and opportunity. We will all miss you as dearly as you miss us, of course, but any who counsel against you answering this call will forever carry the guilt of causing such limitation on you, Quauh. This is your glory. This is your destiny, and you will be remembered through the ages if you fully realize it."

Quauh started to respond but blurted out a sob instead and fell over dear old Lahtli Ayot, hugging him close and wetting his shoulder with her tears.

She believed that he was right, and even dared to hope that such a path of ascension might indeed lie before her if she took this first, giant step. As an admiral, a commander even, she certainly could gain access to the distance-stepping magic of the golden mirrors to come home to visit the Tonoloya Basin.

13

But that wouldn't be for years. Her tears now flowed because she knew without a doubt that if she accepted the commission and departed the next day, as was demanded of her, this would be the last time she shared with Lahtli Ayot. It would be the last time she heard his wisdom, or felt his love, or looked upon his old and wrinkled face with its gracefully dulling colors.

How could she leave, knowing she would never again see this man, who had taken her into his home soon after her sixteenth birthday a few years before so that she could be exposed to and learn of the huge armada ships in the great ports of the basin?

Ayot was really her great-uncle, the brother of her grandfather, but he had become Quauh's second father these last six years.

How could she leave, knowing she would never see him again?

But how could she not?

"Promise me that you will be fierce when you must be," Ayot whispered in her ear. "The sidhe are filthy and they are dangerous and they are clever. Do not be fooled."

He pushed her back to better regard her, holding her by the shoulders, his expression hardening. "Promise me, gentle Quauh."

She shook her head, revealing her confusion.

"Promise me that there will be no gentle Quauh in the east," he clarified. "I have seen you run far out of your way to flip a floundering turtle upright. I have seen you catch a great fish with your bare hands, then kiss it and set it back into the water to swim free. I know that your mother bought a pig for slaughter and wound up serving a stew of vegetables, because that pig became a little girl's pet."

Quauh beamed a smile. "We did eat it."

"You ate it after it died of old age!"

Both laughed, but Ayot's face hardened almost immediately, and his voice went very even and grim.

"Do not ever lose that quality of mercy, but neither misplace it," he instructed. "No mercy to the sidhe monsters."

Quauh didn't even know where to begin with that. She had never met a sidhe and had heard of them only in war stories. Apparently, these wild goblin creatures came in many different flavors, and none of those seemed very appealing.

"With every dead sidhe, the world becomes a more glorious and beautiful place," Ayot told her.

She nodded.

CHAPTER 2

ANGRY GOLDFISH

On the other side of the continent and far to the south, the pirate ship *Port Mandu* rolled easily above the gentle waves, her stern tugging to starboard with each passing swell. She stayed straight enough, though, for she was tied fast to a mooring ball both forward and aft in the hidden cove the buccaneers used to gain access to the mainland beyond the watching eyes of the Tonoloya Armada.

Half the thirty-man crew was ashore then, trading casks of rum and some booty—fine clothes and some shiny but cheap pieces of jewelry they had graciously accepted as payment from the grateful crew and passengers of a Xoconai merchant ship after they had caught her too far from a patrolling warship and shown them mercy. The capture had proven to be a pleasant boarding, with more wine spilled than blood, and the merchant captain had seemed very pleased to convince one particularly nasty old Xoconai couple he was toting about the south seas to pay the ransom.

Indeed, the merchant captain's only disappointment came

about when *Port Mandu*'s gentlemanly captain, known in Xoconai circles as the Polite Pirate, refused to take the elderly curmudgeons along with the booty. The buccaneers had no use for goldfish, as the Xoconai were called, after all.

Port Mandu's captain, Wilkie Dogears, so named for the large flappers that stuck out from his shaggy hair—ears made even more prominent by generous earrings—paced his deck this quiet morning, the sun barely above the horizon behind him. He tried to be patient but found himself glancing to the jungle shore with every other step, watching for the return of his crew. *Port Mandu* had many contacts in the nearby villages, and this stop to unload the contraband would usually be without much tension, except that this time, there were three Tonoloya Armada warships anchored only a few miles up the coast. A lone patrolling warship was a common sight, two a bit unnerving, but three? Three signaled that something important was happening behind the thick canopy of wide green leaves and howling monkeys.

Durubazzi was a dangerous land, thick with giant crocodiles that could swallow a man whole, giant snakes that swallowed the crocodiles whole, and powerful black-spotted orange cats that dropped silently from the canopy on high to kill their oftentimes human prey before the victim even knew the killer was there.

To say nothing of the Durubazzi warriors, of course, fierce and proud, who knew the jungle and had thrived there, where few others dared to walk, for generations untold.

The Durubazzi had gold, though, and the bright-faced conquerors who had swept through the kingdom of Honce a few hundred miles to the north coveted that metal more than anything. Even the dense and dangerous jungle couldn't protect the native folk from the Xoconai legions.

Catching sight of some commotion in the flora, Captain Wilkie glanced to the shoreline, to see his men hustling out of the jungle to the two dinghies they had hidden in the reeds. They scrambled in and rowed out fast, and Wilkie understood when the canopy parted yet again to reveal a team of goldfish soldiers rushing down to the water, a long and light canoe held above them.

Wilkie's crew had enough of a lead to get to *Port Mandu* first, he realized quickly, but he'd never get the sails up and the ketch away before the goldfish came up alongside.

"Just quietly drop it," he ordered the brown-skinned woman sitting near the small chest of gold on the first dinghy that arrived back at *Port Mandu*. "Between the boat and the ship with not a splash."

The woman, Chimeg, who had a round, flat face, grimaced and spat in the water, even paused and looked back at the approaching soldiers. With a snarl, she did as she had been told.

Captain Wilkie understood her frustration—they had worked hard for that gold, after all. He nodded his appreciation, then started suddenly when he noticed a hollow reed pop up at the dinghy's side and the shadow of a man swimming down from underneath the small boat, very obviously in pursuit of the chest.

"We should just kill them and go get our reward," First Mate Jocasta said when she'd pulled herself over the rail of *Port Mandu* to take her place beside the captain.

Captain Wilkie chuckled but otherwise didn't bother to reply. Hunting ships on the open sea was one thing. Tangling with trained goldfish soldiers and magic-using augurs in close quarters on the shore of Durubazzi with three warships close enough to seal them off from any escape was quite another.

The crew had the dinghies tied against the ketch's side, but to their surprise, Wilkie waved them off when they moved to bring the small boats up to the deck for proper storage.

The goldfish in their canoe came bumping up through the two dinghies soon enough.

"I will have your permission to come aboard, captain," said the woman who seemed to be the ranking officer, given the gold ribbons and medals on her wooden breastplate.

"I would have it no other way, good captain."

"I am no captain. I am mundunugu."

"A lizard rider," said First Mate Jocasta, a tall and lanky brown-skinned woman with long, straight black hair—so black that it sparkled in reflection of the climbing sun bouncing off the ripples in the cove. She walked up to Wilkie's side.

It was an interesting turn, indeed. Those ships up north had brought land fighters to Durubazzi? That put Wilkie at ease a bit, as he figured they'd be less likely to give him chase when he sailed out if they had sent a bunch of soldiers deep into the jungle.

The mundunugu warrior and the others came out of their canoe with practiced order, one going into each of the dinghies to closely inspect it, the other eight, led by the woman, coming aboard, with three moving aft and three forward.

The woman and one other came up before Wilkie.

"Why are you here? You are a man of Honce and far from home."

"Freeport, not Honce," Wilkie countered. "I hold no allegiance to Honce. Never have. I care nothing for the place. Haven't been further than Entel in three decades and more."

"You are Wilkie Dogears?"

"I am honored that my name precedes me."

"They call you the Polite Pirate."

"Life is too harsh for added unpleasantries, although I would disagree with the term 'pirate.' I am a privateer; *Port Mandu* is an honest trader."

That brought a pause and a look that showed her to be clearly unconvinced.

The last two goldfish left the dinghies and came onto the deck to aid in the inspection. No sooner were they aboard when Wilkie noticed a shadow coming back up under the dinghies. Then a dark hand came up to grab the reed, which was still floating against the side, pulling it under, then righting it, quite obviously as a breathing tube.

"What did you bring to trade, Captain Dogears?" the mundunugu commander asked.

"Rum, of course," he answered without hesitation.

"Rum for gold."

"Rum for salt, and fresh water, and a box of meat from one of those giant snakes that swim the rivers inland. One of those can feed a boat for—"

"I do not care." She motioned to the man beside her to inspect

Wilkie, and turned to the others who were crawling about the ship. She sent one up the mainmast to the crow's nest.

"Now, if these boats had brought in contraband Durubazzi gold, how do you expect we would have brought it up to the nest without you seeing it?" Wilkie asked her with a laugh.

She turned a scowl upon him and he went silent, but kept a grin splayed across his face as he slowly shook his head. He wasn't concerned, after all, for there really was nothing on *Port Mandu* to implicate the ship in any illegal dealings. Had these soldiers come out before the dinghies had gone ashore, that would have a been a very different matter, of course.

"Have you no Durubazzi crew?" the mundunugu asked as her soldiers began returning.

Wilkie's ears perked up, for she still hadn't inquired about Durubazzi gold, just a Durubazzi person, apparently.

"None here darker-skinned than the woman who now stands beside the captain," one man answered.

"First Mate Jocasta," Wilkie explained. "Of the kingdom of Behren—the great city of Jacintha, actually. Have you been there, good commander?"

The mundunugu shot him a perfectly hateful look at that, for of course, she had not. The desert kingdom between Honce in the north and these southern jungles was no friend to the Xoconai.

"You call yourself a privateer," she said to Wilkie after the last of her soldiers had debarked *Port Mandu*. "Some would say that makes you a buccaneer."

"Some talk too much," Wilkie replied. "I make a living as I can."

"Then make a better one," she said. "We are searching for a Durubazzi man. A very tall Durubazzi man. If you find him and bring him to me—you know where our ships are moored—I will reward you with thirty gol' bears. Old Honce coin, which is accepted in Behren and across the islands. Unmarked and untraceable, so you will not have to explain to any of my colleagues who make note of it."

Wilkie tried not to appear surprised. Reflexively, he glanced to the dinghies, where the shadow had been, and was glad that it was gone once more. Thirty gol' bears? For a single wanted man?

"Interesting. Pray tell me his name."

"Mantili," she answered, verily spitting the word. "Massayo Mantili."

"Thirty?"

"Thirty. Untaxed, untraceable."

"Might I deliver him tied with arms splayed against my prow?"

"Alive," she said. "We want him very much alive."

"And if he unfortunately dies?"

"Alive," she repeated, turning to leave. "And if you happen upon his corpse, you would be better off pretending you never saw it."

Soon after, the goldfish were paddling for shore, and Wilkie noticed that the shadow reappeared under the dinghy right on cue.

"We will bring the boats aboard, Captain," Jocasta said, staring all the while at the same diminutive To-gai-ru woman who had dropped the box of gold.

"Hold, Jocasta," Wilkie replied, holding up his hand. He subtly nodded his chin toward the water.

"You expect that we will dive for the box?" Jocasta asked, rather incredulously. "It's five fathoms, and who knows what's down there waiting for us? Some giant and toothy crocodile, not to doubt. And the muddy bottom's probably swallowed the chest already. A pity we've no powries among the crew."

Wilkie held his hand up again. "Patience," he said. "And look more closely at the shadows beneath the aftmost dinghy. I believe we have a visitor. Indeed, I believe you towed him out here."

Jocasta's expression became a frown when she followed his gaze. "Boomer!" she called.

A gigantic bald-headed and tattooed man with limbs thicker than a typical man's chest came waddling over from the mizzenmast.

"My good Toomsuba," the first mate said when he arrived at her side, switching to the native islander's real name instead of the nickname, Boomer, she often employed for him. She nodded toward the dinghy.

"A visitor," Toomsuba noted. "Goldfish?"

"Go and greet him. Let us find out."

With surprising agility for one of his size, Toomsuba hopped down into the dinghy, sending a wave out in every direction. He fell to the side, looked back at Wilkie and Jocasta with a surprised expression, then plucked the hollow reed out of the water and tossed it behind him into the dinghy. A moment later, he reached his hand down into the water.

He pulled it back almost immediately, dragging a hand, an arm, a shoulder, then the head of a dark-skinned Durubazzi man. As soon as his face broke clear of the water, the Durubazzi began gasping and spitting, having been caught quite off his guard, it seemed, by the removal of his breathing reed.

After sputtering for a bit, the black man lifted his other arm up over the side, bringing with it a length of rope that trailed back under the water.

With a single heave, the mighty Toomsuba hoisted the man clear of the water and over the side of the small boat.

The visitor looked at the giant islander and gave an impressed nod, then turned his gaze to the captain standing at the rail of the vessel and flashed a wide, wide smile and held up the end of the rope.

"I thought you might wish to retrieve the dropped chest," he said.

"Boomer," Jocasta said, nodding.

Toomsuba took the rope from the Durubazzi and began hauling it up. Sure enough, the small chest was fastened at the other end.

"May I come aboard?" the Durubazzi man asked the captain.

"Do," said Wilkie.

When he stood straight, the newcomer was taller than Toomsuba, though not nearly as bulky. He reached for the railing and began pulling himself up, but Toomsuba grabbed him by the back of his pants and heaved him over so forcefully that he tumbled over the rail and fell to the deck at Captain Wilkie's feet.

"Do indeed, Massayo Mantili," Wilkie said. "And tell me why I shouldn't turn you in to the goldfish."

"I saved your chest of coins," the man protested, and Wilkie smiled at the confirmation that this was the man the goldfish were seeking.

"You are worth more to me than the coins in that small chest."

Wilkie watched the man's expression as he fully regained his footing and standing a full foot taller than Wilkie. He could see that Massayo was searching for an answer here.

"Yes, but the goldfish would also be interested in my tale of how I found the chest of coins you tried to hide from them."

Wilkie scowled.

"They want me alive, good sir," the newcomer said. "Of that I am certain."

Wilkie nodded his congratulations at Massayo's cleverness.

"Still, I could deliver your corpse to them," he reminded.

That didn't put Massayo off his guard, Wilkie noted.

"You could. But I would be worth far more to the goldfish alive than dead. And I assure you that I am worth far more to you than I am to them—if I am alive, I mean."

Wilkie stepped back and turned to the side, sweeping his hand out toward the door on the front wall of the raised quarter-deck. "Do come to my cabin and tell me how that might be," he said. "The goldfish seem quite interested in you. Make me understand."

"So do tell me, Massayo Mantili, why you are so valuable to the goldfish," Wilkie said, pouring a shot of whiskey for himself and for Jocasta, then nodding to the tall visitor to see if he was interested.

Massayo nodded. "Why do you keep calling me that strange name?" he asked.

"Why did your mother give it to you?"

"I am not . . ."

Wilkie was moving the glass of whiskey out toward his guest as the man began the denial, but he pulled it back and changed his smile into a frown.

"Let me be very clear here," Wilkie warned. "You are a clever man—perhaps too clever to be trusted. I know who you are, surely. It was no coincidence that the goldfish commander named a fugitive they had been pursuing, while you just happened to ride out here just ahead of them under one of my shore boats. So, do you wish to be clever, or do you wish to remain alive?"

He held the glass back out and Massayo accepted it, gave a little shrug and a grin of surrender, and took a sip.

"They have taken almost everything from me," Massayo admitted. "And I had a lot to give. They got tired of paying for my goods, I suppose."

"What goods?"

"Is your ship soft-painted to slow a wizard's lightning bolt? To seal the hull?"

Wilkie cocked his head in surprise. Almost every ship sailing south of Freeport was soft-painted, which was the term for brushing the hull with the gooey substance created in the Durubazzi jungles. "A bit, of course, as are all . . ."

"That is me, my doing. The *rubair*—rubber—that seals your hull was my doing. We in Durubazzi have used it for years beyond memory, but I found ways to make it better, stronger. And I put together the workers and the needed, and secret, ways and means to make it plentiful enough and very usable on the larger ships. That was my work. All of it."

"The Mantil Works," Jocasta said in recognition, nearly spitting her drink. "Mantil, Mantili. Massayo Mantili."

The tall, dark man bowed.

"I see," Captain Wilkie said. "The goldfish have stolen your business, then?"

"My warehouses," Massayo answered. He considered it a moment, then shrugged. "But not my secrets. It is my own fault. I underestimated their ruthlessness and stockpiled too much. They were not pleased that I was also selling to the buccaneers, and to the Behrenese warships. Now with me out of business, they expect that if they sink a pirate, it won't be replaced by a ship as well-protected from an augur's lightning."

"If they have the warehouses, why are they so eager to get you, then?" Jocasta asked.

"They have what I produced, but they do not know how I produced it, you see?" Massayo replied, and tapped his temple. "Nor does, nor will, anyone else. And of course, if I am free and begin production again, their designs on weakening the buccaneers or the Behrenese fall apart."

"Then you are worth chests of gold to them," said Wilkie.

27

"Chests of gold I dug for them in their mines," Massayo added, his tone full of bitterness. "If you wish to return me to the goldfish, Captain Wilkie, please do make it my body. I'll not slave under their whips again."

"Now I am confused," said Wilkie. "If you were so valuable to them, if you have in your head such valuable information, why would they put you to the whip in the mines? To break you?"

"Because they only recently figured out that I was Massayo Mantili, after beating my friend to death when they thought him Massayo. They could not break him for information of producing the rubber that he simply did not know."

"And you let him die in your stead?" Jocasta asked threateningly.

Massayo stared at her hard but did not respond.

Watching him, Wilkie understood that Jocasta had hit an open sore here, as this man standing before him had to deal with no shortage of guilt.

After a while, Massayo and Jocasta broke their locked stares, and Massayo turned back to Wilkie.

"What are you going to do with me?"

"It would seem that you are indebted to me," Wilkie answered. "To the price of thirty gol' bears, untaxed and untraceable. Do you have thirty gol' bears, Massayo Mantili?"

"All that I have I wear now as I stand before you, unless of course you allow me to count the chest I recovered, which could be considered mine under salvage law."

"I will not, and it is not," Wilkie replied with a laugh. Behind that jest, the captain also doubted this man's claim of having no other assets, but no matter. "We weigh anchor with the slack tide. I haven't the crew to spare to row you back to shore, so if you wish to return to your jungles, you will have to swim."

Massayo gave a knowing grin. "You would let me do that?"

"No," Wilkie answered. "You owe the thirty gol' bears."

Massayo laughed helplessly and held up his hands to either side in surrender.

"And I am in need of crew," Wilkie explained.

"I am now a buccaneer?" Massayo said with a snort.

"What is there for you to fear? The goldfish already hate you. So yes, Massayo, you are now a buccaneer, and on *Port Mandu*, you are expected to know your place. Your hands will be rubbed raw, I assure you, and you will come to cringe whenever you hear Toomsuba's giggles or First Mate Jocasta's snarls as you go about your many, many chores. But you will not complain and will do as you are told, and with all pride and hard effort."

Massayo tilted his head, seeming amused, but Wilkie was quick to quash that.

"Because you know that at any time, you can be my barter to any warship of the Tonoloya Armada."

The amused grin disappeared.

"How much do you know of sailing?" Wilkie asked.

"Nothing."

"Then be a quick learner and make yourself useful."

"He's a tall one," said Jocasta. "We could always use him to scrub the barnacles from our hull."

"I am sure that would please you," said Massayo.

"More than you can possibly imagine," Jocasta answered, and stabbed a finger toward the door, signaling for him to lead the way out.

Captain Wilkie poured himself another drink when the others were gone. He knew that he was taking a great risk here. The goldfish wanted this man badly—the prudent thing, certainly, would be to turn Massayo Mantili over to them and take the gold. That would also be the responsible thing for him to do for the sake of his crew.

But no, he could not.

He didn't really know why, but something in the gut of the Polite Pirate told him that he could not do that.

Even before the coming of the Xoconai, Wilkie Dogears had lived his life by following his instincts, and he wasn't about to stop now.

Not for thirty gol' bears.

Not for a thousand gol' bears.

Soon after, *Port Mandu* glided away from the Durubazzi coast, the shadows of her sails stretching long before her.

CHAPTER 3

AMBITION AND EPIPHANY

"In the Time of Great Darkness, all of Zalanatl was engulfed," the old augur, Yifca, told Quauh. The pair made their way up a mountainside, a great path of uneven stone stairs not unlike the one that Quauh had walked a month before with her lahtli Ayot. Except this one climbed the side of a mountain, ten thousand feet and more, and not the mere five-hundred-foot elevation of the Basin Overlook in Tonoloya.

Looking back, Quauh was amazed at their progress, even from her own youthful body, but she felt strangely energized here, as if something unseen was lifting her feet. To see this augur, who had to be in his sixth decade at least, so easily ascending only made her believe so even more.

She tried not to be distracted by the sounds of the birds and the cold wind blowing down from the mountain through the trees, and the occasional rustle of brush to the side, where a squirrel, a hare, a deer, or even something bigger might be passing by. There were bears here, she had been told, huge and brown and aggressive. But the augur was unbothered and took this trip every week, and so Quauh just tried to enjoy the change of scenery.

She also worked hard to listen to Yifca's tale, his chant of instruction. She knew the story—or was supposed to, at least—from her childhood studies, but she had never been a good student, and it was nothing that had ever really interested her. As she tried to decipher the last line, she inadvertently spoke her question out loud. "Zalanatl?"

Yifca stopped and turned to her, and Quauh worked to suppress her panic. "It is not a word that you would often hear," Yifca said, seemingly excusing her. "Zalanatl, the Land Between the Seas."

"Mayorqua Tonoloya," Quauh replied.

"A slice of it," said Yifca. "We now name our empire such. But there is much land north of our northern border, and more still to the south. Great amounts to the south. And that is where we turn our eyes now. Lands you will come to know, seas you will sail. For that is where we have found the gold, and we need the gold."

"I understand, Augur Yifca," she said with a bow.

"No, I do not think that you do. I do not think that you can, and that is not your fault, and that is why you were brought here for a few days before continuing your journey to the east." He turned and looked up at the great mountain looming before and above them.

"Behold Tzatzini," he said. "The Herald, who holds in the caves near her peak the great magic crystals. For all the Time of Great Darkness, this land was held by the sidhe, who worship

Cizinfozza. With the power of Tzatzini, one of their witches destroyed the embodiment of that god, and thus signaled we of Tonoloya to bring light, to this place and beyond, all the way to the Sunrise Sea."

Quauh nodded. She had heard all of this, of course, for the events were barely a decade old and had shaken her world in the west profoundly. She turned as Yifca turned, to look back down the mountainside, to the great bowl-shaped chasm directly below and the mountain wall to the right—a wall that had been breached top-to-base to the desert below, two thousand feet, when the Xoconai had retaken Tzatzini.

That bowl now housed Otontotomi, the great City of Gold, a place of ancient temples of their god Scathmizzane, a place of power, a place from which the Xoconai had reached out across the continent to the Sunrise Sea. Truly it was the most magnificent city Quauh had ever seen, full of color and power and art beyond comprehension. It wasn't newly constructed—quite the opposite. Otontotomi had been buried for centuries under a vast mountain lake. A lake drained by the Xoconai by breaching the mountain wall, letting the deep, deep waters flow into a much wider, shallower lake on the desert floor, one full of sails every sunny day, one full of fish to feed the people of Otontotomi.

Yifca closed his eyes and began to recite once more from the ancient text, beginning, as always, "They say and it's been told, and we Xoconai did wait, and were promised that Cizinfozza would meet his end, and in that moment would Kithkukulikhan rise and eat Tonalli and vomit Tonalli, to tell we Xoconai of the light renewed."

"The eclipse," Quauh whispered. She remembered that glorious day, one of her earliest memories, when Kithkukulikhan, the dragon mount of Scathmizzane, ate Tonalli, the sun, and then gave it back.

"I am confused, augur," she dared to say, and Yifca's eyes popped open. "Was that day not the signal that the way was cleared?"

"It was, and so we have created Mayorqua Tonoloya."

"But was not the prophecy the creation of Necu Tonoloya?" She cleared her throat and tried to remember the prayer. "Necu Tonoloya, it will be called, and all of Zal . . ." She faltered.

"Zalanatl, child," the augur prompted.

"All of Zalanatl will be Scathmizzane's," Quauh went on, "ruled by the Xoconai between the seas. In the east, we will watch Tonalli ignite her fires as she rises from the great sea. In the west, we will watch Tonalli quiet her flames as she goes to sleep beneath the waters."

"Yes. Well done, child, to recall the prayers of the Last Augur of Darkness. Those words have great meaning to us, and to you, now that you have been summoned to aid in the fulfillment."

"But Necu Tonoloya, not Mayorqua . . ."

"When we expand north and south to hold all the lands will the prophecy truly be fulfilled, child," Yifca explained. "That will be beyond our lifetimes, I am afraid, but know that you will play your part in this great cathedral we are building to Scathmizzane. We are blessed. We have conquered the lands of Honce and own the seas about her, and with that, we have found new and greater sources of Scathmizzane's—of Glorious

Gold's—precious metal, which brings to us power that our sidhe enemies cannot resist. We do not yet have the numbers of macana footsoldiers and mundunugu cavalry to sweep the dark forests and cold mountains of the northlands, and the desert land to the south is filled with fierce warriors and ruled by a great queen who rides a true dragon. Impatience would cost us all. We watch. We grow, in number and in power. And we wait. Everything in its time, child."

"I hope that I see it," Quauh remarked. "Some of it, at least."

"See it? Young Quauh, you will be a part of it. You will chase the sidhe away and perhaps, if you are lucky enough, you will see the fall of Queen Brynn and her desert lands."

Quauh nodded and recalled her lahtli Ayot's words to her about their less-than-human enemies. *Do not ever lose that quality of mercy, but neither misplace it. No mercy to the sidhe monsters.*

The two continued on their way up the long mountain trail. Even with the magical energy lightening their steps, it took them two full days to finally near the summit and come to a small plateau lined with stone houses and holding a pine-encircled lea on its far end. Yifca led Quauh straight across to those pine trees. As they neared, the young woman could hear the singing of many women. Then, as they moved through the tree line, she saw them dancing, a dozen sidhe, dressed only in light, flowing shifts, moving circles within their larger circle as they lightly stepped about the grass. A thirteenth sidhe woman stood in the middle of that ring, beside a single gigantic crystal protruding from the ground, angled back toward Otontotomi.

"I do not understand," said Quauh.

"This is the God Crystal," Yifca explained. "Once for Ciz-infozza, when the sidhe ruled this land, but now for Scathmiz-zane. Below us are caverns of magical crystals, and through this God Crystal, their energy is being sent down the mountainside to the golden mirrors in our city. Their magic flows across the lands. This is how we are able to step through the miles, mir-ror to mirror. You are but three days out of Tonoloya, already hundreds of miles from our home. In five days more, you will view the Sunrise Sea."

"Because of the magic of the crystals."

"It is essential, yes."

"But why are sidhe dancing about it?"

"Because they know how to best bring forth the power. Scathmizzane himself used this power to destroy sidhe cities, to drop a cliff and the monastery upon it into the sea. But he is not available to us now, his corporeal form destroyed—and who knows how long it will take for him to reconstitute it properly and make a glorious return? Even now our scholars are poring over the prophecies to determine—"

"And so we must use the sidhe?" Quauh asked, and she bit her lip when Yifca scowled at her, a clear reminder that she must never interrupt an augur.

"Yes," he answered curtly.

Quauh knew that she should let it drop, but still she asked, "Why do the sidhe so serve us?"

"Because if they do not, we will slaughter their children be-fore them. Slowly, until they change their minds. It has already been done once, and so will be again."

Quauh swallowed hard. The words hit her as solidly as a clenched fist. In her day in Otontotomi, she had been shocked to learn that there were as many sidhe in the city as Xoconai, performing all the menial tasks, never lifting their eyes to look at her or anyone else.

She had convinced herself that this was due to Xoconai mercy—they weren't killing the wretched creatures, at least.

"How long do they dance?" she asked, needing to change the subject.

"When one tires, another will take her place. We have scoured the lands for many miles around, even from the cities far in the east, to find suitable dancers who are attuned to the magical vibrations of the crystals. The dance never slows."

"Could not Xoconai dancers . . ."

"This is Cizinfozza magic!" Yifca snapped at her. "Ours is gold. We steal the magic of the dactyl Cizinfozza, but would you have us pray to him to beg for it?"

"Of course not, Augur Yifca. My apologies."

He spent a long while just staring at her, his face a mask of disgust. "You are young, and so you are ignorant. You will learn much in your travels, so I will forgive you this time."

Quauh nodded, then bowed appreciatively. But deep inside, she feared that she had already learned a lot, and she knew to her very soul that she did not like that which she had learned.

Quauh went back down to Otontotomi the following day with a different escort, a mundunugu warrior riding his brilliantly green, golden-collared cuetzpali, and Quauh uncomfortably astride a second lizard mount. As she was used to the rolling waves under the deck of the small boats she had so often sailed, Quauh thought it would be easy enough to adapt to the gait of the mount, but with the awkward seating position, half-reclined to keep her feet from dragging beside the short-legged creature, and with the lizard's wildly side-to-side shimmying, she wasn't sure whether she would be thrown off or throwing up first.

Still, they made fine time, the lizards moving swiftly down the mountainside, and that same afternoon, Quauh descended the two thousand stairs into the bowl that held the City of Gold.

After the revelations atop Tzatzini, she viewed the place differently, noting the brokenness of the sidhe, their despondence and their slumped shoulders, many limping from too many hours of hard labor. For all the glorious shining and brilliant light, Otontotomi was a depressing place, she thought.

She was happy to be out of there that very night, sailing across the wide lake formed by the breach in the mountain wall, arriving at the first pyramid set with the golden transport mirrors.

"When first we marched east, we could send you in the dark of night," one of the augurs manning the magical portal told her. "But now, magic is diminished, Scathmizzane has gone home to the southern lights, and we need the sun to properly enact the journey."

Early the next morning, the rising sun gleaming blindingly against the polished gold of the structure, Quauh entered the empowered pyramid. She heard the augurs chanting for just a moment before their words morphed into the sound of an ocean gale, a rushing and whooshing noise, and though she couldn't feel any wind and couldn't see the land speeding past her, Quauh sensed that she was moving faster than the fastest ship, faster than the fastest dolphin, faster than the fastest bird. So much faster, indeed, that when she stepped through a similar structure only a few moments later, she knew, she just knew, that she was hundreds of miles to the east. That led to a long march, some fifty miles, to another portal, and so it was repeated four times over the course of a week, until Quauh stood within the great Honce city of Ursal, the seat of power in the land for several centuries—only now, these last eight years, that power had been in the hands of Xoconai.

She found Ursal crowded and stenchful. A place of too much noise and too little light, with tall, hard buildings crowded together and hordes of people, Xoconai and sidhe alike, crowded together, and the stink of urine omnipresent no matter which way the wind was blowing.

Quauh couldn't wait to be out of there, and fortunately, she didn't have to delay for long. Her journey the rest of the way would be by wagon, and a caravan departing Ursal set out later that same day she had arrived. They made fine time along the well-guarded roads, and within a week, Quauh stood on the docks of the southwestern Mayorqua Tonoloya port city of Entel, looking out at the dark waters of the Mirianic Ocean—the Sunrise Sea of Tauilueyatl, in her native tongue.

It proved to be a disorienting moment for the young woman. When her escort mentioned Freeport isle to the south, she looked left.

"South," the woman repeated.

Quauh looked back at her with puzzlement.

"South," the woman said again, pointing to the right.

"But that is . . ." Quauh stopped and realized her error. When she stood on a beach in Tonoloya, she was facing west. Here, the ocean was east of her.

Here, on this coast, south was opposite.

She spent the next few months proving her skills to the armada commanders by day, and training with instructors in the ways of this new land—socially, politically, and militarily. She learned of Freeport, and what she could and what she must not do there. She learned of the kingdom of Behren and the Chezru Chieftain, the famed Brynn Dharielle. She pored over charts and maps showing the seasonal winds, the currents, and the typical track of great swirling storms that were very rare on the western coast, but all too common here.

After all the work, however, Quauh often still had to laugh at herself when she stood at the coast and had to pause and think about which way was north, which south. That habit, that reflex, of looking left for south, right for north, proved a hard one to break.

By the end of that summer, Kueyi Xiuitl of Mayorqua Tonoloya, which the sidhe of Honce considered God's Year 870, Quauh was commissioned as first mate on the carrack *Uey'Lapialli*, the flagship of the Tonoloya Armada's mercantile fleet, becoming the youngest officer in the Tonoloya Armada in modern times.

Lahtli Ayot had told her that she was special, that she had a gift that was very rare.

In that moment, the ceremony where she was awarded a double-braided golden tassel, for perhaps the first time in her life Quauh wondered if those glowing accolades so often put upon her by her family were true.

TWO

JAWS OF THE *CROCODILE*

GOD'S YEAR 872

SUMMER, TWO YEARS LATER

(MAHTLATLI XIUITL)

My dearest Father Abbot Braumin,

My old friend, I am so pleased to hear that you are well of body and of mind as we near your seventy-fifth birthday. What a journey we have had, you have had, from the days of Brother Avelyn through the Demon Wars and now these new trials at the hands of the painted-faced devils of the west.

I assure you that Vanguard remains free and that St. Belfour Abbey is strong in spirit and in numbers. There are whispers in the western reaches of Vanguard and near the Barbacan that a new ranger patrols the areas with the centaur named Bradwarden. He is a man of the west, they say, one who battled the Xoconai, and one who once served beside Tuolonatl in Palmaris.

That is all we know of the situation at present. Whatever the cause, the Xoconai have not threatened us. Nor do their ships pursue ours in the Gulf of Corona. Their new ships, built in Amvoy and Palmaris, sail out of the Masur Delaval, then straight east across the gulf, taking no heed of our sails to the north. No doubt their eyes are in the east and south and the gold trade they have discovered.

That you have received this letter (indeed, I hope that is the case) is proof that we can cross the gulf safely. Our ships are strong and swift, and brothers with gemstones line their decks, ready to rain holy fire and lightning upon any who threaten.

I know that St.-Mere-Abelle shines as the brightest beacon to those who would follow our Abellican Order, and know, too, that your walls bend under the weight of refugees in these dark times. Thus, I beg you, my friend, to fill our ships with food and water and any who would come and live in peace in Vanguard. We have the room and the air clean of Xoconai stench.

Send them, my friend, and know that I will protect them with all that St. Belfour can offer.

The invitation extends to you and my brothers and sisters as well, of course, though I know you will refuse and I agree that you should. You are the beacon, my old friend. Your name, Father Abbot Braumin Herde, brings hope to the people of Honce. If our old land is ever to be liberated, the battle will begin at St.-Mere-Abelle, to the proper misery of the painted-faced devils of the west.

Be well, I beg. The whole world begs.

As always and forever in the love and light of St. Abelle,
Abbot Holan Dellman of St. Belfour Abbey
This Third Day of Octenbrough,
the Eighth Month of God's Year 872,
which the Xoconai, in their arrogance, name as Mahtlatli Xiuitl,
Year Ten of their Mayorqua Tonoloya Empire

CHAPTER 4

THE *SWORDFISH* AND THE *CROCODILE*

Captain Aketz of the *Cipac* lowered his spyglass and looked to Ahmaddi, the skinny Behrenese man standing beside him.

Ahmaddi shifted nervously, which brought a little grin to the face of the Xoconai captain. Aketz Fiatl was not a tall and thick man, standing just over five feet. Few had expected him to survive his earliest days, so sickly was he, and never in his life had he been physically imposing. But he more than made up for that with the severe widow's peak of his raven hair and the set of his small black eyes—too close together beside his thin, long, and hooked nose—which verily glowed bright red as if with unrelenting anger. The ability of Captain Aketz to shatter the nerves of those around him had only grown with his reputation as he sailed these eastern waters, offering no quarter to those who would impede the glory of the growing Tonoloyan empire.

Aketz tried not to laugh and break the spell, but the man's appearance alone amused him. This one was so skinny indeed that his black hair and beard extended out beyond his shoulders!

"What is her name?" Aketz asked.

"The *Swordfish*."

"And her captain?"

"Jocasta. Captain Jocasta. She hails from my village."

"And she is a buccaneer? She sails her ship under the red 'n' black?"

The small man shifted in a strange and jittery fashion but nodded emphatically.

"Or is she just a woman who scorned you?" asked Cayo, the *Cipac*'s first mate and high priest, who was standing just to the side.

"I would not lie to you. Why would I lie to you?" Ahmaddi stammered.

"For the reward, of course," answered Cayo. "And for revenge."

"No, no, she did not scorn me," Ahmaddi said. "No, no. She dishonors my village, but only because she is a pirate."

"If she is a pirate from a village within Behren, does she not sail with a Letter of Marque and Reprisal from Chezru Chief Brynn Dharielle?" Captain Aketz asked.

Ahmaddi swallowed hard, his obvious panic weakening his claim. He was turning in a pirate and he wanted the reward, and more than that, he wanted to stay in the good graces of the ferocious Captain Aketz.

"So how does that dishonor your village? Is she not in service to your queen?"

"Not all of Behren agrees with Chezru Chieftain Brynn," Ahmaddi quietly replied.

"More likely, the reward of gold allows Ahmaddi to care less about such politics," said Captain Aketz, and he snapped his telescoping spyglass closed and shook his head, starting away.

"But that does not take the name of *Swordfish* off her stern," Ahmaddi pleaded.

"A name that means nothing to us," Cayo answered as the captain walked away. The tall and broad-shouldered first mate hunched his golden-colored robes to make himself appear even larger, then leaned over Ahmaddi, making the man appear, and clearly feel, even smaller.

"Because she is new to the waters," Ahmaddi sputtered. "She is just out . . ."

"Convenient," said Cayo. "And you, of course, knew of her, and her intent, before the Tonoloya Armada had ever heard of the ship? Before a single report of a skirmish?"

"Sister ship to *Port Mandu*," Ahmaddi blurted, and Cayo fell back.

"What did you say?" demanded Aketz, who was several steps away.

"Jocasta . . . now Captain Jocasta, who was first mate of *Port Mandu*," Ahmaddi explained. "Captain Wilkie Dogears caught her a ship. That ship, the *Swordfish*. She is his second, his escort, his flank, his . . ." The man held up his hands, searching for a word to better explain in this language, Xoconai, which was not his native tongue.

Aketz came forward again and telescoped his spyglass, suddenly very interested once more. He had never heard of the *Swordfish*, but the *Port Mandu* was a different matter altogether.

"Who have we aboard who knows anything of Captain Wilkie and his crew?" Aketz asked Cayo.

"I will see," the man replied, and rushed away.

"You believe me now?" Ahmaddi asked.

Aketz turned a scowl his way, sized him up and down without bothering to hide his contempt, then went back to his spyglass.

"I will be given the reward, yes?"

"If you do not shut up, you will get wet. Very wet, and very quickly."

Ahmaddi swallowed hard yet again and shifted from one foot to the other, something he continued doing for some time, until First Mate Cayo returned to the captain's side.

"The *Port Mandu* was known to have a Behrenese first mate," Cayo confirmed. He turned to look at Ahmaddi as he finished, "A Behrenese woman named Jocasta."

"Your fellow augurs would minimalize my efforts here to secure the seas," Aketz remarked.

"Captain?"

"They seek better ways to move the gold. They fear the pirates."

"No, Captain Aketz," Cayo answered, shaking his head vigorously. "They know that the buccaneers must be defeated fully and forever, and that Captain Aketz and *Cipac* are the spear to skewer the foul sidhe."

It was a rehearsed line, Aketz recognized. There was a measure of truth to it, perhaps, but he knew that his superiors in Entel were growing frustrated by the continual nuisance of the buccaneers, particularly because of their alliance with the dangerous kingdom of Behren. In normal times, Aketz would have monitored the *Swordfish*, perhaps approached and boarded her to ensure that she had no ill-gotten loot aboard.

But these were not normal times. He needed a prize.

A kill.

"Full sail," Aketz ordered. "Keep us just to her starboard. Do not let her turn for the shallows."

Aketz didn't bother to look over at Ahmaddi anymore, but he didn't try to suppress the grin on his face, even though he knew it would put the little snake of a man more at ease. He couldn't deny the truth of this opportunity. Wilkie Dogears had finally been caught in an act of piracy, only a few weeks before—perhaps even the incident that had allowed him to acquire this ship. Ever had the Polite Pirate escaped Aketz's wrath, and so he would again if Aketz allowed some time to pass, some time for Wilkie to once again charm with gold those Xoconai captains and merchants who listed the wanted buccaneer outlaws. The sister ship to *Port Mandu* would be a prize in this short window of opportunity, no doubt, and *Port Mandu* a bigger one still.

He considered the possibilities. He could shadow this square-rigged sloop and hope it would lead him to Wilkie—he had no doubt that the *Cipac* could sink them both in a single battle. But no, he decided. He'd take this ship alone and get his answers from any who survived the battle.

The *Swordfish* wasn't going to see land again, he decided.

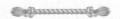

Captain Jocasta paced in circles around the mainmast of the *Swordfish*, glancing up every few moments to Chimeg, who stood tall in the crow's nest, peering intently astern.

"It's a hunter, no doubt," said Calloway, the first mate. "And a big one."

"Many of the big Tonoloya ships are for cargo," Jocasta reminded him.

"How many cargo ships pursue buccaneers?" Calloway came back, and Jocasta stuttered in search of a reply.

Chimeg came down beside the two, then, sliding easily along a rope to the main deck.

"Three-masted," she said. "Rigged both square and lateen, and sailing under the flag of the Tonoloya Armada."

"A frigate. Then it's the *Crocodile*, to be sure," said Calloway.

"Cipac," Jocasta murmured, the formal name of the ship, the Xoconai word for "crocodile." "What would Captain Aketz want with us?"

"Same thing he wants with every buccaneer," Calloway said through clenched teeth. The man slapped a hand against his leg and spun away, spitting curses under his breath.

"We fly no red 'n' black," Jocasta reminded him. "We have attacked no one. To all, how can we be known as anything more than a simple trader? These lanes are filled with traders."

"We have been seen as Captain Wilkie's escort these last weeks," Chimeg noted.

"Or we have been seen as sailing under the protection of the *Port Mandu*," Jocasta decided. "And that is the story we must present."

"Then you mean to let them catch us?" Calloway asked.

"We cannot outrun them," answered Chimeg. "And they remain pointed between us and the shallows, where we can go and they cannot."

"I do not mean to let them do anything," Jocasta assured the first mate. She shielded her eyes with her hand and looked to the westering sun. "Hold our course until the cover of night, then place one of the hourglass decoys and take us hard to port and the open waters."

That brought some raised eyebrows from the two beside her.

"Straight east, then back to the north," the captain explained. "If we can fool the *Cipac* even for a single night, we can run for Freeport before they can catch us."

"And if not?" Calloway asked, but he was nodding in agreement with the plan.

"Then we keep our red 'n' black stowed and present ourselves as simple traders, out on the waves on our maiden voyage."

"A simple trader with that?" Calloway asked, pointing out the catapult on the *Swordfish*'s raised quarterdeck.

"If we again see *Cipac*'s sails when the sun rises, dump it off our starboard rail," Captain Jocasta ordered.

"Dump our catapult?" Calloway's mouth hung open as he finished.

"Do you think that we can fight Aketz? Do you believe that a few throws of that meager war machine will cripple the *Cipac* enough to keep us ahead of her?"

"Permission to speak freely?"

"Of course," said Jocasta.

"I think I would rather be scuttled in a fight than just surrender," Calloway replied bluntly.

"Even if it means your death?"

"Yes."

"Even if it means the death of all aboard?"

"Did anyone here sign their papers without knowing that possibility?" Calloway replied. He gave a little snort. "How many of the original buccaneers are still alive? We all know our fate, captain, and all knew it when we decided that we'd rather live short and free than live long under the weight of Xoconai oppression."

Jocasta looked to Chimeg, who pulled her compound bow off her shoulder and held it tight against her. "As long as I kill more of the goldfish, I die content," the deadliest of archers said.

Captain Jocasta nodded to her dear friend, the only member of Wilkie's crew who had joined her when she had acquired her own ship, taken in a pursuit when the crew had abandoned her to the chasing *Port Mandu*. "Perhaps it will not come to that. Let us see what the morning light shows us."

"Do you believe it will really help?" Aketz asked Cayo and the other augurs who had gathered in his cabin. Dusk was falling about them, with their prey still some distance ahead. They had closed the gap, but Aketz, realizing he could not catch the *Swordfish* before nightfall, had slowed. If their prey knew of the pursuit, keeping them located in the dark night would prove no easy task.

"If you expect it to ignite her sails, then no," Augur Cayo admitted. "But it will dry them to better prepare them for arrows and pitch."

"It seems a lot of work for minimal gain," Aketz said, shaking his head. He looked at the contraption the augurs had brought to him. Its center was a large, multifaceted crystal ball, one set on a pike so that it could be spun. It was surrounded by a quintet of narrow, waist-high sheets of polished gold. "You will take all my augurs from the fight for many minutes to accomplish something minimal or not at all."

"You must be forward-thinking, Captain Aketz," said Cayo. "We have been three years of near-constant sea battles. Our enemies improve their designs. Once, a simple fireball would light up the sails. A simple lightning bolt could split a hull. Now they have perfected gels to wet the sails, and that . . . *caoutchou*, that rubber, to seal their hulls. Our enemies' vessels are growing faster and stronger, and so we, too, must pray to Scathmizzane for guidance that we can continue to properly vanquish them."

"Then you use *Cipac* as a trial platform," Aketz said sourly, his tone reminding them all that Cayo had not been his original first mate, and that he had never meant for the augur to ascend to such a post. Most in the room had witnessed the shouting between Aketz and City Sovereign Popoca of Entel that day two years previous when Popoca had informed the captain of the change in his crew.

Cayo laughed the thought away. "The *Cipac* strikes fear

into the hearts of the buccaneers. With Scathmizzane's golden light, that intimidation will only grow. A trial platform? No, my captain, we view *Cipac* as the only hunter worthy of our efforts, and as we strengthen the power of Scathmizzane-granted magic, your legend will only grow. Truly and clearly, this is the flagship of the Tonoloya Armada in the east. And when we are done, the *Cipac* will be on the lips of every Xoconai throughout Mayorqua Tonoloya, spoken with pride and reverence, while our enemies utter . . ." He paused and looked to his fellow augurs. "What is the sidhe word?"

"Crocodile," answered one.

"Ah, yes, the sidhe from Durubazzi to Vanguard and everywhere in between will tremble and glance about nervously as they utter 'the *Crocodile*' with a very different manner of respect."

All about Cayo, the augurs nodded and murmured quiet prayers.

Captain Aketz knew they were playing on his vanity here.

But so be it. He wasn't a religious man and only attended the services to avoid scandal, but he couldn't deny that the augurs had proven themselves over and over again in the last battles. Whether this new toy they had brought aboard would prove useful or a waste of time, he owed it to them and to Popoca of Entel to give them their trial.

"If it is ineffective, you will fast abandon your attempts and return to the duties of our last battles," he told the first mate.

"Of course, my captain. But by the will and promise of Scathmizzane, it will not be ineffective. Believe, my captain. Believe."

Aketz mulled on that for a bit, then nodded and told Cayo to make sure that the *Swordfish* could not get close to the coast of Behren. Knowing it would be a long and dreary day, the captain then retired to his chamber, climbed into his hammock, and considered the best ways he might use this opportunity—if Ahmaddi wasn't lying—to somehow get to Captain Wilkie Dogears.

The originals were always the best trophies, after all.

With fantasies of scuttling *Port Mandu* dancing in his head, Captain Aketz dozed, sleeping lightly, but enough so that he was a bit confused when he looked across his room to find it dark.

He rolled out of the hammock, straightened his clothing and hair, and went out onto the deck with the stiffened gait, straight back, and high chin expected of Xoconai aristocracy.

He found Cayo standing on the forecastle deck, leaning on the top ladder post, and staring out to the south, at the dark sea.

"Still so far ahead?" Aketz remarked when he joined the first mate, immediately noting the stern light of their prey some distance ahead. "*Swordfish* is faster than we thought, it would seem."

"We were gaining faster before the sun set," Cayo answered. "I do not think we have closed at all since the onset of night."

"She's carrying a second sail set, do you think?" Aketz asked, drawing forth his spyglass. "There are whispers of exotic vessels that can raise side sails like wings to better catch a trailing wind, as we have this night."

He lifted the spyglass and focused in on the distant light.

He couldn't make out much about it, though, for it was simply too far away.

But then he noticed that it was bobbing and bouncing considerably, much more than he would have expected in the calm seas now beneath his own ship's sturdy hull.

He lowered the spyglass and considered that for a moment, even started to ask Cayo about it.

Then Captain Aketz blew a long growl and a resigned chuckle, figuring it out.

"Sinking sand light," he told Cayo.

The first mate looked at him in puzzlement.

"They dropped a raft or a dinghy," Aketz explained. "And upon it, they placed a running light, a large candle, supported on a platform that rested on a bed of fine sand. Like the top of an hourglass, and with the sand running below, slowly, sneakily, lowering the lantern."

"To make it seem as if they remained ahead of us," Cayo reasoned.

"And to make us think that they were indeed pulling away from us."

"So they must be if they are running ahead of this decoy . . ." Cayo didn't even finish the thought before he noted Aketz's amused and perhaps disappointed expression. The first mate realized his error then and just sighed and shook his head.

"How long have we been sailing in full darkness?" Aketz asked, looking up at the stars.

"Less than two hours."

"And how far ahead of us was the *Swordfish* when last you saw the ship itself?"

"Perhaps two hours. No more than three."

"Then expect that we'll be up on this drifting decoy soon enough."

"But the *Swordfish* will be long in front of . . ." Again, Aketz's look stopped him and corrected his reasoning.

"She turned," Cayo said, and the captain nodded.

"You have kept us straight and angled to her starboard?"

"As you commanded, yes."

Aketz looked around the forward rail, then up at the crow's nest at all the assigned lookouts, all seeming diligent, as he knew his crew would ever be. If the buccaneers had turned to starboard to run for the shallows, someone would have likely, or at least possibly, seen *Swordfish*'s silhouette.

Captain Jocasta had trained under the clever Wilkie Dogears. She would know that.

Captain Jocasta had trained under the bold Wilkie Dogears. She hadn't headed for the coast of Behren.

"Half to port, Cayo," he ordered. "All lights out, all decks. Line our port rail with watchers and tell them to keep their eyes staring just above the horizon."

"You think she went to deeper waters?" the first mate asked, the surprise in his voice evident.

"I think she might already be past us out in the east, sailing north for Freeport," Captain Aketz replied. "A ghost in the night, while we are chasing a lantern."

Cayo stepped ahead, peering intently forward, shaking his head as if he didn't believe they had been deceived.

"Should we not find this decoy and ensure—"

"Half to port," Aketz told the man. He produced a small

sandglass and handed it to the first mate. "Ten-minute intervals," he explained. "And with each passage, take us ten degrees farther to port until our bowsprit is aiming straight for Freeport. The pre-dawn glow will show us her sails, and then she is ours."

He saw the first mate's doubting expression, but he didn't give Cayo any signs that it was warranted.

Even though those doubts were valid, of course.

Aketz was guessing, playing his gut here. He knew what he would do if he was being pursued by a ship he could not hope to fight, and he was a fine captain.

Captain Wilkie was a fine captain, too, daring and unconventional.

Now Aketz had to hope that the Polite Pirate had passed that cleverness on to his protégée.

A feeling of uneasiness accompanied Captain Jocasta's awakening senses when the pre-dawn light entered her cabin.

She knew they had executed the ploy perfectly, and by all reasoning, the run to Freeport should be clear and easy.

But she knew, too, that this was Aketz and *Cipac*—the *Crocodile*—giving chase.

She hadn't undressed when she retired, so she gathered up her sword and went out from her cabin quickly.

She looked to the east, to the brightening sky.

She turned to the west, peering into the gloom.

The daylight growing by the minute, and soon the full and ample sails of a three-masted frigate came into view, ghostly in the gray of the marine layer. Jocasta knew that the warship had a better view of the *Swordfish*, with the pre-dawn glow behind her, than she had of them.

"To starboard and out to the open sea?" First Mate Calloway asked, rushing over to her, Chimeg beside him.

"To what end?" Jocasta replied. "That would only admit our guilt."

"Did we not already do that with our ploy?"

"The flag of the *Cipac* was not visible to us then, so perhaps we tell them that we thought her a buccaneer. Now it is visible. Captain Aketz knows now that we know we are being pursued by a Tonoloya warship."

"You don't believe that," Calloway remarked.

Jocasta rubbed the remaining weariness out of her face. She wanted to argue, but he was right, of course. That excuse would not work.

"Wake all the crew and bring them up here," the captain ordered. She moved to the port rail, leaning heavily upon it and staring out to the southwest and the swift-sailing warship. Even if they turned and tried to flee straight away from her, her considerable war weapons would be in range long before the morning sun reached its zenith.

She had barely begun her contemplations when Jocasta was distracted by Chimeg, who had cut her wrist and was bleeding it into a pail. The To-gai-ru had quite a bit of red liquid in the bucket and covered it tightly with a cap of rubber as the crew gathered all about.

"What are you doing?" Jocasta whispered to Chimeg before addressing the others.

"Being clever. I do not intend to die out here without finding every opportunity."

"So, you would prefer that we surrender?"

"You think that a possibility?" Chimeg's tone was almost mocking, and Jocasta winced at the edge in her voice.

The captain shook it away as the crew gathered about.

"We cannot outrun the *Crocodile*, and we know her reputation," Jocasta told them all. "Three choices I see before us. We can dump our catapult starboard and pretend that we are simply a trader heading for Freeport."

"They're close enough to see that," one woman replied.

"Traders don't turn one-eighty after sunset," another man chimed in.

"Or we can strike and surrender," Jocasta continued, trying not to grimace at the doubting comments. "My life will be forfeit, but so be it."

"Others, as well!" someone said.

"Calloway!"

"Chimeg!" another added. "She is the scourge of the sea, raining death arrows from her perch in the nest! Killing her would be a true feather for the cap of Captain Aketz."

Jocasta looked to Chimeg, who merely shrugged. If she was the least bit concerned, she wasn't showing it.

"Still, it is possible that many of you will be spared," the captain told them.

"Spared to work as galley slaves or deck swabs under goldfish whips!" one said, to many agreeing replies of "Aye!"

"Then what's the third choice, Captain Jocasta?" asked the woman who had first spoken. "Tell us the third!"

"We fight," Jocasta said, and before the words had even left her mouth, the cheers rose all around her.

"We cannot beat the *Crocodile*," Jocasta warned.

"If I kill two goldfish afore they cut me down, I'll be dying with a grin that'll follow me all the way to St. Abelle's waiting arms," said that same woman, and again came the agreeing calls and cheers.

"Bah! But he'd only catch the likes o' yerself to throw ye back to the waitin' claws o' the demon dactyl!" another woman taunted, and all had a good laugh.

The captain was taken aback by the remark, the reply, and the cheering, but when she leaned back on her heels and considered it, Jocasta found that she really wasn't surprised. These were buccaneers, pirates, running in waters thick with powerful warships, knowing that every sail could be their last, and that one most surely would. There were only a few ways out of this life: scurvy, dead from the weather, whether becalmed or taken by a storm, or killed at the end of a goldfish macana.

They knew it. They didn't just say it, no, but they *knew* it, and had known and accepted that fate from the moment they had decided that their lives free and full of flavor were worth that inevitably early death.

And now they were showing the truth of that. Jocasta looked all about her crew of twenty-five and saw not a doubt or a regret.

"As she nears range, Mister Calloway," she said, "put her on our stern and fill our thrower with chain. Maybe we will find some luck and take enough of her sails to let us get away."

"Not with a dozen shots," she heard Chimeg whisper grimly, and Jocasta looked down to see the archer sitting by her pail of blood and chuckling softly.

She dismissed the crew and turned to her dear friend. "How many will you kill today?" she asked.

"If less than a dozen, know that I die disappointed."

"Here's hoping that you get a shot at Aketz himself, or an augur."

Grinning wickedly, Chimeg pushed her pail of blood aside and pulled another bucket over. When she removed the rubber cover of this second one, the stench of the chamber pot nearly gagged Jocasta. She fell back and covered her mouth and nose with her hand, watching as the archer dipped her many arrows into the feces, one by one.

"And here is hoping that they die slowly," Chimeg said, taking up her bow and quiver and heading for the crow's nest.

The sheer coldness in her voice unnerved Jocasta. She only heard such a venomous tone from the normally calm lookout when the goldfish were involved. She didn't know much of Chimeg's past, as the woman didn't speak much of her years since leaving the steppes of her homeland in the distant west. Jocasta was certain that something bad had happened to her friend at the hands of the Xoconai.

She hoped Chimeg would get some measure of revenge this day.

Cipac was truly coming on fast, and the *Swordfish* began her starboard turn before Chimeg had even reached the nest. Even then, running straight at full sail away from the warship, the distance was noticably closing by the minute.

Jocasta went to the quarterdeck, all the way to the taffrail, to study the predator—and truly the *Cipac* looked the part. Her bow was flared on either side by side-mounted catapults, readied and pulled to throw, and appearing like the widely opened jaws of a striking snake or, fittingly, like the flared maw of a crocodile.

"Captain, we're coming into range," one of the catapult crew called to her.

Jocasta looked to her catapult, a small thrower, neither accurate nor particularly strong. She glanced back at *Cipac*, at those "jaws," and knew them to be far superior.

"If we are in range, they certainly are," she mentioned to Calloway, who came up the ladder beside her. "And have been for some time."

"They see our catapult," the first mate replied. "Why are they holding their shots?"

Confidence, Jocasta knew, but didn't say. There was no need to heighten the tension any further on the deck of the *Swordfish*.

"But now we can hit them," Calloway pressed.

The words leaked out of Jocasta's mouth before she could reconsider. "They don't care."

She spent only a moment reminding herself that this wasn't

some prelude to a call for surrender, and hearing again in her mind the determination of her crew not to become slaves of the goldfish. She moved past Calloway to the rail. "Fire at will," she told the man, and she went back down to the main deck. Before she had crossed the bottom step, she heard the great rush of the beam and felt the shudder as the *Swordfish*'s first volley flew away.

Captain Jocasta rushed to the rail and watched the chains flying away through the air like a rumba of the flying jaculi rattlesnakes of the Durubazzi jungles. The throw was perfect, a couple of the chains hitting the *Cipac*'s jib, while most soared in against the square foresail.

As she had known, and feared, the heavy canvas held its ground. There were tears, of course, but little to slow the hunter.

She heard Calloway frantically calling for the crew to reload.

Jocasta blew a resigned sigh. She had guided *Port Mandu*'s capture of this light sloop only seven weeks before. She had overseen the reconditioning and the renaming of the vessel, officially inaugurated as the *Swordfish* only three weeks ago.

This was only her third sail since that recent launch, and her first away from the Behrenese coast.

This was certainly the *Swordfish*'s last sail.

Jocasta stepped back from the rail and put her back to the quarterdeck ladder. She took a deep breath, trying to come to terms with the near certainty that her life would end this day. She thought she had been ready for it, but now that the moment fast approached . . .

She had to think of her crew. She had to give them the best

chance to work this into a surrender of some sort, at least, no matter their stated desire to fight to the death.

She turned for the wheel, thinking to help out as the battle closed, but a cry of surprise and concern from the quarterdeck had her rushing back to the rail and peering out at the warship.

She winced at the sting of the brilliant light and turned her head, shielding her eyes, then peeked out carefully at the impossibly bright flare on the *Cipac*'s forecastle, like a bit of the sun itself stolen from the sky. She didn't stare at the source of the light itself, but did indeed watch with unblinking fascination as a different sort of light altogether streamed out past the warship's bowsprit.

Like a living serpent, flat and wide, it swerved left and right, up and down, as the swift-sailing ship bounced and rolled. Slowly, tantalizingly, the unnatural wave of illumination reached forward, closing the gap between the vessels.

"What is it?" she heard Calloway yell out from above her. She looked up to see the man backing toward the ladder.

"Load and throw!" he ordered his artillerists. "Hit it! Hit it!"

The serpent light neared the *Swordfish*'s stern, then rolled upward and over the taffrail.

And the screaming began.

Calloway jumped down from the quarterdeck, tumbling to the planks, then rolled about, his hands trembling as he tried to grasp his face—and both of those hands and his face were beet red, as if he had fallen asleep for a week in bright sunshine.

Jocasta moved for him, but fell back when the serpent light

passed over her, going against the sails, which began to hiss immediately, wisps of smoke appearing in various spots.

The captain had no idea of what to do, of what order to give to counter . . . whatever this was. She had been sailing these seas for years and had never witnessed, had never heard any wild stories of, anything like this.

But the light passed. The sails weren't burning, and Calloway sat up, his face bright red but hardly disfigured.

"What?" he asked, holding his reddened hands out wide.

Before she could answer, Jocasta heard the crocodile jaws of the warship spring, and cries of "Cover!" echoing all about her ship.

Before she even saw the swarming bits of burning pitch, before the air filled with dozens of flaming arrows behind those catapult throws, Jocasta had solved the mystery.

They had dried out *Swordfish*'s sails and her quarterdeck, had turned sea-seasoned and wet canvas and wood to parched kindling.

"Oh, clever bastard," she muttered.

High above the main deck, Chimeg watched the snaking wave of brilliant light reach out from the *Cipac* and wash over *Swordfish*'s quarterdeck, the catapult crew all diving down and trying to cover against the intensity of the magical attack, hands slapping over burning eyes.

The light stung her eyes as well, but she wasn't directly in the line of the attack, and she squinted and didn't turn away. She felt the heat as the light washed through the sails below her, and noted the mist wafting off the cloth.

She, too, understood, and shook her head, knowing the fight was already lost when the flaming pitch and arrows came soaring in.

Fires erupted all about the deck. The sails ignited, flames rushing up the dried canvas, dark smoke billowing from those select areas that had not been fully dried by the magical light. Flames reached all the way up to the crow's nest, some fifteen feet above the topsail, smoke wafting out from the boards below Chimeg's feet.

She knew that she was almost out of time, and that things were only going to get worse. She looked to the fast-closing warship. Seething hatred burned in her eyes. She had always known it would come to this.

So be it.

Chimeg collected her pail of blood, checked the seal, and slung it over her shoulder, then climbed to the rim of the crow's-nest wall. She slung her bow, too, and put a sharp knife between her clenched teeth. Peering through the flames roaring below, ignoring the screams on the deck, she leaped out and called upon the magic in the gemstone set in her anklet, the same type of stone as the one set in the leather band she had strapped around the mainmast just above the topsail.

These were lodestones, gems that could attract and repel ferrous metals, and even more powerfully attract or repel each other.

Now she used the repelling power, the magic and the spring of her leap sending her out wide to starboard, to the end of the rope fastened about her ankle. As she reached the end, she tried to use the magic to slow her downward swing, but still, she hit the top yardarm hard, almost losing the knife from the jolt, and barely catching onto the yard. She steadied herself and secured herself, then cut away the sail, the flaming thing rolling over on itself below her, buying her some time.

She sheathed the knife and pulled her bow from her shoulder. Setting herself solidly on the yard, she studied the warship as it circled to *Swordfish*'s starboard flank, noting the golden object on its forecastle and the augurs gathered about it.

Another wave of arrows flew out, this time without the fires, many sent to sweep the deck of *Swordfish*. Chimeg cringed when she saw her friend Jocasta take a hit.

Chimeg leaped away, back around toward the stern to avoid a volley of arrows aimed her way. She used the magic subconsciously—it had become as much a part of her as her own muscle reflexes. For now, Chimeg went into her dance, the magic of the lodestones giving her the magical pushes to circle the mainmast, to swing out wide, forward and back, starboard and port, and to change direction as easily as she could turn in a run. She stood upright against the rope, hooking her free leg over her tied one for some stability and bracing her back shoulder against the line as she raised her bow.

Stay unpredictable, she told herself over and over, reaching out through her affinity with the stones, sometimes using the base to pull her back, other times to throw her out wider.

Trained from birth to use her core strength in such a way as to keep her upper body steady while her legs absorbed the shock of even violent movements—riding a horse on the steppes of To-gai in her earlier days, and now riding the wild swings of the rope—Chimeg began to fire off a line of arrows, concentrating on that forecastle.

Even with her clever emergency plans, she was certain she was going to die and had already set the parameters of making her ending be worth it.

She would have had the man she identified as the lead augur with her very first shot, except that a goldfish archer rushed before him at the last instant, inadvertently taking the arrow, mortally, in the side of his head.

The augur's eyes widened at that, surely, and he looked from the dead archer right up at the swinging Chimeg, and he dove aside as her second arrow came whistling in, stabbing into the base of the golden item on the forecastle.

The augur went behind the strange weapon, a third arrow clipping him—his robe, at least—in the backside.

Chimeg used the magic to send her far out aft, trying to keep in line with the passing adversary. With the augur out of sight, she quickly adjusted and let fly at another archer, taking her down even as she let fly at Chimeg.

The returning arrow missed as Chimeg swung back in at the mast, her speed heightened by the attraction of the gemstones. She deflected at almost a right angle, the magic shoving her in a swing out to starboard, nearer the enemy ship.

A different Xoconai augur ran to tend the first man she had

shot, and so Chimeg, now so suddenly much closer, wasted no time in putting an arrow into that priest's back, then a second arrow to sting him again when he pitched forward to the deck.

Back she swung toward the mast, and she knew she had to fly out wildly when a swarm of arrows came flying in at her!

But she saw yet another goldfish in augur's robes rush out from behind the magical weapon to sprint across the main deck for the quarterdeck cabin. Instead of going to the pole and using the magic to launch her back toward *Swordfish*'s prow, Chimeg growled in defiance and magically kicked herself right back out toward the *Cipac*.

It felt like a punch when the first arrow slammed into her thigh. It felt like a knife blade as a second sliced across the side of her face, leaving a deep gash from the right corner of her mouth all the way to her ear. Then came some painful sensation that seemed a combination of the first two hits, sharp and dull, when a third arrow jabbed through her left shoulder.

She flinched, but she didn't surrender her shot, and when she reached the zenith of the swing, nearly over *Cipac*'s starboard rail, the augur in plain view below her and running for his life, Chimeg drew back and let fly.

Her missile hit the man atop the back of his head and drove straight down through his skull.

No poison was needed here for a long and cruel demise.

No, this second Xoconai priest was dead before he hit the planks.

CHAPTER 5

CROSSING WAKES

Quauh stood at the prow, one foot up on the railing. She needed to be up here, where the deck was relatively empty, for the carrack had taken on scores of warriors for transport, including mundunugu cavalry and their fierce cuetzpali, and the main deck and the hold were thick with soldiers and the huge lizards, and while the lizards didn't smell, their waste certainly did, filling the hold with the stench of rotted fish.

She held tight to the rope rising up from the bowsprit for support as the *Uey'Lapialli* bounced and rolled through rough seas. They were long out of Freeport—First Mate Quauh's first chance to look upon the independent haven. She hadn't been much impressed. She never left the *Uey*, as few Xoconai officers or warriors rarely set foot on Freeport Island, let alone within the town of Freeport, where the carrack had docked. Still, from the deck, she could see enough to let her know that the place was not for her.

Drunks wobbled along the docks and slept in the shade

beneath them. Whores, male and female alike, exhibited their wares, flaunting them, even, to coax sailors from their ships.

To Quauh's horror, she saw more than one Xoconai visiting with them, walking off with them. Even commissioned sailors of the Tonoloya Armada.

She didn't understand it, any of it, and didn't much enjoy the spectacle, too disgusted to be even the least bit intrigued.

The question did nag at her, however: If the sidhe were subhuman, evil creatures, goblins in human clothing, then why would a Xoconai stoop to engage in such carnal indecency with them?

None of it made any sense to her, and on that morning docked in Freeport, she had wished, and not for the first time, that she had stayed in Tonoloya with her family and Lahtli Ayot.

But now she was out on the sea again, the sails full of wind, the spray flying up with every jolt to splash against her and fill her nostrils with that wonderful smell of brine. And so the doubts flew away and she just enjoyed the moment, the wind, the spray, the smell, and the graceful movements of the schooner to port and the one to starboard of the *Uey*. Escort ships.

Warships.

A reminder that the carrack was carrying something valuable, and mysterious. A few coffin-sized crates that had been loaded and placed in the safest section of the cargo hold. None aboard were allowed to even discuss them and even Quauh, the first mate, had no idea of the contents. She honestly wondered if even Captain Mahuiz knew what the crates contained.

The air was growing warmer now as the *Uey* moved farther

south. But whatever the heat or cold, the winds here surely did not remind her of home, for they carried with them a stickiness and sultriness that seemed to suck the energy right out of her body. Her long yellow hair hung flat and straight back home, but out here, it flared and curled, even, and seemed twice the volume. The lighter linen clothing she had been given for this journey stuck to her even when it was not wetted by the ocean spray.

And the air was only going to get stickier and much hotter, she had been warned. They were sailing for the jungle land of Durubazzi, with no stops intended. And they were taking a roundabout course, far out to sea, avoiding possible problems with any ships sailing under the flag of Behren. The more round-about journey would be much longer than the typical month, and more so because they had to keep dropping sail so that the mundunugu could take their lizards to sea, riding them about to properly exercise the creatures, and also to catch the fish that would feed the mounts and the crews of the three ships alike.

At least there was some benefit to the pauses, with the fish being a welcome break from the salted, spoiling mutton, which had to be picked clean of rat turds, and the hard biscuits that had to be pounded against a plank to eject the weevils and the maggots. Quauh snorted a little bit with amusement as she considered those rituals, weighing them against her continued love of sailing. *Minor inconveniences*, she thought.

But still, the fresh fish were a most satisfying luxury.

Also, she admired the bravery of the mundunugu warriors for riding those mounts into the sea, for she and all the others had witnessed a more remarkable and terrible incident on only the fourth day out of Freeport. Quauh had seen many sharks in her life, both in Tonoloya and in her two years sailing these waters. She had once been caught in the middle of an enormous school of hammerheads, many of them twice her size, while diving to salvage a shipwreck in the west. But never had she seen a creature as powerful as the huge white shark that had come up under one of the mundunugu lizards on that day, perhaps twenty feet of the killer behemoth coming clear of the water after rising right beneath its prey. The mundunugu had been thrown far and wide, fortunately, but the poor lizard had seemed a tiny thing in the maw of that shark, and it was bitten in half before any of them, shark, rider, or lizard, splashed back down into the Mirianic.

But still, the riders went out every day, though now the three ships closed ranks about them, circling while they exercised their mounts and tried to bring in a bit of fresh meat for dinner.

She lived in interesting times, and in a surprisingly interesting place, full of challenges to many concepts she'd thought of as "truths." She liked being challenged mentally more than physically, but even so, nothing was more pleasing to Quauh than standing close enough to the prow of a ship to feel the mist as it cut through ocean waters, the bright sun on her face being mitigated by both water and wind.

The smell and the sparkles of little whitecaps, the whales and dolphins and even the giant sharks.

And the roll of the water beneath the ship—yes, that most of all, for that feeling conveyed so much information to her about the currents and crosscurrents. It was as Lahtli Ayot had told her: she had a gift. Every sensation about her told her something, like pieces of a puzzle, and she could put those pieces together better than anyone she had ever known.

Chimeg swung back toward the mainmast, but instead of manipulating the magic to send her swinging in a different direction this time, she reversed the energy with a thought and let the lodestones pull themselves together, and pull her right to the mast. She grabbed onto it and steadied herself, then bent her attached leg and dropped her free foot down to stand on the yard. Just a quick pause to collect her thoughts, check her wounds, and consider.

Her cheek burned most of all, but there was no arrow there, at least. She had one sticking through her left shoulder, and another stabbed through her bent left leg.

She knew she was in trouble.

Looking down at the deck, though, she knew the *Swordfish* would soon be dead.

Another barrage of arrows swept the deck. First Mate Calloway was down and writhing. Captain Jocasta held a bow and tried to respond, but she was staggering too badly to make any effective shots.

No more than five of the remaining crew were up, and all but one had thrown down their bows and swords.

Chimeg looked to the *Cipac*, fast-closing and with boarding planks readied. She saw a goldfish splendidly dressed and was certain it was Captain Aketz, and beside him an augur dressed in the finest robes of all.

She could get two arrows off. She had a chance here to strike a mighty blow against the goldfish.

She knew she'd be soon dead if she did it, though. She looked to the crew again, to her friends, all doomed, whatever she might try.

With a sigh of failure, Chimeg hooked her composite bow on a peg on the mainmast, then took up the pail of blood. She held the magic strong, binding her ankle to the strap on the mast, but held on to nothing else, and let herself tumble over to hang head-down over the yard, trying to make it appear as if she had become tangled in death to the rigging. She subtly pulled the edge of the rubber seal of the pail, and felt the warm and sticky blood pouring down over her chest, rolling along her neck and chin, matting her hair.

Arms outstretched below her, she let the bumps and rolls of the ship control her swaying. She closed her eyes when the ships came together, hearing the cries and the rush of the Xoconai boarding *Swordfish*. The sounds faded and the darkness of her closed eyes deepened as her consciousness flitted away.

Only briefly, though, but even when she became aware of her surroundings, she hung there for a long while, eyes closed, playing dead.

She peeked down only occasionally, to see Jocasta being

interrogated by the man she thought to be Aketz. Finishing the interrogation, she knew, when he slapped her hard across the face and spun away.

"Prow her!" he yelled, and Chimeg tried not to react and told herself repeatedly that such was of course to be expected.

She knew well the stories and understood the way Captain Aketz played this game.

No one came up to get her. Why would they, since she was showing herself as a perfect trophy to any buccaneers who might see the defeated *Swordfish*? What better warning than a bloody, dead lookout hanging upside down from the highest yard?

The ship had little of value, but its water and food and whatever else the goldfish could find were quickly shuffled aboard the *Cipac*, while the few surviving crew were held sitting in a circle about the mast below Chimeg, javelins and bows aimed their way.

While some goldfish warriors tied *Swordfish* to *Cipac*, others prow-tied Jocasta, arms and legs out wide, bound to the forecastle with her back tight against *Swordfish*'s prow, her feet just above the waterline.

"Prowed," as the saying went among the sailors.

"I am a generous man, and so give you a seaman's chance," Captain Aketz explained to the other captives. "Perhaps some god of luck will look upon you this day and get you to the beach."

He paused and laughed at them, a hissing, wicked sound.

"Whether that god is good luck or bad . . . well, you will have to discover that for yourselves."

With his boarding party beside him, all of them laughing, Aketz left the doomed *Swordfish*.

Once again, Chimeg considered the possibility of righting herself, grabbing her bow, and taking a shot at the vile goldfish.

And once again, faced with a certain moment of death, the To-gai-ru archer could not bring herself to do it.

She was likely doomed anyway, but Chimeg stubbornly held on to a strand of hope.

"I will one day avenge you, my friend Jocasta. Sleep well," she whispered to herself.

"Next seaman who asks me gets fed to the sharks," Captain Mahuiz quietly told Quauh, joining her by the deck galley, where she was waiting for her portion of the fish that had been prepared for lunch.

Quauh didn't have to ask what question was being asked, and understood that she should take great care in even responding at all. So she just smiled at the man. She was quite fond of him, and not just because of his considerable abilities in handling ship and crew. He reminded her of Ayot, though he was likely twenty years younger than her lahtli. The sun and the sea, the wind and the spray, had taken a physical toll, though, and he looked much older than his years. He walked with stiff hips, and his shoulders never settled evenly, for his back was crooked. His eyes had the same gray as Ayot's, and like Ayot, his facial colors were fast dimming. His nose appeared more pink than red, and the blue at its base was hardly more noticeable than the blue of the veins in his gnarled old hands.

With the captain's inviting nod, she took her plate and moved beside Mahuiz toward his door at the quarterdeck, carrying her meal, which was composed of some whitefish she did not know, chopped into bite-sized morsels.

"Weeks at sea can bore many," she did remark as they neared Mahuiz's cabin. "Secrets are exciting, perhaps."

"Even to hold them," the captain admitted with a grin. "Go about the deck and seek out the whisperers—even speculation could prove disastrous. The seas have ears, Quauh."

Quauh nodded. "And those devilish barrelboats are often bobbing unnoticed nearby," she agreed.

"Powries," Mahuiz said with a chuckle. "Formidable little beasties, and aye, always listening, trying to find an advantage."

"Or a reason to take on a ship as formidable as *Uey'Lapialli*."

"I think our flanking vessels might have a word with them if they tried, as well," Mahuiz said. "See what you can learn."

Quauh started to respond, but a call from the warships to starboard rang out loud and clear. "Sails! Forty to starboard!"

The captain and the first mate turned reflexively.

"Sails to starboard!" confirmed their own lookout high above. "Fifty to us!"

Quauh ran for the forecastle, the captain close behind. Up on the higher deck, she pulled out her spyglass and pointed it toward the indicated area.

"Two ships: a three-masted frigate and a sloop behind," she told Captain Mahuiz when he shuffled up behind her. "A sloop with lowered sails."

She stepped aside and handed him the spyglass, indicating the general direction.

He began nodding almost as soon as he lifted the glass to his eye.

"Back one's flying the red 'n' black," he said. "Red sailfish, or might be a swordfish, on a black field."

"Buccaneers," Quauh remarked. "But with a three-masted—"

"*Cipac,*" the captain interrupted, leaning forward as he continued to peer through the spyglass. "That is *Cipac*, for sure. Captain Aketz has caught another one!"

He stepped back and handed the spyglass to Quauh, motioning for her to take a closer look, and while she did just that, Captain Mahuiz went to the rail overlooking the main deck. "Captain Aketz, the *Crocodile* of the Mirianic, has rid us of another foul pirate!" he yelled down to the crew, and the cheering began, joining that of the two warships.

Quauh studied the distant ships more carefully, noting the huge flag trailing the sloop. *Yes, a swordfish*, she thought.

"Why is he letting them fly the red 'n' black?" she asked quietly, not expecting an answer.

"To let everyone who views the spectacle of the death sail know that another pirate is destroyed, or soon will be," Captain Mahuiz answered. "He is towing that sloop to her doom."

"The death sail?" Quauh had never heard the expression. She turned to the captain.

Mahuiz was looking back, then to the west, then up at the sun. Gauging their position, she thought. Finally, he nodded.

"He will tow them to the north side of Serpent Isle, likely, and there, cut her free," the captain explained.

"Free?"

Mahuiz chuckled. "Free of him, but not of the tide. They've no sails to raise."

"Serpent Isle?" Quauh remarked. She had heard the name before but could not place it.

"Comes by its name honestly, not to doubt," said Mahuiz. "But no matter for those pirates aboard the captured sloop, for they'll not likely get anywhere near the dry land."

He patted Quauh on the arm and started away. "If I am not back on deck at eighteen bells, come and wake me," he said. "I wish to view the stars tonight."

Quauh nodded, then turned back with the spyglass to regard the distant ships. She wasn't quite sure what to make of Mahuiz's cryptic references, but she was glad indeed that another of the infamous buccaneers would trouble the Xoconai ships no more.

CHAPTER 6

FIRST MATE MASSAYO

"I hear ye been waitin' for yer *Swordfish*," a scruffy-looking powrie told Captain Wilkie, who was sitting with Massayo at a table, trying to enjoy his late supper. The tavern was no more than a large awning, the ocean breeze blowing warm onto the coast of Dinfawa Island this day.

Wilkie leaned back and considered the red-capped dwarf. He was pretty sure that he had seen this powrie before.

"You with Captain Thorngirdle?" he asked.

"Nah."

"Then who?"

"Ain't sailing much o' late. Too much coin to be earned ashore."

Wilkie's smile showed his suspicion. He looked to Massayo and nodded.

"You have information?" Wilkie asked.

"Would I be interruptin' yer meal if I didn't?"

"I do not know. Would you?"

"Ye looking for the sloop, or ye ain't?" asked the powrie.

"I'm waiting for her."

"She ain't coming."

Now Wilkie came forward in his seat, as did Massayo. "What do you know? And what will it cost me?"

"Could use a meal and a drink or ten."

"Then make it worth my coin. And yes, I've seen how much you bloody caps can drink."

That brought a smile, and the dwarf licked his thick lips. "The *Crocodile* got her," said the powrie. "She's in tow and takin' water. Listing, but she'll make it."

"To port?"

The powrie laughed.

"If you stay ashore, how do you know this?" Massayo demanded.

"Every red-cap huntin' pack knows me well," the scruffy fellow answered, puffing out his barrel chest. "Name's Finneas. Finneas the Gaff, at yer . . . nah, at me own service. Might that ye've heard o' me."

"No, actually," Massayo replied.

But Wilkie said, "Oh, indeed," at the same time.

"The gaff?" Massayo echoed, arching his thick eyebrows. "There is more than one meaning to that particular word."

That brought a glare from the powrie.

"Gaff hook," Wilkie remarked sternly, and he narrowed his eyes when Massayo looked to him. "Of course I've heard of Finneas the Gaff, and 'tis a pleasure, good man, to finally make your acquaintance."

The powrie continued to stare at Massayo. "Bah, but I've

pedaled with most of 'em, even Thorngirdle's Six Bits, and that when it was only called Two Bits. I been runnin' these waters since afore yerself was born!"

"Enough, if you please, and forgive the ignorance of this newcomer to these waters," Captain Wilkie intervened.

"A lubber, eh?" the dwarf snorted.

"You said that the *Swordfish* would make it," said Wilkie. "Make it to where?"

Another snort. "North side o' Serpent Isle, o' course," he answered, still staring at Massayo. He turned to Wilkie after he answered, and added, "Ye might get there afore 'em if ye're fast out o' port."

"See that this fine fellow's tab is covered for the night, then find all the crew you can and get them to the ship," Wilkie ordered Massayo.

"Haha!" laughed the dwarf, and he shuffled away.

"You know that little wretch?" Massayo asked.

"No, but he doesn't need to know that," Wilkie told him. "You disappoint me, my friend. I thought your charm your greatest asset."

"Not so much with powries."

"Even powries that may hold the key to rescuing our friends?"

That set Massayo back in his chair.

"You want us to engage the *Crocodile*?" he asked a moment later, shaking his head. "To go against Captain Aketz? She carries a hundred archers, at least."

"We won't get near *Cipac*, because *Cipac* won't go anywhere near the north side of Serpent Isle."

"But your little friend just said—"

"Aketz will cut *Swordfish* loose a half mile out, or more. He won't play with that current or tide, or the many reefs. And the water west of the island is too shallow for *Cipac*, and too near the coast of Behren, so that's where we'll be, tucked behind the tall mound that centers Serpent Isle."

Port Mandu was out of port soon after midnight, sails full and catching a brisk and warm wind off the desert sands of Behren. Scope in hand, Captain Wilkie never left the bow. They covered most of the hundred miles northeast to Serpent Isle by the time and as the eastern sky began to brighten, the large, dome-shaped mound of the island came into view.

"Half sail!" Wilkie called. "Steady at the helm and ready at the rigging. On my calls."

Wilkie was glad as the pre-dawn glow brightened. The waters in the triangle created by Serpent Isle, Dinfawa, and Freeport were indeed shallow, and thick with reefs, particularly as one neared Serpent Isle. Like every buccaneer, Wilkie knew them well. Even with that familiarity and his agile ship and skilled crew, he knew, too, that every sail near this lump of rock had to be taken very seriously.

Soon, still before the sun broke the eastern horizon, they had crew all about the rails, poking and pushing at every nearby rock, dropping sounding ropes, and finally, still some distance southwest of the island, dropping the anchors, forward and aft, and the sails.

"North side, Finneas said," Massayo reminded the captain, coming up beside him.

"Aye, but this is as close as we can take her. Toomsuba, ready the dinghy."

"How many will we send with him?" Massayo asked.

"One, just one."

"Who?"

Captain Wilkie handed him the spyglass. "You get just far enough to the north to get a clear look to the open waters northeast of the place."

"Should we go ashore?"

"Serpent Isle," Wilkie replied very evenly. "And the name doesn't come from the shape of the place, but from the inhabitants. Little bastards, but swarms. You might survive a dozen bites. A dozen, ha! That would take about fifty steps, if you're lucky."

"So I am to simply witness the death of the *Swordfish* and our friends?" Massayo grumbled.

"Very likely, yes. But Massayo is clever—at least, he tells me that he is," Wilkie replied. "I trust that you will figure your best course, if there is one."

Massayo looked down at the spyglass and shook his head, smiling helplessly. Another test. Captain Wilkie always had a test for him.

"Boat's in the water," Toomsuba called.

Still grinning, chuckling even, Massayo started for the stairs to the main deck.

"Oh, and do understand," Wilkie called to him, turning him about, "Toomsuba knows these waters well and knows that lump of rock quite well. You'll not coax him out of that dinghy until she's tied back up against *Port Mandu*. Never. If you lit it on fire, he would sit in it and melt before he ever stepped foot on Serpent Isle."

Massayo blew a sigh.

Soon after, he was crouched at the prow of the dinghy, a long spear in hand and a saber lying right beside him in easy reach, looking for rocks and watching for snakes. Behind him at the oars, Toomsuba rattled on and on about how the little gray devils almost never approached a boat, but it was known to happen.

"They usually eat at dusk," the giant islander said, over and over and over, obviously trying to convince himself as much as his shipmate.

They came around the northern edge of the island just as the leading edge of the sun crested the horizon, and far to the east, Massayo noted sails, lots and large. He figured they belonged to *Cipac*, and as the light grew, he realized that she was turning to starboard, to the north, and as she cleared, he saw a second ship, much smaller and with no sails flying.

"*Swordfish*," he muttered.

He turned about. "It's the *Swordfish*," he told Toomsuba. "Still far out. We can get to her."

The big man laughed at that notion.

"Then signal Captain Wilkie and let him get *Port Mandu* around the south side . . ."

"*Crocodile* would see him and catch him," Toomsuba said, shaking his head.

"Then row, my giant friend."

"Captain Aketz knew where to put her, and the tide has her," Toomsuba explained. He did take up the oars, though, and began pulling hard. "Look for rocks and push us off, and look for snakes and push them away," he told Massayo. "They swim, and we do not want to swim with them."

Massayo turned a nervous look upon the giant islander, who glanced back over his shoulder and smiled widely, showing an enormous gap to the right of center in his upper teeth. It made him appear almost childlike, Massayo thought—there was something truly disarming about this huge man who could pick him up and snap him in half as easily as if he was a dry twig. Toomsuba would be smiling if he ever did that, Massayo understood. The man was perpetually amused.

"Hey, rubber maker," Toomsuba said. "Do you know how to tell which of the snakes are full of venom?"

"Their size?"

"Nope. The little ones have little teeth, but they bite. It is very easy to tell which will poison you out here."

"How?"

"If they are snakes out here, they will poison you," he explained, and he laughed heartily and continued his rowing.

Lovely, Massayo mouthed, and turned to the waters ahead, gripping his pole as if his life depended on it.

The water grew shallower and clearer as they neared the island. More than once, Massayo had to direct the rowboat away from a rock, and once, he overbalanced and nearly plunged headlong into the water. His face barely inches from the surf, he noted his first serpent, slithering about at the base of the rock he had just poled, long and gray and moving with great ease through the crystal-blue water.

It wasn't the last snake he'd view. Toomsuba brought them in tight around the northern edge, close enough for Massayo to spot snakes in almost every crevice along the rocky coast. How badly he wanted to tell his giant friend to turn the boat around!

But now he saw the *Swordfish*, much closer and so clearly out of control, caught by the tide and with no sails, and apparently no rudder to turn her. She lurched forward, angled diagonally, then rolled back as the swells washed under her, then forward again.

Now they were close enough for Massayo to see the person—he knew at once that it was Jocasta—tied spread-eagled against the prow.

Far, far out, the *Cipac* had dropped her sails. The bastards wanted to watch, obviously.

"Keep pulling hard, Toomsuba," Massayo said, snakes be damned. He didn't know why he had said that, for he had no idea of what they might begin to do to help their doomed friends. Even if they somehow got up aside the *Swordfish*, they'd be caught in the same killer tide—and it was murderous indeed, Massayo recognized as they came around that northern tip, to see the great jags and sheafs of stone awaiting the *Swordfish*, waves crashing in with tremendous force and thunderous reports.

Massayo noted a second figure then, hanging upside down from the topmost yard. He put his face in his hand for Chimeg, the woman who had become his best friend in the two years he had been sailing with Captain Wilkie, the woman who had almost convinced him to join the *Swordfish* when Wilkie had granted Jocasta her command.

Only Wilkie's elevation of Massayo to bosun with a promise

that he would soon fill the vacant role as first mate of *Port Mandu* had convinced Massayo to stay.

It wasn't lost on the tall man that good fortune alone was the only reason he wasn't on that doomed ship.

Toomsuba continued to row hard, bringing the boat around to the eastern coast of Serpent Isle. He had to give it a wide berth, though, with the tide threatening to pull them into the rocks.

Even if he had cut a straight line to intercept the *Swordfish*, they wouldn't have made it.

The sloop was caught fast by the tide now, rushing forward in greater swells, pitching hard to starboard so violently that her forward rail almost dipped under the water with each wave.

Massayo watched, transfixed.

Jocasta was still very much alive, stubbornly shaking the water from her face with each pitch. He saw her eyes go wide with horror, her mouth opened wide in a gurgling, water-filled scream as the last waves lifted that prow and launched it head-long into a great shelf of rock.

Massayo looked away and tried to growl through his agony.

It took him a long while to look back, to see the ship being lifted and thrown repeatedly into the stones. Jocasta was gone, most of her anyway, for he could still see her right arm swinging at the end of the rope.

Screams carried across the waves, sailors in the water and others stubbornly and foolishly holding on to the shattering *Swordfish*.

"There is a small beach. If they can get to the beach," he

heard Toomsuba saying, but it hardly registered against the horrors, the sights and the sounds, playing out before him.

A huge wave came in right under *Swordfish* and lifted it up high and threw it, clear of the water—other than the bottom of its keel—for a heartbeat, over the first bank of rock and into the second!

Massayo heard himself screaming, and that was the only way he even realized that he was. In that moment of utter shock, watching the ship verily explode as it crashed down on the stone, there came one brief moment of hope. For up high on that pitching, then snapping, mainmast, Massayo saw Chimeg, dear Chimeg, invert suddenly and brace herself.

As the mast struck the ledge and snapped, Chimeg somehow—was it the magical gemstones, perhaps? Massayo wondered—lifted straight up from the splintering beam into the air and came down behind it, landing on her feet, but hard, before crumpling down out of sight.

"Get me there, Toomsuba! I beg!" he called.

The big man responded by pulling even harder, driving the boat along and against the relentless pull of the incoming tide.

Massayo kept his eyes peeled on that ledge, the broken mast leaning against it, the top of the mast shattered along it, hoping that Chimeg would show herself again. More than once, he reacted only at the very last moment to slap aside a swimming snake or to deflect the hit from a submerged stone.

He noted more movement in the water—not snakes, but fellow buccaneers, some splashing, some bobbing facedown, and also barrels and crates, planks, and a sizable portion of

Swordfish's quarterdeck, all of it being swept around the rocks toward a small beach at the end of a short inlet.

Toomsuba was already rowing hard that way, turning the small boat to ride the tide.

"Use your weapons now," he told Massayo. "No more rocks."

Massayo replaced the long pole in the boat and drew out a cutlass and a hatchet, fidgeting nervously and rolling them about in his hands, ready to cut in half any snake that came too near. Not all his friends were dead, he noted. One man turned at the sight of the rowboat and tried to swim for it, but a swell caught him and drove him far into the inlet toward the beach.

"Hurry," Massayo urged. He saw a second man stand up in the shallow waters, stumbling for the beach and slapping at something on his side.

Massayo didn't have to see it to know it was a snake.

In the rescuers rushed, coming up on the man battling the snake, whom Massayo recognized as Calloway.

Calloway, the first mate of the *Swordfish*, who would likely take that title from Massayo if he came back alive.

Reflexively, Massayo hoped the boat wouldn't get to the floundering man in time. The world was a wicked place and you had to take what you could, when you could. Would anyone blame him? He was weary of scrubbing decks and pulling lines. He was a leader, a man who had built a powerful and rich company, only to have it stolen by the goldfish. Why should he settle for being one of many in a crew, serving beneath people who didn't have his intelligence and cleverness?

For a moment, he hoped for Calloway to die, but just a moment, and one that left him shaking his head in shame.

"Pull, Toomsuba!" he yelled emphatically, desperately, as if trying to exorcise the demons of his dark thoughts.

Calloway went under just before the boat reached him, but Massayo threw down his cutlass and hatchet and dove to the rail, holding tightly, bracing his feet, and putting his arm, his head, and shoulder under the waves.

He grasped Calloway's shirt and felt something wriggling beneath his hand!

With a growl of denial, Massayo heaved the man up, and outraged beyond fear, he grasped the snake and flung it far away, then grabbed Calloway again and pulled him up to the rail, calling for Toomsuba.

He couldn't get Calloway over, and the man had at least one other snake on him.

A huge hand, thick and wide, slapped down beside Massayo's, and with strength that mocked Massayo's efforts, Toomsuba hoisted Calloway over the side and dropped him into the boat.

As Massayo tried to grab for his cutlass, Toomsuba stomped a snake flat. He was bitten by a second serpent on his forearm, so the islander paid it back in kind, stretching it out and biting it back, then flinging the severed body into the sea, leaving the head stuck in his fleshy arm.

A third snake lifted its fanged maw toward Massayo, who wisely leveled his cutlass, waving it only slightly, just to the left of the serpent.

The snake threw itself at Massayo, its entire three-foot length coming right from the decking.

Across came the cutlass, slapping the living missile aside and right out of the boat.

Toomsuba patted him on the arm for that one, then hoisted Calloway and rolled him over, checking for more serpents before settling the groaning, wounded, and likely poisoned man into the back of the small boat.

The waves had driven them nearly to shore by then, and Toomsuba went for the oars.

Massayo gasped when he looked to the beach, to a sailor stumbling about, to the swarm of snakes about him and upon him, biting him over and over again. He stumbled and staggered, flailed and spun, showing snakes hanging from his neck and his face, and when he fell, he was covered by dozens of snakes.

Toomsuba was turning the boat then, and Massayo wasn't about to argue—until he heard a cry from the top of that large stone block, from over the ledge near the broken mast.

"Half to starboard!" Massayo ordered. "Get me to the rocks."

"Massayo the mad!" Toomsuba argued.

"It's Chimeg!" Massayo yelled back.

Toomsuba paused for just a heartbeat, then pulled hard with his right hand, the port oar, swinging the rowboat hard to starboard.

"There are snakes in those rocks," he warned Massayo, but he kept rowing.

Massayo ignored him. He hoisted the cutlass and the hatchet and set himself, one foot atop the prow. As the rowboat neared, he sprang, leaping forward to the nearest of the stones, slipping and splashing, but moving on, leaping to a second, higher perch.

"Give me as much time as you can, but do not come after me," he ordered Toomsuba.

He was no longer consciously thinking or picking his path with any foresight. He was just moving constantly, trying to keep ahead. He saw snakes before him in the shadows of the overhanging stones. He felt snakes slap against his hard boots on several different strides. He knew that snakes were trailing him, chasing him.

He pushed it all from his mind, leaping and scrambling along the broken stones, trying to get higher up the side of the high mound, every now and then stabbing into a crevice to strike a snake before it could strike at him.

Everything was a blur around him. Instinct and reaction guided his every move. Somewhere deep inside, Massayo understood that if he paused long enough to consider this stupid rescue, he would likely throw himself from the rocks in a desperate attempt to get away.

But no, he kept going, leaping and scrambling, stabbing and chopping, pulling himself over every ledge without even thinking of what coiled monster might be awaiting his rising face.

Somehow, impossibly, he got to the last ledge, some eight feet above him. With no choice, he tossed both of his weapons over it, then leaped up, catching it with his hands, his booted feet digging against the stone to propel him up and over, where he scrambled over it, grabbing for his cutlass, eyes darting all about.

He saw no snakes. None at all up here.

He reached for his hatchet, but hesitated, for there was Chimeg, collapsed beside the broken mast, one hand on the leather strap fastened about the beam that held her corresponding gemstone.

Massayo ran to her and gently rolled her, calling her name. Not knowing if she was living or dead, he put away his weapon and heaved her over his shoulder, or started to, before laying her back down once more and retrieving that gemmed strap and her wonderful composite bow.

Now he hoisted her over one shoulder and stood straight, looking all about for an escape. He couldn't go back the way he had come up, surely.

He walked to the edge and called down to Toomsuba.

"Over there!" the huge man yelled back, pointing across the rocky formation toward the other side.

Massayo swallowed hard when he realized the spot the big man was indicating: an undulating pool sheltered from the brunt of the waves, but swelling with every incoming rush of water, just to the side of the shattered *Swordfish*.

Massayo was fifty feet up from the sea. He'd have to go down a bit to get to the end of a lower jut overlooking that pool, but still he'd be perhaps forty feet above the pool—and who knew if there were rocks hidden under the dark water?

He turned all about again, looking for an easier path. But he couldn't go inland, obviously, for the sheer number of aggressive serpents.

He looked down at Toomsuba and nodded emphatically,

and before his better senses could overcome him, he scrambled back down to the landing below the high ledge, settled his friend more comfortably on his shoulder, and began his next run.

He leaped across a five-foot expanse to another stone and stumbled along, stomping a snake on the narrow spear of stone before him. He could see the pool and he tried to judge the incoming swells, and in the end, with more snakes coming up around him onto this jut of stone, he just had to trust his luck, and he didn't slow when he reached the end, flinging himself and his dear friend into the air.

They crashed down hard into the pool, Massayo knifing down far enough to bang his feet on the bottom before propelling himself right back up. He grabbed Chimeg and got her face out of the water, then pulled as hard as he could for the opening between the rocks, his hope soaring when he saw the prow of his rowboat appear just beyond them.

To his surprise, two other sailors from *Swordfish* were in that boat with Toomsuba and Calloway.

It was hot in Tonoloya, particularly in the valleys west of the ocean. The sun, which shone down from cloudless skies upon the place for all but the winter season, radiated strong heat and could blister uncovered skin in short order, and when the winds came down through the canyons in the northeast, they carried such velocity and heat that they could dry clothes out in a matter of heartbeats.

Quauh wasn't unused to heat, certainly, but never had she imagined the level of sweat and stickiness she had experienced as they neared the coast of the Durubazzi jungle. Her eyes stung from sweat, and no amount of wiping it away seemed to help. The humidity sapped the strength from her limbs and made her want to simply melt upon a hammock.

But they had made the journey, with the *Uey'Lapialli* docked on a long wharf—the only man-made structure in sight— alongside one of the escorting warships, while the other moved about at battle sail out near the mouth of the small harbor.

A host of soldiers waited on the wharf as Quauh supervised the sidhe slaves in unloading the few crates. She meant to ac- company them as they made their way from the wharf into the jungle but was stopped by a fierce mundunugu commander, who told her that it would not be necessary.

Quauh looked back to the deck of the *Uey*, to Captain Mahuiz for instruction, and the old man just shook his head and waved her back to his side.

"The mundunugu are without humor," Quauh noted when she joined him, the bearers and the escorting soldiers disappear- ing into the thick brush.

"They have been fighting sidhe for more than a decade," Mahuiz answered. "All of them have lost friends, and indeed, lost their humor as well. Another casualty of this war to restore the empire." He patted the young woman on the shoulder. "Prepare the ship for departure. Only the warship out in the harbor will accompany us home."

"When the bearers return?" Quauh asked.

Mahuiz shot her a puzzled look. "They will not be coming back," he said, and Quauh understood from his grim tone the implications and finality of that statement.

She stared at him and knew from his returning look that she wasn't doing a good job at hiding her revulsion.

Mahuiz looked all about, making sure that no others were near enough to hear.

"There were mirrors in the crates," he whispered. "Transport mirrors. The buccaneers have become too much of a nuisance for the augurs. They know too much about what is coming out of the jungles bound for Mayorqua Tonoloya."

"They will send the gold and other goods all the way to Entel with the mirrors?"

"No, of course not. That would be far too distant a journey. Our leaders have secured some nearby islands, where receiving transport mirrors will be secured and hidden. We will still send our cargo ships to Durubazzi, but for lesser loads. The true hauls will be found elsewhere, away from the spies of the sidhe buccaneers.

"I have had more than enough of these troublesome pirates," he added. "Let us hope this new plan works."

"I thought that Captain Aketz was proving successful in ridding—"

"Sidhe are like insects, my young friend," Mahuiz interrupted. "You slap one and a dozen others bite you. Let the buccaneers chase the ships carrying lesser treasures."

Quauh nodded and let it go at that. She stiffened in a proper salute, then turned to go about readying the *Uey* for departure, but paused and looked back to the spot in the jungle wall where the mundunugu and the bearers had disappeared.

A pang of guilt stabbed at her. She had sailed with those sidhe for weeks, had watched them from afar. There were two families there. Among the bearers were several young sidhe, barely adults.

They were all about to be slaughtered.

She closed her eyes and remembered what Lahtli Ayot had told her. There could be no mercy.

She had to try to believe that.

Massayo leaned back in his chair in the lone tavern on the island of Dinfawa, a pirate refuge near to the coast of Behren. He had recovered from the trials of Serpent Isle over these last couple of weeks, physically at least. He would never forget the images, though, most particularly the poor sailor who had stumbled onto the beach to be brought down and covered by the small vipers that gave the island its name.

He was not a religious man, following no god in particular, but many times in the last days, Massayo had thanked fate, or whatever forces might be out there, for that pool below the ledge, deep enough and rock-free.

Chimeg sat across from him, and when he looked upon her, his heart swelled. She was such a good person, such a capable shipmate, such a deadly ally. He had saved her, though he still couldn't believe he had made that run, and he felt embarrassed whenever she or anyone else thanked him. It was almost as if it wasn't him at all who had done the heroic act, but some other spirit that had found its way into his body and controlled his movements.

Massayo didn't feel like a hero, because he knew that if he, if this true person called Massayo, had spent a moment considering the path before him, he wouldn't have had the courage to take it.

But he had, and Chimeg was here with him, and that was all that mattered.

Across the way, the crew of *Port Mandu* began entering through the open tavern door, two by two, one group after another, all thirty of them. Last of all came the two sailors, both women, whom Toomsuba had pulled from the water when Massayo had gone after Chimeg, followed by the huge man himself, and behind him came Captain Wilkie and Calloway. Calloway leaned heavily on a cane and walked shakily, appearing a shell of his former self, and the whispers were that he would never fully recover from the half-dozen snakebites he had suffered before Massayo and Toomsuba had gotten to him.

Toomsuba, though, who had been bitten only once, had quickly and fully recovered.

Again, a play of luck, Massayo realized, and the fragility of life and health twisted at his sensibilities.

The entire group made their way across the tavern to form a circle around Massayo and Chimeg. Captain Wilkie led Calloway in and helped him into a chair at the small table. On the captain's signal, drinks were brought to the entire crew, and then to everyone else in the tavern as well.

"To the *Swordfish* and Captain Jocasta," Wilkie said, hoisting his glass. "As fine a buccaneer as the Mirianic's ever known!"

The room exploded in a rowdy "Hear, hear!" with many echoing the name of the pirate.

When the cheering had settled, Wilkie motioned for the crew to huddle in closer.

"And now we're without our sister ship," the captain began. "But so be it. We've sailed a decade alone, and so we will again—for now. But now it's time we reorder a couple of things going forward."

"Calloway!" one man said.

The venom-battered man shook his head.

"Mister Calloway's days at sea are at their end," Captain Wilkie announced. "He is staying right here in Dinfawa until the end of the season, when we'll take him home to Port Seur."

A cheer went up for Calloway.

"*Port Mandu*'s officers have been in flux since we got the *Swordfish*," Wilkie said. "That's no secret. But now, with all that's happened, it's past time we set it out in full." He looked to the woman across from Massayo. "Chimeg . . ."

The first mate, Massayo believed.

"Our dear Chimeg is back aboard," Wilkie said. "I'll make no secret of the fact that I offered her the position of first mate."

Cheers went up for Chimeg.

"But she has refused me," Wilkie silenced them by saying. "She wishes to be our lookout, only that. To serve her friends as their eyes—and arrows—above. And she has told me who should be my second, and I could not agree more." He stood tall and lifted his glass again. "My friends of *Port Mandu*, I give to you First Mate Massayo Mantili!"

Massayo's jaw hung open, the rousing cheers only adding to his surprise. He knew the choice to be a good one; in truth, the best one. He believed himself smarter than anyone on *Port Mandu*, more worldly, more clever, better at understanding their goldfish enemies—he could speak the Xoconai language, even, along with several other tongues. And even though he had been on the ship, indeed on the waters, for only two years, none were better suited to the post than he, not even his dear friend Chimeg.

So, as the moments passed, he accepted the cheers and the title.

First Mate Massayo.

THREE

TO RULE THE SEAS

GOD'S YEAR 874

SPRING, TWO YEARS LATER

(MAHTLOMEYI XIUITL)

Most holy and revered Father Abbot Braumin,

I hope this letter finds you well and thick with the blessings of Saint Abelle and Saint Avelyn. The work in Entel continues, and your fears about the growing discontent were not without merit. Let any thoughts that the Xoconai wish to maintain this city as it was before the war flee your mind. They are here in large numbers, and their augurs are often seen about the grounds of St. Bondabruce, no doubt whispering corruption into the ears of the De'Unnerans who remain plentiful within.

The election for city sovereign was, as we feared, wholly unfair, even more so than the one that put Popoca into the position in the first place. Now he has solidified his gains and corrupted the institutions about him. He will rule Entel for as long as he desires, unless he crosses Grand Augur Apichtli himself. And that is not likely, Father Abbot. City Sovereign Popoca serves one purpose here: to take as much gold from the lands in the south as possible, and send it west to his Xoconai masters.

If their god, Scathmizzane, offers blessings, I fear that Popoca is thick with them.

He is unrelenting in calling for more forces and ships from Ursal. He revels in every ingot that is taken through their magical mirrors to the west. He greets every ship that sails into port, low in the water from the weight of their precious metal.

I fear that your concerns about his inroads with St. Bondabruce might have been understated. Our friend is there now, but I have heard nothing. I do not know how he was received, or if he even still survives.

We must hope for the best and prepare for the worst.

Yours in service,
Acting Abbess Elysant of St. Rontlemore

CHAPTER 7

CAPTAIN WILKIE DOGEARS

"That?" Captain Wilkie Dogears said with a great bellow of laughter. "That is how Massayo will command the sea?"

Massayo, the target of Wilkie's mocking, came out of his fighting crouch and moved his right hand slowly nearer to his left, releasing the tension on the bands of the contraption that was affixed to his left wrist and being held in place by the flesh between his thumb and index finger. Tall, lean, broad-shouldered, and well-muscled, Massayo seemed the complete opposite of his captain, who was thirty years his senior and becoming thicker and rounder with each passing year. Massayo was Durubazzi, his skin very dark, his hair tightly spiraled, while Wilkie's skin, though browned and ruddy from his life at sea, was very pale naturally, and the captain's hair flowed bushy and long, even from his generous beard, which was often described as a fat and dead raccoon, its ends braided and tied with black ribbons.

Massayo sometimes wore a beard, but it was always perfectly trimmed. Always, meticulously and perfectly trimmed.

"This is but a tiny model of the bullhead," he replied.

"It's a child's toy."

Massayo sighed, then turned, pulled back the bands to their limit, and let fly the small stone settled in the pocket of the slingshot. It zipped across the common room and shattered an empty glass on an unoccupied table.

"Ye're payin' for that, don't ye doubt!" called the tavern keeper from behind the bar.

"Well now, you can break glass!" Wilkie loudly exclaimed with feigned excitement. He stopped abruptly and looked about, as did Massayo. They had, as was often the case, put in to the small island of Dinfawa, off the coast of Behren. This hamlet, and this tavern in particular, did not turn away the pirates. Indeed, the tavern keeper himself had spent many years sailing under the red 'n' black. Most of the folk living here, and most of the crews moored about the low island, were Behrenese, and so, while accepting of the visitors from the north and south, there remained a measure of caution about them. Given the startling display by Massayo, most in the tavern now had their eyes locked on Massayo and Wilkie.

And more than one had a hand on the hilt of a khopesh or a scimitar.

"Do try not to get us kicked out of port before I can find a strong drink, a hard woman, and a soft bed," Wilkie whispered to the tall man.

"It is just a model," Massayo replied, holding up the slingshot and ignoring the attention. "Though do not underestimate even this hand slingshot. In the hands of a skilled shooter, such a toy, as you call it, can prove quite deadly."

"I will believe you when I see Chimeg or one of the others trading their bows for one of those . . . slings."

"Slingshot," Massayo corrected. "You do not spin it. You merely draw it like a bowstring. And it can be deadly."

"I can imagine my discomfort if you shot it into my face while I was taking a great draw of my ale," Wilkie replied.

"It will break more than glass."

"It won't break the hull of a goldfish warship."

"It is a model!"

"And how would you begin to pull a band of *rubair* that is large enough to throw a large-enough stone with enough force to damage a ship?" Wilkie asked quietly, so that none around would hear.

"A fair question," Massayo agreed. "I am working on a proper balance for that right now."

"Well, know that you're not going to be taking up the entire deck of *Port Mandu*'s forecastle," Wilkie insisted. "Besides, you'd probably strip the lines from the bowsprit with your shot before the stone ever cleared our own deck!"

"These are minor issues that can be resolved," Massayo insisted, but Wilkie was already turning away, shaking his head.

"Your escort ship will show you the way and take from you your doubts," Massayo called after him, drawing another great laugh from the captain.

"I'll be dead and buried before Massayo finds the gold to buy a ship to properly escort *Port Mandu*," Wilkie replied without turning.

The edge in his voice warned Massayo off. It had only been two years since the loss of Jocasta and her crew of the *Swordfish*. Still, he could not so easily let that go. "But your previous offer remains?"

Now the captain did stop, right before exiting the tavern. He turned slowly to regard Massayo, his generous smile shining from under the black frame of his untrimmed beard and thick mustache. "'Twas not an offer, Massayo Mantili. 'Twas a promise, and a request, one you have earned, and one you have shown to me to be . . . mutually beneficial. I call you first mate, and never have I known a better second. And know that I'll sail with more confidence with Captain Massayo sailing beside me. But as we agreed, you must provide the coin for the ship and the crew."

Captain Wilkie spoke it all very deliberately and very loudly, and none in the crowded tavern missed a word. And he ended with a bow to his first mate, a show of such great respect that Massayo felt his cheeks flushing with gratitude.

However, with typical Wilkie Dogears aplomb and an exaggerated derisive snort, the captain added, "But Massayo the gambler will never find the gold for anything more than a leaky dinghy!"

Massayo laughed along with the rest of the tavern. He truly loved that deceptively ferocious man, his mentor, his friend. He also understood that Wilkie's public display this day was meant as much as an expression of his continuing determination to keep the trade routes free of Xoconai oppression as anything for Massayo's benefit.

But, too, it was indeed for Massayo's benefit, another reminder of the generosity of his mentor. From the beginning, Captain Wilkie had seen him, and not just the shadow under the dinghy. As soon as *Port Mandu* had sailed away from Durubazzi that fateful day four years before, Wilkie had shown great interest in this man, Massayo Mantili, who had once been a clever and successful businessman, so much so that the goldfish were offering thirty pieces of untraceable and untaxed gold for his return—alive.

That last part was the most important, Massayo understood, for it gave Wilkie some sense of the value Massayo might prove to him. Thus began the mentorship. Captain Wilkie had taught Massayo how to sail, had spent hours showing him the ship and the sea, and most of all, had shown him how to coexist with the others sailing these waters, even the fierce Xoconai.

How many times on their visits to Freeport over the last two years had Captain Wilkie and Massayo run into a goldfish sailor from a merchant ship they had recently raided, only to have that victim of *Port Mandu* greet them with a wide smile and offer to buy the most gracious and merciful Captain Wilkie, the Polite Pirate, a drink?

More than any of the technical lessons of sailing or even of maneuvering in a ship-to-ship battle, this lesson was the most valuable, Massayo knew. Captain Wilkie was cleverly and successfully walking a truly remarkable line, combining honor and piracy, ferociousness and mercy. It was working, with the notable exception of Captain Aketz, who was more driven by pride and legacy than by any sense of propriety. But only for Captain Aketz, it seemed. For all of the other Xoconai, captains and crew alike, there were drinks for gracious Captain Wilkie Dogears.

Massayo Mantili had paid attention.

"They are all laughing because they know he is right," said Chimeg, walking up to take the chair beside Massayo.

He looked over at the slight, brown-skinned archer-acrobat from the steppes of To-gai, his most trusted confidante and dearest friend. It struck him then how truly thin she really was, carrying the frame of a young teenager, her smile more girlish than that of a woman in her early thirties. Not her dark eyes, though, Massayo noted. The eyes of one who could kill without mercy, they showed the darker side of Chimeg. She was still *Port Mandu*'s lookout, having repeatedly refused any offers from other buccaneer captains, and they all wanted her, and even promotions from Captain Wilkie. She was content up there on high, swinging about unpredictably, acrobatically, aided by the gemstone in her anklet and in the leather strap around the mainmast, and ever ready to let fly one of her feces-dipped arrows with impossible accuracy.

She had become as famous as Captain Wilkie himself. The mere sight of Chimeg whirling about atop *Port Mandu*'s mainmast had goldfish sailors all along the coast diving for cover.

"Your faith is encouraging," Massayo replied.

Chimeg just shrugged. "I have already pledged to you should you prove him wrong." She paused and gave a little smile to the tall man. "Or perhaps it was an easy pledge, being generous when it would not cost me anything."

"I will get my ship soon enough."

Chimeg shrugged again.

Massayo directed her gaze across the tavern to their enormous friend, bald-headed and covered in tattoos, with arms the size of a large man's thigh, and a belly girth to make a centaur proud. He was facing away from them and in the shadows of the far corner, but there could be no mistaking this one.

"You have continued to talk to Toomsuba?"

"Boomer hears me, but he just laughs. He always just laughs."

"I—we—need him."

"Captain Wilkie pays him two shares," Chimeg reminded her friend. "And he is worth more. Can any seaman on the Mirianic set the sails more firmly?"

"We need him."

"Every captain sailing the Freeport-to-Durubazzi run likely feels the same. Even the goldfish would pay Boomer to pull their rigging."

"I do not need him on my rigging."

Chimeg gave him a curious look.

Now it was Massayo's turn to grin. He reached down to his slingshot and gave a little tug on the bands. He understood the tensile strength of the bands he needed for his bullhead idea. If any man alive could draw those bands, it was this giant Ata'ino islander. Toomsuba weighed thirty stone if he weighed a pebble, Massayo knew, and while there was a generous amount of blubber involved in that measurement, it covered a mass of muscle and power that could not be underestimated. Massayo had feared that he might need to buy and train a mule to pull the bullhead bands, but if a mule could pull them, then so, likely, could Toomsuba.

"Keep engaging him," Massayo begged Chimeg. "Offer him whatever he wants."

That brought a sour look.

"Well, not that. I mean two shares, maybe three . . ."

"I already offered him *that*," Chimeg replied anyway, her feigned frown disappearing.

"Wait. You offered *that*? To Toomsuba?"

"Look at him. Have you ever seen a man of that . . . size?" She smiled—Massayo liked it when she smiled, for it was not a common occurrence, and even less so since the disaster at Serpent Isle.

"And he refused you?"

"No, he accepted that offer quite eagerly. But that part of the bargain had nothing to do with your plans for this ship you will likely never purchase. That was all for my pleasure, not your gain."

"And for Toomsuba's pleasure, yes?"

Chimeg shrugged. "He just laughs through it all. But yes, he keeps asking for more."

"Laughs, or laughed?"

Another shrug. "The nights are long at sea."

"You said 'that part of the bargain,'" Massayo prompted.

Chimeg shrugged.

"Then Toom—Boomer will join with us when I get my ship?"

Chimeg shrugged again, giggled as she rose, and walked away.

Massayo felt quite pleased by that last bit of information. He glanced about, then scooped up his glass and made his way to a different table, one that was more out of the way. There he fell into a seat and pulled paper, ink, and quill from his pouch. He unfolded the paper and smoothed it on the table, then went back to his drawing, his design for the bullhead.

With levers to turn it, gears to change the angle of the throw, and a rail to slide it side to side so that the throw wouldn't take out the bowsprit lines, it was already becoming more complicated than he had initially believed. And it was going to be expensive to actually fashion the thing, he knew, even though he already had the prepared rubber he would need.

Very expensive, still, and all of that only if he could even find someone skilled enough to make this new weapon. He did know of one man who might be able to fashion the gears and bolts and rails, but putting the whole of the bullhead together would be a different matter, as would mounting the massive slingshot on the forecastle of any ship.

Wilkie's parting taunt had been offered in a spirit of jovial jousting, but Massayo heard the ring of truth in it.

Wherever would he find the gold he needed?

"You have to show it!" Harbormaster Hadil of Dinfawa shouted back at the black-bearded powrie. "That is how we do it, and

119

there is a reason that we do it. Our strength, our hope, is in solidarity."

"I got five other boats pedalin' aside me," answered Captain Thorngirdle.

"Then take five other pennants," answered Hadil, and she gave an exasperated blow to flip a strand of her very curly blond hair out of her face.

"We're under the water! Where're ye expectin' me to fly the damn things?"

"Just run them up your deck bracing poles when you can. Even after you make the catch."

"The kill," Thorngirdle corrected, and he pulled the shining red beret off his head and shook it in his fist at her.

"As you wish," Hadil told him. "But please, good captain. You fly the red 'n' black because it tells the world that you are part of a larger and greater league. I am of Behren, under the protection of Chezru Chieftain Brynn Dharielle. Even the Xoconai—the goldfish, if you will—wish no trouble with her. And so, I tell you now, as a friend to the pirates who irritate the wretched goldfish, that the pennant will serve you well if ever you find yourself in the midst of Behrenese warships."

Thorngirdle gave a great sigh and plopped the beret back on his hairy head.

"Look, I have even designed these small flags for you." Hadil held open the pennant. The field was black, with a red beret in the top corner and five smaller ones running across the flag in a row beneath it. "Is that not fitting for Six Bits?"

Thorngirdle's expression softened as he regarded the small flag. "Ye got six of 'em, do ye?"

"Only one like this, but five others you can give to your fellows for now. I wanted to ask your thoughts before making them all." She hesitated as the door opened and Captain Wilkie Dogears entered the office, giving a nod to Thorngirdle, who returned it.

"What'd'ye got in yer mind, then?"

Harbormaster Hadil paused before answering, noting how much Thorngirdle looked like a miniature version of Wilkie Dogears, with their shaggy heads of black hair and wild beards, Wilkie's tied with ribbons, Thorngirdle's shaped with dung. "I'll make the other five with the same larger beret as for your boat, the *One o' Six*. With the others, I'll make one of the bottom berets a bit bigger than the others, in order, for *Two o' Six* all the way to *Six o' Six*. If that suits you, I mean."

Thorngirdle's widening grin told her that she had finally, at long last, won the stubborn powrie over. She gave him the pennant and five others with simple black fields outlined in red, and he even tipped his beret to her before rushing out of the office.

"They are the most stubborn of creatures," Hadil told Wilkie.

Wilkie wasn't about to disagree. "Six Bits is heading out?"

"Barrelboats don't shy from the storms. They're positioning for a strike, or they might be looking for stragglers they can catch out alone. All whispers say the goldfish warships are caught south behind the storm."

"Where might Captain Aketz be?"

"Far south," said Hadil. "He's got the *Cipac* prowling off the coast of Durubazzi, by all accounts. They had a big strike, and you know how the goldfish covet gold."

Wilkie nodded. "The powries have better luck in foul weather, no doubt. Barrelboats have such an advantage."

"Aye, but who would wish to remain inside one for more than a few heartbeats?"

Wilkie conceded the point with another nod.

"Is *Port Mandu* putting out?"

"Thinking on it. Up the coast north a bit, maybe to Djinnit to do some repairs and scrape while waiting for the storm to pass. We're once more to Freeport before the winds turn."

"Not many leaving before the storm, so go when you will." She pulled a harbor mark from her desk drawer and handed it to him. "Not that any would question you, but if so, here's your leave. Any port in Behren, but you'll find Jacintha's mooring balls crowded."

"Won't go that far," Wilkie replied absently, and Hadil noted that the perceptive captain was watching Thorngirdle through the window as the powrie moved back toward his docked barrelboat. "Any goldfish been about?"

"A few," Hadil answered. "Nothing unusual." She kept her eyes on Wilkie, who continued to watch the departing powrie, and understood his interest. Even though barrelboats could handle the storms, why would Thorngirdle be so eager to go out at this time?

Hadil smiled. What she enjoyed most about watching the

many buccaneers who came to her harbor was the way these fellows could smell intrigue.

Captain Aketz of the Tonoloya Armada paced the quarterdeck of his frigate, the pride of the eastern fleet. The *Cipac* had put more pirates at the bottom of the Mirianic than any other three Xoconai warships combined. At more than 130 feet and with a crack crew of two hundred proven sailors and proven fighters, the hunter was fast and deadly and could clean a deck of pirates with a single volley of arrows. City Sovereign Popoca of Entel had put great resources into Aketz's ship and mission, and expected, and had thus far realized, great returns.

Which was why it was especially galling to Captain Aketz to be serving as a decoy in this all-important mission. He with *Cipac* and a battle group that included three other warships had escorted two fat-bottomed carracks to the Durubazzi coast, and waited here while those lumbering cargo ships were loaded with heavy chests for the return north.

Not loaded with gold, however, but with items far more mundane and far less valuable, even a few crates that were filled with rocks, simply to make it look like they were low in the water with the precious shining metal.

The *Cipac*, a grand and beautiful frigate, was a swift and deadly predator, and Aketz a skilled hunter. He had designed the armaments and supervised their installation. He had drilled his crew to precision and had spent countless hours working with the archers to ensure the best coordination in their volleys to quickly cripple pirate crews.

He had given Popoca everything the man had asked for and more.

And now he was a decoy.

Many times, the captain looked to the north.

He thought Popoca's ruse was a clever one.

He respected Popoca and loved the man.

But Aketz, in his heart, hoped the ruse would fail.

CHAPTER 8

SIX BITS

Captain Quauh of the carrack *Uey'Lapialli* rested her hand on the main boom to steady herself as the *Uey* rolled about in swells nearing twenty feet, the darkness of the chasing storm, a veritable wall of opaque dark gray, all too clear behind them to starboard. Had she miscalculated, she wondered, in leaving port with the southern skies darkening?

She shook the doubts away. It hadn't really been her choice to make, after all.

The tall, thin woman, standing straight-backed and steady on the rolling seas, brushed her long yellow hair back from her face, her Xoconai colors shining even under the gray clouds. Not yet even twenty-five years of age, Quauh was so very young for her commission, let alone the level of responsibility that had been put upon her at this particular time. She had been on the *Uey* for several years, yes, but this was only her third voyage as the carrack's captain.

She reminded herself that she had come by this command honestly. Captain Mahuiz had not died, allowing her to merely inherit the post. Indeed, he had been the one to recommend her, citing her exemplary work as his first mate on several long southern runs, particularly in two that had included bloody ship-to-ship battles.

"You are here because you belong here," she told herself quietly, her words not even reaching her own ears in the howl of the wind and the crash of the waves.

She stood on the high quarterdeck, staring out to the darker waters to the east across the mighty Mirianic. They were running north, far off the coast of the kingdom of Behren, though occasionally, those in the crow's nest spotted the distant desert land.

With her broad, square sails, the *Uey* was among the fastest cargo ships in the growing Xoconai armada, and one of the largest, at more than seventy feet and with a crew of threescore and ten skilled sailors. The wind had begun strong off the hot sands of Behren this day, but even in that following breeze, the overladen *Uey* had been lumbering along. She was rated at 120 tonnes and weighed every bit of that now and more, her planks groaning, her hold full of gold panned on the treacherous rivers in the dangerous, monster-filled, steamy jungles of Durubazzi.

Now, though, the storm out in the deeper waters had drawn nearly even with them, and Captain Quauh watched with growing concern the increasing luffing of the sails as the winds encircling that hurricane rolled around from the northeast. The *Uey* needed speed, she knew, and that was becoming more and more difficult.

"We had to go," she said under her breath, chasing away her second-guessing insecurities. Weathering the storm in port had not been an option, particularly with so many unsavory characters bringing their ships into that same sheltered harbor on the island of Watouwa for exactly that reason. Had she not put out to sea, Quauh and her crew would have been sitting in the bay surrounded by pirates, and any whisper of the tempting cargo in her hold would have been the end of the ship and the crew.

"Not seeing any, anymore," the first mate, a thick-limbed Xoconai named Matlalihi reported, as if reading Quauh's mind. "Wretched *tepits*." He spat over the rail.

Everything about this man was exaggerated and over-the-top, Quauh thought. His muscles, his emotions, his reactions, his yells, even his teeth and his wide and square jaw. Whispers of "A set of choppers fit for a horse" often followed Matlalihi. He wore his shirt unbuttoned almost to his navel, showing off his large chest and plentiful body hair, and accented that bravado look with a thick chain of silver links.

Too thick, like everything to do with Matlalihi.

"Tepits," Quauh echoed, and she snorted and shook her head, her long and wavy golden hair gathering about her shoulders. The name translated to "little," and Quauh didn't think it fitting of those she feared to be now pursuing the *Uey*, or worse, laying a trap for her. They were dwarfs, yes, but hardly diminutive in any manner other than height. Barrel-chested and as tough as anyone Quauh had ever known, the *estli-kau*—or as the humans called them, the bloody caps, or powries, were simply too formidable to be labeled in such a deprecating manner.

Quauh understood the desire of the fleet commanders to minimize the enemies of Mayorqua Tonoloya, but she also realized that if her crew underestimated these enemies, they'd find a fast trip to the bottom of the dark ocean.

"Don't doubt, Matlalihi. They're out there."

"Surely they cannot pace us in those half-drowned tubs," Matlalihi replied with an emphatic snort. "Our sails catch the wind while they turn blades with their pedaling feet, and in tubs more beneath the waves than above!"

"No, they cannot pace us, as the wolves cannot pace the fleet deer."

"Then we left them far behind."

"We left one of them far behind," Quauh corrected. "One that was likely in place simply to monitor our passing. The estli-kau powries hunt in packs."

Barely had she finished speaking when a lookout called down from on high, "Barrel to the starboard-forward!"

Quauh and Matlalihi looked out to the northeast.

"Clever bastards," Matlalihi muttered.

"Leeward, you'll note," said Quauh. "To sail faster, we will have to sail through them."

"Them?"

"Packs," Quauh reminded. "Put the crew to fighting stations. We will not get by them unscathed."

Matlalihi ran off, shouting "Quarters," leaving Quauh alone on the quarterdeck. The captain looked to the sails, measuring the wind, hearing the protesting groan of the heavily laden *Uey*'s main and mizzen. She knew that she couldn't push the carrack much harder, but knew, too, that she wanted no part of a fight with powrie barrelboats with her hold heavy with gold.

"Second barrel!" the lookout yelled, and before she even continued, Quauh could guess where it was: starboard and farther to the north.

The pack was herding.

"Keel over!" one of the pedaling powries yelled when the barrelboat lurched upward, then leveled and swerved hard to port.

"Benoyt!" screamed the gray-bearded commander of *Six o' Six*, a surly old fishbiter named Pinquickle. "Kick her four bits to port, ye dope! Put us straight to the swells or I'll throw ye to the sharks!"

At the back of the barrelboat, which really quite resembled an elongated barrel, Benny McBenoyt kicked the bar beneath his right foot repeatedly. His audible response was simply a growl, but in his mind, all sorts of curses bounced about, some for Pinquickle and others for just being out so far in a barrelboat on seas this high. A barrelboat was designed to have more of her hull underwater than atop it, much more, but with these kinds of swells lifting and breaking, she was catching too much air, and often at odd angles.

No powrie could work a rudder better than Benny Mc-Benoyt, and he knew that he was doing a truly impressive job even now, since no less than two of the other five in the hunting pack had already rolled over at least once, and this boat, chasing the goldfish ship's taffrail, had a lot more to do than simply hold steady, as with the other members of the hunting pack.

They went up again and all twelve aboard were jarred to the right this time, then lifted as the barrelboat dropped off the wave and crashed into the low wake behind.

But the ten pedaling kept pumping their legs, Benny kept fighting the unwanted swerves, and Pinquickle kept swearing.

Until Pinquickle was spitting salt water, for the powrie captain went up the tower and popped open the hatch just in time to eat a bit of a wave. He coughed it all out, then urged his boys on harder.

"*Uey*'s slowin'!" he shouted to them. "She's seeing our waiting hunters and she's got a luff in her sails, what ho and whack the goldfish!"

"What ho and whack the goldfish!" the pedaling dwarfs returned, using the term that all the powrie and other sailors of the Mirianic seaboard used for the Xoconai, because of both their gold-colored uniforms and their golden skin.

Benny didn't join in the chanting that ensued. He kept his focus on the rudder's foot controls before him, fighting hard to keep *Six o' Six* straight and perpendicular to the swells. The sooner they got the bright-faced humans to strike their colors, the sooner the barrelboats could get back inside protected shoals and calmer seas.

And hopefully, with barrelboats using gold for ballast, instead of sand and rocks.

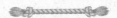

"If a barrelboat rams us below the waterline with the weight we're carrying, we will be swimming like a stone," Matlalihi reminded Captain Quauh.

She didn't turn to regard the man, her gaze locked out to the southeast and the approaching storm, then swinging north to try to get some idea of the barrelboat locations (though she spotted none), then around back to the west and the shallower waters.

She settled that gaze over Matlalihi's shoulder, to the two teams of Xoconai sailors trying to carefully maneuver the giant wheeled arbalists to the starboard rail. She nodded approvingly at their efforts, confident that the weapons could put one of those heavy eight-foot spears through the hull of a barrelboat.

Getting a good shot at one of the mostly submerged, hard-to-spot craft was an entirely different matter, she knew, particularly in these rolling seas.

"They won't ram us," she finally answered Matlalihi. "They know why we are running, know where we came from, and know what we are carrying. Mayorqua Tonoloya's gold won't do them much good at the bottom of the ocean."

"The estli-kau are deep divers, I am told."

"We have fifty fathoms beneath us," she reminded. "They will call for us to strike our colors."

"And?"

Captain Quauh arched an eyebrow at the ridiculous question before answering, "And hopefully one of those arbalist teams will have a proper answer ready."

Matlalihi smiled and nodded at that, but Quauh noted a twitch, a grimace perhaps, as he did. Was he so hungry for a face-to-face fight with powries? He grabbed the rails of the ladder and slid down to the main deck, barking orders to prepare the captain's preferred answer.

"Get two sets of hands on each wheel," she called down to him. "And have every free hand at the sheets. When we turn, bend her low, Matlalihi. You make the yard tickle the waves!"

"My heart, my arm, my very life for Captain Quauh!" he shouted back properly. The man's heightened emotions and responses caught Quauh as uncharacteristic, but she considered their situation now and took it as a sign that this was likely the most desperate predicament she and her crew on the *Uey* had known in their years of sailing the southern waters.

Captain Quauh caught a glimpse of the pursuing barrelboat then, its signature ramming beam protruding from a swell for just a moment before the water broke over it yet again. She scanned the length of that breaker, then nodded, confirming her guess that this one was the raiders' last resort. She rushed down the rail and across the main deck, Matlalihi swept up in her wake, right behind as she climbed to the forecastle.

"Set the arbalists starboard, just forward of the mainmast," she told her first mate. "You tell them to make their shots score. It is all on them, Matlalihi. All our lives on them."

"Red cap waving!" came a cry from above, and Quauh nodded and scrambled up to the forecastle and to the prow. She spotted the powrie immediately, standing wide-legged, leaning against a beam, and likely tied to it, as the barrelboat rolled about some hundred yards ahead.

"Strike and be spared!" he was yelling, or seemed to be

yelling, for with the sloshing seas, Quauh and the others couldn't make him out clearly. It was obvious enough, though, given the situation.

"Pass the word that the dwarfs will put half of us to the sharks, whatever they might promise," the captain whispered to a couple of nearby crewmen, and the pair ran off.

The *Uey* closed, but caught a wave sidelong and pitched. Captain Quauh winced at the sound of the arbalists rolling and crashing about the main deck. The handlers were on them fast, trying to pull them back to starboard, so intent on their work that they simply left one of the crew who had been caught between the war machine and the port rail writhing on the ground, grabbing at her shattered legs.

As swell after swell rolled from the east, Quauh spotted another barrelboat, then a third.

And beyond them, the blackness of the swirling storm.

She had to delay. She wanted those arbalists to send a powerful message before the inevitable chase ensued.

"Steady!" she barked out, and she saw the crew straining with the sheets, and though they weren't in her line of sight at that moment, she knew well that the four pilots on the double wheel were fighting mightily to keep *Uey* in line and perpendicular to the swells.

Trusting in her crew, Captain Quauh went to the prow and stood tall.

Now merely fifty yards ahead, she saw the dwarf standing on the barrelboat. Closer than that, she saw the second boat.

"Be smart, Matlalihi," she whispered under her breath,

and to the powrie negotiator, she yelled, "I am Captain Quauh of the Tonoloya Armada, aboard the MTS *Uey'Lapialli!*" She repeated those letters, MTS, Mayorqua Tonoloya Ship, officially commissioned, a reminder as clear as the golden dragon on the main pennant that this was no privateer, but a true representative of the Xoconai.

"We know yer name and yer gold," the powrie shouted back. "Ye wantin' to talk or ye wantin' to swim?"

Quauh resisted the urge to glance back over her shoulder, not wanting to give her next move away.

"We are wishing to sail home to Entel port," she replied.

"And ye might well do so, and might well do so faster when ye're ridin' higher in the water, ayuh? Might even outrun the storm once yer sails ain't groaning under the drag."

"Matlalihi!" she yelled.

"Hard aport!" the First Mate ordered, and he leaped at the wheels, adding a fifth set of hands, and the crew at the sheets hauled for all their lives.

The *Uey* was too heavy to be nimble, but clever Captain Quauh had timed her call for the turn perfectly. The masts and yards groaned in protest, the five at the wheel turned it, and so turned the rudder, just a bit, but it all happened as the next swell rolled under the boat, and the angle of that wave bent the carrack over and spun her hard.

As soon as that swell passed and the *Uey* settled, the arbalists let fly. One harpoon missed badly in the rolling seas, even though the powrie marked that boat as less than twenty-five yards to port, but the second ballista sent its missile flying in low, skimming the ocean like a surfing Durubazzi tablist riding his footboard before a wave to the beach. The spear hit right below the wide-legged negotiator, whose "Bah!" was erased by the hammer's crack.

The whole of the barrelboat lurched backward, the negotiator flying forward to bend at the waist, staying atop the craft only because he was indeed lashed to that vertical beam.

It didn't much matter, though as the barrelboat began immediately taking on water, more dwarfs climbed up and out of the hatch.

Running the wave to the west, the *Uey* crew who witnessed the barrelboat's seemingly fatal roll burst into cheers.

Captain Quauh couldn't see the spectacle from the forecastle, but she understood clearly enough what had happened. She muted her response.

There were at least four more barrelboats in pursuit, five if her guess as to the name of this particular band proved correct, and she knew well that these powries weren't about to surrender such a treasure as sat in *Uey*'s hold over the loss of a single craft.

She knew, too, that the storm was chasing them all, that they were running to shallower, reef-filled waters, and that the shores of Behren were not that far in the west.

Lady Dharielle's dragon could fly quite swiftly, she had been warned.

"Hah, but she's running into the settin' sun!" Pinquickle called to his eleven crewdwarfs. "Aye, and won't her pretty square sails make a fine vision to follow? Bend yerselfs at the waist, boys, and dig yer legs in hard. We'll be chasing her through the night, and here's hopin' she gets herself into shallower waters, where we can put her to the bottom instead o' begging the goldfish for a strike o' colors, what!"

"Ho hoi!" the crew yelled back. Not Benny, though, who was too busy fighting every twist and swerve of the waves. The thought of an extended chase, whatever the outcome, wasn't sitting well with him, as he was already aching from the rough seas. And all that was only exacerbated when another of the crew yelled back to Pinquickle, "Oy, cap'n, should we might shift our seats a bit?"

"Flip yerselfs now left 'n' right," the captain told them. "Front to back one at a time, that ye're drivin' harder with yer fresher leg."

"Oy, but cap'n?" Benny started to say, but another made the point more clearly, asking if someone should swap places with the steering powrie.

Pinquickle shot that notion down fast. "Quit yer bellyaching, Benny McBenoyt," he barked. "Earn yer damned gold!"

Benny said nothing—what would be the point?—and focused on battling the swells. He had the toughest and most demanding job by far on the barrelboat, but he reminded himself that working the rudder meant that he'd be the last out when the fighting started, and maybe some of the others would have caught all the javelins the goldfish threw their way.

He also reminded himself that if he failed in the job demanded of him, the whole raid could fail. *Six o' Six* was the chase boat, the back gate to lock their victim in the corral the other five were weaving about her. If Benny couldn't keep her in position, the *Uey* might turn back to the south and catch a favorable wind and so be out and away from the trap that had been meticulously planned and set in place.

"They cannot still be out there," Matlalihi said to Captain Quauh long before the dawn. The night had started full of stars, but they were gone now, blocked by the outer bands of the swirling storm—a storm that had accelerated as the *Uey* had turned, and now, as if the powrie barrelboats weren't enough of a concern, the laden ship's chances of outrunning the hurricane had greatly diminished. "They cannot."

Quauh tried not to mock the man with her incredulity. These were powries, and he understood that. Of course they were still out there!

"Let us hope," she humored him.

Even as she finished the remark, a bright light sparked in the east, then soared up into the air and arched in their direction, flaring brighter and brighter as it went. It came down from on high as a flare, illuminating the area, showing the sails of the *Uey* clearly to any nearby.

"*Tletletepo,*" Quauh said in response to Matlalihi's slack-jawed expression. "The thin strips of gray metal. The powries make some quarrels of them for their crossbows."

"To light up the night," the first mate replied. "So they are still out there and they certainly see us."

"They never lost sight of us."

"We have had full sails for much of the run!"

"And powrie legs can turn their propellers tirelessly. They never let us out of sight, and they didn't light up the night about us for their benefit."

"Then why?"

In response, Quauh glanced over her shoulder to the east, where the coast of Behren was now in sight—or would be when day broke, certainly.

"The clever dwarfs are telling any eyes peering out from the desert sands of Behren that we are in their waters," Quauh explained.

Matlalihi glanced over his shoulder nervously, for the Mayorqua Tonoloya had no treaty with Behren, and no leave to be anywhere near the shores of the kingdom ruled by the warrior queen, Chezru Chieftain Brynn Dharielle.

"They are going to demand again at dawn that we strike colors."

"Then we fight."

"You know who they are, yes?" the captain asked.

"The powries?"

"Six Bits," Quauh told him, and he seemed confused for only a moment before the name seemed to spark recognition, and his eyes widened in a combination that was perhaps shock and horror.

"You have heard of them?" Quauh asked, not quite registering Matlalihi's expression.

"Heard about them, aye," Matlalihi replied. "I thought they were a myth."

"Oh, my friend, they are very real."

"You have fought them before?"

"Not as captain." Quauh shook her head. "But I have seen their work. Their reputation is not exaggerated. They know how to fight. Six boats, each with a dozen powries inside."

"A fair fight, then, for we have a like number and the high ground."

Captain Quauh just shook her head. She knew that going against them with an even number meant that you were sorely outnumbered.

"And might only be five now," Matlalihi added. "One boat ate a spear and might be on the bottom, or at least is sure to be far afield."

Even five are too many, Quauh thought, but did not say.

"Turn us parallel to the coast," she told him. "We will ease *Uey* back to starboard a bit at a time, trying to stay in deeper water—they know what we are carrying and won't sink us if we stay deep—and stay ahead of that storm."

"And if they catch us and demand a strike?"

Quauh wore a grim expression but didn't answer.

"You cannot be thinking of surrendering?"

"If they lost powries to our spear, they will kill twice that number when we are taken if we strike colors. If we fight them and they take the *Uey*, we will all be fed to the fishes."

"And when we fight them and defeat them, let the fish eat powrie meat."

"Go. Run us parallel now," Captain Quauh told him, and she waved him away. She knew about Six Bits, indeed, and understood that there was little chance of any victory here. If they fought off the boarding powries, one of the barrelboats would drive its ram through *Uey*'s hull. The carrack was well-built and could possibly survive that, or even two such strikes.

But then they'd never outrun the storm, and low in the water, overladen with heavy gold, their outlook would seem very grim.

Quauh looked up to the sails. Their only chance was to outrun the powries as the dwarfs inevitably tired.

But the wind was swirling, the sails blowing tight, then luffing, over and over. The outer bands of the rotating storm in the southeast were gusting from starboard forward, while the sunbaked sands were countering with the steady, hot desert breeze.

Another flare fired up into the air behind the *Uey*, a stark reminder that Captain Quauh's ship was being herded.

And into waters she did not know.

She went to her cabin, telling herself that she needed to get some rest—she had long given up on any thoughts of sleep. Still, she knew that she would need to be sharp and at her very best in the morning, or even before if the powries stopped the *Uey* from turning parallel to the coastline. She heard Matlalihi barking his orders and cheering the crew on, promising a bloody row in the morning that would turn the waters red with powrie blood.

Quauh expected that Matlalihi was half-right.

Almost certainly, the waters would turn red.

"Drink yer rum, ye waggyskals, so yer brains're rolling to keep up with yer bellies!" Pinquickle ordered, as did the captains of all the other barrelboats. Unlike the sailors on tall-masted sailing ships or the oarsmen of the open-decked knorrs and balingers favored by the Behrenese, powries pedaling in a barrelboat didn't really fear the giant ocean storms. Skimming along, mostly submerged, such a craft could take a tremendous beating. A barrelboat would be tossed about, certainly, and often rolled in the swells, but a skilled crew could roll it back upright easily.

The barrelboat raiders of Six Bits were filled with the most skilled crews the powries could muster in the south Mirianic, perhaps as skilled as any powrie crew outside of their homeland on the Weathered Isles, far to the north and east.

As morning came to the Mirianic, the waves grew higher and sharper. The sound of rain began to drum on the top of the barrelboats.

"She's gonna have to strike!" Pinquickle began to sing to his crew, who took up the ditty:

Rollin' left and rollin' right,
Her yards'll scrape the sea
And soak her masts and lay 'em flat,
She's no way left to flee!

So take her quick
And kill 'em fast
O'er the rails they fly!
Show us yer measure

And get to her treasure
Below the heavy sky!

Faster! Faster! Fast ye must be!
With a belly o' gold
Her planks'll fold
And not a coin for thee!

But oh, what ho!
She's got to know
She's not a chance to fight
So give her a shout
And tell her what's 'bout
She's gonna have to strike!

In the back, straining with all his might, feeling helpless as a white gull in a cyclone, Benny McBenoyt put every bit of remaining strength he had into his stretching legs, trying desperately to flatten both wings of the dual rudder to create some drag, at least, to slow the pitch and roll of *Six o' Six*. He wasn't singing with the others.

He was just sweating and aching and wondering why Pinquickle had held him in the rudder throughout the run.

Six o' Six lurched hard to starboard, came over the top of a wave, and pitched down hard, sending the powries in a crush to the curving port wall.

"Benny McBenoyt, ye fool!" Pinquickle yelled. "Ah, but you'll be number seventy-two afore I'm letting ye count thirteen!"

142

Benny simmered at the thought of a demotion, given his tireless efforts, but he didn't doubt that possibility of the threat from the ever-nasty Pinquickle. He growled it away and kicked hard and fast with his left leg, flapping the rudder, fighting to realign *Six o' Six.* He gripped his sidebars hard, feeling the sea through them, trying to judge the angle of the swells to keep the run perpendicular to the sudden mountains of water. He closed his eyes and focused, trying to block out the continuing berating of Pinquickle.

But that first promise had stung him, for he almost expected it now, and also didn't doubt that perhaps Pinquickle had left him on the rudder all night—too strenuous a task for any powrie—for exactly that reason: to put him at seventy-two. For the captain was talking about the shares of the booty here. As helmsdwarf on *Six o' Six,* Benny was twelfth in line to pick his share of the treasure: the six captains and the helmsdwarfs of *One o' Six* through *Five o' Six* ranked ahead of him.

A simple demotion could drop Benny to thirteenth, but a "break-a-rank," an egregious failure, would throw him to the very end, seventy-second of the seventy-two!

He tried to keep his gray eyes closed so that the scoundrel Pinquickle wouldn't notice the murderous hatred flashing in them.

He tried not to growl threats that the surly Pinquickle might hear.

He tried, but failed, at both.

For all her doubts, Captain Quauh did fall asleep in her cabin. She didn't know for how long, but she came awake quite abruptly when she was thrown from her bunk. Books and flagons, a bottle of wine and a flask of water flew and smashed all about her.

She scrambled to her feet, nearly falling over the other way and only catching herself on her hammock when the *Uey* rolled back to even keel—or almost even keel, for the carrack was listing to port now, only a few degrees, but noticeably so to the seasoned sailor. She stumbled out of her chamber, stuffing her arms through the sleeves of her long double-breasted pilot coat, dyed golden and with thick silver buttons to fasten the heavy wool. She managed the rolling of the deck brilliantly with widespread steps, while she untangled the bright red sash of her long weapon.

Captain Quauh wanted her fearful crew to see her standing firm even with no handhold, and to see that formidable two-handed macana strapped across her back, to have that assurance.

Water streamed off the main deck, barrels and crewmen all scattered about and discombobulated, a testament to the violence of the approaching hurricane.

"Rogue wave, captain!" a woman up above called down to her. "Crossing swells leaped astarboard and sent both their weights against us!"

Quauh brushed her hair out of her face, the locks already soaked from the driving rain. Out to the east, the sky was brightening under the angry black clouds of the hurricane. She called for First Mate Matlalihi, sending some others rushing about to find the man, then slowly turned about to watch the actions of her skilled and veteran crew, making sure that they knew their duties in the battle she expected would soon erupt across her decks. She removed her weapon, and sheath, which had been belted tightly against her back, and loosened the strap on the scabbard. Most macanas were about three feet long, handle to rounded bat end, but Quauh's was a bastard design, fully five feet long and fashioned to be wielded with either one hand or both. She looped the weapon's sash over her head, adjusting it for an easy draw over her shoulder, plopped her bright gold, red-trimmed, and black-plumed tricorne on her head, and made her way to the forecastle.

And there she stood and she watched, trying to find a new gauge for their position, the storm, their enemies. She said nothing when Matlalihi joined her.

"The wave sent some crates tumbling," the first mate explained. "I've got ten hands restacking the gold, to put us to even keel, but I'm hardly seeing the point of it."

"Do you think I care what you're seeing the point of, Mr. Matlalihi?"

"Of course you do not."

"And?"

"And should not, captain," he replied appropriately, but hardly seemed convinced.

"Should we bother to cover the crates with cane again?" he asked.

Captain Quauh, her gaze locked on the dark waters to the northeast, gave a slight shake of her head. It hadn't been simply a guess by the bargaining dwarf back before nightfall. The powries knew about the gold. She didn't know how they knew.

But they knew.

Thus, she was not surprised when one last flare went up from a barrelboat, some two hundred yards to starboard amidships.

They hadn't outrun the stubborn, bowlegged devils, and the storm had gained, its fury more clear to see, east and south, as the day brightened with the rising sun.

But it brightened only a bit, for the rain poured down and the seas were rolling, the wind coming in powerful gusts. The mere thought of a ship-to-ship, or ship-to-barrelboat, fight seemed absurd to Captain Quauh this morning, but these were powries, and bloody caps of the notorious Six Bits. Everything she had ever heard about them seemed disappointingly true.

By this time, from the calls of the lookouts and her own observations, Quauh realized that five barrelboats were within a hundred yards of the *Uey*. None were even trying to hide—why should they, after all, when the rolling waves made using the heavy war machines of *Uey* impossible, and had the barrelboats disappearing with every swell?

Quauh, Matlalihi, and the rest on *Uey*'s top decks watched in amazement as a powrie appeared on the boat nearest their prow, the bowlegged dwarf scrambling up out of the hatch with surprising ease and disregard, casually navigating the rolling craft to the vertical support beam, where he strapped himself in. He turned his attention to the carrack and crossed his arms over his thick chest.

"Hey, Cap'n Sparkleface, ye ready to talk now, or ye thinking to shoot one o' yer puny spears at me boat?" he yelled. "And know that if it's that, ye'll get a hold full o' rams afore ye pull back yer drawstring!"

"Shoot the wretch," Matlalihi whispered, but Quauh kept her hand up high, holding her bowmen and atlatl throwers at bay.

"How long do you believe we stay afloat if even one of those barrelboats breaches our hull below the waterline?" she asked.

"We shot the first," Matlalihi protested. "And I am only noting five of the six barrelboats coming against us now."

"That was in deeper waters," Quauh reminded him. "If they had put us down out there, they would never have retrieved our gold. Now we're not more than ten fathoms."

"Then we should have fought them out there!" Matlalihi yelled, loud enough for others nearby to hear.

Captain Quauh grimaced and tried to find an answer to that. But she had none that would make her crew feel better about their present dilemma. She had hoped against hope that the *Uey*, even so heavily laden, could outrun and evade the powries and get back on course through the night.

Still, she didn't regret her choice, even with its failure. Out in the deeps or here in shallower seas, she had understood from the moment she had taken a good measure of their attackers that the best she could manage if it came to blows was a draw—and one that meant the death of everyone involved.

Captain Quauh and the Xoconai admiralty had gone to great lengths to try to disguise MTS *Uey'Lapialli*'s true purpose. They hadn't sailed all the way to Durubazzi to collect their treasure, but only to Watouwa, a relatively small and insignificant island in the southern waters known as the Eileanan Sea. Watouwa was known for its sugarcane, only that, because the wider world, or even the vast majority of people on the island, did not know that the Xoconai had planted a pyramid with some gold transport mirrors deep in her jungles, amid the waves of giant ferns and swaying palms. The Durubazzi gold was making its initial voyage with magic, away from the many buccaneers ever about the jungle coastline.

Even so, and even here where none should have known about the huge shipment, the loading of the *Uey* had been secretive, with the gold ferried aboard in small crates in the dark of the island nights, and with those crates covered immediately in layers of cane. Their primary defense in their run back to the north and Entel was to appear not to be valuable enough to attract the attention of such notorious pack hunters as Six Bits, who didn't waste their time on such middling targets. Any single pirate along the southern reaches of the shipping lanes would have no chance battling against the *Uey*.

Those hunting packs would never bother with a ship full of cane, particularly not with such a storm rolling up the coast.

But here the *Uey* sat, facing one of the most notorious packs of all. How?

Someone had tipped them off, Quauh knew. She very likely had a traitor aboard.

She filed that thought far away for another time, and hoped that she'd have another time.

"C'mon then, Sparkleface!" the powrie called. "I'm getting rained on here and it's washing me second breakfast out o' me beard afore I get me chance to eat it. Ye gonna strike or sink? 'Cause them's yer choices."

"What are your terms?" Captain Quauh shouted back, and a chorus of gasps and muttered protests and curses sounded all about her.

"Two crew to the sharks and we'll let ye pick 'em. That's for killin' me friend on *One o' Six*, poor fat fellow. And yer gold, o' course. All we can carry."

"We carry sugarcane."

"Aye, sure ye do! That's why the water's lickin' yer rails. Stop yer lying, Sparkleface. Strike and we'll take whate'er gold we can hold and leave ye the rest. Keep making me stand in the rain, or lie to me again, Sparkleface, and we're adding a third goldfish to the sharks for our bargain."

"You cannot surrender," Matlalihi whispered.

"Two killed or all?" Quauh whispered back. "Half the gold or all the gold?"

"C'mon now!" the powrie roared. "Ye know ye can'no outrun the storm with so much ballast anyway!"

"The safety of all my crew!" Quauh shouted back.

"We'll bring the bounty down to one if the one's yerself!" the powrie countered, and Captain Quauh closed her eyes, considering the box that she had just foolishly constructed around herself. The Seafaring Code of the Xoconai Armada forbade any captain from accepting such an offer and the sacrifice, of course, for a captain was worth the entirety of her crew and more. But convincing Matlalihi and the others of that wasn't going to be an easy proposition.

Did she have enough support here to save herself?

A great gust of wind bent the *Uey* to port. Not too far in the east, a bolt of lightning crackled across the sky, sending a thunderous boom.

"C'mon!" the powrie yelled. "Strike or . . ."

The dwarf's last word was lost to those on the *Uey* in the sudden and unexpected jolt, the explosion of a ram driving through the thick hull of the carrack, for a great swell rose behind the *Uey*, a barrelboat floundering atop it. And that wave broke just back of the carrack, launching the powrie craft clear of the water.

It came down from on high, plunging through the *Uey*'s port wall just below the afterdeck, and there it hung, back end angled up, sticking from the carrack like a harpoon sticking from a whale.

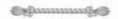

"Benny!" screamed Pinquickle, or more like, "Bennnnnny!" when *Six o' Six* flew off the wave, diving down.

No less terrified than the captain, Benny pumped his feet, but there was no resistance, not through that terrifying eyeblink of falling, not in the moment of collision when he was slammed into the bracing pole centering the rudder works and the other ten crew went bouncing and tumbling forward, living missiles flying for the shrieking captain.

The sudden stop left them angled and dangling, and Benny's

pumping legs still felt no resistance, for the tail end of the barrelboat wasn't in the water.

In fact, little of the powrie craft was actually in the water at all, other than the long ram up front, but the impact had cracked the barrelboat's hull along several seams, and as the waves rolled by, the hungry sea began pouring in.

"Ah, ye dog, McBenoyt!" Pinquickle sputtered. "What've ye done?"

Nothing. The answer was nothing. Benny had positioned the barrelboat perfectly, he knew from the consistency of the angle of descent all along the hold, but the wave had simply overwhelmed the small craft.

Still hugging tight to the vertical beam, he watched his shipmates sputtering and battling and punching, trying to climb over each other and to the hatch or to climb higher for the stern, as more water flushed in with each roll, flooding the front.

With each roll of the *Uey*, Benny realized, and he understood what had happened and why they were now stuck at such a ridiculous angle.

He also understood what would happen to him if Pinquickle got out of this, for the vicious captain would surely blame him, and publicly, to deflect his own culpability. Pinquickle couldn't blame the sea, of course. No powrie would ever blame the sea or a storm.

Benny said nothing in reply, but he studied the jumble of tossed powries carefully, measuring friend or foe coming nearest, his boot ready to kick back any he thought supportive of the captain. He glanced to the side, to his long and curved knife and his small crossbow.

"Ah! By the rolling luck o' the salt-spittin' gods!" the powrie standing atop the other barrelboat shouted when he realized what had happened. "Just take her, boys! Get as much as we can afore she's dragged into the reefs!"

Dazed and bruised, Captain Quauh began to pull herself up from the base of the rail, thinking herself lucky that she hadn't tumbled over—a fate that several of her crew hadn't escaped, apparently, given the shouting all about the decks. She heard Matlalihi barking commands behind her—to the powrie, she realized—then felt the man's strong hands hooking under her arms, helping to hoist her.

It took her a moment to understand his shouting and to decipher his meaning.

"Strike! Strike!" he was screaming. "We're done for!"

Upright now, the captain saw the barrelboats nearing, powries coming forth. The first bowlegged dwarf up atop each boat stepped back from the perch post, moving to a second, lower rail. There, the leading pirate kicked out a peg, releasing an unseen counterweight, apparently, or freed a spring or bowstring, for a sharp report followed, bars righting like the arms of a catapult on either side of the narrow barrelboat, throwing forth a long and weighted rope ladder from the craft's stern.

Clever bastards, she thought.

But her clearing thoughts were drawn back to Matlalihi and his curious response.

"We strike!" he shouted again, then added, "Here's yer pay!"

And he pushed Quauh forward over the rail.

She felt her legs go flying up as she tumbled, and she instinctively twisted and threw back her right arm. The first mate came forward behind her, determined to shove her clear, but she somehow slipped the force of his push as she fell free, and he bent just enough at the waist for Quauh to grab onto the heavy silver chain he wore about his neck. She hooked her right hand and had the presence of mind in that heartbeat of time to turn her wrist and so twist the heavy chain about it.

Matlalihi made a strange guttural sound and clutched at the rail, just barely holding on, and holding a free-swinging Captain Quauh below him as the thick silver links dug into the back of his neck. He slapped frantically with one arm to try to break her free, but her hand and wrist were too tangled.

So he pulled out his long knife as a mate rushed up to help brace him.

Quauh knew she was doomed and that a wet death awaited her, but stubborn as ever, the captain wasn't going alone! She got one foot against *Uey*'s hull and kicked off, swinging outward, far outward as a swell rolled under the ship, leaning it over her.

She braced and bent with all her strength, getting both legs up in time for the swing back into the hull.

"I'll take your hand!" Matlalihi promised, flashing the knife.

Quauh planted both feet against the hull just below the rail. She clenched her jaw, blocking out the pain when that knife dug hard into her wrist and hand, resisting the reflex to thrash and try to get away.

She had to wait, just a moment.

Another swell rolled under the *Uey*. With all her strength, both feet fully braced, Captain Quauh forced her legs to straighten, pulled herself away from the side.

Over the rail went Matlalihi, and when the woman helping him lurched forward beside him, the rail cracked and splintered and all three dropped from the forecastle, splashing into the dark waters of the stormy Mirianic.

CHAPTER 9

AH BUT THE SEA, SHE ALWAYS WINS

C aptain Quauh still had the silver chain in her hand as she thrashed about to get back up to the surface, and it wasn't until she got her head out of the water, sputtering and spitting, that she even realized she was holding it—or that its clasp had broken and first mate Matlalihi was no longer wearing it.

She would have let it go, except that it was tightly wrapped about her sorely wounded wrist and the pressure felt good. She glanced about and hoped its previous owner was far below.

She dismissed that thought and all thoughts about the man, and focused on staying alive, bobbing in the swells, trying to avoid the rolling ships: her own and a quartet of barrelboats crowding about.

Powries streamed up the rope ladders, firing crossbows, while Quauh's crew tried to respond with arrows of their own. Few hits were scored either way, with the seas rolling heavily and the rain pelting down.

Quauh couldn't believe what she was witnessing, such folly for the promise of some gold. Even if they got aboard the carrack and won the fight, did the powries really have a chance of getting back to their bobbing barrelboats with their plunder? In these seas?

But on they went, firing their crossbows, clearing the way for the lead boarders to get over *Uey*'s rails.

The powries were going to win, she knew, as the sounds of fighting grew louder on *Uey*'s decks. She had battled one in single combat once, had hit it a dozen times before the little beast even stopped smiling, and the stout fellow had never stopped coming for her until its life had fully flown—and only because three of her crew had filled its back and the back of its head with javelins and arrows! On land, a powrie was worth a pair of Xoconai warriors.

On the sea, even more.

For the bowlegged powries didn't stumble on a rolling ship.

Quauh knew that she should get back aboard the *Uey*. She was the captain, and the Seafarer's Code was clear on such a matter.

But how?

Her only chance would be to use one of the powrie rope ladders, but there were still dwarfs on those barrelboat decks, one on each, securing the hatch against the splashing waves and bracing the ladders.

She started for the nearest craft—what choice did she have?—but pulled up short when she saw Matlalihi swimming up to it, and the fallen woman, whom Quauh now recognized as Oliloc, her deputy quartermaster, close behind.

So much came clear to Captain Quauh when the powrie

deckhand reached down toward Matlalihi's outstretched hand. And so much more came clear to her when that same powrie paused in helping Matlalihi just long enough to put a crossbow bolt into the face of Oliloc. The bloody cap then pulled the *Uey*'s first mate aboard and guided him down the hatch.

"Matlalihi the traitor," Quauh whispered quietly, shaking her head.

Captain Quauh swam the other way.

The powries were climbing up the angled pedal benches of the barrelboat as if using a ladder, but Benny breathed much easier when he saw those who had managed to get out of the flooding going for *Six o' Six*'s hatch instead of continuing on for him.

At least one of his mates was dead down in the mass of bodies and water far forward, and probably more, but now a second of the crew went out through the hatch, then a third.

He felt a sudden shudder as *Six o' Six*'s ladder was launched.

He heard the fighting outside, on the decks of the goldfish ship, and became even more hopeful. Might they win in spite of the accident? Maybe because of it?

Perhaps, just maybe, Benny McBenoyt would get through this.

"Y'always been a lucky swine-poker," he reminded himself, and put his head down right before a crossbow bolt drove through the right side of his chest, just below his shoulder.

Benny was smart enough not to lift his head, but he let it

loll to the side just enough to note Pinquickle tugging himself over the powrie who was trying to get out of the hatch, with the ornery captain trying to reload his crossbow.

So predictable, Benny thought. The hateful fool would let himself drown in the barrelboat if it meant he could dip his beret in Benny's fresh blood.

Benny noted his nearing adversary pause, and fully expected a second bolt to come his way.

So be it.

Benny rolled down to the left and turned limply so as to shield his head and heart, and stifled his grunt when the expected missile buried itself deep into his shoulder, perpendicular to the first one and not so far above it.

"We gotta be out!" he heard another of the crew yell out from the deck above. "We're winnin' on the *Uey!*"

He heard, too, the continuing approach of Pinquickle.

"Come and dip yer caps!" the captain called back, inviting the others to bask in Benny's blood.

Aye, Benny thought, and out of the corner of his half-closed eye, he saw the flicker of red as Pinquickle reached his hand holding his beret toward Benny's blood-spitting chest wound.

Benny struck like a snake, rolling under, right shoulder back, left rushing ahead. He threw himself out from behind the supporting beam, left hand holding that curved knife and stabbing up and out.

Ah, but he was perfect, he knew, and he snarled with glee! The tip of the blade went in right under Pinquickle's chin and dug deeper, curving up under the captain's skull as Benny just let himself fall farther forward.

Pinquickle dropped like a gutted cod, straight down atop the back side of the nearest pedal bench, his right arm shaking in death throes and still extended, still holding his bright beret—a nicer bloody cap than Benny's, to be sure, and dipped in the blood of many more victims.

And now it was Benny's new bloody cap. He pulled the cap from the gurgling Pinquickle's hand and wriggled himself a bit more from behind the bracing beam so that he could bathe that cap in the dying captain's gushing blood.

"Aye!" he yelled to those few beyond Pinquickle still in the craft and still alive. "Dip yer hats, boys, and feel the sticky salve o' life!"

He plopped the brightly glowing beret on his head, then reached back and grabbed Pinquickle by the collar, tugging the dead captain forward, rolling him about to free him from the tangle of a pedal station. With a great shove, he lifted the dead dwarf up high enough so that the next roll sent Pinquickle tumbling back over his heels, slamming into a pair of powries who had almost made it to the hatch, and sending the whole lot of them crashing down into the flooded prow and sloshing drowned powries.

Benny cackled with glee. His wounded right shoulder wasn't helping him much, but he managed to get back up, almost, and behind the supporting beam, almost. He put the knife between his teeth and reached for the crossbow, an old saying about shooting fish in a barrel coming to mind as he saw the two alive trying to extricate themselves from the watery mess below.

But the barrelboat jolted then, planks splitting, a flood of water rushing in.

Up higher went Benny's end, then right back down again, hard, slamming the water.

The fighting on the *Uey* suddenly sounded louder, and it took Benny a long while to even realize that he was staring up at the dark clouds, the rain pelting down to splatter against his face.

The barrelboat had split in half, Benny's end tumbling tail down into the sea, and there she bobbed and there she bounced, water splashing over the jagged planks.

"By a Honce-man's mother's empty teat," the dwarf cursed. The wreck was fully upright—there was no way Benny could hope to climb out of it with his twice-shot shoulder.

He wondered how long it would take for the swells to swamp the bouncing bucket and feed him to the fishes.

Quauh had grown up thousands of miles away, across the continent and on the shores of a different ocean, one larger but not nearly as stormy and dark and roiling as the mighty Mirianic. She had learned to sail as a very young girl, but before that, had learned to swim, to play in the waves, to let them take her on a wild ride to the beach with a board to lie upon or without.

She had survived a capsizing in that other ocean, and an even worse incident when shifting winds had luffed her sails at exactly the wrong time, preventing her from getting around the long line of rocks that had been piled to protect the harbor of her small hometown. Quauh, still not yet a woman, had watched her small boat rolled into those rocks by a line of swells, and there reduced to driftwood.

She too had been swept into that same jetty and had to fight for every inch of water against the tide. She had wriggled between a pair of large boulders to put her back against a third, and there she had waited for the tide to turn, hour after hour of waves crashing in, drenching her, slamming her back against the stone.

She hadn't cried out but could hear the others screaming for her, up over the jetty, out of sight, fearing the worst.

When the tide had finally subsided, they came for the girl, thinking her surely drowned or bashed to death. What they had found instead was an angry and defiant Quauh sitting in a puddle against that same stone, staring at the sea, her hair matted with water and brine and blood, her clothing torn and stained dark.

Her eyes unblinking, staring, staring down the ocean.

Her lips stretched in a grin.

She had beaten the sea, had cheated the water gods of another victim.

And so she would again, she told herself as she struggled untethered in deep, rolling, and sloshing seas, fighting for every inch of water against mountainous swells, kicking and pulling determinedly to get to a nearby barrelboat.

Up she went, lifted by a swell, and from there, she spotted

the powrie bracing the boarding lines of his barrelboat, one foot on the bottom rung of the rope ladder, the other inside that rung as he gripped the outer lines with all his considerable strength, trying to keep everything as steady as possible. His gaze remained glued to the top of that rope ladder, which was hooked over the rail just above the top of the ladder to the *Uey*'s high afterdeck.

Quauh glided in quietly, going with the waves instead of battling them. She dived low under another roll of the Mirianic, and while under, drew her long macana off her back, only to find that she could hardly grip it with her right hand. Working fast in the relative calm beneath the waves, she used Matlalihi's chain to secure the weapon to that wrecked hand, then kicked hard and wriggled like a dolphin to get up for some air.

When she surfaced, she was much nearer the barrelboat than she had anticipated, and whether the sound of her spitting water or just the sudden appearance, the powrie let go of the boarding line and turned to her with obvious surprise.

Quauh knew that a single strike of her weapon, fine though it was, wouldn't fell the dwarf, particularly since she was below him and treading water, and so had no weight to put behind the blow.

She kicked and thrashed and pulled herself as far out of the ocean as she could, though, and was glad indeed when a wave caught her and lifted her even higher. Down she came from above, bringing her long, tooth-edged paddle up high over her head. As she descended, she snapped forward and brought her arms jerking down before her.

She missed the dwarf.

She hit the ladder's securing ropes, both the one right before her and the second, across the hull, at the spot where they were secured to the barrelboat's metal cleats.

Quauh held on to her weapon as she went back down, her arms going above her head as she dunked beneath the waves, for she had to take care not to change the angle of the blade she had set. Her weapon was hooked to both lines, the rocking and rolling sea loosening and tightening the tangle repeatedly, sawing at the ropes.

She came up to see the powrie leveling a crossbow at her face.

The back rope snapped right before the dwarf fired, the sudden tug twisting him and sending his shot wildly wide. He shouted a protest, or tried to, for then the nearer rope snapped and the ladder came free.

And the *Uey* swayed to port, leaning away.

And the powrie, his legs tangled about that first rung, went flying off, skipping like a stone across the swells as the ladder hauled him wildly for the *Uey*.

Getting up on the barrelboat was no easy task, but Quauh managed it somehow, and managed, too, to keep her prized weapon. She climbed to her knees, then stood at the bracing pole and stared as the *Uey* and her crew died.

High above the fighting on her ship, she watched as the *Uey*'s lookout fired his last arrow. Like ants on a sap-covered tree, a host of powries climbed the rigging for him, long knives held in clamped teeth. The lookout was paying them little heed. He was looking away from Quauh, to the west, shouting frantically, "Reef! Reef!"

When she finally sorted out his warning, Quauh fell to her knees and turned for the hatch. She figured out its turn-and-twist motion soon enough and flipped it open, then crawled inside, meaning to go fully in and secure it against the sloshing seas.

She glanced back, though, and froze in place, first watching the powries getting to her crewman, her trusted lookout, blades flashing.

Despite the water splashing in about her, Quauh simply couldn't turn away, particularly a moment later when her beloved ship jolted so suddenly, planks screaming as if in pain, masts and yards and rigging shuddering violently.

She watched the MTS *Uey'Lapialli* die.

Captain Quauh fell into the barrelboat hold more than climbed down, then pulled the hatch closed, entering a foreign world indeed. She marveled at the groaning belly of a powrie barrelboat, glowing in the blue light of luminescent fungi hanging in jars as living lanterns the length of the cylindrical hull, shining on the pedaling stations and the rudder assembly.

There was no manual, no notes or appendixes in the Seafaring Code to help her now, and Quauh was quite sure that there were simply no actions she might take to actually control the world about her.

It was luck now, and only luck, for her.

She crawled far aft and braced herself about the beam there, setting her feet against the rudder pedals. But she wasn't a powrie, particularly not a skilled helmsman like Benny McBenoyt. Quauh couldn't *feel* the sea, not like this.

Port or starboard, did it really matter?

It was all just luck.

And now the storm came on in full, throwing the boats, throwing the swimmers, throwing the corpses and the flotsam and the jetsam, and throwing Quauh, battering her so fully that at one point she bit clear through her bottom lip and spat out a tooth.

She vomited and she screamed, and screamed some more, at the top of her lungs, just as she had screamed in the hours fighting the swells against the jetty in another ocean. She screamed in anger, not fear. She screamed in denial of the storm, of the howling wind and crashing waves and thunderous reports so continual and loud that she couldn't even hear herself screaming.

She screamed because if she didn't, she would have to take stock of her situation, and then she knew that she would know despair.

She screamed until there was one great twist and roll, a full flip diagonally that sent the barrelboat diving under the water like a dolphin plunging down from on high, and suddenly, there was silence.

Peace, and silence.

But oh, what a clever craft was a powrie barrelboat, its buoyancy greater than its ballast even when half-flooded, as was this one. *Five o' Six* leveled and she rose, and she bobbed above the waves once more, into the thrashing liquid jaws of the godly Mirianic, which cared not for the renewed screams of the Xoconai captain.

Screams that were ended by the next sharp swell, which

threw Quauh face-first into the curving side wall, where she slumped and found peace once more in silent blackness.

***

With his injured shoulder, it proved to be a great struggle, but Benny finally managed to climb up the now-vertical row of pedals and get his good arm up high, clasping the jagged, broken wood where *Six o' Six* had split in half.

Above him, lightning creased the sky, the thunderous retort all but lost in the endless crashing of the waves and the roaring of the wind.

Benny's tub was riding lower now, as it was half-filled with seawater and rainwater, and every rolling wave beneath him sent a bit more splashing in, and the unrelenting rain poured down. He didn't like his chances and understood that he was running out of time here.

Struggling, kicking, scraping his feet and pulling with all his might, the powrie inched up the side wall. He grimaced mightily as he lifted that second shoulder, feeling the bite of two crossbow quarrels deeply embedded within it. But he finger-walked that right arm upward, gnashing his teeth and spitting curses for every movement, until that hand, too, had the lip.

Grimacing and growling in pain, Benny pulled himself up just high enough to peek over the side.

He sucked in his breath with surprise to find the goldfish carrack lying on her side not far from him, like a great whale skeleton, her masts and yards shuddering and shaking and

166

splintering as the waves pounded relentlessly over her in her tenuous and disastrous perch on the reef. She was more than halfway over to port, the tips of her yards and a good part of her rigging already in the water. She had little fabric left in her sails, just torn rags whipping in the wind.

Little remained of her stern castle as well, with every other plank, it seemed, blasted away. But there stood *Six o' Six*'s front half, embedded in her tail, stabbing her to the bitter end.

Despite the seemingly imminent end of his life, Benny began to laugh at that strange sight of half a barrelboat sticking up into the air from the carcass of a dead ship. "I threw that spear! Haha!" he congratulated himself, though of course, he had done no such thing. The Mirianic had thrown that spear, despite Benny's best efforts to prevent it.

But he laughed again anyway, and then even more raucously when he realized that the wretched pelican-throated Captain Pinquickle was probably still in that part of the barrelboat, bobbing and bouncing like the dead fish Benny always knew the old dwarf to be.

"Good boat, stupid captain," the powrie muttered. He looked around. All sorts of wood bobbed in the water about him, mostly pieces of the *Uey* as she broke apart. He might be able to crawl out and find a better raft, he thought, and he began to plot. Or better still, maybe he could find a suitable piece to put atop this bucket of his, to lessen the water flowing in.

"Aye," he muttered, and he looked all about with focused purpose.

Another crack of lightning stretched across the sky above

him. He noted bodies in the water and wondered if he might get some new clothes.

"Why not, eh?" he shouted at a goldfish sailor who went floating by, and he even pulled himself up higher and tried to reach out to snag the corpse. He didn't come close, and he slipped back into his tub, and barely held on with only his wounded arm. He struggled and kicked against the side, trying to hold his place, trying to reset his good hand up on the rim, and at last he did, and yanked himself up, then nearly let go in surprise when a huge bolt flashed down, splitting the darkness, and issued a boom that pealed loudly above all the other noise and shook Benny to his core.

He thought that perhaps the lightning had struck the *Uey.* He wasn't sure, and before he could sort it all out enough to make a better guess of it, he realized that the carrack was now quite a bit farther away from him. When he had first peeked over, he was about level with her taffrail as she lay there, but now he had already drifted past her masts.

So possibly, he realized, he was past the reef, as well.

Before that thought could put any hope in the waterlogged dwarf, he noted a greater darkness over to his right, farther out at sea. For a moment, he thought it another ship, her tall decks and sails blotting out the clouds.

For just a moment. But no, it couldn't be, for the hull of the thing seemed to be growing taller and taller, too high for any ship Benny had ever heard tell of.

"Oh, by me own hairy arse," the dwarf muttered when the white beard of the monster gave it away, some forty feet above the hull of the *Uey*, and charging fast like some rampaging giant.

A wave. An enormous, monstrous, murderous wave.

Benny just sighed and let go, skidding and bouncing to splash into the water that had collected in his makeshift bathtub. He looked up through the opening now ten feet above him, watching the lightning flashes in the angry clouds.

But then they stopped, or rather, they were blocked, as the black giant lifted, lifted, then crested and began its dive.

Benny's raft went up on its side, rising with the swell. Then it was flying and tumbling, with Benny holding on for his life and screaming, because he didn't know what else to do. The broken hull of *Six o' Six* crashed down and bounced again and again, then went racing along in the froth, driven by tons of water. Benny and the boat flipped too many times to count, and not always at the same time and place for the rider and his craft. Benny stopped counting anyway, for suddenly he was flying free, launched from the broken barrelboat into the air.

He splashed back down in the frothing wave and kept the good powrie sense to hold tight to his bloody cap. On and on it went, the water driving him and tossing him and flipping him like a child's toy.

Tumbling and spinning, tumbling and spinning, and then crashing against something more substantial, scraping at his skin as he was still driven forward. Then driven down hard, feeling like a team of horses had just galloped across his back, planting him facedown into the . . .

. . . into the mud.

He sputtered and rolled free, and the water grabbed at him on its retreat, but he dug his claws into the sand and held on.

Facedown in the mud.

On a beach.

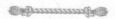

Quauh had no idea of the passage of time. She opened her eyes, her head pounding, her face caked in dried blood, her hair matted with blood and salt water, her every joint aching, particularly her right wrist, which had felt the bite of Matlalihi's knife. She was still in the barrelboat, and it was mostly dry, and upright.

It was still rocking, though, forward and upward, then down and back, predictably and rhythmically, and the Xoconai sailor who had spent her entire life by the sea and out upon the sea understood at once that it was the surf rolling her and not the tempest.

She unwound herself from the beam and the pedals, stretched the pain from her limbs, and crawled to the short ladder and the tower to the barrelboat hatch.

She held her breath and lifted the hatch to peek out.

The glow of pre-dawn lit the sky behind her. To the north, she saw the darkness of the storm, rushing away.

And before her, the unmistakable silhouette of land, the tide pushing her in. Over to her right, north along the beach, she saw some small fires and heard some commotion, and it took her only a few moments to realize it to be the powries, so many powries.

And her crew, or what remained of them, she realized

when she heard one woman being run down by the dwarfs, to be dragged away screaming and pleading for mercy.

She lifted the hatch a bit higher and turned her gaze out across the black wall of rain in the northern waters, then back to the lighter sky in the east.

The water was full of wreckage, and almost all of it from the *Uey*. Captain Quauh had lost her ship, and had lost a sovereign's treasure hoard of gold.

A not-small part of Captain Quauh wanted to just sink below, close the hatch, and stay in the barrelboat until she died—or better yet, scramble out and swim to the deeper waters in the east until she simply could not swim anymore.

She had lost her ship.

There could be no greater dishonor.

She had lost the gold the city sovereign of Entel had worked tirelessly to procure.

That travesty went beyond mere dishonor to some practical possibilities of punishment.

She did close the hatch and put her face in her hands—in her good hand, anyway, for she crushed the wounded one against her breast—and tried to figure out what she might do. Nothing, she realized, at least while she remained in this boat. For she couldn't pedal it and couldn't steer it, and it would soon slide onto the beach, in any case, where the powries would almost certainly swarm it and reclaim it.

So Quauh did the only thing she could, as she had done when she had missed the lip of the jetty in that distant harbor and that other ocean, as she had done bobbing in the tempest-driven sea.

She threw aside her despair and her fear, threw open the hatch, and rolled off the port side of the barrelboat, putting it between her and the powries on the beach. She replaced her macana across her back and she swam, buoyed a bit by her dark-fern breastplate. She went as far as her weary and battered limbs could take her before she came upon a large piece of wreckage and hooked onto it, then slumped near unconsciousness and rode it all the way in to the island.

It wasn't until her impromptu raft banged against a rock, jolting her fully alert, that Quauh realized that the wreckage carried a bit of unintentional lagan within it: a rather large and sturdy chest, battened tight and locked, which surely would have sunk like a stone if not for the buoyancy of the tublike wreckage that had carried it so far.

A wave rolled under Quauh and the raft, followed by another jolt.

Quauh climbed up a bit and peered ahead, to find that the raft had drifted even farther to the south, off the edge of the beach and into a rocky spur.

It scraped the stone again and began to turn to Quauh's left, and she hand-walked the other way, trying not to get caught between the raft and the stones. She noted then that there were many rocks all about, a beach of giant stones weathered by the forces of wind and ocean for centuries untold. Two spurs jutted out, a channel worn between them, and into that channel went the wreckage, the very next wave bringing the impromptu raft skidding on a bed of small, surf-smoothed stones.

CHAPTER 10

A LUMP OF SAND IN A SEA OF ROCKS

Walls of stone ten feet high and thirty feet long brought mixed feelings to Quauh as she moved in front of the makeshift raft. She was shielded from the powries on the beach down to the south, yes, but she couldn't see much about her beyond this narrow channel. Coordinating her movements with the flow of the incoming waves, she tugged the raft higher across the small stones. She could see the high-water mark some dozen feet farther along the channel, and with the tide coming in now, she knew where she had to put the raft to keep it ashore.

Beyond that point, the ground sloped up more quickly, spilling out above the stony side walls. Up there, it was more dirt and brush than water-washed stone, and Quauh paused and spent a long while just staring at the landscape in the growing light, looking for some movement among the leaves and flowers, the frangipani and the white spider lilies, and the small powder-puff trees. Her gaze lingered longer than it took her to feel comfortable that there was no one hiding up there, because she knew these plants. She had seen them in southwestern Tonoloya far, far to the west, in the waters where she had sailed as a young girl.

The world so suddenly became smaller for Quauh in that moment. She didn't know why—she had seen these plants in this region before, of course—but there seemed to be something so very familiar to her here in this secluded little spot. Maybe it was the smell of the flowers washing down on her, or the temperature of the water as it swept in about her ankles, or the aroma of the weeds in the stones about her. Whatever it was, for the first time since she had traveled over the mountains and crossed the great plains coming east to Quixi Tonoloya, Quauh felt as if she was still home, still that same little girl who had taken all the western ocean could throw at her and had thrown it back in a stream of curses and utter defiance.

But she wasn't mad now, strangely. Her wrist ached, for it was surely seriously wounded, but she didn't really feel the pain. Not in this moment. She didn't even feel defiant, or triumphant, in this moment, this one moment, this reprieve from the pain and the guilt of losing her ship and her crew.

But no, Quauh kept all that out of her mind for just this moment.

And then she understood. It was the aromas and the wash of water, yes, but more than that, it was the sound! The waves sent water rushing up into the channel, and when it receded, the pull of the water made those rounded stones click and chatter as if speaking to each other. It was barely perceptible in the hum of the wind, but when Quauh closed her eyes, she couldn't miss the sound, and once she identified it, it seemed to become magnified, grabbing her attention fully.

She recalled a rocky shoreline back home where she had often fished and dived for shellfish, and a channel there with similar stones, clattering and chattering in their conversations during the ebb and flow of the waves. She had only heard it a couple of times, but those precious few memories could not have been clearer to her than in this moment. Memories she had shared with her father, who had taught her the ways of the sea, the eternal sea, the sea from which they all had come and to which they would all return.

Yes, her papah. She could almost feel his eyes upon her now, his strong chin nodding his approval and reminding her that her work was far from finished here.

She had taken the hits of the powries, of Matlalihi the traitor, and of the sea, and she had emerged from the surf yet again, that little girl who found her way.

He would be proud, but it wasn't time for that kind of self-satisfied puffery right now.

Thus, the moment proved fleeting. Quauh wasn't safe; far from it.

The waves helped her in getting the half shell of flotsam and the chest it contained up high enough into the rocky channel and onto the tide-smoothed stones so that it wouldn't slip back into the water even when the tide was highest. She still didn't know what to do with the found treasure. She couldn't possibly lift it, or even drag it. Quauh had watched them load the *Uey* back on Watouwa Island, with four strong and very large people handling the chests with a block and tackle, thick carrying poles, and a wheeled base. This laden chest was easily ten times her weight.

But again, she found that the sea was her ally here, for the jostling and the bouncing, and likely more than one slam against a rock on the way in, had broken a top corner of the chest, enough to allow Quauh to wedge her macana under the lid and create leverage for her to pop the lock.

She glanced around reflexively once again to make sure she was alone, then threw the lid open and stared in awe at the top layer, sixteen bars of pure, solid gold, four across and four deep. Just looking at the depth of the container, she came to understand that there were four such layers. Sixty-four bars in this chest, each of them worth more than Quauh would earn in a full career of captaining ships for the Tonoloya Armada.

The chest and the curved flotsam that held it were grounded here in the shallow on the small stones, and there was no way Quauh was moving it without the power of the ocean buoying and pushing. She looked around, knowing that her opportunity was short on time, then grabbed up a bar, tucked it tight against her side, and hoisted another. With fifty pounds in her arms, the Xoconai struggled and stumbled across the pad of rounded stones, but she kept going, up and to the left-hand wall of stone, toward a narrow crack in the great gray slab.

No, it wouldn't suffice, she realized immediately.

So she went up, up the ramp of stone and dirt, then crawled atop the block, lying low as she crawled about in the dim light of pre-dawn, peering into every crack. She glanced over to the north, to see an expanse of sea-rounded stone shelves, pocked with pools and dotted with boulders. The northern edge of the channel arm wasn't as smooth and solid, not a singular block of rock like the ones forming this channel. Still, all the boulders there, too, were fully settled and had been here for centuries, but they weren't mortared together or fitted by craftsmen, which meant that there were crevices between some, open holes, even, with pools of water down below.

Quauh dropped a bar into one such hole and heard a splash below. She strained her eyes and noted that the bar wasn't fully submerged.

In went the second.

Back and forth she crawled, into the channel to the chest, collecting two golden bars at a time, then only one as her strength began to give out with each climb and crawl. Rain-soaked and sweat-soaked, the woman reminded herself with every struggling step of the many implications here. She needed this. The *Uey* had been commissioned by City Sovereign Po-poca of Entel and by Grand Augur Apichtli himself, and that vicious old priest wasn't about to be merciful to a captain who had lost thirty-five chests of gold—more than two thousand bars of the precious, all-important metal, the lifeblood of Xo-conai magic and beauty.

She gathered up the last two bars together, anxious to be done, stumbled back to the rocks, and dropped them atop the pile below. Then she rushed about, collecting armfuls of wet seaweed, and that, too, went into crevice to conceal her treasure.

Quauh rolled to her back atop the channel arm and took

some much-needed deep and relaxing breaths. She noted that the commotion down to the south along the beach was growing, however, and the storm was moving far away, with a clear sunrise just beginning to peek over the eastern horizon. She pulled herself over the northern ridge of the channel arm and nestled down at its base in a shallow created by a huge boulder that had crashed into the giant block in some century past, settling like a mole against the giant gray slab.

She had to hope that they wouldn't find her.

Panic hit her as she closed her eyes with the realization that she had left the chest sitting there on the wreckage in the channel, opened and empty!

She tried to rise, but Quauh discovered that she could go no farther. Battered and weary, truly exhausted, she had no choices left. She needed to rest.

She rolled to the very base of the channel arm, rolled to her side and brought one arm up over her face, then fell fast asleep.

A pair of eyes locked onto the lean form running back and forth from the flotsam in the channel. He didn't know it to be the captain of the *Uey*, but he recognized that it was indeed a goldfish human and no fellow powrie, of course.

"What're ye about now?" he asked himself repeatedly through the process.

He wanted to go down and investigate but held back,

thinking it wiser to let this person be done with the work, what-ever the work might be, before he had to kill the damned thing.

Over the channel arm went the woman at long last, and still the powrie hesitated. As the dawn began to break out over the water before him, he drew his long, curving knife and began creeping down from the brush into the channel, toward the broken tub of wood, shifting and floating a bit now that so much had been removed and the tide was coming in strong and hard.

He rushed to the north wall of the channel and there paused.

How Benny's eyes widened when a wave smashed against the wreckage, nearly flipping it and rolling out its contents.

A chest!

An empty chest.

The powrie almost laughed aloud. He knew well what the carrack had been hauling!

He had to move now, Benny realized, but in which of the three possible directions? Should he run to the flotsam and push it out into the surf, to be taken by the swells so that his friends who had settled down the beach didn't note it in the growing light? Or should he rush to the top of the channel arm, where the human had hidden the treasure? Or over the arm completely to put an end to the one other person who knew the secret?

"Aye, that," he decided, and he crept back up to higher ground, thinking to circle the arm and come at her from the other direction.

"Hey there, mate!" Benny heard from the side. He glanced to the sea nervously and noted with great relief that the chest had rolled out a bit, swamped, and now was almost completely out of sight in the still-dim light. Even if they found it, they might simply think it had broken open and spilled its gold out on the sea floor.

Benny turned to see a trio of powries approaching along the southern beach.

"Oh, but that's McBenoyt o' *Six*," said one, a grizzled old dog named Columbine.

"Aye and heigh-ho, Benny," added another, Reeker, the helmsman of *One o' Six*.

Columbine, too, had been serving on that first boat, Benny recalled then.

"So, *One* made it, eh?" he replied, quickly moving past the right-hand arm of the rocky channel, sheathing his knife as he went. "We thought ye lost when the harpoon skewered ye."

"Small hole and one pedaler killed to death," Columbine answered. "We got out and got her rolled back to right, then bailed."

"Aye, and talking o' harpoons, nice throw there, McBenoyt!" laughed the third, a young, red-haired sprite, with limbs so thin they seemed like willow branches hanging out of a barrel. Benny didn't know this one's name, nor his boat, but he found immediately that he didn't much like the fellow. It occurred to him that this one might hold a seat that Benny might be taking on a surviving boat after he had left the sprite's corpse bobbing in the surf and had buried the chuckling fool's heart deep into the beach.

"Oh, but ye should've seen it, mates," the teasing, spindle-armed powrie told Columbine and Reeker. "Flew from the wave, did *Six*, like a throw from the Himself, MacLlyr! Might that 'twas inspired, or might that *Six*'s helmsman forgetted which way the waves was rollin'!"

That brought a laugh from the other two.

"Aye, we heared as much," said Columbine, nodding to Benny. "Good fortune's what we're guessing, since we got the treasure and a lot of goldfish blood for our caps."

"Got what treasure?" the young redhead argued. "The damned gold's out at the reef, sunk deep with *Uey*."

"Ain't so deep," said Reeker. "And we'll get all we can carry." He motioned for Benny to come along, then turned to head back down the beach.

Benny hesitated, considering the situation, the human on the other side of the narrow channel, and the hidden gold.

No, he decided. He wasn't about to say a word.

He followed his mates down the beach to the gathering a few hundred strides away.

Captain Quauh had a moment of true confusion when she opened her eyes to see the last vestiges of sunset off in the west.

Hadn't she collapsed at the break of dawn?

She had slept through the whole of the day, she realized. The woman rolled from the stone to her feet, crouched defensively behind the side of the stone, and perked up her senses, fearful, for something had startled her from her sleep. But she saw no threats nearby—had she really been fortunate enough to remain hidden throughout the whole of a sunny day?

Put me deep in the groun' so cold
I'll be dead 'fore I e'er get old . . .

The voices drifted on the breeze across the jetty between her and the other survivors. She couldn't miss the solemnity in the powries' song and knew it to be a dirge. Yes, they probably had many friends to bury.

Done me fights and shined me cap
Now's me time for th' endless nap.

Quauh gathered her sensibilities and took a quick look at her surroundings in the dying light, then carefully scaled the nearest rocks to the top of the channel formation. Carefully and very slowly, for her torn wrist was already percolating, swollen now and oozing blood and a bit of pus, and the whole of her forearm showed an angry redness. She made it to the top, sucking in her breath in stinging pain with every movement—the wrist was surely broken, and it appeared infested, looking angry and sickly. Down the beach, within a circle of standing torches just above the high-tide mark, the powries huddled and sang, arms interlocked, all eyes staring at the ground—at the graves, Quauh understood—before them.

Done me fights and shined me cap
Now's me time for th' endless nap.

It shook the Xoconai a bit to see and hear such soberness and yes, humanity from the bloodthirsty powries, but still, she felt little sympathy for their losses. She knew what would have happened to her if the treacherous Matlalihi had turned her over to them. The bloody-cap dwarfs came by their reputation honestly and mercilessly. She had never heard of powries before coming to the east. Here, they had been a scourge for centuries, with accounts of their raids found in the annals of recorded history contained in every Abellican abbey. With only rare exceptions, these written accounts had been scribed by monks filled with obvious fear and loathing.

Certainly, Quauh's experience with the diminutive powries since coming here and getting out onto the Mirianic had substantiated those same descriptions.

Were there other sides to the strange little people? she wondered. Whatever she might think of the Bearmen, or the folk of the Wilderlands, the powries were a different matter altogether. Perhaps her Xoconai leaders were correct in proclaiming all the others to be sidhe, goblinkin, less than human, but the powries could not be compared in any way to that. First, there were no female powries that she had ever seen—or maybe there were no male or female powries. Just powries. Just grumpy, growling, fighting, tougher-than-stone powries. Whispers said they had no sex, that when they were away from their island homeland, they procreated from burying the hearts of their dead and performing a ceremony, as she was witnessing right now, it seemed. Those hearts would regrow, the powrie resurrected and clawing his—or perhaps its?—way out of the dirt, as an adult powrie exactly as he, or it, had been, with full memory of the previous life.

Were there even powrie children? There were certainly none to be seen here along the shores of the mainland. None in Freeport or anywhere else that anyone had ever noted.

According to the common lore, those powries whose hearts could not be readily recovered, buried, and consecrated with song would wander as ghosts back to the Weathered Isles, far to the northeast, and there would be reborn, or more precisely, re-created, stepping from the fires of the volcanoes again as adult powries, only this time without the memories of who they had once been.

Quauh didn't know how much, if any, of these stories were true. As she didn't know if the bloody-cap dwarfs were men or women or neither, or something in between.

She let those thoughts flitter away then, for they were notions for another day, if she could manage to ever have another day with time to contemplate. The sun was setting, and Quauh didn't dare stay here by the rocks on the otherwise open beach. She used the rocks for cover for as long as she could, then sprinted up the sandy bluff, dodging the many scraggly plants that were trying to gain a foothold there, and over the top into a forest, thin with trees down here near the water, but thick with underbrush. She moved along to the south, trying to position herself close to the powries so that she could get a better idea of what they were doing and what their intentions might be.

One barrelboat came onto shore, another headed out. After the burial of the powrie bodies that had been recovered on the beach, in the surf, and bobbing out in the deeper waters by the reef, the stoic dwarfs went about their business with the same sense of ruthless purpose that had brought them out into these stormy waters in the first place.

The hearts of nineteen of the seventy-two powries of the pirate team known as Six Bits were in the ground on that beach, and another eight powries were still missing, and likely sitting in the bellies of some sharks or trapped in the sunken wreckage of the *Uey* or the two wrecked barrelboats, *Six o' Six* and *Three o' Six*.

But so be it. The lost fellows would be replaced—the list of bloody-cap dwarfs looking to join Six Bits was long and thick with quality. In a stroke of great luck, *Five o' Six* had been found just sitting on the beach, bobbing in the surf, and *One o' Six* had rejoined the victors, with only one casualty, a crewman who had caught the arbalist spear when it had driven through her hull.

Thus, they buried the hearts of their dead comrades with their berets, sang their ceremonial dirges, which would inspire regrowth of those lost fellows, then towed the remaining corpses of heart-gutted powries and goldfish humans out to the north in deeper waters to let the sharks have their meals far away from the reef.

Because the reef was the point of it all, to be sure, or more particularly, the point of it all was the gold that had settled on the ocean bottom all about that reef.

Benny McBenoyt kept a low profile through the day, for among the working powries were no less than half the crew of *Six o' Six*, including one dwarf who had watched the skirmish inside the ruined boat that had led to Benny's killing of Captain Pinquickle, the sixth-ranking powrie in Six Bits.

The seawater had washed Captain Pinquickle's blood from Benny's long knife, but surely hadn't washed the memories of Pinquickle's murder from any witnesses.

As a precaution, or more likely, a stay of execution, Benny joined up with Columbine and the other pedalers from *One o' Six*, for these were the powries ranking right behind him among the seventy-two of the pirate band, and since two of the barrelboats had been lost, it was likely that one of these dwarfs would be promoted to helmsman on one of the replacement vessels. Benny expected that they'd welcome him in their midst if for no other reason than to bend his ear.

All went well for a short while, *One o' Six* spending more time on the beach while the three lesser crews did the funeral runs to the north, but with the eastern sky still dark, a powrie moved by and paused, staring at Benny.

"Y'out o' work to be doin'?" Columbine yelled at the gawking dwarf, who just replied with a quick glance at Columbine, then dropped his gaze back over Benny as he slowly walked away.

The whispers began almost immediately, and ended abruptly when High Captain Thorngirdle of *One o' Six* roared, "Benny McBenoyt!"

"By the howls of an angry grizzle bear, who'd ye murder?" Columbine joked right beside Benny.

"Stopped me own murder," Benny muttered back. "With me knife."

"Sounds right."

"Me own murder by me captain."

"Oh," Columbine said, and stepped away from Benny, as did the others in his group.

Thorngirdle, a great beast of a powrie, wide and muscled, with a wild black shock of curly hair and a beard that reached as wide as his shoulders, and with a beret so coated in the blood of his enemies that it glowed in the night, fixed his gaze squarely on Benny and lifted his hand, motioning for Benny to come to him.

Benny had been in Six Bits for nearly a decade, and this was the first time he had met the withering gaze of the great and deadly Captain Thorngirdle. He didn't much like it.

He swallowed hard and reminded himself of the warmth he had felt when his knife had gone up through Pinquickle's chin and into his brain. This predictable situation would almost certainly be the price, he had known in that moment of murder—at least, if the sea didn't take him first.

Benny walked out as the other powries on the beach, who numbered more than thirty, since only one barrelboat was then out on the water, formed a circle about him. The whispers began anew, and Benny heard the name "Pinquickle" spoken more than once, confirming to him the source of Captain Thorngirdle's angry tone.

"Yerself's Benny McBenoyt?" Thorngirdle said when Benny stopped right before him.

"Aye."

"Helmsman o' *Six o' Six?*"

"Aye."

"I heared ye threw the boat like a spear at *Uey*."

That brought a fair bit of laughter from the circling powries.

"Two waves crossed right afore us and pushed us up," Benny explained, bringing his outstretched hands together, fingertip to fingertip, to mimic the wave movement. "Up we went with it, and th' water dropped faster . . ." He stopped and just shrugged, for it was clear that Thorngirdle didn't want to hear it.

"Ain't blamin' yerself for that, helmsman, but do tell me, where's yer captain?"

Benny swallowed hard.

"Yerself ain't blamin' me, boss captain, but Captain Pinquickle to be sure were. Put two bolts into me, he did." Benny pulled back his shirt enough to reveal one of the missiles, the front half of a crossbow quarrel still embedded and the wound still looking mighty nasty, although the magic of the bloody beret had begun the healing process already.

Thorngirdle eyed the wound, then snorted dismissively as if it was nothing much.

"And he was coming for me, trapped as I were up behind the rudder workings."

"Coming to whet an' wet," Thorngirdle reasoned. "To feed his cap—aye, and that's the one ye're wearin' now, ain't it? The one ye're wearin' and the one that's still sticky with Captain Pinquickle's gushing blood, eh?"

"He'd've killed me. I killed him first," Benny said with a shrug.

"He might've. That's his choice, eh, by the rules? So yerself choosed to kill him and take yer chances o' getting' away with it?"

Benny could only shrug again, and Thorngirdle nodded and seemed satisfied with the answer.

"I'd've done the same," the boss captain admitted. "Ye played the odds with nothin' more to lose than ye thought ye was losing anyway."

"Aye."

"We'll bury yer heart and sing for ye," Thorngirdle offered graciously.

Though he wasn't very pleased at the prospect of having his heart cut out, likely while he was still alive and watching, Benny returned the offer with a meager smile and a nod of gratitude. They would perform the ceremony! Benny would rise from the grave in a matter of a few months, and with his memory, his very identity, intact.

This was far better than he had expected. They could have just fed him to the sharks, and then his ghost would have had to walk all the way back to the Weathered Isles, and then Benny McBenoyt would be no more, for the new one he became wouldn't know the old one he had been.

He gave a greater and more sincere smile of thanks to High Captain Thorngirdle.

This was the powrie way. Their population now was the same as it had been a hundred years before, and a hundred years before that, and, so they believed, a thousand years before that. There were only a certain number of powries, and that was all there'd ever been, and that was what there'd be forever, so they believed.

"Ye need not do more work," Thorngirdle added generously.

"Happy to dive for ye," Benny offered, but the boss captain shook his head. He looked past Benny and called to Columbine and the others of his crew, "Put him with th' other prisoners."

Columbine and Reeker rushed up and grabbed Benny by the arms.

"No fightin' now," Thorngirdle told Benny.

"I know what I did. I know the price," he replied.

"Good man, then. Now don't ye be killin' any o' the goldfish, and if they're plottin' some trouble, ye tell me. The better ye do, the quicker I'll make yer death and the louder we'll sing for yer return."

"Appreciate it, boss captain."

Soon after, Benny found himself sitting in a shallow pit dug in the sand with a handful of battered, wounded, utterly defeated goldfish sailors. Pickets had been set around the ring, but getting out would have proven little trouble—except for the powrie guards standing all about, weapons in hand. No one was going to make any escape attempt here, Benny knew at once. The distraught men and women all just sat with eyes downcast, trying to come to terms with what seemed to be their obvious fate.

All except one, a large man with wide shoulders, who paced back and forth, spitting curses and insisting that he be taken to the boss.

"What worth a powrie's word, then?" he kept growling at the nearest guard, who was eating a large raw fish and responded only with a shrug or a burp, or both, and a look of utter amusement.

"Your captain will not be pleased with your choice," the large man warned, poking a finger the powrie's way. "He knows who I am, and well! You tell him that Matlal—"

"So might be that I just cut yer head off, dip me cap, and throw ye to the sea, eh?" the powrie interrupted, dropping the fish and drawing a long, serrated knife, which he waved from on high before the man's face.

The protesting man seemed to deflate, clenching his bound fists and spinning about to simply collapse on the sand, sputtering curses.

Benny smiled, understanding. He hoped he might be given the chance to watch this obvious traitor torn apart before he was put to his own death, and made a mental note to ask Boss Captain Thorngirdle if he'd afford him that final pleasure. It wasn't that Benny McBenoyt had any particular problem with traitors. Hardly that.

But there was something about watching the incredulous expression on the face of a double-dealer right before the blade dropped that always amused him.

She awakened with the sunrise in her eyes, bright and painful. Her right arm still pressed against her breast—indeed, secured there by dried blood—the captain pushed herself up to her left elbow, then rolled with a grunt to a sitting position. The morning was not chilly; the sweeping wake of the storm was funneling hot winds up from the tropics. But still, Quauh was shivering as she huddled there on the bluff. She was weak from hunger but had no desire to try to eat anything. She tried to avoid the truth, but she looked down at her swollen arm—her entire forearm now, and not just the broken and gashed wrist.

She rocked back and forth, angry that she had been thrown from her ship, even though she could see what remained of that ship collapsing farther out on the reef a couple of hundred yards out from the beach. She could have died with the *Uey*, as was expected of a captain, as was honorable. In that event, the death of Captain Quauh would have been spoken of in heroic and reverential terms back in Mayorqua Tonoloya, a young prodigy captain who had stayed with her ship and battled storm and powrie to the bitter end.

What a pity that she was lost to us so young, they would say of her.

Looking down at the beach, at the powries methodically going about their salvage operations, Quauh was still fairly certain that she would die here, and likely very soon. But the whispers would go out from this place, of course, carried with the recovered gold, that she had abandoned her ship, or that her crew had thrown her from the ship—neither event evoking any semblance of honor.

She would become the patsy of this utter disaster, she understood, a way for City Sovereign Popoca to deflect any blame for the daring plan to send an unguarded carrack to collect such a hoard of Durubazzi gold. If it had worked, if the secret cargo onloaded at Watouwa Island had made it all the way to Entel, the margin of profit would have been tripled above the norm, the decision to use the golden transport mirrors for the first leg out of Durubazzi would have been validated, and Popoca would have been hailed a genius.

But this failure would not be tolerated by Grand Augur Apichtli, Quauh knew, and so her name would be cursed throughout Mayorqua Tonoloya, easily so with her dying on land instead of on the *Uey*.

Quauh thought of her parents, three thousand miles away. They shouldn't have to suffer this insult.

The resilient woman growled that nonsense away and focused her attention down to the beach. Two barrelboats were anchored out by the reef, leaving only a score of powries on the sands, plus one sitting within a ring of sharpened and secured sticks along with a handful of *Uey*'s crew.

Perhaps she could get down there and take out the powrie guards, she mused. One or two at least, helping her crew to get out, arming them with their jailers' own long knives and hand axes, and leading the fight for freedom. She couldn't be certain, but perhaps the barrelboat that had floated her to the beach was still out there to the south.

Could a half-dozen Xoconai manage to propel a powrie barrelboat?

The idea was preposterous, of course, Quauh knew. A few Xoconai fighting a score of powries?

But she held on to the fantasy and kept plotting, because she needed to. Sitting there shivering, knowing her reputation doomed, feeling her life slipping away, it was all she had. After she had schemed out the whole of the fight, to no satisfiable possibility, she thought she might just lie down and fall back to sleep, fully expecting that she would never awaken.

Perhaps that would be the best way to die, given her options here.

A moment later, she heard a hiss behind her, and realized suddenly that dying in her sleep, too, was simply no option. She turned about, her bright amber eyes popping open wide, to see a large gray-brown lizard, longer than she was tall, with huge black claws ending the five toes on each foot. One swipe from those powerful legs would end her days.

The lizard lifted its tapering snout high, long forked tongue flicking out and flopping to the side before being sucked back into the maw. Then it hissed again, opening wide those jaws, showing rows of hooked fangs, teeth that would hold on with a bite and prevent escape. Everything about the creature seemed filthy, for truly this was an ugly beast, quite unlike the beautiful cuetzpali lizard mounts.

Quauh reached down to the side to retrieve her long macana. Grimacing, she forced her right hand out as well to help grip the weapon, ignoring the waves of accompanying agony. She noted the silver chain she had used to secure her torn hand and wrist off to the side, but had no time or way to get to it. She slowly rose to stand tall, hoping to intimidate the predator, and hoping, too, that she wasn't revealing herself to the powries on the beach down below.

The lizard swayed back and forth on its long forelegs, hardly seeming afraid.

Quauh tried to stay focused, to fight away the fear, expecting the beast to charge.

The shake of a bush behind it caught her attention.

A second lizard.

Then a rustle to the left, then the right, and suddenly, all the jungle before her seemed to be shaking from the movement of the hunting pack.

Quauh imagined herself knocked to the ground, the giant lizards covering her head to toe, tearing off bits of her body with those teeth, and with her alive to feel all of it.

She swung her macana around, letting the motion and the weight of the thing turn her about and launch her into a charge over the lip of the ledge, running, falling, rolling down the bluff. And screaming all the way.

She didn't want to scream. She wasn't even aware that she was screaming. She just kept moving, ignoring the throbbing in her arm, up her shoulder, and through her whole body. At some point she lost her prized weapon, but she didn't care, and just kept propelling herself forward any way she could.

She heard the calls before her, powries raising the alarm, but she didn't care and didn't slow.

She rolled up to her feet as the ground leveled on the beach and stumbled forward, stepping fast in a futile attempt to keep her legs under her.

Then she was down, facedown, spitting sand, holding her breath in expectation of the monster lizards chewing at her feet and legs from behind, expecting a powrie spear or crossbow quarrel to plunge into her from the front. Instinctively, Quauh reached her left hand up over the top of her head, trying to cover.

And she heard the click of crossbows from ahead, and the hiss and roar of lizards from behind—and not far behind.

Then the hollers and whoops of the bloody-cap dwarfs, who came running up to her and past her, banging their weapons against their shields, if they had one, and against their chests for those who did not.

The fighting began behind her, and Quauh dared to roll to the side so that she could glance back.

One powrie ran out to the left flank of a lizard, the beast turning and snapping.

A second powrie leaped atop it like a rider and began wildly and viciously chopping at the creature with his hand axe, pumping and striking over and over.

Not far behind to the side of that fight, Quauh saw a lizard struggling weirdly, and it took her a few heartbeats to realize that the beast had been shot in the face, neck, and shoulders near to a dozen times, the powries clearly focusing their volley on this one alone. This was the same one she had faced up on the bluff, she believed, and so likely had been leading the pack in the chase.

The strategy came clear as the other lizards continued their charge only up to that thrashing, dying lizard. They set upon it with hungry fury, biting and clawing, tearing off strips of the tightly scaled, leathery skin, or chomping at the open flesh below the strips, removing great chunks of bloody meat and organs.

The victim fought back a bit, pathetically, but was so overwhelmed that Quauh almost felt sorry for the thing.

That would have been her, eaten alive.

Strong hands grabbed her by the shoulders then and started dragging her away. She turned back to protest, to try to break free, but there stood a third powrie between the two that were dragging her, his crossbow flipped in his hands as he punched out.

The butt of that weapon hit Quauh right between the eyes and the world started spinning.

She felt as if she was floating, in a dream more than the waking world.

"That like Brynn's dragon?" she heard one powrie say, or maybe she just imagined it.

"Nah, ye dolt. Brynn's got one that flies and breathes fire to toast yer chestnuts."

Quauh heard a groan escape her lips.

She got hit again on the head, a solid smack from the butt of the crossbow. She was still moving, being dragged across the sand, but now she wasn't floating, no. She was falling, far, far away.

Though he was consumed by his own dire predicament, Benny McBenoyt couldn't ignore the ranting of the wide-bodied goldfish man, a stream of curses and protests that increased exponentially when this newest prisoner from the ship was thrown in with them. She was dressed in a fine but dirty peacoat—not a cheap garment, certainly, and one that implied a high rank in the goldfish navy.

She rolled about in delirium, right arm tight against her chest, left arm pressing it tightly, and Benny wondered why his fellows hadn't just put the poor thing out of her misery. She didn't seem long for this life, in any case. He considered sitting on her face and suffocating her, but instead just sidled up to her and put a hand across her shoulders to stop her from hurting herself more in her thrashing.

"Ye'll be goin' away soon, pretty Sparkleface," he said. "Won't hurt much longer."

To his surprise, the woman awakened fully and glared up at him. "Let go of me!" She slapped at him, as if his very touch was hurting her.

Benny did so, and moved away, but stopped fast and pulled off his beret. "Here, put it against yer wound. It'll be helpin' a bit."

She stared at him with obvious suspicion, then turned her gaze to the extended hand, then back at Benny.

"Ye really got anything to lose, Sparkleface?"

She snapped the beret from him and put it gingerly over her wrist. Only a moment later, her eyes widened with surprise, and she dropped her left hand over the bloody cap to press it more fully against the garish wound.

"Aye, ye see?" said Benny with a grin.

She didn't reply, but softened her expression just a bit.

"That big goldfish, there, he don't much like ye, eh?" Benny asked a little while later, when some more guards came over and the large Xoconai leaped up to assail them with his typical invective.

"Traitor," she whispered.

"Aye, that's what I been gatherin' from his haranguin'. Loudmouthed blusterbus, eh?"

"Tell Boss Captain Thorngirdle!" the man roared at the powries. He swung about, and Benny thought he was pointing at him—and was more than ready to leap up and toss the fool onto one of the pickets!—when the man went on, "Her! Do you not know who that is? You fools, she is Captain Quauh. Captain! The *Uey'Lapialli* was her ship!"

"Don't take much to get that one to flap his face, do it?" Benny said with a laugh. "He just keelhauled ye, didn't he, Captain Quauh?"

"Traitor," Quauh repeated, a bit louder. "He knows your commander's name. Matlalihi the traitor."

Matlalihi heard and spun about. "I will kill you myself!" he promised, and came forward a threatening step.

Just one, though, for Benny hopped up in front of him and pulled out his long knife. "I'll be needin' more blood for me beret. Ye mind if I'm takin' it from yerself?"

Matlalihi glared at him, even puffed out his chest and leaned forward over the dwarf, but unlike Benny, who was there with a good measure of trust and respect from his captors, the human prisoners hadn't been allowed to keep any weapons. Captain Thorngirdle wasn't about to allow the humans to murder Benny, after all.

Outside the pickets, one of the three guards ran off to the main powrie gathering, and it didn't take long before he was coming back with all the dwarfs behind him, including a most impressive fellow with a giant black beard.

"That be Thorngirdle," Benny turned back and whispered to Quauh. "Ye take care yer words now, Sparkleface."

The powrie moved a bit farther from Quauh then, for his own sake. He reached out and tugged back his beret, too, and just shrugged when she looked at him in surprise.

"I tried to give her to you, as we agreed," Matlalihi told Thorngirdle. "We were about to strike our colors!"

Benny snorted and looked to the prone Quauh, who just shook her head in disgust.

"But then your barrelboats attacked," Matlalihi went on.

"I heared it all, mate," Thorngirdle said. "But here we be."

"I did as I promised!"

"Ye did, indeed. But here we be."

"You are collecting the treasure," Matlalihi pointed out.

"And burying more'n two full crews o' me boys and a pair of boats, to boot."

"That was not my fault."

"Aye, so I heared."

"Then let me out and give me my end."

"The *Uey* is yours, as we agreed," Thorngirdle said, turning and moving a bit to the side to afford Matlalihi a good look at what remained of the carrack. "And when ye get her running again, we'll leave ye be, as we agreed."

Matlalihi sputtered on that one for a long while before finally spitting out, "The gold! I demand my share. I'll buy another . . ."

"I got twenty-seven boys to replace, and two boats o' me own to buy," said Thorngirdle. "There's yer share. The strike should've come afore ye shot a damned harpoon into me own boat and killed one of me boys right in front of me own eyes."

Matlalihi stuttered a bit after that remark, Benny noted, and the powrie wasn't surprised when the desperate goldfish traitor spun around and jabbed his finger toward Quauh.

"Her!" he yelled. "She stopped me from completing our surrender. That is Captain Quauh. I know not how she managed to survive, but there she sits. She has value. Take her to recoup your losses. The Xoconai will pay large sums for their prized Captain Quauh."

"That you?" Thorngirdle yelled to the woman. "Th' *Uey* was yer boat, then?"

Quauh pulled herself up, closed her eyes for a moment to stave off some dizziness, then nodded.

"I am Captain Quauh of the Tonoloya Armada, sailing out of Entel."

"Lot o' words to just say yes," Thorngirdle teased. "What say ye? Ye think yer friends'll pay a hefty price for yer head?"

Quauh snorted. "Probably more for just my head." She nodded toward the reef. "There lies my command, and the treasures sought by the city sovereign of Entel." She shrugged again. "He might pay you a pittance so that he can watch my neck stretch."

The honest response brought some gasps. Benny looked at

the woman with more concern than he would have expected he'd ever feel for a human, let alone a human woman, and let alone a goldfish.

Thorngirdle, though, laughed heartily. "Strange way to beg for yer life."

Quauh merely shrugged.

"I'll be considerin' it, then," the powrie boss captain assured her, and turned to leave.

"Do not listen to her lies!" Matlalihi yelled at him.

Boss Captain Thorngirdle froze in his half-turn, paused there for a heartbeat, then slowly turned about to cast a withering glare at the man.

"I'm listenin' to many things, Matlalihi," he said in a truly threatening, too-steady tone. "And I alone choose what I'm wantin' and not wantin' to believe."

"Then let me cut off her head for you," Matlalihi said.

"Ye really want to, don't ye?"

"No more than I want his," Quauh interjected. "Traitor. Lower than the sidhe."

"Aye, I do," Matlalihi answered, not even turning to regard her.

Thorngirdle stood there nodding and hmm'ing for a few moments before looking back up at Quauh.

"Hey, Benny," he called, and to the shock of all the powries, Benny perhaps most of all, the high captain of Six Bits removed his cap and tossed it, spinning like a saucer, toward Benny.

"Help her find a bit o' strength," Thorngirdle instructed him. "We lost some friends and could use a bit o' fun."

Benny dove into the sand to catch the prized beret, then held it before his eyes with sincere reverence. Truly, it was the most gloriously bloodied cap he'd ever seen. He could feel the magic thrumming within it, affording health and strength.

He finally looked up, to see Thorngirdle still looking his way, as if waiting to meet his gaze.

The boss captain winked—a measure of respect that Benny McBenoyt had never before known—and walked away.

Benny went right to Quauh. "This'll chase away the percolations for a bit, and might bring ye a fighting chance against the traitor. But the healin' won't be lastin' long when me boss captain takes back his cap, so I expect ye best get up and stretch a bit. Ye've a fight coming quick."

"Ending quick, you mean," Quauh corrected, and, as if to accentuate the point, the woman nearly fell over to the side when she reached out for the beret.

Benny wouldn't give it to her. He pulled it back and waggled a finger to chase her reaching hand away.

As she settled, he came forward and wrapped her wound with Thorngirdle's cap. He could see from Quauh's face the immediate relief it offered.

"C'mon, get yerself up," Benny ordered, rising beside her and lifting her wounded right arm with his. He took her other hand and helped her to her feet.

She nearly fell again, but he held her there.

"Give me your knife and I will end her here and save her the embarrassment," Matlalihi said from across the way.

"Good," Benny whispered to Quauh. "He thinks ye can'no fight."

"I cannot," she replied.

"But ye will," Benny promised, and he plopped his own beret atop her head. "Ye'll get yer chance, but it won't be holdin' for long. Ye got to take him down fast."

Quauh's expression was truly incredulous.

"Aye, why am I carin'? One goldfish or another, eh?"

"Eh," she echoed, and Benny nearly laughed aloud at her powrie imitation.

"Same reason Thorngirdle's carin'," he explained. "Aye, ye're right in that he and meself won't be crying when ye go to yer grave—aye, but what's this run o' life more than a flicker o' time, only to be repeated again and again? Ye die, ye come back and start over." He shrugged. "But when ye're here, ye don't be a damned traitor. Now, stretch yer legs and make yer plans. Ye kill him fast, or ye got no chance."

A moment later, Benny took back the beret he had taken from Pinquickle and now called his own and plopped it on his head, then carefully pulled Thorngirdle's from the wound— which appeared far less angry than it had when he had applied the magical cap.

He directed Quauh's attention back toward the entrance of the makeshift prison, to see the return of Thorngirdle and the other dwarfs, one carrying a pair of conventional macanas, another carrying Quauh's longer two-handed weapon.

"Get the extras out o' the pit and place yer bets fast, boys," Thorngirdle ordered.

CHAPTER 11

THE VALUE OF ENTERTAINMENT

Quauh's right hand felt better from the healing properties of the magical berets, but she couldn't begin to ball it into a tight fist, and realized that there was no way she could secure her large macana with it. She knew Matlalihi's martial prowess quite well—the man could spin his twin macanas deftly and strike with true power.

Quauh winced as she merely thought of blocking one of the strong man's heavy blows. The vibrations through her wounded wrist and hand would likely drop her to her knees in agony.

Her thoughts whirled furiously as she sought a solution—the powrie captors bearing the weapons were coming into the pit now. She could wield her large macana with one hand, true, but feared she would be far too slow for the ferocious Matlalihi. Perhaps she should ask for a smaller macana or some other one-handed weapon.

If only she still had the silver chain.

As she pondered that, she noted that Benny hadn't been pulled out by his brethren, but still lingered in the pit.

"Do you still have your knife?" she whispered to the powrie when he walked near to her.

"Aye, but not for yerself," Benny answered. "They got your toothy paddle."

"I do not want your weapon, no," she replied, and began to remove her golden peacoat. "Quietly move behind me, I beg, and cut a strip from the tail of my blouse."

The powrie's stare went from confusion to a sly grin, and he nodded and moved behind her as she shrugged the coat to the ground. A moment later, he came back around on her left, brushed against her, and covertly handed over the strip of cloth.

"Bah now," he yelled. "Are ye boys going to let me bet on the fight? One last bit o' excitement for old Benny McBenoyt afore ye cut out me heart and bury it?"

"Bah, Benny, but ye ain't that old," no less than Captain Thorngirdle answered. "And o' course we'll let ye bet—yer whole share that ye won't be getting!"

"I'm puttin' me gold on the girl," Benny told them, turning back to wink at Quauh.

Several powries howled that they'd cover the bet, for sure, making Quauh realize that they weren't giving her much of a chance here—and in truth, neither was she. She noticed that Matlalihi had gotten back his twin macanas and was working them in a fast and impressive warm-up routine.

She managed to toss a nod of thanks to Benny—certainly, he had only bet on her to lift his spirits, since he was about to die anyway.

But Quauh meant to make that bet pay off. When the

approaching powrie held out her macana, she took it purposely with her right hand, then grimaced in true pain as the weakened wrist failed her and the long weapon dipped fast, its tip settling on the ground.

That brought laughs and more calls to cover Benny's bet.

Quauh used her very real discomfort to half turn and shield herself from the onlookers, and there, she very quickly and securely tied that broken right wrist and torn hand to the macana hilt, as tightly as she could. When she turned back around, she lifted the weapon high across her chest, tucked in close, left hand gripped below the right.

She tried to remain confident as Matlalihi began to approach, but she was well aware that even if she'd been at full health, she wouldn't really have had much of a chance of beating this warrior. Matlalihi had served with the macana warriors before taking to sea, while Quauh had known no more than two actual melees, the one with the powrie where her shipmates had killed the thing in her earliest days in the east, and another with a Behrenese woman three times her age.

"Sails!" came a cry from the beach, and all eyes turned to the sea, and yes, the billowing sails of a sizable ship out on the horizon.

"Get on with it, then," Thorngirdle told the prisoners before turning to his sailors and yelling, "Bets are done!"

Quauh noted that Benny walked past Matlalihi, and despite her predicament, couldn't help but smile when the powrie said, "If ye kill her, might that they'll let me fight ye next."

"I would enjoy that," the proud man replied.

"Oh, but ye would'no."

Matlalihi didn't turn to regard the departing powrie, but kept his stare aimed squarely at Quauh.

Oh yes indeed, she knew, the first mate wanted to kill her.

Quauh took a deep breath and lifted her weapon. It was quite a beautiful thing, a polished darkfern handle wrapped in leather, attached to a four-foot-long darkfern paddle, almost a half-foot wide and an inch thick, its tip and thin sides lined with the large, serrated teeth of the white sharks that prowled the waters of the western sea. The triangular tooth capping the weapon was nearly half a foot wide and tall, while those on the side were even in size at about half that.

She felt the balance of the weapon as she slowly turned to face Matlalihi. Darkfern was almost unbreakable and quite light—and Quauh was glad of that now with her seriously injured hand and wrist.

Matlalihi grinned at her wickedly and twirled his smaller macanas in tight circles at his side.

"Are you ready to die, Captain Quauh?" he asked. "I could make it quick, if you please."

"Shut up, traitor."

"Traitor? You could have surrendered the *Uey* and offered yourself and avoided all of this. Your hands are red with the blood of your crew."

Quauh knew that wasn't true, but the words stung her anyway. She had lost her ship. Everything aside—the powrie pirates, the great storm, even Matlalihi's apparent treachery in dealing with Thorngirdle—that loss remained her responsibility.

She swallowed that sting and recalled the scene of Matlalihi swimming to the barrelboat and being helped aboard by a pirate.

He, Matlalihi, had doomed the *Uey*. He was the reason Six Bits had known to watch for her, had known of the special cargo tucked into her hold.

With that anger rising, Quauh widened her stance and crouched defensively.

Her hand was throbbing already. She knew this wouldn't be a long fight.

Matlalihi ran a couple of steps her way, jumped up into the air, and brought his macanas in a crossing spin before him, then landed and launched forward.

Out went Quauh's macana, stabbing like a spear to fend.

The large man batted it hard with a powerful right cross and went spinning out that way, forcing Quauh to move fast to her right to stay out of his reach. She felt the waves of agony rolling up her right forearm—if she hadn't tied her wrist so tightly to the weapon, she surely would have dropped it!

She covered her wince of pain with a scream, a primal roar. She reflexively let go of the macana with her left hand to wave an invite to Matlalihi, taunting him.

But she regretted it immediately and gripped the weapon more solidly as the end began to dip.

Matlalihi was coming on, but he skidded to a stop and continued to circle left to right about her, staring curiously, grinning knowingly.

"Kithkukulikhan's giant pecker," she cursed quietly, realizing that she had just revealed her weakness. She ended with a growl and forced her destroyed hand to tighten on the handle, then roared through a series of sudden, short horizontal swings both to drive Matlalihi back and try to convince him that she wasn't as injured as he now believed.

But shortening every swing, breaking the momentum of the cutting paddle, brought a wince, and even her voice in her covering roars occasionally cracked from the sting of pain.

Her bluff, she feared, hadn't been very effective.

She did drive the man back, however, and the speed of her reversals prevented him from stepping in behind any cuts to strike at her.

He circled fast, darted forward, then back, and went back the other way.

Working her.

She turned with him, stabbed out her long weapon at one point and got it whacked twice in alternating blows by Matlalihi's smaller paddles, each impact feeling as if the man was reaching inside her forearm and strumming her tendons and muscles, a sudden and shockingly painful sensation. Again, if her weapon hadn't been tied to her hand, that hand would have fallen from the hilt and she probably would have hugged it in close to steady herself. But she couldn't, so she just stabbed the macana ahead again to force the bouncing, dodging man to stay back.

He hit the macana again, hard, and Quauh stumbled out to the side, recovering quickly, but hearing the cheers from the onlookers—almost certainly from those powries who had bet on Matlalihi!

She caught the stare of one powrie in that moment: Benny,

looking back at her, shaking his head. The bloody cap began mouthing two words with exaggerated movements and silent exclamation, for her benefit, surely.

He knows!

Then Benny threw his hand up against his own forehead and turned as if in a swoon, before coming out of it suddenly, fists out in front.

Quauh made little sense of it at first, and the distraction nearly cost her everything when Matlalihi drove his right-hand paddle against her macana, then leaped into the opening behind it, hitting it again with a left-hand backhand to keep it out to the side. Another step had him in striking range, so Quauh threw herself to the right, wisely letting her legs fall out from under her and turning her back.

She got hit hard on the left shoulder blade, the small teeth lining Matlalihi's weapon poking through shirt and skin, and only her fall moved her fast enough directly away from the serrated edge to prevent Matlalihi from dragging the blade across to create a long and deep gash.

She turned as she dropped to protect her right hand, hitting the ground on her butt and throwing herself immediately into a roll backward over her shoulders and head, then back up to her feet, stumbling to move farther from the turning, relentless Matlalihi. Yes, Benny was right, Quauh understood. Matlalihi knew, without doubt, and all her growling and stubborn determination weren't going to hide the truth.

In that roll back to her feet, Quauh suddenly understood Benny's message to her.

Matlalihi knew that she was pretending to be healthier and more able to fight than she was, but what he didn't know was exactly how bad her injury might be.

Use it, her mind screamed.

She began to pant and stumbled to the side as she tried to set her feet wide defensively.

Matlalihi came on, leaping, weapons spinning, then came in hard, batting Quauh's stabbing weapon left, then right, then up—and each impact sent her weapon out farther than what would normally be expected, and drew a gasp or a yip from Quauh, though she tried to pretend to cover those with a follow-up growl.

Matlalihi was smiling widely, she saw. He ducked low and to the side on her next thrust, then came up hard with both paddles underneath her long weapon, driving up and shoving his right hand up and across in an attempt to pull the long macana from Quauh's hand.

And it would have worked if she hadn't tied her weapon so tightly to her throbbing—and it was indeed now throbbing!—wrist. She stumbled back and clenched her teeth in agony as she forced her weapon to reverse its movement and come cutting back down. She had no choice, and even with her desperate and painful effort, only barely got the weapon down fast enough to force Matlalihi to sidestep, thus allowing Quauh to retreat the other way.

She knew she couldn't keep this up, but she was afraid of attempting the endgame now, for that would require such a desperate win-or-lose ploy.

Matlalihi made up her mind for her by stepping back and smashing the side of her descending weapon.

A wave of fiery vibrations ran up Quauh's arm. Her knees wobbled, her eyes nearly closed, tears of agony rimming them.

But she held her feet and rolled about to her left, almost three-quarters of the way around, before her weapon's tip dropped to the sand and she nearly fell over it.

Her pause there in that pose wasn't faked. It took her a long moment to clear her vision and her mind. "Matlalihi," she whispered, focusing on what she knew of the man.

He was coming in fast, of course.

She knew well his killing move.

Gathering everything she had left to give, Quauh swung about, dropped to her knees, and swept her weapon across with all her strength.

Matlalihi was already up in the air, his signature killing leap, weapons raised for a brutal downward double strike.

Quauh's long weapon got there first, cutting right behind the man's left knee. She pushed off hard with her own left leg, turning out to the side, but continued her cut with all her remaining strength. She felt the serrated edge digging through, cutting muscle and tendon and ligament.

She almost passed out again from the agony, but she held on and dug through it, and as she stumbled to the dirt, took some satisfaction and some hope in the feral shriek that came forth from the man.

It took Quauh a long time to come up from that roll to her hands and knees. Her *hand* and knees, actually, for the cloth had finally come free, releasing her right hand's grasp on the weapon—and there was no way she could hope to settle that mangled hand on the ground for any kind of support.

She blinked through the pain and clenched her jaw, hissing and sneering, and only finally looking over to Matlalihi.

He, too, was on the ground, half sitting, his left hand grasping the side of his ripped leg, trying to stem the blood. He met Quauh's gaze and roared in outrage.

Quauh scrambled away from him and managed to get back to her feet, stumbling with every step.

He tried to come on, but the wound was too fresh for him for properly get that leg under him for his crawl. With a roar of defiance, the powerful man got his good leg under him and began to force himself upright.

But Quauh rushed in, macana held only in her left hand, but tucked under her upper arm and pointed like a spear, and when Matlalihi set himself in a half crouch, up on his right leg, his left weirdly out to the side, Quauh turned out and circled him, going out around that leg, forcing him to turn or get stabbed.

But he couldn't swivel from that crouch, not well, and down he went to the sand again.

Quauh kept circling—he was using way more energy than she in trying to keep up the turn from his seat, and he was still pouring blood.

She slowed but kept going around him, and anytime Matlalihi made a move to stand, she sped up suddenly, forcing him to drop back and spin faster.

Some powries were booing openly now, while others just laughed.

"Do ye mean to do this all day, then, woman?" Captain Thorngirdle called to her.

"He'll bleed out soon enough," Quauh promised, gasping though the pain. "This fight is already over."

That brought more boos, and also cheers—and Quauh realized from the volume that most had indeed bet on Matlalihi.

"It's a boring way to win a fight, lass," said Thorngirdle. "We're only keepin' ye alive for the entertainment, don't ye see?"

"As long as that one dies first, I accept your judgment."

Her words, her proclamation, her circling movement . . . all of it now was just the feint, for she sped up suddenly, one step, then two, then, when she thought Matlalihi was moving almost without thinking, when she judged that his mind was devising a way to stem the bleeding long enough to survive until Thorngirdle had seen enough, Quauh struck, moving as if to stride to the right, but dropping her foot short, digging it into the soft sand, and suddenly throwing herself at the sitting man.

His macana came across in a backhand to whack at her down-angled blade, but too late. The tip of Quauh's weapon speared Matlalihi on the side of his right hip, and his hard parry only sent it ripping across his own flesh.

How he howled!

Quauh stumbled to the side and fell to her knees again. She glanced back at her enemy and tried to compose herself.

She had time to recover, for Matlalihi was too consumed by his own garish wounds to come for her in that moment.

With a deep breath, Captain Quauh stood straight and nodded to the powries, to Benny, who was smiling, and to Thorngirdle, who offered an approving wink.

Quauh stalked over to stand behind Matlalihi, who was trying hard to even maintain a seated posture.

"Do I have to finish him to claim my victory?" Quauh said as firmly as she could manage.

"Nah," Captain Thorngirdle replied.

Quauh heard Matlalihi exhale with relief.

She found that very satisfying as she brought her weapon up and over her right shoulder, leaning forward, then falling forward, as she sent it down with all her remaining strength onto the top of the traitor's head.

She wasn't even holding the weapon any longer when she pitched face-first to the sand, barely holding on to consciousness.

Then not at all as a warm blackness overcame her thoughts, and as a warm and sticky substance flowed over her extended right hand.

"He's for the sharks," a powrie complained. "I ain't paying a dead man."

Others grumbled similarly, poking stubby fingers at Benny McBenoyt, who just stood there smiling, palm out and up, fingers flapping for his payouts.

"Ye keep talking and I'll be puttin' a lot more hearts in the ground," Captain Thorngirdle warned the complainers as he walked up to Benny's side. "I'll keep murderers in me crew, but damned to the eight-armed menace if I'm to let them what won't pay their bets!"

The losing powries grumbled and moved off.

"Don't be supposin' that ye'd bury me gold with me heart," Benny said to the captain.

"Not likely, no."

Benny nodded his chin out to sea, where a few other sailing ships had joined with the first they had spotted. "That's *Port Mandu*," Benny said of that first, a sleek two-master. "Wilkie Dogears's ketch."

"Aye," Thorngirdle agreed. "And to be sure, Wilkie's planning to be the go-between twixt ourselfs and those others floatin' around out there."

"Behrenese," Benny said.

"Aye."

"So ye'll be needin' a barter with Wilkie Dogears, who's always favoring ransom and good sailors."

"And what's yer deal, then?"

"Ye take me gold that I just won, and take me own share from the carrack to boot."

"And give ye to Wilkie, who'll welcome a good helmsman."

Benny looked Thorngirdle in the eye and shrugged.

Thorngirdle held that stare for just a few moments, then said, "Hmm, well, I didn't really want to kill ye anyway. Not many can throw a barrelboat like a spear, even if ye did murder a captain."

"Wave threw the barrelboat, not Benny," Benny said.

"Ye think it a good time for arguin'?"

"A godlike throw, if I say so meself," Benny quickly corrected himself, and puffed out his chest.

Thorngirdle laughed. "Back in the pit with ye. Ye're still a prisoner. But find a piece of jetsam—flat plank or something— and get yer champion tied tight, arms out."

Benny's grin became a frown, and he glanced back into the pit with surprising resignation. But he knew that Thorngirdle was correct in his assessment of the extent of the Xoconai's wound. He went down to the water and quickly found a suitable piece of wreckage. The longer they waited to do what needed to be done, the worse it would be.

"Wait," Benny asked, "ain't she dead anyway?"

"Weren't Benny dead a minute ago?"

Benny nodded and went back into the pit to see to Quauh, a captain of the Tonoloya Armada who would likely be a valuable acquisition to the Behrenese sailors, or to a man like Captain Wilkie Dogears of the *Port Mandu*.

Her ears tuned into the buzz of words—they were talking about her!—before she managed to open her eyes. At first, Quauh thought she was floating, lying on her back with her arms stretched out to either side.

Her right arm was somewhere beyond pain now, into a sense of dull, endless death and decay. She felt more sick than shocked with the continual fiery agony coursing through her.

Finally, she blinked open her eyes and found herself staring up at the cloudless sky above. A face came into view, that of a powrie, black-bearded and gap-toothed.

"Ah, she's awake," he said. "Not good for her!"

He walked around above her as she lay prone, and a metal rod moved past Quauh's view, one with a flat head glowing orange with heat.

The woman blinked to full awareness. She tried to sit up but found that she was tied down tightly at her elbows to a wooden plank stretching below her shoulders and out wide to either side. She lifted her head to protest, but the words caught in her mouth as Captain Thorngirdle moved toward her, raising a cleaver up over his strong shoulder.

Quauh cried out in fear, thinking she was about to die. That yell became a scream of shock as she watched the cleaver sweep down to her right, then morphed again into a scream of pain when the blade fell hard through flesh and bone, slamming into the wood upon which she was bound.

And the scream changed in tone when the hot brand came down behind it, burning her flesh. Her eyes were closed again, but now simply in a desperate effort to chase away the agony and the shock.

It was over quickly, though it seemed an eternity to poor Quauh. When she at last opened her eyes once more and looked over to the right, she saw Benny there, sorting some bandages, and saw, too, her severed hand and wrist and part of her forearm lying on the sand. The pain didn't abate, not at all, and it grew all the more terrifying and agonizing to Quauh when the smell of her burning flesh filled her nostrils. She pulled against her bindings and kicked her legs, turning her hips as she tried to twist herself free.

Benny fell over her.

"Hold, girl, hold. We had to take it or the rot would o' taked yer life! Them wounds weren't goin' to heal. Look at it. Look at it!"

He kept repeating that and kept holding Quauh down tightly until at last she calmed and glanced again at her lost limb.

The green color of it.

The swelling.

She knew that Benny had done the only thing that could save her, but the pain, the shock, and the sheer anger and sense of violation did not go away. Quauh stopped thrashing, though, and just fell flat once more, closing her eyes and sobbing and wishing she would just die then and be done with it all.

She felt Benny bandaging her burned stub soon after, every wrap sending shocks of pain up her arm. But she didn't yell at him or at anything, didn't even look his way. She just lay there, empty, wondering what the point of it was, since the powries were just going to murder her anyway.

At least Benny untied her from the plank when he was done with wrapping her stumped arm.

A short while later, after many deep breaths, Quauh even managed to sit up, and after the waves of dizziness passed, she was able to better survey the situation about her. She was still in the pit, along with five of her crew, three women and two men. Benny was there, too, sitting up by the wider-spread pair of pickets through which the prisoners were being shuffled in and out of the makeshift prison. He seemed in good spirits now, laughing and talking with the powrie guards.

Off to the side, she noticed another person, lying facedown on the sand and wheezing.

Matlalihi wasn't quite dead yet.

A sad chuckle escaped Quauh's lips. What a waste it had all been. This traitor had cost them all so very much, had cost most of the crew their lives, and for the *Uey* crew in the pit with her and the traitorous first mate, could there be expectations of anything but misery and a forthcoming execution?

How Quauh hated Matlalihi! She only wished she had the strength then to go over and finish the skunk.

No, not to finish him—not yet. To torment him and make him whine in agony for as long as she could manage until he at last expired.

Quauh looked away and silently scolded herself for such terrible, dark thoughts. She was not that person. She was an officer in the Tonoloya Armada, a person of dignity and decency.

She chuckled again, helplessly this time, when she considered her haughty nonsense.

Yes, in her heart, undeniably, she wanted to torture Matlalihi until his last breath.

She took another deep breath then and forced herself upright, standing simply to show her fellow Xoconai and their captors that she could, that she had not been and would not be beaten. Benny and the guards looked at her, Benny flashing a smile, then hopping to his feet and finishing his conversation with his fellows.

Quauh looked past him to the beach, where the powries were continuing their work. A group was coming in then, carrying boxes and gold bars and other baubles they had apparently just retrieved out at the reef. All of them had something wrapped about their necks, like a rope, except that it was glowing.

"What are they doing?" Quauh asked when Benny finally came walking over. Her voice was still shaky, as were her legs, but the stubborn Quauh would not allow herself to fall back down.

"Salvaging," Benny answered. "Finishin' up. See them sails? Behrenese boats, and we're not wanting them to see what we got."

"We?"

"Well . . ."

"What are those powrie divers wearing?"

Benny looked at her curiously.

"Around their necks, I mean."

"Eels. Glow eels. Gets dark down there. Yer boat broke up in five, six fathoms. Long way down, long way up, and dark. Can't be finding the treasure without 'em. And can't find the sucking tubes without 'em, so they'd have to come above the water for every breath."

Quauh scanned the water farther out and noted powries on small rafts moving about. Every now and then, one would pick up from the water what looked like an inflated bladder and give it a squeeze.

Quauh didn't reply for a long while, digesting and marveling at the cleverness and resourcefulness of the bloody-cap dwarfs.

Perhaps they were monsters—certainly, they were not merciful and decent creatures—but there was no denying their intelligence.

"Breathing tubes," she muttered.

"Aye, but ye can only go down a bit under the water and still suck the air, or the damned hose collapses."

"Hose? Stockings?"

"Nah, a tube, made from the *caoutchou*."

Quauh looked at him curiously.

"The *caoutchou*," he repeated. "Ah, but what do the Bearmen call it? Stretchy stuff from the Durubazzi trees." He lifted one foot and bent his leg so Quauh could see the sole.

"Rubber?" she asked.

"Aye, or *rubair*. Good on the bottom o' yer shoes for holding steady on a wet deck. Good for plugging holes in yer boat."

"I would expect that a hole in a barrelboat could pose a bit of a problem."

Benny laughed.

Over to the side, Matlalihi made a sudden wheezing sound, louder than before.

"Why is he still alive?" Quauh asked.

"Won't be for long. Ye split his skull good." He laughed again. "Look," he bade her. "Bugs're crawling in. Haha!"

Despite her disgust, Quauh reflexively glanced Matlalihi's way, and indeed, beetles crawled about the gash on his head, some disappearing within.

"Bet that's feelin' fine, eh? Bugs crawlin' about yer brain! Ha!"

Quauh didn't answer and focused her attention once more on the beach, particularly when she recognized one specific box

223

set down among the pile of salvaged treasure. That one had come from her cabin, she knew. Her heart sank.

"What d'ye know? That yer coffer?" Benny asked after obviously following her gaze to the desired item.

The powrie handling it broke the latch and flipped the top, then dumped out some gold coins and a small, painted carving of a Xoconai mount.

"My brother carved that for me when I first went to sea," Quauh told the dwarf.

"That's one o' yer riding lizards."

"Cuetzpali," she confirmed. "He wanted me to remember what I was missing by choosing a commission to sail instead of an appointment to the mundunugu riders, as he had done."

"Ever regret it?" Benny asked after a few moments, surprising her. "Not just now, I mean," he added with a little laugh.

"Not even now," Quauh told him, and she meant it.

"Aye, the sea calls ye, don't it?"

"Aye. Our visitors are sailing in," Quauh noted, and saw, too, that the powries were suddenly scrambling to bury that which they had recovered.

"Chezru Chieftain Brynn's armada, and a corsair friend we know who runs about with her letter o' reprisal tacked on his mainmast."

Quauh's face tightened at that last bit of information. She knew well those orders from the dragon-riding queen of Behren. City Sovereign Popoca of Entel had warned all the captains to beware the coast of the desert lands, for the pirates running there were doing so with the blessing of Brynn Dharielle, with her full permission to attack any Xoconai ship sailing too close, and a promise of a market for any goods they looted.

"So, they will want your treasure."

"Thorngirdle'll talk 'em down, and he's got other things to trade, aye," Benny replied with a wink, and the dwarf began walking away, saying, "Everyone's looking for workers, aye."

"We'll be given as slaves?"

"Workers," Benny corrected. "Chezru Chieftain Brynn ain't much fond o' slaves. And if ye live long enough, ye'll get to buy yerself free."

"I am a commissioned captain of the Tonoloya Armada."

"Ye might not want to be sayin' that as if it's a good thing," Benny warned her, and he moved back to talk to the pit guards.

Quauh played that advice in her head over and over again. As a commissioned Xoconai captain, wouldn't the corsair, or Brynn's people, think her more valuable in trade back to Entel?

But then again, Quauh knew what awaited her in Entel, if she ever managed to return to City Sovereign Popoca. She would be offered a sword upon which to fall.

And if she chose not to do so, she would surely be stripped of her commission and, if not imprisoned, then marked with a tattoo of shame on her forehead and exiled from Xoconai society. She looked at her stubbed arm. She wouldn't be able to find a position as a seaman or even a cabin girl on any respectable boat—on any boat at all, likely.

If it came to that, if she was traded back to Entel, Quauh would take the sword.

She sat there for a long while, cradling her busted arm,

watching the powries finish their salvaging operations and noting the ships as they neared, striking sails, lifting oars, and dropping their anchors. Three were Behrenese cogs, she knew from their oars, single-sail design, and shallow draft. They were fast and agile and designed to hunt in packs among the shallower waters near the coast.

The fourth showed no oars, a full sailing vessel, and of a design less common among the pirates: two masts and lateen sails, but with a jib and a staysail. This was a fine example, she could see, with new sails and polished planks.

A laugh from Benny turned her back to the situation at hand, the dwarf walking back over to her.

"The cutter is your corsair acquaintance?" she asked, focusing her gaze on that ship as it settled just beyond the reef. They lowered a boat, and a handful of sailors rappelled down the vessel's side to get in and get it moving, almost as if they were trying to beat the dinghies dropped by the three cogs to the beach.

"Aye, Wilkie Dogears," Benny replied. "First in, best bribes. But she's a ketch, not a cutter. Bigger an' tougher."

Quauh responded with just a snort, realizing that she and her crew were almost certainly the primary barter for those bribes. "She's a cutter ketch," she corrected the powrie, but quietly, and eliciting no response.

"Fine sailor is Captain Wilkie," Benny went on. "Fine crew, and one to get better when Benny joins." He turned and winked at Quauh. "Took a chance, figured ye to be so angry that ye'd take down that dog no matter the pain. Traded all me winnings for me life, and Wilkie's had a good share o' powries in his crew on *Port Mandu* over the years."

Quauh let that digest for a moment. Benny had bought his life, and with far less loot than she . . .

"Benny," she said as he started away, and she grabbed his arm to stop and turn him. "I have a secret."

"No ye don't, lass," he answered with another wink.

Quauh's hand fell away as she tried to sort out the confident and cryptic response as Benny trotted off.

She watched him go, then sent her gaze out to the sea once more. She hardly looked at those other three rowboats when the ketch's landing vessel came in close enough for her to pick out the individuals aboard, for she found her eyes locked on a single figure, a tall and lean but wide-shouldered man standing at the prow, one arm over his bent knee, the other on his hip.

His skin was too dark to be called brown. No, he was black, with black hair tight and curly to his head and his face. He had a wide mouth that flashed a bright smile under that beard and mustache, a wide nose, and giant eyes.

Quauh couldn't take her eyes off him. She had never seen such a sculpted figure, as if every detail of the man had been planned by an artist.

As the boat glided into the shallow waters, scraping sand and rock, he didn't even flinch with the jostling—indeed, so still was he that he seemed more a figurehead than a living creature. He wore tight pants that went just below the knee, and a blousy white shirt open almost to the waist, its edges flapping in the breeze and showing droplets of sweat glistening on his muscular chest.

When the rowboat beached, he easily and gracefully sprang from the prow, not slowing to help the others drag it up out of the surf.

On long legs, the tall man—and he was as tall as any man Quauh had ever seen—strode with purpose and with no signs of trepidation at all up to the powrie band.

Another figure, much shorter and very slender, ran up behind him, and Quauh couldn't tell if it was a man or a woman, for they wore a hood with a long cowl. This person ran stiff-legged, one arm tucked tight to secure a longbow slung over one shoulder.

"To-gai-ru," Quauh whispered, noting the color of this one's bare skin and the layered clothing. And the bow—could any in the lands shoot a bow better than the folk of the south-central high steppes?

As they neared Captain Thorngirdle, the To-gai-ru pulled back her hood—yes, it was a woman, with a beautifully round and flat face, cheekbones high and, penetrating dark eyes, and long black hair, braided to one side.

The way Thorngirdle and the tall man shook hands, smiling widely and launching right into conversation, told Quauh that they were well-acquainted. She noted, too, that the mood of the two darkened noticeably when the other three rowboats came ashore, the Behrenese sailors rushing up to join the parley.

Fingers pointed, and the talking, mostly from the men of Behren, became very heated, very quickly. She didn't understand a word they were saying, but the tall black man did, and seemed to be translating for the powrie commander.

Soon after, a pair of powries came to the pit, collected Benny, and led him over to the group. Thorngirdle then began jabbering at the black man exclusively, the powrie high captain even turning his shoulders to use clear body language to exclude the Behrenese contingent from the conversation.

Benny stepped over to the tall black man, who shook his hand and motioned for him to go and stand with the To-gai-ru archer behind him.

As he had told her, he had bought his freedom, Quauh knew, and she was surprised at how much that pleased her. The powrie had saved her life and had supported her in her fight, but he had also, after all, harpooned her ship with his own.

But yes, for some reason she couldn't quite yet appreciate, she was glad that Benny McBenoyt had apparently been spared.

She shrugged and chuckled softly, imagining the life that Benny would make for himself with the gold Quauh had salvaged. She wanted to be mad at him, but she couldn't quite get there.

Now Thorngirdle was arguing with the Behrenese sailors, with the tall man working furiously to translate the increasingly heated exchange back and forth between them. For a while, Quauh thought there would be a fight right there on the sand. She even began plotting her escape route if they all got involved in a brawl.

But then Thorngirdle turned about and snapped his fingers at some guards, who rushed to the pit and began hauling out the Xoconai prisoners, hustling them across the way. Quauh was still in the pit when the first of those prisoners arrived to the gathering, to be thrown at the feet of the Behrenese negotiator. That man clapped his hands and brought a pair of his companions rushing forward to kick the woman repeatedly, then bind her arms tightly behind her back, before roughly hauling her up to her feet and running her to the nearest landing boat, where she was unceremoniously thrown over the rail to crash down inside.

So it went with all the others, one by one, with Quauh bringing up the rear. The powries shoved her forward and the Behrenese man motioned, but Thorngirdle held up his hand to keep them at bay, and turned instead to the black man.

"Massayo?" he asked.

"She has lost a hand," the tall man, Massayo, replied. "What use would she be to me?" He looked back to Benny when he finished, and the powrie nodded enthusiastically.

Thorngirdle grabbed Massayo by the arm and pulled him low to whisper in his ear.

The tall man's bright eyes widened indeed! As did his toothy grin.

"All right, then," Massayo declared. "We will take the useless one."

The Behrenese negotiator blurted out a protest Quauh could not understand, and another argument ensued, this time between him and Massayo, neither speaking words she could understand, perhaps, but in a battle that she surely recognized.

They were fighting over her, and again, surprisingly, Quauh found herself hoping that the pirate—though he was likely a bloodthirsty and brutal murderer—would win out.

When it finally ended, Massayo pulled a small pouch from his belt and flicked it to the Behrenese man, who weighed it for a moment, tossing it up and catching it repeatedly, before at last nodding in agreement and storming away with the others.

The To-gai-ru woman moved up to Quauh and took her roughly by the arm, pulling her down to the boat. She didn't throw Quauh over the side, as the Behrenese had done with the other prisoners, but rather, helped her onto the stern bench to sit with Benny.

"What just happened?" Quauh whispered to the powrie as Massayo concluded his business with Captain Thorngirdle.

"Cap'n Thorngirdle weren't fighting under the red 'n' black, and he's got no letter o' reprisal," the powrie explained. "Them Behrenese sea dogs would've come ashore, all two hundred, and taken our booty. But Massayo there claimed the strike of yer boat was Cap'n Wilkie's fight so as to keep the Behrenese off our backs—mostly."

"So Captain Thorngirdle paid off Captain Wilkie with us?"

"Three gold bars for Wilkie, aye, and a bit for Massayo. Meself and yer jacket to start."

"And what of me?"

"Yerself too. Yerself just joined the crew of *Port Mandu*, sailing under the red 'n' black o' Captain Wilkie Dogears," the powrie explained. "Make yerself useful and do as ye're told, and might that they don't feed ye to the sharks."

"You told them," Quauh accused.

"What?"

Quauh's face tightened, but she held her tongue and feared that she had just confirmed the cryptic guess this powrie had made earlier.

Benny laughed at her. "Why would I be doing that, ye dolt? Why would I be tellin' anyone yer secret?"

She didn't quite know how to respond to that, trying to figure out how it made any sense.

"You don't know my secret," she insisted.

"I watched ye put the gold bars in the rock pile."

Quauh licked her parched lips at the unassailable answer, one Benny certainly couldn't have bluffed. "And you didn't tell?"

"'Course not! And it's our secret now, not yer own, and don't ye forget that."

Quauh leaned back against the stern plank, her jaw hanging open. Questions rolled about her thoughts. Why was she here and not with the others of the *Uey*? Was it because she was the captain and more valuable in trade to the Xoconai than indentured to the Behrenese?

But Benny had just claimed that she was now part of *Port Mandu*'s crew. How did that make sense, particularly since she wasn't even able-bodied anymore? She started to ask the powrie, but noted that Massayo, the To-gai-ru archer, and the others from *Port Mandu* were returning to the dinghy, so she just sat back and told herself to take things one at a time. She was still alive, and that was something.

But exactly what that something might be, she could only begin to guess.

She was no more Captain Quauh of the Tonoloya Armada, so it seemed.

Now, apparently, she was a pirate.

CHAPTER 12

CABIN ARREST

Quauh was somewhat taken aback by the size of *Port Mandu* as the dinghy approached, or rather, the lack of size. She was long enough, fifty feet by Quauh's rough estimation, but very narrow, with a beam barely above a dozen feet. She had a very tall mainmast sporting a triangular lateen-rigged mainsail of typical size for a ketch, though it only went about three quarters of the way up that mainmast, with the crow's nest much higher. Her mizzen was typically proportioned to the ship, as were the jib and staysail up front. To her surprise, though, she noted a third small sail up front, a second staysail— or maybe a second jib.

Quauh had never seen that design before, and it gave her pause as she climbed up from the dinghy to the deck. She understood immediately that *Port Mandu* wasn't built for cargo, but for speed and maneuverability, particularly in shallower waters. The captain's gaze kept going back to that strange jib design as the dinghy crewman came up behind her and pushed her along. Her experience solved the clues quickly and made her realize that it would take some clever sailors to properly handle those three small forward sails efficiently, but if they did, was there any wind at all that *Port Mandu* couldn't use to serious advantage?

"Well, what did you get?" barked a man (though his gruff speech pattern made it sound more like "whajagit"), forcing her sensibilities back to the situation at hand. She immediately connected the man standing before Massayo to the name she had heard, Wilkie Dogears, because he did indeed have large ears, sticking out wide through his long and thick black hair. And to make it even more obvious, those flappers were adorned with huge feathered earrings that hung down to his collarbone, like the bouncing ears of an Alte Anxellin shortsnout, a breed of dog Quauh's family had kept for all her young life. He was a thick man, with a round belly and broad shoulders, though nowhere near as tall as the towering Massayo. His beard was huge and full, ringed with hair spikes all about the bottom, braided and tied with metallic baubles, silver and gold.

His waistcoat, pants, and boots were black, trimmed in red, and fancy—or once-fancy, for the clothes, like Captain Wilkie himself, had clearly spent many years at sea.

"They hadn't much to give," Massayo replied. "Their prey ran aground at the reef and broke up." He pointed to starboard, toward the obvious skeleton of the *Uey*, and Quauh grimaced and did not look. She didn't need to see her failure again.

"Not much they showed you, you mean. You know the little darlings buried what they looted."

Massayo shrugged. "Did you want me to start digging up

the beach with all the damned Chezru soldiers about? I'd have started a fight there, and Captain Thorngirdle would have left us all dead on the sand. You would have cursed my name all the way to the beach beside the Behrenese boats for the revenge fight."

Captain Wilkie flashed a smile that was more gold than tooth, and laughed heartily. "Aye, but might be that I like cursing you."

"Might be that I like being cursed," Massayo retorted. "But I'm no fan of lying bloody in the sand. It sticks to you, then, you know?"

They both laughed then, cut short when Wilkie repeated, "Well, what did you get?"

"Thorngirdle slipped me three bars of gold before the Chezru got ashore," he said, nodding to a small box the dinghy crew had put at the top of the ladder. Then he held up the golden coat, Quauh's coat, which he had carried across his arm.

Quauh held her breath, expecting to be exposed.

"A goldfish captain's coat?"

"Aye," Massayo answered, "and a pity that we didn't get the captain who was wearing it. Still, I expect that some Tonoloya warship would take it in trade for passage. They prize these symbols."

The big man turned, grinning, and slyly—so slyly that she wasn't really sure of what she had seen—gave a wink to Quauh.

"Better for you, then," Massayo said to Wilkie, turning back. "I will take this coat as my own cut of the booty and leave my share of the gold for you."

Wilkie's face widened in surprise.

"And new crew for *Port Mandu*," Massayo continued, stepping to the side to fully reveal both Benny and Quauh to the captain.

"Bah, but another red-capped runt," huffed Wilkie. "We haven't enough of them now, what?"

"Better than most others, this one," said Massayo. "He can help on the wheel. Helmsman of one of the lost barrelboats."

"Then why's Thorngirdle giving him away?"

Massayo looked to Benny and nodded for him to answer.

"Because I cut me cap'n chin to top-skull," the fierce powrie said, and spat upon the deck.

Quauh fought hard and futilely to hide her shock at Benny's candor.

"Hmm," said Wilkie. "I expect that he deserved it?"

"Oh, aye," said Benny. "'Twas him or me, so 'twas him."

"Helmsman?" Wilkie asked Massayo.

"Good one, by all I been told."

"Chain him in reach of the wheel," Wilkie ordered some crewmen, and they hustled Benny away. "And keep him there until he's come to know that this captain ain't so deserving as his last!"

The stunned Quauh still couldn't close her jaw.

"And what o' the pretty goldfish, then?" Wilkie asked. "She's not to be much help with a fresh stub."

"She's mine," said Massayo. "I'm keeping her for my cut of the gold."

"The jacket was your part of the gold."

"Would you rather I take a torn and bloody jacket and a

torn and crippled goldfish, or the half bar of gold I'm owed?" Massayo asked.

"Not sure what she's worth, though," Wilkie replied. "We come up on a goldfish warship and she's likely the trade that'll keep us above the waterline."

"Well then, in that event, she's for *Port Mandu*, but until then, she's mine, just mine, and the jacket. Fair deal?"

"Not fair for you," answered Wilkie. "But Massayo's ever been a strange one. Keep her locked in her quarters. She shows that sparkling face on the deck and I'll take no responsibility for the actions of the crew."

Quauh noted that his voice rose at the end of the proclamation, drawing nods and smiles from many nearby pirates. He had done that for her benefit, she understood, a clear warning of the consequences of any escape attempt.

"You hear that, goldfish?" the captain confirmed.

"Aye," Quauh answered meekly, playing the role.

"She got a name?"

"I just call her Lefty," said Massayo, drawing some laughter. "She deserves nothing more."

"Well, put the lefty to good use then, Mr. Massayo," Captain Wilkie ordered.

"Oh, but I'll get my money out of that one," said Massayo. He called out to a nearby crewman. "A bottle of whiskey to my quarters. I'm not losing this one to mortification."

He nodded to the man and woman behind Quauh, and they roughly pushed and pulled her to a small bulkhead far forward on the prow. They opened the door and helped her down a short ladder into a tiny triangular room, one without a porthole, which was made even more obvious when the hatch was again closed, leaving her in pitch-blackness.

She tried to keep calm, taking many deep and slow breaths. Massayo had just said that he meant to get his money's worth, but what that might mean terrified the young Xoconai. She didn't know exactly what this arrangement might entail, but she wasn't anxious to find out.

She fumbled around in the darkness for a short while before finding a bedroll to curl up on. She couldn't even straighten her legs as she lay there in the tiny accommodations, and couldn't imagine how the towering Massayo could be comfortable here.

Yet another reminder to her of life at sea. So many people, herself included, gave up so much comfort for the smell of the brine, the rolls and sounds of the waves, the night sky unhindered by the lanterns and commotion of a city.

How much comfort they gave up for the feeling of true freedom.

She heard the footsteps of the crew rushing about up above, then the rattling of the chain as the anchor was hoisted, and finally she felt the sudden pull as *Port Mandu* rushed away.

Quauh could only sigh. She tried not to feel sorry for herself.

At least she wasn't as bad off as Matlalihi the traitor. Was he still alive, she wondered? Was he feeling the bugs crawling through his cracked skull to nibble at his brains?

She hoped he was.

That wicked thought alone comforted Quauh. Whatever

might happen to her, at least she had paid that wretch for his treachery.

She didn't measure the passage of time as she lay there in the darkness, sometimes dozing, mostly not, feeling the roll of the waves beneath her, telling her that she was part of something bigger than herself, something eternal, something that considered the follies of mankind a mere nuisance, if even that. However many ships might be sunk, however many bodies might be thrown into the sea, the waves would only shrug.

She was startled, her eyes stinging, when the hatch opened and the sun shone in on her. A large form came down the ladder—Massayo, she realized, before he closed the hatch behind him.

A moment later, a small lantern flared to life.

No, not flared, she realized when she was able to see it more clearly, for this, like the lights the powries had taken with them in their diving, was a glass filled with water and small, glowing eels.

"Ah, so you have helped yourself to my bed," Massayo said.

Quauh rolled up to a sitting position and shrank back against the wall. "Is that not why I'm here?" she spat back venomously.

Massayo laughed. "No, no, nothing like that. We'll just let Captain Wilkie and the others think so, because if they believe that you are my woman, bought and paid for, then they will not bother you in such a manner."

"Should I be grateful?" she asked, her voice dripping with sarcasm.

"I think you should, yes."

The man's bubbly reply caught her even more off guard. "What do you mean to do with me?"

"What would you like? To be given back to the Xoconai, I expect. For now, I just came here to offer you a bit of whiskey." He held up a half-filled bottle. "You have been through a lot, I hear."

Quauh swallowed hard and didn't reply, and Massayo laughed.

"So you don't want me to give you back to the Xoconai? Why? Because this is your jacket?" He tossed the old peacoat to the bed beside her. "And because your ship lies broken across a reef, the parts that aren't at the bottom of the sea, at least, and your boss's gold is lost?"

"You know?"

"Of course. I survive because I know."

"Why didn't you tell Captain Wilkie?"

"Because you are irrelevant to Captain Wilkie, and he does not need to know."

"But I'm relevant to you, and so you will trade me to the Xoconai."

"Is that what you wish?"

Again, she hesitated.

"What would they do to you, Captain Quauh?"

The woman remained silent, lowering her gaze.

"Would they reinstate you to a command with your arm shortened?"

That brought a sad laugh from Quauh. "It has nothing to

do with my arm. There are many captains still sailing with worse wounds."

"Then why? For the loss of a ship? Certainly such things are not unheard of."

"Not this ship, and not this gold."

"So I ask again: What would they do to you?"

Quauh met his gaze. "If I am very lucky, they would brand my forehead with the red hourglass, a symbol of eternal shame. If I am only quite lucky, they would give me a sword, that I might do the honorable thing."

"Honorable and stupid are not the same thing," Massayo interjected.

Quauh spent a moment trying to digest that before continuing. "Most likely, they would behead me, and privately, a quick and clean death. But if I am unlucky, they will hang me and let my body remain dangling above the wharf as an example."

"That is ridiculous. You were outnumbered and caught in a storm. How can they hold you accountable for such a—"

"The captain is accountable. Always accountable. It is, in the end, that simple."

"But your anticipated fate seems extreme. Are there no captains in the Tonoloya Armada who have lost a ship?"

Quauh didn't answer.

"Ah, then it is the gold," Massayo reasoned. "The *Uey* was very low in the water indeed."

She glared at the man, who laughed in reply.

"Fear not, Capta—I mean, Seaman Quauh. I have no design

or desire to turn you over to your people. For now, at least, you will remain aboard at my suffrage and serve me."

Her eyes narrowed even more.

"Not for that," Massayo said, pointing to the bedroll. He laughed again. "And not for the gold you hid in the rocks. I do not need you for that, of course, since the powrie named Benny knows where you put it. No, your first task will be to help me better learn your language. I can understand it quite well, but my accent does not well serve the bitten endings of goldfish words."

"You want me to teach you to speak Xoconai?"

"Yes!"

"Then what?"

"I do not know. We will see."

She could tell that he was lying. He had something specific in mind here, beyond her helping him with his language skills. But what? And why? Why was she here? If they weren't simply thinking to ransom her back to the Xoconai admiralty, then what might Thorngirdle have told Massayo to make them believe that bringing her here was worth anyone's while?

"You know, you may begin to see the world a bit differently as the days pass by," Massayo said, as if reading her mind. "No one aboard this ship has not had a very different life than the one they now know and love."

"Are you asking me to embrace the idea of becoming a pirate?"

"Pirate?" he said, as if she had wounded him. "Good lady, *Port Mandu* has a Missive of Reprisal tacked upon her. We are not pirates, but privateers, sailing with the blessing of Chezru

Chieftain Brynn Dharielle, a great and powerful woman, and one with whom your Xoconai leaders want no trouble." He winked. "She has a dragon."

"So I have heard."

"Ah, but have you seen it? You should hope that if you do, you are under the red 'n' black of Captain Wilkie Dogears, and not on a goldfish vessel venturing too near her shores."

"I am ever so grateful," she deadpanned.

Massayo laughed and clapped his hands. "But again, that is for another day, likely one far, far away. Behave yourself, Quauh, and serve me well in my language lessons, and I will get you up on the deck as often as I can manage, under the sun and under the stars.

"Ah yes, Quauh," he continued after she had inadvertently tipped her feelings at that possibility. "I see the sparkle in those clever, golden-orange eyes of yours. I, too, have been on the sea for many years. You hate this room in the darkness, of course! That is why I have brought you this lantern. But even then, you want to feel the sun and the spray and the wind on your face, and I want to give you that. So, behave yourself and let me help you."

He rose and stretched, then stepped upon the ladder.

"Why?"

His grin back at her unnerved her, strangely. "Benny said that you were his friend, and Benny is now my friend, and I now have a lot of gold."

Leverage, she thought, but did not say. Massayo wasn't sharing his little secret with Captain Wilkie, it seemed.

"A lot of gold that will serve me and my friends quite well," he added, again as if reading her thoughts. "I hope you will become my friend."

"Why?"

"Do not underestimate yourself . . ." He crouched lower and softened his voice as he finished with, "Captain Quauh."

"I'll not betray my fellows with information . . ."

"One does not ascend to the rank of captain in the Tonoloya Armada without great knowledge of the sea and of the vessels who sail her. And no unaccomplished captain in that fleet would be given the task that was assigned to you, with the hurricanes spinning and the pirates thick in the waters. I have examined the locations and the fight that lost the *Uey*. I have heard the story from Benny, who trailed you most of the way. No captain could have saved the *Uey* short of striking her colors unconditionally. With these options you have described were I to return you, it would seem as if these comrades you'll not betray have already betrayed you."

He retreated from the small room then, climbing back to the deck, but left her the glowing lantern, for which Quauh was quite grateful.

Quauh was on the deck of *Port Mandu* for the next dawn, walking with Massayo. The coast of Behren was clearly visible now to port—they were sailing northward. Quauh had never really seen the desert land this near to shore, and she listened carefully as Massayo pointed out various landmarks, and even a small port village as they passed, the brown-skinned Behrenese villagers offering waves, even blowing horns in recognition of the ship.

"They want us to put in," Massayo explained. "For rarely is the hold of *Port Mandu* empty."

"Is it now?"

"No, we've a load of scrimshaw from Durubazzi and rum from the islands, but we'll find a better market by the end of the day. This is Jhazir. It is just a fishing village."

Quauh noted the many small oared boats dotting the waters, along with a few small sailboats, and even a pair of two-masted vessels, though smaller than *Port Mandu*—thirty-footers, perhaps.

"They've little to offer in trade beyond fish, and we are all sick of fish," Massayo explained.

"And next?"

"Djinnit, a favored market city on the central coast. We should make her harbor near to sunset—were it dark now, you'd see her lights in the northwest."

"Jinnit," Quauh echoed, somewhat.

"Djinnit," said Massayo.

"That's what I said."

"No, you bit off the front of 'Dji.' I want to hear a bit of breath before you say 'Jinnit' to soften the beginning. It is not home to juniper-berry liquor. It is Djinnit, warm and welcoming. The name means hospitable, and indeed the people are, even to unthreatening goldfish. Though you should hold your purse close if the children with too-clever fingers are running about. We are well-known there, and they have a second harbor well-protected from storms, and a soft beach where we can tug *Port Mandu* right up onto the sand to clean and tighten her hull. You will get to know this village quite well, and perhaps come to love the place as I do."

That brought a suspicious look from Quauh. Was Massayo hinting that he really did mean to sell her?

"We will be there for a few weeks," Massayo said with a wide grin.

Again, he seemed to be in her thoughts. Her shifting expression and resigned sigh tipped that off and turned that grin into another one of Massayo's belly laughs in response.

"You'll not be chained, good lady," he assured her.

A cheer from the shore drew Quauh's attention, then brought confusion, for many people were standing on the docks and on their boats, staring at *Port Mandu* and shouting huzzahs and yipping in unison.

"What?" she started to ask, when she realized they were staring up higher than the ketch's deck.

Quauh spun about, shielded her eyes from the rising sun, and looked up, fearing that she might be getting her first look at this dragon she had heard so much about.

But no, it was no dragon drawing the cheers from the folk of Jhazir. It was the To-gai-ru woman she had met with Massayo on the beach. It didn't take Quauh long to understand the cheers, for the woman was putting on quite a show of flying up there. She glided about on a rope attached to the top of the mast, which extended a dozen feet and more above the topmost rigging.

She had her foot in a loop at the bottom of the rope and was only half-heartedly holding on to it as she swung about, for she had a bow in hand, drawn and loaded.

She went out wide, then came back in fast toward the mast, and Quauh clenched her teeth, expecting a collision.

But no, the woman soared in, but then, as if pulled by some unseen force, she went flying out to starboard, and in a wide, swinging loop that brought her coming around over Quauh and Massayo, and in that swing, the woman inverted—never losing the level of her bow, as if ready to shoot throughout the entire movement!

"Chimeg is practicing, as she does every morning," Massayo explained. "And showing off, do not doubt."

In the archer went again, flipping back up just in time to avoid clipping the top line of the triangular mast. Out over the port side she went, then back in for the mast pole, where, again, she was thrown out wide into another twirling and twisting spin.

"How is that possible?"

"You would have to ask Chimeg," Massayo replied. "She wears a bracer on her wrist, like so many of the To-gai-ru people, and another strap on one of her ankles that I am sure is possessed of some magic. And look closely at the mast, just above the rigging."

Quauh shielded her eyes and focused on the mast. There was a bit of a perch, no more than a small, circular girdle of a crow's nest about halfway between the top of the mast and the top of the rigging, but that was nothing unusual. Below that, though, she noted something tied about the mast, but she couldn't make out much about it.

"You would have to ask her," Massayo said again when Quauh turned a curious look his way. "I do not understand it. All I do know is that the enemies on rival ships are not pleased when Chimeg begins her flying dance. I don't know that I have ever seen her miss her mark, from any angle. Even among the To-gai-ru riders, this one must have been quite special with her bow."

Quauh just nodded and looked up, unable to tear her eyes from the acrobatic display, Chimeg's complete control of her body and of her bow. With all the spinning and inverting, the rolling about and the sudden changes of direction, the set arrow never once seemed to shift out of line.

If what Massayo had claimed was true and Chimeg could shoot accurately throughout these acrobatic spins and inversions and rolls, she would prove a formidable and troublesome enemy indeed. Quauh could only imagine the frustration of her own archers on the *Uey*, trying to hit that ever-swerving target while Chimeg was spitting arrows into their faces.

Certainly the folk of this fishing village appreciated her act. They cheered and cheered until *Port Mandu* was far to the north.

"I'll not put you to work today, with your wound so fresh. You can return to my cabin and rest," Massayo offered. "Or you can remain topside and watch the sea and the coastline, or go talk to Benny, if that is your desire." He paused and gave her a wry little grin, then moved closer and whispered, "But don't you or Benny tell anyone else about our golden secret, okay?"

Quauh just stared at him, then spent the rest of the day

staring at the sandy coastline of the desert kingdom, almost expecting a dragon to fly into sight at any moment.

As promised, the city of Djinnit came into view, her spirelets, towers, and domes silhouetted before the giant orange globe sinking into the western horizon. Pennants flew everywhere, topping every structure, every tent, and each of the tall masts of the multitude of swaying ships moored all about her large harbor.

As the ketch moved in, Quauh was drawn to the forward port rail. She could feel the energy of the place—and could hear it, the heartbeat of many drums and the vibrations of horns. And the voices, many voices, chattering and singing. The woman couldn't hide her anticipation and intrigue. The aura emanating from Djinnit seemed more akin to that of the Tonoloyan cities in the west than anything she had known in the eastern lands.

She didn't get to go ashore until the following afternoon, on one of the last ferries from the moored *Port Mandu* to the short wharf of Djinnit. Massayo was with her, as were Benny, Chimeg, and a mountain of a man who seemed as if he could rock a sizable ship just by walking across her deck. He wasn't quite as tall as Massayo, but outweighed Port Mandu's First Mate by a hundred pounds at least. His frame was like that of a stout powrie, only many times enlarged, but unlike the spindly-limbed dwarfs, he was thick-limbed, with muscles upon muscles. Maybe he could not rock a sizable ship, but he could likely lift it from the water!

He worked both oars on the dinghy—there wouldn't have

been enough room on the bench seat for another to comfortably sit—grunting with every stroke, pulls so powerful that they lifted the front of the rowboat from the water.

His skin wasn't nearly as dark as Massayo's, more of a brown with a golden tinge to it—it seemed to Quauh the most even blend of her own and Massayo's, as if they had a child whose skin coloring was the most perfect mixture of the two. He wore no shirt and showed a multitude of tattoos, even on his face, where a black line crossed about his eyes like the bandit mask of a raccoon. That animal theme was all about him, with images of the wide-snouted southern crocodile, the fearsome jaguar, the exotic, bright-colored, large-beaked birds so common on the islands, snakes and smaller lizards, and a curious and cute little fellow on his left shoulder that seemed like a large-headed cross between a Tonoloya roof rat and a small bulldog.

He wore no shoes, either, and had tattoos atop his feet as well. Indeed, all he wore were two pieces of jewelry—a small wooden figurine hanging on a rope around his neck and a single earring on his left ear, dangling a pair of square-cut lavender gems, circle-cut in the middle to show a richer and darker amaranthine—and a purple cotton skirt.

And yes, that was indeed *all*, Quauh discovered from her seat on the back bench of the rowboat when the giant sat down wide-legged.

She shifted uncomfortably in that moment of revelation and looked up to see the huge man scowling at her; indeed, looking at her like he was quite hungry and she was the main course to be served.

Quauh quickly looked away.

Beside her, working the rudder, Benny giggled more than once, finally releasing the poor woman from her embarrassment by whispering, "He's laughing at ye behind the mask."

And then the mountainous man did laugh, a great, hearty bellow of pure joy.

"Ah, yes," Chimeg said from the front. "Do tell us, Quauh of the goldfish, what does an Ata'ino warrior wear under his skirt?"

"His rudder. Aye, Toomsuba?" Massayo said, clapping the giant on the shoulder.

"Rudder?" Quauh echoed, shaking her head.

"More than anything else, it guides a man where to go," Massayo explained.

The three before her in the boat laughed at that, but Quauh noticed that Toomsuba did close his legs a bit, which she surely appreciated, but Benny beside her merely snorted, "Peoples," and gave a square-toothed grin. "Ye're all spending so much time worrying about what's down twixt yer legs that ye're forgettin' what's most important in life."

"Oh, and what is that, Benny McBenoyt?" Chimeg asked the powrie.

"Blood!" Benny and Toomsuba said in unison, and both cheered. Benny lifted the bright beret he had taken from Captain Pinquickle high, and all of them laughed heartily.

Raised in the disciplined ways of the Xoconai navy, where such frivolity wasn't accepted, Quauh didn't quite know what to make of the banter, but she couldn't help but smile.

"Are you saying that you have no desire for women?" Chimeg pressed him. "Are there no girls in your powrie homeland?"

"Nope, not a one."

"You are all boys?"

"Bit o' both and neither o' either," Benny said proudly. "Got no time for the sweaty bumping games what seem to concern ye all."

"You don't make love? You don't have children?" Chimeg seemed quite confused, something Quauh could understand in that moment.

"We clang our mugs together, not our nethers," Benny said. "We sing together and dance together, fight together, and dip our caps in the blood of our fallen enemies."

"I have heard you curse your mother's empty teat," Chimeg reminded him.

"My mother's a jug o' whiskey," said the powrie.

"It amazes me that your people still walk the world, then," Massayo remarked.

"Ah, but we're eternal beasties, don't ye know? A higher level o' being than ye poor mortal things, free o' the silly hunger that makes folks like yerself distracted from what's what."

"The ones floating facedown in the sea did not seem so eternal," Quauh said before she could bite back the words.

Benny turned on her, his face as if set in stone, and a chorus of gasps arose from Chimeg and Massayo, while Toomsuba snorted like a waking bear. For a brief moment, Quauh thought she would be thrown overboard.

But Benny howled and slapped his knee, then sobered

immediately, flashed an exaggerated wink at the woman, and quietly assured her, "Them boys'll be back soon enough. We sung the song o'er their buried hearts."

The banter continued until they got to the shore, where Toomsuba hopped out into the water, ran to the prow, and tugged the boat and her four passengers high up onto the sand.

"You three go to hear Captain Wilkie's orders," Massayo told Chimeg, Benny, and Toomsuba.

"You are the first mate," Chimeg reminded him.

"And therefore, I already know what he will say, of course," Massayo told her. "And you," he said to Quauh. "You are to stay with me. Have you been to a Behrenese city before?"

"Only Freeport."

"Freeport is not a . . . well, you will see." He motioned for her to follow and led her off the beach, up onto the avenues of Djinnit.

"Is it true what Benny said?" she asked him as soon as they were out of earshot of the others.

"About?"

"About his people. A bit of both and neither of either?"

"Who can know? I have sailed with dozens of powries and seen scores more in the port towns, but never a bloody-cap woman. But then, I suppose, who could tell? Never seen one interested in a human lady, either, or a human man. Not in that way.

"What he told you about burying powrie hearts to resurrect the fallen was true, though," Massayo added. "I have seen it with my own eyes. Truly unnerving to see them crawl from the dirt, confused, their bodies not fully under their control, their memories scattered. It is often days before such a returning dwarf can even speak—they are more zombie than alive in the earliest days. But yes, it is true, and they eventually recall their identity and history."

"A gift from their god."

"More a reason they have no god—or at least none that I've ever heard them speak of in prayers. Their life is here, eternally, so they believe, so why worry about an afterlife?"

Quauh, who was not very religious, though wise enough never to admit such to any of the zealous augurs of Scathmiz-zane, considered that for a moment, then nodded.

"But no sex," Massayo said suddenly, and lightly. "Why would they want to live forever?"

Quauh froze a bit at that bawdy remark, particularly given the tone of the man—since he apparently owned her now. She tried to cover it up with a bit of a smile, but knew it was strained without having to look into a mirror. She was totally inexperienced sexually—personally, at least. She had of course served on ships with randy crews, full of trysts onboard and in port. It wasn't that she had any problem with the concept, just that she had little desire for it, or knowledge of it, or, at least to this point, much curiosity about it. Her career had been her life and her fulfillment. She fell behind a step in her hesitation, and Massayo swung about, seeming concerned for a moment, then figuring it out.

"Come along, good captain," he said. "You need fear nothing from me."

"To where?"

"To see Djinnit, that you can learn of these desert people. You might be spending much time among them in the future, of course."

"As your servant? Your slave?"

"I already told you, never that."

"Then what?"

"That will be for you to determine."

"So I can leave now if I choose, and make my own way through Djinnit, or to wherever I wish?"

Massayo smiled. "Yes." He stopped and so did Quauh, staring at him.

"I think you would be passing on the best opportunity of your young life, though," Massayo went on. "But the choice is yours. I do not need servants and abhor the thought of owning another human being. Can you say differently?"

"Do you always speak in such a cryptic manner?"

"If I tell you too much, how could I let you leave?"

Quauh crossed her arms over her chest, which only reminded her of her new infirmity. It truly surprised her that she had to be reminded, for there was no pain in that stumped arm, and no infestation that she could note. Powrie berets were powerful healing magic, she now understood. But still, she had only half of her right arm! Reflexively, and more than a little because of embarrassment, she quickly dropped that right arm down by her side. "Show me about this place you call Djinnit."

Massayo motioned her up beside him and did just that, and despite her stubborn defiance, Quauh couldn't help but be enchanted by the sights, the sounds, and even the smells of the city. It reminded her of home in many regards, except that not even the most decorated of Xoconai cities had such a brilliant display of color. Reds and yellows, greens and such shining orange to shame the sun itself, fluttered all about the place—and it wasn't just the variety of the colors, but the sheer brightness and richness of them. She could imagine these people spending days and weeks dying the fabric. And years and years making the carpets on display in several of the tents! Such workmanship and pride!

Musicians seemed to be on every corner, and there was no dearth of talent here, with fine melodies and harmonies drifting lazily down many side streets, uplifting strings and drums putting a bounce in the step of every person traveling down others.

Many looked at her with obvious interest, staring at her. She got the feeling that they had seen Xoconai before, but probably not many walking freely through a Behrenese city. One old woman, her face wrinkled with experience, ran up to her and said something she couldn't understand. Quauh looked at her apprehensively.

"She wants to know if your colors hurt," Massayo interpreted.

"My colors?"

"Your face."

"No, of course not."

The old woman nodded and asked something else.

"She wants to know if she can touch it," Massayo explained.

Quauh arched an eyebrow at the man, who just shrugged and nodded, mouthing, *She means no harm or disrespect.*

It was an uncomfortable, almost alarming, notion to Quauh, who did not like to be touched. But she did bend low, and the woman traced her fingers over her red nose, then the blue and white flaring to either side of it. Then the old woman clapped her hands together before her, bowed to Quauh, talking excitedly all the while, and after yet another bow of gratitude or respect or both, skittered away.

"She said you are very beautiful," Massayo translated. "She also mentioned having a grandson who is about your age."

That brought a higher arch of Quauh's eyebrow and a wider smile from Massayo in reply, and Quauh had to wonder if he had added that last part on his own, probably to embarrass her yet again.

On they went. At one tent, Massayo purchased two small pita breads of a sweet, finger-sized fruit, and handed one bowl to Quauh.

"I saw these on Freeport, and on the island of . . ." She let her voice trail off.

"Watouwa," Massayo finished. "Yes, Captain Quauh, we know where the *Uey* got the gold and the sugarcane to cover it. You have seen these—dates, they are called, and come from a particular type of palm tree plentiful along the coast—but have you tasted one?"

"They do not look very pleasing." She cradled the bread under what was left of her right forearm and picked one date up, but dropped it immediately back onto the bread and wiped her fingers on her trousers. "Sticky."

"Sticky sweet," Massayo agreed. "Try it. So many possibilities are open before you right here and right now. Are you really going to ignore them, and if so, then why?"

Quauh plucked up a date and popped it into her mouth.

"Beware the pit!" Massayo warned, just in time.

By the time they had reached the other side of this small market square, Quauh's dates were all devoured, as was the pita. As Massayo finished his as well, he flashed that huge smile at her, then held up a finger, clueing her into a growing chorus down the end of a narrow alleyway. He grabbed her by the hand and rushed off, coming out of the alley onto another market square, and near to a group of musicians, playing and singing a bouncy and happy tune. Before them, people danced and clapped in time with the backbeat.

"Will you dance with me?" Massayo asked, and before Quauh came out of her noncommittal shrug, the large man brought her left hand to his shoulder, put his own right arm about her waist, and pulled out her right arm as he began to quickstep around.

He slid his arm as if to take her hand, then hesitated, an uncomfortable moment hanging before them.

Her hand that was no longer there.

The moment was gone in an instant, Quauh pulling back in shame and seething anger, bringing her torn right arm up across her chest and tucking her chin over it, then covering her face with her left hand.

"My good lady," Massayo stammered. "I did not . . . the music . . . the mood . . ."

"You have no blame here."

Massayo came up close and again touched her as if to dance.

"Please," he said when she looked up to match his gaze. "The music is joyous and the company grand."

She didn't embrace the notion, but neither did she resist as Massayo gently took her arm again and began the dance. He led beautifully, with surprising grace for a man so tall.

"You see," he said to her, "no one notices and no one cares."

"You think me ashamed?"

"I think you in turmoil in many directions, as anyone would be having suffered your last experiences. But it will pass, Captain Quauh. All of it. You have my word. When we get to Freeport in the autumn, I will take you to a man who can help with your infirmity. Crippling wounds like yours are not uncommon, though not as common on the arm as with lost legs. What do you think we should use as a replacement? A hook? Hooks are very useful, though you will need to be very careful in time of itch."

She couldn't help but laugh a little at his joke, and even after, her smile remained in gratitude as Massayo was truly trying hard to make it all better for her.

"Or maybe a blade," he suggested. "With a sheath, of course, so that you do not roll upon your own arm and kill yourself in your sleep, or kill your lover if you find one—and I am sure that a woman as beautiful as Quauh has little problem in such affairs."

Quauh smirked at his feeble attempt to butter her, and at yet another reminder of that uncomfortable subject. But she couldn't deny that she appreciated it, for it was clear that Massayo wasn't saying such things to embarrass her, nor facilitate such an affair between them. He wasn't trying to take advantage here, with her so out of sorts and vulnerable. She was confident of that, even though she understood that a true rake would want their intended victim to believe exactly that.

"But yes, I have a friend who will be of great help, and now we have enough gold so that we can do it right."

"We?"

"My friend and I. He is a talented fellow indeed, and owes me as I owe him, as is true with all my friends."

"And you will have him repair my arm as much as he can? And you will pay for it?"

"Yes. But not just I. We will pay for it. It was Quauh who cleverly salvaged and hid the gold, not I. I and our dinghy companions will help you retrieve it, and so we will use it for the benefit of friends."

"So now, I too have become a friend of Massayo."

"Does that trouble you?"

Quauh was about to make some clever retort, to cook up something sharp to say that would sting the man, but instead she paused and considered the question sincerely. "No," she answered, to her own surprise. "It pleases me."

"I, too, am pleased. As I told you before we even sailed past Jhazir, I had hoped that you would become my friend."

"But why?"

"I told you that, too. I do not underestimate you. Not in any way."

The music stopped and all the dancers turned to clap, as did Quauh, before sighing and slapping her one hand against her thigh instead.

"Come," Massayo told her. "We must secure a wagon."

"Where are we going?"

"Captain Wilkie will not bring *Port Mandu* to the sand for her scraping and tightening for at least a few days." He nodded out to the south, where some masts could be seen far from the open end of a side street. "There are already two other ships tied up on the beach, and there aren't enough trees there to properly secure a third. Chimeg and the others will return with a more precise timeline, likely, but we surely have several days to linger about."

"But why a wagon? Where are we going?"

"Back to Jhazir, of course."

Quauh looked at him with clear puzzlement.

"Captain Wilkie has offered me my commission," Massayo explained. "He has been seeking an escort vessel and has offered the opportunity to me if I could find my way to purchase a proper vessel and hire a worthy crew."

Quauh was sure that the sea breeze would blow her over in that moment if it found its way past the huddled buildings along the street. So much suddenly began to make sense to her, even though a hundred questions bounced about her thoughts. That last part, *hire a worthy crew*, echoed in her mind most of all.

CHAPTER 13

CAPTAIN MASSAYO

They rolled out of Djinnit in a small, wobbly cart pulled by a huge and fat horse. Quauh, who had learned to ride a cuetzpali lizard, had been intimidated by the mounts used by the people east of the mountains, which had her sitting several feet off the ground, with a wide bulk beneath her that made it hard for her to see the land she was moving across. But even the largest of those mounts seemed tiny compared to this behemoth, whose shoulder was several inches above the top of her head and who weighed a ton, quite literally.

Fortunately, she wasn't riding, as Chimeg had claimed that seat and wouldn't surrender it, and Quauh wasn't even asked to walk up front guiding the beast—Benny and Toomsuba took turns at that. She got to sit in the cart with Massayo and the powrie or the giant man, whichever of them was taking a break, although she often got out and walked to settle her stomach from the constant jostling along the bumpy trail. For indeed, this was more a rut-filled and worn path than anything that could properly be called a road.

The journey took about four hours, and they had a lovely view of the Mirianic Ocean all the way, as the trail continued along a high bluff overlooking the beach. Quauh spotted several sails, but they were all small boats, day boats, single-masted sloops and square-rigged craft that couldn't safely carry more than a handful of people.

She saw the masts of some larger vessels when at last they came in sight of Jhazir, much like the ships that had anchored near *Port Mandu* out by the island.

"Those are commissioned Behrenese ships?" she asked Massayo.

Massayo pointed out three of the five moored outside Jhazir. "Yes. The one in the middle was at the island when we rescued you."

She started to respond, but his use of the word "rescue" put her off her guard. She looked from the boats to the curious man.

"They are good enough people, these Behrenese," Massayo assured her. "Even the sailors in service to Chezru Brynn Dhari-elle, who, too, is a very great lady, from what I have been told by people who know her."

"They don't seem to like the Xoconai."

Massayo shrugged and smiled, a reminder that he wasn't enamored with the Xoconai, either. "Your people invaded and waged war on her ally—a nation that had been as a sister land to her since before she wore the crown of Behren. An ally nation she had helped to overthrow the demon King Aydrian and his murderous army. Not only did your people wage war

263

on Honce-the-Bear, but after the blood had dried, your people broke the truce that had been agreed upon by all parties, one that was favorable to the Xoconai, considering that you were the invaders to Honce. That is the true story, is it not?"

Quauh shifted uncomfortably. "I do not know. I was just a child when all that happened. I came to the east at the orders of my superiors."

"But you do not care how they came to be in the east?"

Quauh swallowed hard and had no answer, and was grateful when Massayo let her off the hook by smiling warmly. "Sometimes even the ranks of the victors are filled with victims, eh?" he said, and let that uncomfortable conversation drop.

The cart rolled down from the high bluff and moved among a settlement composed mostly of tents scattered about a smattering of small houses of hardened clay and wood. Many of these people were probably nomads, Quauh realized, noting the items about the tents, which often included a donkey and even a couple of horselike animals she did not know, tall and with humped backs.

She made a mental note of these strange mounts, thinking that the information might prove useful to her commanders back in Entel.

But no sooner had she done that when she realized that she really didn't care what might prove useful to her commanders back in Entel. No matter what information she might bring back, it wasn't going to make any difference if they got their hands on the captain who had lost the *Uey'Lapialli*.

She slumped back against the wall of the cart, overwhelmed by her feelings.

Only in that moment did Quauh truly come to appreciate that she had no desire to return to serve her commission. Ever. Even if she was forgiven for the loss of the *Uey*, she was suddenly seeing her service in a very different light. Maybe it was Matlalihi's treachery, or maybe it was because she was being surprised at every turn by the banter and compassion of these people now surrounding her, people from all over the region, people from the dense jungles of Durubazzi, to the islanders, to the Behrenese. Even to the powries—Quauh was truly stunned at how much she had come to trust Benny already! He could have cut her out of the stolen treasure, and cut her heart out of her chest, without a thought.

The dissonance within her had her sitting and shaking her head. For all her life, all she had known were the societies of the Xoconai—she had never, in all her life, spoken to anyone who was not Xoconai nearly as much as she had on the rowboat coming into Djinnit alone. Even after crossing the continent to serve in the east, her interactions with the conquered people of Honce had been less than minimal.

Now her eyes were opening. Could she really think of people like Massayo as "sidhe"? Were these goblinkin? Lesser beings than she, than Matlalihi?

She didn't know.

They pulled to a stop on a dirt avenue just outside a market square that looked very much like a scaled-down version of the bazaars they had just left in Djinnit, at least from the side. When they entered, Quauh noted that this was more of a local market, fresh food and wood and peat for fires, and without the booths in Djinnit set up for trading durable goods.

But the vendors were getting durable goods in return, it seemed. Boats were coming in to resupply. The children of locals were rushing over to get this night's dinner.

"Do the vendors here make trips to Djinnit with the cloth and cane and art pieces they get from the crews?" she asked Massayo.

"Indeed. And there, they sell them to other crews for more. Jhazir is the place where boats get their short-term needs. Most that you see here are sailing south from Djinnit before going on a longer journey. Also, this is the place where a clever captain or first mate can off-load some goods that might attract too much attention in a larger market like the city to the north."

"But you said there were commissioned Behrenese ships in this port."

"And they have captains and first mates," Massayo replied with a wink. "No time to bargain, no time to tarry," he called back to Toomsuba, Chimeg, and Benny, who were loitering at a booth that sold dates.

"I am late for our important meeting and our departure."

"Back in the wagon again today?" Quauh asked.

"Oh, no, we only procured it to come to Jhazir. The woman where we left it will rent it to someone traveling back to Djinnit. She is the sister of the stableman who rented it to us, I believe."

Quauh looked at him curiously.

"You will see," he promised.

They moved out of the square and down to the docks, to the large building that served as home and office to the harbormaster and her enforcers. There, Quauh waited with the others while Massayo entered a side chamber, haggling with a woman sitting behind a very clever and ornate desk made of driftwood and sea glass. It was quite a beautiful piece of furniture and reminded Quauh of the one used by the harbormaster in her distant childhood home.

Once again, the parallels, seeing the commonality between these people in the east and her own people in the west, had her off-balance, challenging her long-held beliefs.

"You cannot expect me to pay such a price for a boat I haven't yet sailed!" she heard Massayo shout at the woman.

"If you change your mind, I give you back your coin when you return," came the reply. "If you will not trust me with the coin, why should I trust you with the boat?"

"Because you know me, and know my captain, whose ship comes to Jhazir several times each season."

"I need more than this pittance. In good faith."

Massayo came to the doorway and blew a frustrated sigh. "Benny?"

"Bah, me bosses'll take me heart and eat it if they learn of it," the powrie grumbled, but the way he was moving and the dramatic exasperation in his response told Quauh that the powrie and Massayo had set the whole situation up to play out along this exact script.

Benny reached into his pocket as he approached and brought forth a second bloody beret—his old one, which he had replaced with the one he had taken from Captain Pinquickle's corpse.

He pushed past Massayo, pulling back his arm as if he wasn't going to let the harbormaster snatch it from him.

Again, this was all scripted, Quauh recognized.

"If I don't get this back when we come back with yer scow, ye'll be needin' more than it to keep the blood under yer skin, don't ye doubt," he told the woman, dropping the beret onto the desk.

"Back to pay me the balance on the boat."

"Bah, but that cap's worth more'n yer boat by itself," Benny grumped, but he was smiling when he came back out, even tossing a wink at Quauh.

The added deposit finished the deal, and soon after, the five were out on the seas, sailing a sloop whose name was covered by a piece of hanging fabric. Benny took the wheel, with Toom-suba handling the rigging, calling for assistance from Quauh now and again.

Quauh mostly watched Chimeg. The To-gai-ru woman scrambled up the mast with ease and settled on the perch while she organized her rope and the leather strap that secured the second gemstone to the mast.

"I hate this top rigging!" she called down to Massayo. "How am I to serve properly as anything more than a set of eyes?"

"That's all I ask of you at this time, my friend!" he called back up to her.

"She's angry because she cannot set up her swinging?" Quauh asked Massayo.

"She is To-gai-ru. She is always mad about something."

"I heard that," came the call from above. "Even on this perch, do not doubt that I can hit you exactly where I wish to hit you."

"She's not ever going to be happy with this boat," said Quauh.

"This is very temporary," Massayo assured the Xoconai.

"So this isn't really a test sail so you can decide whether or not to buy the ship? Why, then? And where are we going?"

"We are going to get the money to properly buy the sloop."

"But you said it was temporary."

"It is."

"You are not making any sense here."

"Do you think we can hide a chestful of gold bars on an open cart?"

As that sank in, Quauh found her response sticking in her throat.

They moored the boat that evening under a sky full of stars, very near to the black silhouette of the small island where Quauh had lost her ship and her way of life. They seemed to be almost exactly where *Port Mandu* had been anchored when Quauh had been bought from the powries and brought aboard—a time that seemed so very long ago to Quauh.

"Should we perhaps move a bit farther from the shore?" Quauh asked Massayo even before Benny and Toomsuba had properly set the anchor.

Massayo arched his eyebrows at that.

"Those lizards might be swimmers, are likely night hunters, and our rail is very low on this sloop."

"Well, if the lizards fancy us for a meal, they won't have to swim to get us," Massayo replied. "We will only be here for a few hours."

"We are going ashore at night?"

"We're going ashore as soon as Chimeg can get the dinghy launched. Go and help her, if you would."

Quauh paused for just a moment, then sighed and went to assist the To-gai-ru. She hadn't gone far when she heard Massayo call out, "Benny, are your friends ready to be brought out of the ground yet?"

"Nah," the powrie replied. "Got to give 'em a few months to grow, and the more ye give 'em after that, the more they'll remember who they were."

"That a good thing?"

"Do ye want them knowing how to handle the sea?"

Quauh wasn't sure if that was a good thing or a bad thing. The five of them could handle the sloop, but a few more wouldn't hurt, certainly. Still, not all the powries were like Benny, she knew, and the idea of being outnumbered by bloody-cap powries on a single boat in a wide sea wasn't very appealing to her.

The tide was beginning to recede when they neared the rocky shoreline and fumbled about, trying to find the right place.

"Listen for it," Quauh told them. "Just be silent and keep the oars up for a bit, and we'll know when we have found the right channel."

"Clicking stones," Benny agreed.

The tactic worked, and the dinghy came into the same channel where Quauh had beached her flotsam raft the morning after the battle.

"Should I lead them to the gold or will you?" she asked Benny, more than a little slyly.

Benny seemed to appreciate the sarcasm. "I saved yer life, Sparkleface," he reminded her, and he did indeed take up the lead, soon enough coming to exactly the place where the treasure had been hidden. Fortunately, surprisingly, they didn't encounter or even see any of the lizards on that short journey, and even better luck, the gold was still in the hole. They began hauling out the bars as soon as Benny jumped in and pushed the seaweed blanket aside.

"Just fifteen bars for the first trip," Massayo instructed, loading one of the five sacks they had brought. "I'll take Chimeg and Benny back to the boat to unload, then come back while Quauh and Toomsuba bring the rest down to the channel for a full second . . ."

He stopped talking at the sound of clicking—crossbows clicking!

"Aye, ye bring 'em all down to yer boat now, hey?" came a voice from the darkness, and a short, stout figure hopped up on top of the rock wall and lit a torch to show them his smile.

Benny recognized him.

"Six Bits," he whispered to Massayo.

"Well met again," Massayo said to the powrie on the rocks. "I am First Mate Massayo, sailing with Wilkie Dogears on *Port Mandu*."

The powrie hesitated. "*Port Mandu*? Bah, and stick yer finger in yer nose. That ain't *Port Mandu* out there."

"Ye're the one what dragged me to Massayo, Columbine o' *One o' Six*!" Benny called out.

Columbine held up his hands to signal the others to hold their fire. "Benny McBenoyt?" he asked. "That yerself?"

"Only self I got, ye dog, and what's Six Bits doing lurking out at this lizard-infested rock?"

"Ah, ye clever dog! Ye had some gold hid away. That's how ye're still drawing air through yer yap. Well played!"

"I heard only three crossbows cocked," Quauh whispered quietly to Massayo. "Four powries, including the one with the torch."

"The bloody caps are steady-handed and fine shots," Massayo warned.

"Here now, what're ye jabberin' about?" Columbine asked.

"We're arguin' about whether to cut yerselfs in for a share or fight it out with ye to keep what we got," Benny answered before Massayo could. "Doubt that Captain Thorngirdle's looking for a war with Wilkie Dogears."

"Got nothing to do with Thorngirdle," Columbine answered, and his tone and the fact that he referred to the powrie boss without his title offered some tantalizing possibilities to Benny and his friends.

"Ain't no Six Bits," said another voice from the darkness, and Columbine turned that way and seemed to growl.

"Well now," Benny said. "What's that about?"

"Come now, friend," Massayo added. "We can fight or we can bargain, as has always been the way between Captain Wilkie and your kin and kind. Are we really to be enemies over this, when there might be agreements to be reached?"

"Come on, now, Columbine," Benny said. "Ye got three crossbows leveled, but ye ain't bringing me or the big one there down with one shot. And that one there?" he added, motioning to Quauh. "Aye, but ye'll find out why the goldfish made her a captain! No two o' ye'll stand long afore that one."

Far from being flattered, Quauh realized that Benny had just made her a prime target. She wanted to kick the little rat, but she really couldn't argue the logic, considering her infirmity and the skill of the others who would fight beside Benny.

Columbine paused for a bit, then asked, "What're ye offerin'?"

"Ten bars of gold and you go your way," Massayo answered.

"Ten? O' how many?"

"Or," Massayo continued, "perhaps you tell us the truth of your situation here and we find better terms for all. On my word, we will honor a truce here."

Again, the powrie paused, but then hopped down from the rocks and walked toward the group.

"He's in desperate straits," Quauh whispered. "Something happened with this group."

"Aye," Massayo quietly agreed.

"Name's Columbine," Benny informed them. "Sailed on Thorngirdle's own boat, *One o' Six*."

"So, no Six Bits?" Benny asked when Columbine stopped before them.

"Too many o' them goldfish hunting us now," Columbine said. "Thorngirdle decided not to buy more boats. Not now, at least. Only kept two, and brought back th' other three captains and helmsmen to his own crew."

"He cut ye out," Benny remarked.

"Two Bits now," Columbine continued. "They're chasin' smaller and along the shores, if they be piratin' at all, until the goldfish hunters're bored and go home."

"How much he give ye?"

"We got our honest cut."

"But ye thought ye could come back here and pull out a bit more, eh?"

"Eh. We saw ye come in. Didn't know what ye were about."

"Just four bloody caps, then, trying to salvage a bit of treasure," said Massayo.

"More'n four," Columbine countered.

"Just four," the tall man stated again. "If I let Chimeg over there make a move, you will be down to three."

"Two," Chimeg corrected. "I usually move twice."

"But why are we talking like enemies?" Massayo asked. "You seem to be in need of work, and we are in need of crewmates. And we have a lot of gold and will find fine drinking and carousing in Freeport soon enough."

"Wilkie's hirin'?"

"Not Captain Wilkie. Captain Massayo, who sails as second boat to *Port Mandu*. And out there is my ship, the . . ." He paused and looked around, then at Benny, when he smiled and announced, *"Pinquickle's Folly."*

"Oh, but I'm likin' that!" Benny exclaimed. "Haha!"

"Oh, then, and how many ye got, Cap'n Massayo o' *Pinquickle's Folly*?"

"Five here and twenty more out there."

Columbine snorted. "Bah, ain't a light on her decks. Ye got five here and no more'n that, or ye'd have brought a fighting force to the beach."

"And you have only four," Massayo countered.

"Aye, four," Columbine admitted.

"And aye, five," Massayo admitted, and the two laughed. "So, deal?"

"Pirate proper split?"

"Two parts to Wilkie off the top. Pirate proper split on the rest."

"We'll fill her out, and we got a dinghy, or what's left o' one, ye can tie up and drag along." Columbine spit in his hand and held it out, and Massayo did likewise, taking the hand with a firm shake.

"C'mon, boys!" Columbine called.

Sure enough, there were only three others, including the red-haired sprite.

"Ye takin' the wheel o' that sloop, Benny McBenoyt?" Columbine asked.

"Aye."

"Good enough." The powrie looked to Chimeg curiously. "The flyer? Surprised Wilkie let you go."

Chimeg didn't answer.

"And what's she doing here?" Columbine asked with a snicker, indicating Quauh. "Barter for when we get to Freeport?"

Quauh stiffened and glared at the dwarf.

"Oh, hardly," Massayo answered. "And watch your tone, Columbine. Show proper respect when you address First Mate Quauh."

That surprised all of them, clearly, and Quauh most of all. She stared at Massayo, who flashed her that huge smile and a wink. "Underestimate her at your peril," he finished to Columbine, but really, to them all.

"And what's this one's name?" Benny asked Columbine when the red-haired sprite came up beside him.

"Aushin," the sprite answered.

"And that one's Perridoo, and over there's McKorkle," Columbine added, pointing out the other two. "Both worked *Three o' Six* but got bumped out in the new alignment."

"Hmm. Okay then, well met, boys," said Benny. "And yerself, Ohshit, get in that hole and start pullin' out bars."

"Aushin!" the young powrie corrected.

"That's what I said, Ohshit. Now get in the hole or the rest of us're finding a wee bigger share."

Aushin shuffled nervously and looked to Columbine, clearly begging for support.

"Ye heard Benny McBenoyt," Columbine told him. "The helmsdwarf what throws a barrelboat like a spear, eh? Might that Cap'n Pinquickle'd done better listening to him, don't ye think?"

Crestfallen, Aushin's jaw drooped. He went to the hole, mumbling curses, but very much under his breath.

"Kids," Benny said to Columbine. "Didn't get his heart buried last time he got killed to death, eh?"

"Nah, but I been told he was a fine warrior in his previous life."

"Shame when that happens. Got to teach 'em all over again."

"Ye sound more'n happy to give him a lesson, eh?"

Benny flashed a wicked smile.

Only a short while later, for few could work with the tirelessness of powries, the last of the gold bars were secured under the planks of the floor of the lower hold. "Good for balancing her," Benny quipped as they hammered the flooring back into place. Soon after, *Pinquickle's Folly* raised her sails and journeyed back to Jhazir without delay, where Massayo paid for the boat, then returned with a surprise: a trio of Behrenese musicians signed on to perform and to serve as deckhands.

"What is life without music?" was all the explanation he offered, introducing two young women, the sisters Dalila and Ibtisa, and Dawoud, a handsome young man with dark eyes that seemed to continually scan everything put before him. The three unloaded an assortment of instruments and bags of clothing, while Massayo called Toomsuba down to the dinghy to help him with an enormous keg of rum and a second full of salted fish.

"We make our own music," Columbine protested. "Who can out-croon a powrie, eh?"

"I have heard your solemn dirges," Massayo came back at him. "We have too few crew to risk losing some who throw themselves over the rail in despair!"

That brought a laugh all around.

"Come now, weigh anchor, hoist the sails, and let us get to Djinnit, where we can better supply, get our colors from Captain Wilkie—he's been waiting for this day for some time and is ready for us—and properly commission *Pinquickle's Folly*. I have a painter friend. And a builder friend . . ."

"Ye seem to have a lot o' friends," Aushin remarked from the hatch to the hold.

"That's how he stays alive," Columbine scolded, then with a wink to Benny, added, "Ohshit."

The sloop was back into Djinnit late the next day, now crewed by twelve. All but Quauh and Benny went ashore—nine to join up with *Port Mandu*'s crew to prepare for the repairs, while Massayo went off on other business, including informing Captain Wilkie of his purchase and collecting the colors.

Quauh spent the next couple of hours pacing the deck, trying to make sense of . . . everything.

"Nervous, eh?" Benny called down to her from the crow perch. "Not to worry." He pointed to port, to the next nearest ship, *Port Mandu*. "The folk already know we're with Wilkie."

"I am not worried, Benny. I was just looking forward to going back into Djinnit." Hearing the words surprised Quauh, for she was caught off guard by how much she truly wanted to go back in and explore that fascinating and lively city.

"We'll be in and about the port for weeks. Nothing but day trips, so we can sort our places and stations and learn better how this little tub o' gum-stuck wood handles on her turns and holds together in the rolls. Ye'll get yer chances ashore."

"It really is a lousy little tub, isn't it?"

"We'll get it into shape, but Captain Massayo's not think-ing we'll have her for long. I'm doubtin' he'll even put his own invention on her."

"His own invention?"

"Made his name selling the *caoutchou*. Look around close at th' other ships moored. All got *caoutchou* lines on their hulls, with metal wires inside. Seals the wood from leaking, and more than that, keeps the shock inside when they're taking lightning—from the sky or an enemy monk or wizard.

"He was a rich man once," Benny explained. "Until ye goldfish went to Durubazzi and cut deals with treacherous bosses for the gold. Massayo got pushed aside, his business stolen. The goldfish even sold him into service to dig and pan for the gold, until he escaped. Surprises me that he let a goldfish like yerself aboard, and didn't just kill ye." Benny shrugged. "He's a bigger man than meself, ha!"

Quauh took it all in, another few brushstrokes to the tapestry she was painting of the truth of the world beyond her parochial understanding. Massayo had even danced with her, and made her first mate, and she found that she wasn't the slightest bit suspicious of his motives. Again, perhaps he was just very, very good at deception . . .

"Then what?" she called up to Benny. "What will Captain Massayo do after he's rid of *Pinquickle's Folly?*"

"I got me suspicions, but not much to tell ye yet. What I do know is that Massayo's not wantin' to sail in the shadows of Wilkie's mainsail for long, and that he only bought the *Pinquickle* to get the gold off that lizard-thick rock. We'll know soon enough. So enjoy yer days, good lady, good First Mate Quauh. Dance and merrymake! We'll be finding some real fun afore the summer's surrenderin' to fall."

CHAPTER 14

CAPTAIN FURY

"**D**o you know what they call me?" the diminutive Captain Aketz said to the boy who was cleaning his cabin in *Crocodile*'s quarterdeck, though the captain never glanced back at him, just continued staring out the window across the open water to the west.

"Do you?" he asked again, and this time he did glance over his shoulder at the nervous kid.

The young boy, an orphan from Entel, knew better than to look up and match stares with Captain Aketz. He just kept sweeping.

"Fury," Aketz told him. "Captain Fury." He gave a little laugh. "Look at me. I am barely larger than you, and what are you, ten years old? Perhaps twelve? Captain Fury! I rather like it. And do you know why I like it, boy? Because it shows that these stupid sidhe underestimate me. Yes, *Cipac* is formidable, but because I am clever in design and not just a brute. I know how to use the tools, you see?

"Captain Fury!" He said it as if announcing a god, and

laughed as he finished. "They think me brutish, and so remain blind to the traps I set. Like this one. Oh, they have me, don't you know, boy? They have me! They have us. Outmanned and outgunned. Helpless and so very far from shore."

He laughed again and looked back to the west. Nothing but water as far as the eye could see, and much farther than that, even. *Cipac* was a long way from her ports and her patrol routes.

By design.

"Sail!" he heard from up above.

"Boy, do come here and sweep this mess from the window jamb," Aketz ordered, and he pulled open one of the large windows at the tail of his ship.

The cabin boy hustled over and leaned out, lifting his broom to brush whatever it was that had caught Aketz's eye.

Aketz grabbed the broom and tugged it away as he grabbed the boy by the back of his belt and hoisted him up, over, and out the window, sending him flailing into the ship's wake.

"It is a shame that these animals know how to speak," Aketz lamented, closing the window so as not to hear any pathetic screams. "It would be so much easier to confide in them if they had no way to relay such private thoughts."

He sighed, shook his head, placed the broom to lean in a corner, and exited the cabin, stalking across the main deck to the foredeck, where his first mate stood with the augurs.

"The *Dancing Dolphin*?" First Mate Cayo asked him when he arrived. "That's Whirley's schooner, isn't it?"

"A good ship," Captain Aketz replied. "Too good for a filthy buccaneer like Whirley."

Cayo looked around at every horizon, and they all looked the same. They were far out of the typical shipping lanes south of Freeport, nearest to the bend in the land masses called the Leeward Isles, with no land in sight. Few ships came out this far, for beyond the elbow formed by the Leewards, there was just the open, violent Mirianic, and the islands themselves were no welcoming harbor for Xoconai, Behrenese, or buccaneer alike.

"We came all the way out here for Whirley?" Cayo asked, shaking his head at the mystery of why Whirley or any buccaneer might even be out this far to the east in the first place.

"No," Aketz explained, motioning for the spyglass, which he put to his eye immediately. "He's coming all the way out here for us."

"You did get a spy on the *Dolphin*."

"Oh, I did indeed, and as far as Captain Whirley knows, we're out here light in crew and low on supplies and arrows and ballista bolts." Aketz lowered his spyglass and turned a perfectly wicked expression onto his augur first mate. "And Captain Whirley knows that when we return to Freeport to resupply, we're to meet with three other warships to pack hunt until we bring him to Entel to be hanged. His Letter of Reprisal was canceled by City Sovereign Popoca and Grand Augur Apichtli."

"Canceled? The letter is from Chezru Chieftain Brynn Dharielle. What jurisdiction—"

"Popoca and Apichtli are testing her limits," Aketz explained. "Whirley was assured in Freeport that the red 'n' black and his letter meant nothing now, and that the Tonoloya Armada would spare no expense in seeing him hanged."

"City Sovereign Popoca would spare four ships to chase the *Dancing Dolphin?*" an incredulous Cayo asked.

"Of course not. But if you were Whirley, with all that information, what would you do?"

"Even were we light in crew and supplies, the *Dancing Dolphin* would have little chance against *Cipac*," Cayo insisted.

"She's not alone, not hardly."

Cayo started to respond but bit it back. He turned to the forecastle rail overlooking the main deck to see the chain netting sprawled across the planks, two corners tied to the low ballistae, and with weighted ropes lining them all about.

"Two Bits," Cayo said.

"Three Bits now, so they claim. All the better, I say."

Cayo took a deep breath and was glad that *Cipac* really wasn't low on warriors and supplies. His light-wave magic had been highly effective against the sailing ships in the last couple of years but was fairly useless against the low-riding barrelboats. They had encountered the bloody-capped dwarfs only a couple of times, but both had resulted in melees and had sent a score of Xoconai sailors to the ocean in shrouds. He didn't really want to fight them again, but Captain Aketz seemed more than eager.

He studied the chain netting and shook his head.

"It will work," said Captain Aketz. He smiled as he considered his coming victory and the gain to his already formidable reputation. The buccaneers called him Captain Fury now, and he quite liked the compliment.

He meant to kill them all, and the thought saddened him, for then who would be left to fear him?

"They call me Captain Fury, you know?" Aketz told him, and Cayo nodded. "Surely a brute with such a reputation wouldn't be clever enough to turn their ambush into a trap."

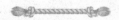

"Not this time, ye bastard," Captain Whirley of the *Dancing Dolphin* said, his mustached lip curling into a feral snarl. "Hunting me, are ye?" He had taken the Letter of Reprisal from his mainmast and tagged it on his great red peacoat. He wanted Aketz to see it, and to know what Captain Whirley thought of the hubris of the goldfish leaders to believe they could cancel it.

He lifted his spyglass to view the approaching ship, large and fast, and with the unmistakable jaws of those prow-mounted side catapults to identify this unmistakably as the *Cipac*. His snarl turning to a wicked grin, the powerful buccaneer, thick-bodied and intimidating to all around, slowly lowered his spyglass to scan the water between the two ships.

He caught the motion of the barrelboat only a hundred yards ahead of the *Dolphin*, moving in pace with the schooner. *Three o' Three*, the third boat added to powrie captain Thorngirdle's hunting pack, playing her role perfectly.

The *Dancing Dolphin* would keep the *Crocodile*'s focus high and forward, while the powrie hunters jammed her forward and turned her to put her deadly front guns off-line. Thorngirdle and *One o' Three*, and his second, commanding *Two o' Three*, would sandwich Aketz port and starboard, rocking her, locking her, while the *Dolphin* did a deadly dance about her.

"He thought we'd run," said Cara Blue, who'd served as Whirley's bosun ever since she had lost her own ship to *Cipac* a year before.

"He's filled with the cheers of his Entel bosses," said Whirley. "He thinks he can beat us all. In a fair fight, he'd be right, but what a fool to be thinking that we're to fight him fair."

"To come out this deep for a fight with powries is the move of a fool indeed," Cara agreed. "Even if you beat the dwarfs, they'll put holes in your boat, and we're a long way through rough waters to find shore."

Whirley lifted his spyglass once more. "Come on, ye dog. Show us yer damned light and be done with it, and then we'll put ye down."

"Buckets are filled and ready," Cara Blue assured him. All the buccaneers knew of *Cipac*'s wave of light to lead the attacks—the stories of the *Swordfish*, and three subsequent sinkings, had been whispered a hundred times to every sailor on the Mirianic seaboard.

Now they knew to duck from the wave and were ready to drench the sails and rigging immediately after it passed. As long as *Three o' Three* could delay those catapults, the *Dolphin* might well get out of this wholly unscathed, and what a feather in the great cap of Captain Whirley that would be!

"Hold yer nerve and straight in for a rake when the powries turn her and crunch her," Whirley told the bosun, who nodded, more than ready to pay back Captain Aketz.

She had watched him keelhaul her bosun and her first mate and feed half her crew to the chummed waters as soon as the sharks had begun their frenzy. He had left her tied to the mainmast in the drifting and slowly sinking wreckage, and only the good fortune and brave acts of a passing Behrenese ship had saved her that day.

Now she was more than ready to give the goldfish wretch his proper payback.

Captains Wilkie and Massayo and others of their sister ships sat in a tavern on the tiny island of Prickly Reef, the so-called "Gateway to the Mirianic," a mere blot in the rough waters just northeast of the northernmost of the Leeward Islands.

The tavern, Gut Thorns, wasn't even open yet, the small island wholly deserted, for its operation didn't begin until the ninth or tenth month of the year, when the season of hurricanes was ended. The proprietors left enough good whiskey, rum, and ale there, though, and the few buccaneers who knew the secret did come here occasionally to just be at ease. They didn't have to deal much with the hostile islanders of the Leewards here, for the place was deserted during the storm season. Here in this isolated paradise, they had no bother from the noisy Behrenese merchants along the mainland villages, nor the bustle of Free-port, and were out beyond the reach of the goldfish.

So they'd sometimes journey here when they were in the far east and the northern limits of their hunting zones, but coming here was not without some danger, even beyond the obvious perils of the underwater dangers that gave the island its name.

Captain Wilkie would usually wait for a storm to blow through before venturing to Prickly Reef, but even that was no guarantee that another vicious hurricane wouldn't soon follow. And there were thieves, as well, Leeward Islanders from the much larger Scrub Island to the south, who would spot the sails or masts and row their small boats out to steal what they might find in the dark of night.

The proprietors of Gut Thorns were never seen, but the buccaneers always held up their side of the agreement, cleaning up the place whenever they visited if a storm had put it amiss, and leaving proper payment for the use of the tavern—more than would be paid by the Leeward Islanders in the season when the establishment was properly open, but less than the cost of drink and harbor fees in the ports to the west.

The buccaneers would also pay for information when it was left for them—whatever value they deemed it—as was the case this day.

"I do not understand," said Quauh, shaking her head as she struggled to read the badly penned letter. "How can the grand augur cancel a Letter of Reprisal from the queen of Behren? Are these letters simply an assurance from the queen that she will buy your ill-gotten booty?"

"*Our* ill-gotten booty," Massayo corrected her, bringing some laughs.

"He can't," Wilkie Dogears explained. "'Course he can't. But that's not the point. They're putting out this word to tell everyone that the *Dancing Dolphin* is fair game—mostly to tell Captain Whirley and his crew. And they're warning away, or trying to, any merchants or fences who might deal with the ship."

"It's a threat," Quauh replied.

"Aye."

"An empty one?"

"Not if Aketz sees the *Dolphin*'s red 'n' black anywhere but Freeport Harbor," said Wilkie.

"He can't touch them in Freeport," Massayo explained, "whatever the grand augur might decree. That would begin a war before the sound of the first battle stopped echoing."

"Captain Aketz will attack any ship flying the red 'n' black," Quauh said, trying to make sense of it. "Why is this different?"

"It's telling Captain Whirley that if he was to *Crocodile*'s starboard and we, or any others, powries or buccaneers alike, were to *Crocodile*'s port, *Crocodile* would turn to starboard in full battle station and with no quarter offered. It's an open threat, and one that's sent other buccaneers sailing south before a season's end, to be sure."

Quauh sat back, trying to digest it all. "It is a stupid game we all play out here."

"Only gotten stupider since you goldfish came calling," Wilkie said.

There was no consternation aimed at Quauh in the statement, and none around her gave her a stern look or a sidelong glance. They considered her one of their own now, she understood, though she still wasn't sure if she liked that or not.

Better than being murdered on that island with the snakes swarming to eat her corpse, she figured.

While most of the others spent the day drinking and sleeping in the shade of the trees beside the tavern, Quauh walked the white sand beach, taking in the smell of the ocean and the brilliant sparkles on water impossibly blue, rolling in lines of whitecaps over the many reefs offshore. She focused on a line off to the west, the waves climbing high over one reef and becoming brilliantly translucent with the setting sun directly behind them.

She thought she'd just stand there until the sun dipped below the ocean—perhaps she'd see the green flash of that moment this night!—but became distracted and startled when she spied a powrie rising above the waterline to her left.

It took her a moment to realize that the fellow was standing atop a barrelboat. He jumped off and splashed his way to the shore, as another came onto the deck. Then another and another, until six of them, half the crew, gathered on the beach.

They saw Quauh, and more than one drew a knife. She held up her hand unthreateningly and slowly backed away, and she was glad indeed when Benny showed up at her side.

"They think ye're a goldfish," he said.

"Aren't I?"

"Aren't ye? Can't be a goldfish and a buccaneer, now can ye?"

"Then I aren't," Quauh said with a powrie brogue, and Benny laughed and nodded his approval before hailing his fellow bloody caps, who had obviously relaxed at the sight of him.

The group came over.

"What hey, but it's true that Wilkie's got a goldfish in his crew," one remarked.

"She's Massayo's," Benny explained. "As is meself. Sailin' on *Pinquickle's Folly.*"

"Yer old cap'n's sure to like the name when he comes out o' the ground in a year, what," the powrie replied.

"What're ye boys doing here?" Benny asked.

"Hidin'."

"Hiding?" Benny and Quauh asked together.

"Aye. The *Crocodile*'s about, just to the west, and in fine hunting form."

That brought an exchange of concerned looks between Benny and Quauh.

"And what of the *Dancing Dolphin?*" Quauh asked. "Any word of Captain Whirley's boat?"

"Only heared that he's not runnin' from Aketz, and that he's got some help that yerself might know well, Benny McBenoyt."

The sun dipped below the horizon.

The first stars came out.

The ships closed, neither turning, and between them, the powries continued their quieter charge.

"Keep it low," Captain Aketz told his first mate, who stood with the other priests by the wave weapon.

Cayo nodded but didn't stop his chanting, the droning priests building a humming charge from the large crystal set within the golden mirrors.

"One-fifty!" the lookout called down.

"Blind those powries and turn that schooner to kindling," said Aketz.

"One hundred yards!" cried the lookout.

The augurs loosed the energy, the wave of light reaching forth, skimming the water like a serpent—a hot serpent that sent wafts of hissing fog all about. It crossed over the barrelboat, showing it starkly as it passed, and certainly blinding any powrie foolish enough to be looking through the crude periscope of the craft.

On it went to the *Dancing Dolphin*, splitting over her bowsprit and riding her forecastle back to the sails.

"Barrel to port!" cried the second lookout.

"Barrel to starboard!" shouted the third.

Captain Aketz's tight, thin-lipped grin creased his face from ear to ear.

"Got them!" he said of the barrelboat, now less than fifty yards ahead, for the hatch popped open and out came a powrie tugging a large box. "Again, now!"

The augurs released a second pulse. The powrie, opening the box, didn't even notice it until it was too late.

The dwarf glanced over his shoulder at the last moment, then turned back, spitting curses at the sting on his face and his eyes.

He should have shut the box instead.

"Second wave!" cried several on the *Dolphin*. "Cover! Cover!"

The captain and crew scrambled to shield themselves from

the painful beam, which was easy enough to avoid. Whirley and the others were surprised by it. Why would the *Cipac* waste the effort?

They got their answer before the wave ever reached their ship, for the powrie on *Three o' Three* was readying the magnesite flares when the wave swept past, and the metal immediately ignited in a great flaring white-hot fireball. The shocked powrie yelped in pain and went tumbling off, which was the only chance he had at survival, as it happened, for the splashing of the sea against the barrelboat sent water into the chest of flares.

When those flares were lit, powries took great care to prevent any water hitting them, for if they got wet in that state . . .

The explosion on *Three o' Three* sent a shock wave rolling out in all directions, and blew the barrelboat apart, leaving twelve powries in the water, half of them dead before they ever got wet.

As soon as the wave passed the *Dolphin*, Whirley jumped up, his jaw hanging slack.

"But the gods," he muttered. "Get us out of here, mate Blue. Get us out of here!" He leaped about, shouting to his shocked crew. "Fire! Fire! Throw everything we have at them! Hard to port!"

He glanced back and closed his eyes. Like the hunting monster that gave this goldfish warship its name, the *Cipac* only seemed to be coming on faster.

And her great jaws swung from either side of her prow, filling the air with burning pitch.

And her archers, a hundred archers, sent forth their barrage of flaming death.

Three o' Three was supposed to ram and turn the hunter, but *Three o' Three* was gone, just gone.

Captain Aketz grabbed the rails of the forecastle ladder and slid down to the main deck, nodding to his ballista crews. "Fifteen yards out, no more," he reminded them.

The gunners nodded, but neither took their eyes off their incoming targets, powrie barrelboats speeding in to intercept quite rudely, port and starboard. These were seasoned sailors, veteran gunners, who could gauge distance perfectly to fifty yards with eyes alone.

The barrelboats rushed in. Port fired first, for that barrelboat was nearer, both ballistae throwing their heavy spears out, beyond and to either side of the approaching barrelboat, draping the metal net they carried between them over it, tower to stern and beyond, where it sank right into the craft's propeller.

The craft lost speed and momentum immediately, as did the one coming to starboard.

And immediately, the appointed crewmen, strong Xoconai lads and lasses, began spinning the ropes weighted with heavy blocks, launching them out of the spin into the water at the side and behind the trapped barrelboats. Those ropes were lashed to the metal netting, a score of small anchors tugging the stern of each of the barrelboats down, down.

The barrelboat to starboard actually had enough forward movement to bump against the *Cipac* as she sailed out from between the intended crunch, but it had little momentum about it, and did no damage, and even amused the Xoconai archers on the quarterdeck as a powrie tried to open the netted hatch. They taunted the dwarf and put arrows all about him.

"One destroyed, two dead in the water, and the schooner on fire," First Mate Cayo said to Captain Aketz. "That was a fine minute's work."

"Supported by a solid month of planning and drilling," Aketz reminded him. He wanted nothing to be taken as luck out here, nothing to diminish his brilliance in this, his most impressive battle yet.

"Pedal!" Thorngirdle yelled to his struggling crew. "Pedal!"

"She's stuck!" one yelled back, groaning and putting all his weight into the pedal, to no avail.

"Rudder's dead, too!" said the helmsdwarf at the back.

One o' Three groaned in protest, her prow going up as if on a swell. But no, Thorngirdle realized, they weren't climbing with a rolling wave. Their stern was sinking!

More splashes could be heard about them. On a nod from the captain, a powrie scrambled up the short tower and tried, unsuccessfully, to open the hatch, then came back down fast, holding an arrow that had cut across his cheek.

"Weights?" Thorngirdle asked.

The shot dwarf nodded.

One o' Three upended, stern down, and the dwarfs went

tumbling, Captain Thorngirdle bouncing among them all the way to the tail.

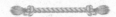

Miles away on Prickly Reef, the great flare lit the sky beyond the horizon as if the sun itself had changed its mind and jumped back out of the water.

Quauh saw it, as did Benny and many others ashore and on the moored ships.

"How far?" asked Massayo, rushing to join Quauh and Benny.

"Beyond three miles, clearly," said Quauh. She nodded her chin toward *Pinquickle's Folly*. "Chimeg's in her nest. She'll give us a better guess."

"Get Toomsuba and get the boats," Massayo ordered Benny. "Be quick and collect the crew ashore."

"What are you thinking?" Quauh asked the captain when Benny had gone.

"*Crocodile?*" Massayo asked more than answered. "Maybe Whirley found her."

"Or Captain Aketz found him," said Quauh.

"We're not going to know out here," Massayo replied.

"And we might find out too intimately if we go out there," Quauh reminded him, and the tall man nodded.

"We get to *Pinquickle* and get ready to sail," he told her. "And go tell Captain Wilkie, who's sure to join. I'm not getting caught here. We'll sail in the morning when the sun's up, when we can see the *Crocodile* from a long way off. Far enough so that he won't catch us."

"And if it is Captain Whirley and he and his helper ships won the fight?"

"Then we'll take them back here and buy them enough spirits to keep them drunk through the summer," Massayo assured her.

They spent a nervous night on *Pinquickle's Folly*, as did Wilkie and his crew on the ship beside them. No one slept, all eyes looking outward for some sign. From above, Chimeg guessed the flash, whatever it might be, at five or six miles, at least, and she could see a fire out there, a ship burning.

"Like the *Swordfish*," Massayo muttered, not liking that information. If it was a fight between the *Cipac* and the *Dolphin*, he doubted very much that the *Cipac* would be the one burning.

They sailed out with the sun rising behind them, straight to the west, then southwest. Soon after they cleared the crossing currents and treacherous reefs, going to full sail, they noted a thin black line of smoke from sea to sky out in the west.

The two ships widened the water between them, ensuring that at least one could get away, and approached more cautiously.

Long before Chimeg and her peer on *Port Mandu* shouted down confirmation, Massayo knew it to be the *Dancing Dolphin* out there ahead. He knew well the profile of Captain Whirley's schooner.

She sat dead in the water, rolling and turning with the quiet swells, her sails and rigging burned away, her masts standing naked, yards askew, like old, dead trees in a moor.

No other boats were to be seen. Whatever or whoever had hit them—and Massayo was quite certain that it had to be the *Crocodile*—was long gone.

"Too far to tow the trophy in," Massayo said to Quauh.

"Do you think there's anyone aboard her?"

Massayo gave her a skeptical look. "Alive?" he asked, and he could only shrug.

They bumped through wreckage as they neared, and passed among bodies floating in the sea—parts of them, anyway, in water red with blood, the rolls of the reddened waves occasionally cut by a dorsal fin.

"Gaffs to the rails," Quauh called, on the off chance that they came upon something or someone worth saving.

But no, the destruction and death seemed complete.

"They chummed the damned water and fed 'em all to the sharks," Benny growled at one point, tugging up his gaff and the left shoulder, neck, and head of a dead powrie.

"That's Captain Malachi, *Two o' Three*," Columbine said.

"Got one!" came a cry to starboard, and all on the deck turned to view *Port Mandu*, which had pulled up alongside the dead *Dolphin*, her boarding planks already set. Quauh and Massayo watched as a sailor was cut down from the mainmast, a woman who fell limply into the arms of her rescuers.

"Cara Blue," Massayo said.

"There, to port!" cried the musician Dalila, jumping up and down and thrusting her finger to the north.

Massayo and Quauh ran over, fearing that she had seen the hunter's sails. Their fears turned fast to curiosity, though, when they noted the object that had caught Dalila's eye: a sharp beam pointed skyward and bobbing in the water.

"That's a barrelboat or I'm a golden-haired Durubazzi," said Aushin.

"Good one, lad," McKorkle congratulated, and the younger powrie beamed with pride.

"Take us there, Quauh," Massayo ordered.

They got gaff hooks into the beam, which was now clearly the ram of a barrelboat, soon after, then pulled it and secured it to the side, but they hadn't the winches, beams, or manpower to hope to pull it up.

"She's netted!" Columbine noted. "And anchored down!" He fell back as he finished, for a huge shark drifted past, putting away any notion of anyone diving down beside to try to cut those ropes.

"Put a rope on it," Quauh ordered, just get it up enough to get air below the ram. "Toomsuba!"

They tugged and fought but could only shake their heads. Quauh ordered the boat secured and sails to full, so they could tow it away from the carnage and the sharks, and once the water seemed clear of the hungry fishes, she went into the water herself with a knife to try to cut the barrelboat free of its drags. She actually made some headway, and when she came up, Columbine was next down, then Perridoo, Aushin, and McKorkle all at once.

For all their efforts, they did manage to cut away enough anchors to put the craft higher in the water, high enough for Benny to sit on the ram and chop away at the hull to make a small hole. As soon as he got through, he could hear the weak voices inside, pleading desperately for help.

It took the rest of the morning, but they finally extracted seven powries alive from the wreckage, including none other than Captain Thorngirdle, who called back to those still in *One o' Three* to get the hearts of the dead five.

"We saw a great ball of white fire," Massayo said to Thorngirdle. "Was that Aketz's doing?"

"Aye, but not on his own. His light wave caught a box o' flares and set them to burnin', and we're guessin' that a splash o' water caught the flares and blew *Three o' Three* and her crew to little bits."

"And *Two o' Three*?" Massayo asked.

Thorngirdle shrugged. "Guessin' they got the same treatment as us, and luck alone kept us from slippin' under the water. *Two o' Three*'s likely out there near the *Dolphin*."

"But on the bottom," Massayo reasoned.

"Bad death" was all Thorngirdle would reply.

Massayo patted the powrie on the shoulder and walked away, calling Benny to his side.

"Water ruins the flares?" he asked.

"Nah, only if they're burnin'. Then ye're not wanting to be near 'em."

"Can you get back into *One o' Three*?"

Benny shrugged.

"Salvage what you can, including her flares," Massayo told him. "Let's bring some powrie ingenuity to *Pinquickle's Folly*, eh?"

"Eh," Benny agreed, and he hopped away. When he was

done with his work, salvaging little besides a flare box, some soaked clothing, and three kegs of fresh water, they cut the ruined barrelboat away and sailed back to the wreckage, coming up beside *Port Mandu*, who had pulled away from the dead schooner. Massayo and Quauh went aboard their lead ship to speak with Captain Wilkie.

"Cara Blue," Wilkie told them, indicating the battered sailor sitting against the quarterdeck's front wall, wrapped in a blanket, her eyes vacant, expression blank with shock. "First mate. Only survivor. They keelhauled Whirley, and when he came up somehow alive, they did it again. And all the while, they chummed the waters, drawing in the sharks, and fed all who survived the fight to them, hanging them head-down from a beam one by one and taking bets on how long before a shark might leap up to tear off each one's head."

He stared at Quauh the whole time he recited the gory description. She tried to hold steady against his accusing gaze, but surely her heart was broken, and she found herself greatly ashamed.

"The flare we saw was a barrelboat," Massayo explained. "Aketz killed three of them besides the *Dolphin*."

"We knew he was formidable, and vicious," Wilkie replied.

"We got Thorngirdle alive, along with a few of his crew. His boat's wrecked, and the third of the pack is likely below us. Maybe to the bottom, maybe only halfway down, netted and weighted with anchors."

"Let's sail about and see what we can see, but we're not lingering long," Wilkie told him.

The two ships circled the area for more than an hour, all hands lining the rails and peering into the gloom of the Mirianic for some clue of *Two o' Three*.

But they never found her, and they filled their sails with a following wind, sailing straight to the south inside the arm of the Leewards. Two full days passed before they dared turn west, sailing back for the protected islands near to the sands of Behren.

Quauh spent her free time at the forward rail, digesting all that she had seen and all that she had heard.

Thinking.

She heard the voice of Lahtli Ayot in her mind, warning her of the sidhe, demanding of her no mercy.

How hollow it sounded now.

"Yerself okay there, Sparkleface?" Benny asked her at one particularly difficult point. The powrie plopped down beside her.

"I am okay, Benny," she assured him, though she heard little conviction in her voice.

"What'd I tell ye when we started, eh?"

Quauh looked at him curiously.

"We'll be finding some real fun afore the summer's surrenderin' to fall. Haha!" said the dwarf.

"Fun?"

"Aye. It's all a game, girl. So just play it and take yer laughs where ye might and let go yer pains soon as ye can."

"You heard what Captain Aketz did to the crew of the *Dancing Dolphin*."

"Aye, and to Three Bits. And might be that we're finding the same bad deaths." Benny shrugged. "That's the game, and that's why we play when we can. That's why Cap'n Massayo's got musicians aboard, and why me and me boys drink and gamble and put our fists into each other's eyes, and why yer kind drinks and gambles and humps till they fall to the floor for a long nap, eh."

"Eh," Quauh said half-heartedly.

"No one's blamin' ye, Sparkleface, not even Cap'n Wilkie, who told Cap'n Massayo that he was sorry for starin' hard at ye when he was telling o' the murders."

He clapped her hard on the shoulder.

"Me one-handed friend, are ye a goldfish or are ye a buccaneer?"

Quauh thought about it for just a heartbeat, before giving a helpless little laugh and replying, "I'm a buccaneer."

In that moment, at least, she meant it, for in the face of the actions of the man now tagged as Captain Fury, it seemed to her to be the more moral choice.

CHAPTER 15

THE WIND AND THE SPRAY

They parted ways with Captain Thorngirdle and his remaining fellows back in Dinfawa. The powrie commander
promised to rebuild his pack. "Six Bits," he kept insisting all the
way on the long sail to the west and the coast of Behren. "Three
weren't enough. Six Bits!"

To the surprise of Captains Wilkie and Massayo, the five
powrie crew members serving on *Pinquickle's Folly* declined
Thorngirdle's offer to rejoin his hunting pack.

"We're doing good work here," Columbine told the great
powrie.

"Aye, and learning lots to take with us when we're back with
our own later in this life or the next," Benny agreed.

Thorngirdle wasn't happy with the decision, but these boys
and their captains had saved his life, after all, and from a death
from which he could not have been reborn with his memories
intact.

"Ye're fore'er on me good side, unlessin' ye're giving me a
reason to put yerselfs on me bad side" was his parting salute to

Wilkie and Massayo, to which Wilkie responded by giving him a bag of gold, enough to buy a new barrelboat.

"It's a loan," Massayo explained. "One we'll need to call in someday, as you call in your own."

Smiles and handshakes followed.

Standing at the side, Quauh wasn't smiling. She wasn't upset, just confused by the level of comradery here among these thieves and killers. She knew she shouldn't be surprised, but yet again, she was.

Port Mandu put out of Dinfawa only a couple of days later, but *Pinquickle's Folly* remained in port for the better part of a month for repairs and refurbishment. It had all been arranged before they had sailed across the sea to the Leewards, for Massayo had at last assembled a team of builders and parts to at last test out his design.

He unveiled it, the bullhead, to Captain Wilkie the day of the man's return to Dinfawa.

"You're a damned fool" was Wilkie's initial response as he walked around the war machine. A beam in the shape of a huge Y centered the circular platform of the weapon, with a huge strap of rubber hanging limply, affixed to each fork of the Y. "It's taking the whole of your forecastle!"

"Not much of a forecastle," Quauh remarked with a shrug.

Wilkie turned to her with a snort. "Not much of a boat," he said. "And not much of a weapon. Can it throw a load as strong as the catapult on *Mandu's* quarterdeck, or as far?"

"No," Massayo admitted. "Not this one, but a larger . . ."

"Larger?" Wilkie huffed. "It'd sink your ship!"

This ship, Massayo thought but did not say. Captain Wilkie didn't know about his gold stash, or about his greater plans going forward, and for now at least, he wanted to keep it that way.

"We've no room on the *Pinquickle* for a catapult like yours," he did reply. "We would need a smaller one, of course, and that would be nowhere as good in range and load as this bullhead. And the bullhead loads and throws more quickly, and more accurately—far more accurately."

Wilkie snorted again. "Show me."

Pinquickle's Folly put out of port and sailed to the southern side of Dinfawa, out of sight of the small village. There, Quauh lined her up facing the rocky cliffs, and the gunnery crew showed their work, Benny and Aushin loading the pocket, then helping Toomsuba tug back the band and set it on the trigger pole.

Massayo's grin was ear to ear, and he never took his eyes off Captain Wilkie as he told Quauh to let it fly. That grin became a toothy smile indeed as he watched Wilkie's eyes open so wide that they seemed like they might just roll out of their sockets.

The rock flew across the expanse to slam against the cliffs.

"We can shoot it higher or skim it lower simply by which notch we set the tie in on the trigger pole," Massayo was explaining, but Wilkie clearly wasn't listening.

"Calm water and a mountainside for a target," Wilkie said with sigh and a headshake.

Massayo knew he was impressed, and understood well that he wasn't about to admit it or show it.

"How might you do in the rolling swells?" Wilkie asked.

Massayo could only shrug.

"Well, we'll know soon enough," Wilkie announced. "I got a good lead on the way in, and we're out tomorrow. We've sailed beside each other enough to be ready for a fight, and you've your dream weapon, whatever that might prove worth. Season's getting late and the isles of Inudada are readying for our winter respite. Past time for the *Port Mandu* and *Pinquickle's Folly* to show the goldfish that there's a new pack in town."

"Aye!" Massayo and all the crew cheered.

All except for Quauh. This was it, she realized. To this point, they had been gambling and drinking, sailing and rescuing who and what they might from the fight far in the east, but now, it seemed clear, they were about to live up to their names.

Pirates.

Pirates against the Tonoloya Armada and merchant fleet.

Pirates against her own people.

"The plan, first mate?" The hunt was on, the spray whipping, three ships in a line. First, the prey, a carrack named *Golden Augur*, flying under the flag of Tonoloya, but not under the markings of a warship. This was a private ship, a merchant and not of the Tonoloya Armada. Closing fast on her stern came *Pinquickle's Folly*, having just run past *Port Mandu*, the small refurbished sloop showing all the speed and agility Massayo had hoped for.

"Stay to port," Quauh answered Massayo, who stood behind her, between her and the wheel of *Pinquickle's Folly*. When she glanced back at the man, she did a double take, curious. Almost continually when out on the water, he had been wearing her old coat, the golden coat of a commissioned Xoconai captain, which he'd had altered in Djinnit early on by a seamstress friend so that it would fit him. But now he'd changed back into his simple leather jerkin. Was he afraid of the ramifications? she wondered. Of what the Xoconai might do to a pirate wearing a pilfered captain's coat?

"Port's that way, you know," Massayo said dryly, pointing to his left, toward Behren and shallower waters.

"Stay to port," Quauh insisted, and at the wheel, Benny snorted.

"We want to drive them to the shallows," Massayo reminded her. "Not keep them out in deeper waters. You understand that we do that by getting up on the deeper side of our prey, yes?"

"Aye, and that beach is left when I'm facing forward, right when I'm facing stern," said Benny. "The beach is port, eh? We're wantin' them to go to port—ye think they're to turn and ram us, do ye? Or did losing yer hand take all notions of left and right from ye?"

"Stay to port," Quauh said again. She turned to see the captain and Benny exchanging glances, with Benny's expression clearly incredulous. She was pleased to view Massayo, though, for while he looked confused, there was a wry grin underneath it all revealing that he was beginning to recognize that she had a plan here, and one that he had not thought of on his own.

That trust in her reinforced all the claims he had made those two months before, when bringing her aboard as his first mate instead of trading her to the Behrenese or selling her back to the Xoconai.

"The typical move would be to run abreast of her starboard," Massayo said quietly. "Then angle in to force her nearer to shore."

"They've no chance at fighting us both," Quauh explained. "They know it, and they probably already know how this will end—and they'd prefer that culmination to be in deeper waters, not beached near to a land so hostile to them."

"That's why we're not givin' them the choice, eh?" said Benny.

"If we run up on them to starboard, with *Port Mandu* closing fast from behind, they'll turn starboard and try to fight past us," Quauh explained.

"So we fight," said Benny with obvious enthusiasm.

"They will not go shallow, in any case," Quauh continued. "If we go port, they're going to see their chance and hard turn for deeper waters."

"Which is what we do not want them to do," said Massayo.

"She's at battle sail now, but she'll go full sails, and she's square-rigged," Quauh emphasized. "Fill the bullhead thing you made and installed with chains and aim it high when she opens wide her sails."

Massayo laughed and nodded and seemed impressed. "If they do not turn, though, we will be in for a long chase—maybe too long."

"*Golden Augur* will turn. She's big and wide, and wants higher seas beneath us all, do not doubt. Her archers will have the advantage if we are rolling in the swells. When we come up on her, she'll go at once to half mast, as if conceding that we're about to fight, but then she'll turn and go to full sails, and quickly, thinking to surprise us while we are only then dropping to battle sail. That will be our chance."

"Hmm," mumbled Benny, with no sarcastic argument following.

"Her captain doesn't want a fight," Quauh explained. "The *Golden Augur*'s got more passengers than crew, and many no doubt wealthy and influential. Getting robbed is a terrible thing, aye, but having important Xoconai killed in a sea battle is far worse."

"Keep us port, Benny," a convinced Massayo told the helmsman.

"Some song, if you will!" Quauh yelled to the band, walking forward across the deck. "Horns and drums, and a fast heartbeat!"

Dalila, Ibtisa, and Dawoud rushed from their stations to the small "pit" Massayo had built amidships, which was really just a portion sectioned off with gardening ties to keep them separate and keep the large chest with the instruments secure on the rolling deck. The captain had spent a lot of gold in refurbishing the little sloop—particularly since, by all accounts, including his own remarks when in private, he wasn't planning on having it for long.

"And keep those sails full! Get us up on her!" she added to Toomsuba, who tugged at his guide rope with a bit more enthusiasm.

By the time she got to the prow, walking beside the new bullhead, the song and music were loud about her, with Ibtisa blowing a horn, Dawoud thundering a fast cadence on a drum fashioned of a hollow tree trunk and deerskin. Dalila strapped a curious stringed instrument—a score or more of strings, Quauh noted—about her waist and over her shoulders. Braced against her abdomen, the body of it seemed to be made of some melon husk, with a long hardwood neck running up and out diagonally from her, with more than half its four-foot length covered by multiple tuning rings. She plucked the strings almost equally with either hand, left and right, along the gourd body, producing delicate and distinct notes, reminding Quauh of the clavichords she had heard in the west. And though the construction of this particular instrument seemed somewhat cruder, Quauh could not deny that the music was equally enchanting and sophisticated.

Dalila was a small woman, but there was nothing small about her voice!

Ho, ho, the sails, loaded with wind!
Ho, ho, the crew, loaded with gin!
Ho, ho, the bullhead, loaded with chains,
Run her, boys, run her, for fun and for games!

Quauh held on to a guide rope at the prow of *Pinquickle's Folly*, feeling the wind and the spray on her face. How she loved that feeling! She glanced to the side, to the large fork in the throwing Y, taller than she. Between them hung that thick strand of rubber, the *caoutchou* sap material from which Massayo had once built his thriving business. The band was fastened to each of the beams securely, and at the back end of the bullhead, some seven paces toward midships, was the trigger post.

Quauh smiled when she recalled Massayo showing her his model of this weapon, which he had then called a sling-shooter. He had drawn back the small *caoutchou* band in that demonstration, pinched between his fingers and holding a sling bullet, then let it fly, quite accurately and quite impressively.

Despite the testing and practicing against the southern cliffs of Dinfawa, though, this "bullhead" had Quauh more than a little skeptical. She glanced to Toomsuba—yes, he was stronger than any man she had ever known, but could he really pull that band in rough seas and set it with any accuracy?

In the end, she had to just shrug and let it go. This was Massayo's call, and he had made it, and now he had to prove it all out. Quauh's job was to get them the desired shot.

The crew joined in the song around her, the music blending perfectly with the rush of wind and the splashing. Oh, how Quauh felt her blood rising then! The chase! A pang of guilt found its way through. They were chasing a Xoconai ship here, one full of her people.

That flicker couldn't ignite anything too strong within her, however. Her sensibilities would allow her to sustain no guilt for more than a fleeting moment, for the rush, the smell, the sounds of the hard-charging sloop proved to be simply too exciting.

Pinquickle's Folly came fast over one swell and pitched down hard, like a bucking cuetzpali, rocking Quauh where she stood—but she had her sea legs as well as anyone ever could, and the impact below the swell just reminded her of the power of this beast, the sea, they were riding, and riding so joyously and swiftly, with billowing sails and the spray, oh the spray!

"Golden Augur, you say?" Massayo said from beside her. She hadn't even noticed his approach.

Quauh pointed to the stern of the ship, the lettering of her name emblazoned upon it. *"Golden Augur,"* she read.

"You do not know her?"

"I am trying to remember, but no. I've heard of her and seen her in Entel's port, but I know nothing of her crew. She's no warship, but like any ship sailing this far south, she's a capable fighter, I'm sure."

"Well, we have a good plan," Massayo said with a smile and a nod of appreciation to his fellow planner.

Quauh took the compliment in stride. Her thoughts were spinning around now, the focus of a hunter looking for advantage. "Go and get your captain's coat, Captain Massayo," she said, and turned her head to look the man in the eye.

"Your coat?"

"It is yours now these last weeks, is it not? And no, I do not ever want it back."

"I thought that wearing it would make our intended prey this day less likely to strike her colors."

"I think that seeing you in it will signal to them that we are formidable," Quauh replied. "Here in the east, there are merely two score of those coveted items, and they are hard-earned through grueling experience. When our prey turns and we rip her sails apart because we are not surprised by their turn, they will have a choice to make. Seeing the captain of the pirate chasing them wearing the coat of a vanquished Xoconai captain will help them to make the correct decision."

"Privateer, not pirate," Massayo corrected with a wink and a wry grin. He ended the conversation with a nod and headed for his cabin.

Quauh was watching him go when Chimeg yelled down from above, "Catapult!" Quauh spun back to see a ball of fiery pitch rising from the afterdeck of the ship before them, arcing in the air.

Quite a shot, she thought, when the ball splashed sizzling into the water no more than a few yards to her right. It should have been unnerving, and would have been to a less veteran sailor, but for Quauh, like the wind and the spray and the music, the enemy's throw proved merely exhilarating.

"Come on, boys!" she cried to her crew above the song. "Fill those sails and get us up beside her!"

She ducked then, instinctively, as an arrow cut through the air very close to her.

"Chimeg!" she yelled, and looked up.

And then, so quickly, she understood the value of this To-gai-ru acrobat.

Back in Dinfawa, *Pinquickle's Folly* had been altered to Chimeg's specifications, the mainmast extended, with a second beam rising a dozen feet above the top rigging. The crow's nest had been relocated up there and fashioned more completely than the simple cross plank set up below, now showing the typical half-barrel design. Quauh hadn't put much significance in that alteration given the other repairs and the massive alteration of the bullhead. She figured that the higher mast gave Chimeg, or whoever was on lookout, a more secure perch, and a place to put some water, or arrows, or a warm coat.

But then, a few feet below the crow's nest, Chimeg had added her own touch, in the form of that leather strap set with a gray stone that wrapped about the very tip of the original mainmast. A similar stone to the one in the anklet she had donned before climbing up to her post. A couple of feet above that strap, Chimeg had also added a foursome of quivers, full of arrows, strapped to the extending pole.

Now the woman came forth from the crow's nest, bow in hand. Instead of using the walls of the perch for defense against the incoming fire, she put her foot in the loop at the end of a short rope and leaped from on high. She came down upright at the end of the line in a swing just above the top rigging, and as she swooped about the mast, she plucked an arrow from one of the quivers, nocked it in the same movement, and sent it flying out at one of the archers at *Golden Augur*'s taffrail, who dived aside just in time.

Quauh kept her eyes on Chimeg, thinking the woman mad, for though she was swinging on that rope, such swings were predictable and any decent archer could correctly lead her.

Except, Quauh then realized, and a smile creased her face, there was nothing predictable about Chimeg's swings. At one point, she went out wide with the roll of the ship and came swinging back fast for the mast, and Quauh grimaced, expecting a brutal impact despite the display she had seen in the calmer waters near the fishing village.

As with then, at the last moment the To-gai-ru deflected from the mast before ever hitting it (and still plucking another arrow from the tied quivers, leaving the quiver on her back full), flying out to stern in a circular flow. Around she went to starboard, one arrow flying—and taking down the same archer who had dodged her first shot and was now trying to get back to position.

A second arrow went out, and Chimeg changed direction immediately. Instead of continuing forward along the starboard rail, she somehow cut straight across, just behind the mast, and out to port!

Quauh blinked, thinking that her eyes deceived her. It was one thing to watch this type of movement in practice in calm seas, but quite another in an actual fight, and even more astounding to see the accuracy with which the woman could shoot in the midst of such swings and tumbles! She continued to stare, mouth agape for another few heartbeats, as Chimeg flew zigzags, shortened wide swings with startling suddenness, and was always back by the mast without ever colliding with it. Her stream of arrows reached out at *Golden Augur*'s stern, and the rain of arrows from the fleeing ship turning into a sprinkle of misaimed shots from archers who couldn't come near to hitting Chimeg, and who dared not show enough of themselves to take an arrow from the deadly woman.

Quauh had never imagined such a display, let alone witnessed one.

"Where's my first mate?" she heard Massayo yell, and she moved out from her position on the other side of the bullhead and called to the man, who was indeed now dressed in the golden jacket that had been her own.

Massayo bounded over to her, hands up, questioning.

"They know what to do," Quauh assured him.

"You are supposed to remind them every breath."

In response, Quauh pointed straight up.

"Ah," the captain replied, nodding. "You have never seen Chimeg truly at her work before. You are forgiven your distraction."

"It is amazing, and wonderful."

Massayo flashed his wide and toothy smile.

Pinquickle's Folly leaned left then, easing to the west to make her run up *Golden Augur*'s port rail.

"Twenty yards, yardarm from yardarm, Benny!" Quauh called to him. "Don't bring us up too close. And Toomsuba, take up that rope and ready the bullhead!"

"You think she'll turn?" Massayo asked.

"I know she will. But be ready, captain, they will be quick in their starboard turn," she warned. "When they drop the side-drag, their turn will surprise you."

"Side-drag?" Massayo asked. "An anchor?"

Quauh tensed up, realizing from the response that she was about to give away a Xoconai secret, a fairly recent innovation the western people had put upon their more lumbering ships that had not been replicated in the east. The part of her that had allowed her to rise through the ranks and become a commissioned officer, the loyalty and dedication to duty, wanted to avoid this conversation.

But the other part, the part of her awakening to the realities of the cruelty her people were inflicting upon the people here, who were not sidhe, who were not lesser humans, battled back. She was alive now, and free to sail, to command, because of the powrie at the wheel and the captain of the sloop standing right beside her.

"Some of the heavier ships carry one to port and one to starboard. An anchor, yes, heavy and hooked, and dropped just behind midships. When it catches, it is like having a paddle in the water on a canoe."

"It becomes a pivot point."

"Yes, and they will cut it free when the hard turn is executed."

Massayo lifted his gaze to the carrack, clearly intrigued. "I will learn more about this when we find the time," he said, nodding and smiling.

Quauh nodded back, still torn about whether she should have revealed that information. She felt like a traitor, and why not?

Wasn't she exactly that?

"They would kill me for losing the *Uey*," she whispered under her breath, a needed reminder in that moment of doubt.

"And I will scold you if you lose *Pinquickle's Folly*," Massayo said, startling her, for she hadn't even realized that she had spoken the personal reminder aloud. "But I will not kill you, on my word," he added lightly, and flashed that smile and a wink to Quauh.

She knew that he wasn't lying, or at least, she had to believe that.

"And I trust you in your insistence that she will turn," the captain added.

317

"Her captain assumes that anything we will throw against her beyond our arrows will be grape and that we'll run past her and fast pivot so that we can try to rake across her low deck as she passes. We cannot get that shot over her high taffrail with any angle to strike down anyone on the deck, obviously."

"Then perhaps she'll turn to port to ram us."

"Not with Wilkie chasing. The captain of *Golden Augur* wants no part of that fight. And besides, she's going to turn before we are."

"You seem very sure of yourself, First Mate Quauh."

Quauh started in response as if she had been slapped, but Massayo smiled all the wider. "That was a compliment," he explained, then called out for his band to pick up the cadence, and called to Benny to be ready to pull the sloop around to starboard to its very limits. Then he restated Quauh's order to Toomsuba, and told Aushin and McKorkle to help him.

Pinquickle's Folly filled her sails and began her run, gaining fast. A second ball of pitch flew out from the fleeing Xoconai ship, this one clipping *Pinquickle's* starboard rail, spitting across the deck and lighting small fires.

Chimeg answered by swinging out wide to port and plucking one of the cannoneers right from the raised catapult platform with a barbed broadhead, driving into his shoulder and throwing him to the deck, howling in pain.

Now came the most dangerous part of the plan, with *Pinquickle* rushing up alongside the prey. Arrows flew all about. *Golden Augur* had a dozen archers still firing, many of them trying to hit the lone archer flying about up above.

Then *Golden Augur* had eleven.

Then ten, as the To-gai-ru acrobat soaring about up above plied her craft.

Chimeg took a hit in the leg but kept returning fire and kept swinging.

"Come on," Massayo growled, keeping the beam of his mast between him and the enemy ship.

"Turn, turn," Quauh whispered beside him, as if trying to urge the merchant ship. She glanced stern and saw that *Port Mandu* was at full sail and charging ahead, but still a long way away.

The powrie Columbine shouted out in pain and sprawled to the deck, clutching the vibrating shaft of an arrow sticking from his shoulder. Then Dalila was clipped just under her ear. She grabbed the wound with her hand, then brought it back before her eyes, covered in blood.

Quauh grimaced and whispered, "Turn," yet again. Had she been wrong?

Pinquickle's Folly pressed ahead of the slower carrack, her stern passing midship, then to the prow and beyond, and the arrow barrage lessened from *Golden Augur*, though Chimeg kept her line of bolts flying out from on high.

Now was the moment, Quauh knew, as did Captain Massayo, she could tell from his suddenly tense expression.

Would the carrack turn port or starboard?

Would she run or would she ram?

She ran, as suddenly hard starboard as her crew could manage, dropping the side-drag anchor to catch the floor and help tug her around. Her beams and planks creaked and groaned in protest—one sailor even slid across the deck and flipped over the starboard rail, hanging on desperately, his feet skimming the ocean in the ship's deep lean. *Augur*'s crew was skilled, clearly, her sails pulling up full before she had even completed the turn.

The others couldn't get to the hanging sailor in time, though, and so he went into the dark and cold waters, and Quauh couldn't help but grimace in sympathy.

She let it go and focused on the carrack. She had performed quite a fine maneuver, and despite her own change of allegiance, Quauh the Xoconai felt proud of her kin on this supremely practiced crew.

"Benny!" Massayo and Quauh yelled in unison, but the powrie was already spinning that wheel!

Pinquickle's Folly dug deep into the water in her pursuing turn, Benny plying the wheel furiously to square her up to any swells. Toomsuba, carrying two arrows stuck into his large frame, dug in his heels and tugged that band of rubber toward the triggering finger.

"Get off the deck, dwarf!" Toomsuba yelled at Columbine, who dragged himself up to his knees, then feet, then went back to the rigging.

"On my count," Massayo told Quauh. "You earned the trigger."

Quauh nodded.

"You keep them off us!" Massayo yelled up to Chimeg, who responded by dropping the first Xoconai archer who came to *Golden Augur*'s taffrail.

Chimeg swung out far to starboard as *Pinquickle's Folly* bent and groaned in her fast turn, and so suddenly, they were directly behind the Xoconai carrack again.

But now *Golden Augur* had her sails blossomed full, and now they were running straight east, away from the shore.

Back to the south, *Port Mandu* veered to starboard, taking an angle to intercept, but she was still a long way away.

Toomsuba set the bullhead. With help from Aushin and McKorkle, he got the weapon's pocket in place, fully loaded.

Up went the sloop over the high swells, prow up, then down. Quauh knew that she and Massayo would have to time it perfectly, coming up the front of a swell, to properly angle the shots. And they were running out of time. They weren't far behind, but they weren't going to run with the heavy carrack in these high seas for long.

The carrack, with its side-drag, had turned inside the sloop, remarkably, but the work of Benny and Toomsuba and the team, under the crisp and decisive commands of Captain Massayo, soon had the small vessel back in line directly behind their prey, just as before, except that now *Golden Augur*'s sails were opened wide and full of wind.

Massayo looked across the deck to his first mate and the trigger for the bullhead.

"On my two-count," he yelled to Quauh.

She nodded in reply. The angle of the catapult shots would be wholly determined by the angle of the prow—the bullhead's firing angle could not be easily adjusted on the fly.

At full sail now and in the middle of the flattened wake

of the larger ship, they were gaining on their prey, but barely, and with the swells rolling beneath them, Quauh knew—and expected that Massayo knew, as well—that a single off-angled breach of a swell could spin his smaller vessel enough so that it would take them a long time to recover and rejoin the chase. She wasn't surprised, then, when she heard Massayo call out to her, "Next climb!"

Pinquickle's Folly pitched down over a rolling wave, the prow coming clear for just a moment before splashing down and sending the spray up in her face. Before she had wiped her eyes, the swift sloop began to scale the next wave.

Up went the prow. Up, up, the carrack lost from sight for just an eyeblink before it ascended the wave ahead of them.

"One!" Massayo yelled, then, "Two!"

But Quauh hesitated, something within her overruling Massayo. She felt the roll of the ocean, heard its voice, understood not only this swell, but the next they would soon be climbing.

That one was correct, she knew.

"Two!" Massayo yelled again. "Let fly, first mate!"

She didn't have to glance his way to know he was coming at her. But the moment was lost, *Pinquickle's* nose rolling level and down.

She closed off the yelling—it was more than Massayo shouting at her now—and listened only to the sea, whose voice she knew so very well.

Her eyes weren't even open when she felt the climb, when she knew not only the swell beneath her, but the next in line that was now lifting the *Golden Augur*. She tugged hard on the trigger lever and the whole ship shuddered with the release, the *caoutchou* band contracting like a striking viper, presenting the basket forward with such suddenness and violence that the sheer rush of it had Quauh holding on to the rail with whitened knuckles.

Only then did she understand the true potential of this strange bullhead weapon, for the contraction of that band showed more power than any ship-mounted catapult she had ever seen—and she had seen the finest designs of the finest navy in the known world!

So shocked was she by the display, by the sheer power of the throw, the chains spinning out with tremendous speed, that it took her a moment to even consider the shot itself—and she heard Massayo's cheer, now from right beside her, before even looking at that which he was cheering.

The throw had gone in perfectly, with great spread of the flying, spinning, weighted chains, which were sharpened at every juncture. They blew through fabric and rigging lines alike, splintered the yards, clipped and removed *Golden Augur*'s taffrail, and removed, too, a pair of archers huddling there.

Poor fellows.

Much of *Golden Augur*'s starboard rigging was simply gone, and now half the mainsail flopped about, waving wildly in the strong winds.

The Xoconai carrack was slowing and wavering on her course, and Benny began the expected left-hand turn to get them north of the prey, with *Port Mandu* coming up from the south.

"Hard to port!" Massayo screamed to the helmsman, and his desperation was clear and Benny pulled all the harder, *Pinquickle's Folly* leaning deep and turning hard—so much so that the next wave rolled under her to starboard and sent her back some distance, her sails luffing.

But that was good, Quauh understood, if the others did not, for their prey only had her port side-drag left. *Golden Augur* was going to turn and fight broadside, with all she could manage before the second pirate ship could join in the battle.

"No, Benny, starboard!" she yelled. "Starboard! Bring us around behind her!"

"What are you doing?" Massayo began to yell at her, but as Quauh had expected, the carrack's port side-drag anchor dropped, and the struggling ship began a left-hand swing.

Pinquickle's sails flapped and luffed repeatedly as the sloop turned and rolled with the swells, but once Benny got her aimed to starboard, those sails caught the wind anew and sent her on her way.

Arrows flew at them from the carrack, but the two ships never got close enough for the *Golden Augur* archers to do much damage, and by the time they were behind the floundering larger boat, Chimeg's continuing rain of arrows had the carrack's aft section fully under control.

"No rush now!" Quauh called to the crew. Out of the corner of her eye, she noted Massayo staring down at her.

"I said two," he told her.

"The sea told me that you were wrong."

"But I am the captain."

"And I am your first mate, and it was my responsibility, from you, to make the shot count." She looked up and guided his gaze with her own to the floundering carrack. "It counted."

Massayo burst out in a great laugh. "Keep us away from her until Captain Wilkie joins."

Quauh nodded, but assured him, "She'll strike her colors, do not doubt. She's not up for this fight now, and she cannot run."

"If you think me pleased, you are wrong," Massayo said, but his smile betrayed him. He leaned forward and whispered, "If you keep showing such brilliance, I may have to kill you so that my crew doesn't mutiny and put you in charge and feed me to the sharks."

Quauh beamed with pride and excitement, those feelings overwhelming any doubts she might have had about hunting a Xoconai ship.

The carrack rolled with the swells, meandering. *Golden Augur's* crew didn't cut the drag anchor free, which was very telling to Quauh.

"They've little control," she informed her captain, who nodded with every word, having clearly come to the same conclusion. "They're using the side-drag for some measure of stability."

"They're trying to keep us behind their high stern rail to give their rigging teams some time to repair," the captain explained.

"Load for a second volley?"

Massayo considered it for just a moment. "Load the bullhead and tug it back to ready," he instructed Toomsuba. He glanced starboard to measure *Port Mandu's* progress. "But I do not think we will need it."

"Unless it is to convince their captain to strike colors, since we are simply not going to allow them to repair that rigging."

"Always an option."

"Keep us on her stern, off thirty yards," Quauh called to Benny.

The powrie replied with a grunt and a groan, then spat repeatedly.

"No," Massayo called out in contradiction, surprising Quauh. "No, not yet. Circle her, Benny, at fifty yards." More quietly, to just Quauh, he added. "Let's take a good look and see what they've got, and let them know that we can, quite literally, run circles about them."

"They have a capable catapult crew," Quauh warned.

In response, Massayo looked up at Chimeg, who was against the mainmast then, solidly so, as if she had fastened one boot to it. She stood there comfortably, her bow up and ready.

"Dear Chimeg," he called up. "Do kill anyone who goes near to that catapult."

Chimeg flew out suddenly to port, as if some great gust of wind had hit her and hurled her.

An arrow cracked into the mainmast where she had been standing.

Out at the end of her rope, the To-gai-ru suddenly wasn't far from *Golden Augur*, and she let fly and made the would-be assassin pay dearly, as confirmed by a sudden cry of pain from the carrack.

Back she swung toward the mast, but she turned a right angle as she neared, and swung out toward *Pinquickle*'s stern. "As you wish," she calmly replied.

"How is that even possible?" Quauh asked Massayo.

"The shooting or the swinging?"

"Yes."

"Her people are equestrians, always sitting a horse, and they are the finest archers in the world. Our dear Chimeg is surely skilled even when rated against that talented group. She grew up shooting while riding or even standing on the back of a galloping horse. The rest of her aerial act is magical, both that band and her anklets. Some of her arrows probably are, as well—she had some fitted with tips of material that can seek out certain metals, I am told."

"Why would she want to shoot into metal?"

In response, Massayo held the pose of an archer and looked to his hand drawn against his breast. "A bracelet? A necklace? A belt buckle? You tell me."

Up above, Chimeg went soaring back to the mainmast, and there held.

"They are trying to repair the starboard rigging," she called down.

"Do make it difficult for them," Massayo answered.

Chimeg shouldered her bow and quickly climbed back into the crow's nest. A few moments later, some smoke rose from that high perch. Out leaped the archer, swinging down fast, her nocked arrow showing a glowing, rounded tip. She swung back in, then flew off fast to port, propelled again on unseen magic. Up high above the starboard rail of *Golden Augur*, she tapped the arrow tip, which flared brilliantly, then drew her bowstring and let fly.

No cries of pain followed this time, but many calls of "Fire!" and some smoke, just a bit, began to rise from the carrack.

"A small bit of pitch won't burn her sails," Quauh said.

"Aye, but a powrie flare might, particularly if it is well-placed. Chimeg will weaken some corner of those sails and the ropes to which they are tied. She will keep our enemies busy."

Pinquickle's Folly moved away, then, out to fifty yards, and began her turn to port, running an eastern hurricane's rotation around the wounded carrack. By the time they were crossing the carrack's bowsprit, they noted *Port Mandu* dropping to battle sail and approaching the carrack's port.

Massayo climbed up onto the rail. "You would do well to strike your colors, commander!" he yelled across. "We have no desire to slaughter civilians, surely, but know that you are not escaping."

It took a few moments, but a call came back, "State your terms."

"Would you do all the work and take all the fun from me?" came a third voice, that of Captain Wilkie Dogears, addressing Massayo. To the carrack commander, he called, "If we must fight to board you, there will be no terms, not for you, and not for any goldfish aboard!"

"I ask only for the safety of my crew and passengers," the carrack commander returned.

"And yourself, I presume?" Wilkie shouted.

"I am vanquished. That is at your suffrage, Captain Wilkie Dogears."

"Ah, you know me! Then you know that I do not take

pleasure in killing. Drop your sails, drop your bows, and show your crew in full!"

"We have a deal?"

"We have a deal."

Massayo patted Quauh on the shoulder. "Your insight and judgment likely saved many lives this day," he told her.

"Does that please you?" she asked as he walked away.

Massayo stopped in his tracks and turned back to look at her, his expression a mixture of surprise and wound.

Just the reaction Quauh was hoping for.

With *Pinquickle's Folly* still circling like a hungry shark, *Port Mandu* sidled up to the Xoconai ship and dropped her boarding planks.

Quauh noted that Captain Wilkie himself led the way across onto the deck of the surrendered ship and was greeted by the Xoconai commander, who offered his macana. Quauh breathed a sigh of relief when she considered the next group crossing the boarding planks, for among them was the Xoconai sailor who had flipped over the rail in their desperate evasion—*Port Mandu* had slowed enough to pluck the poor sailor from the ocean, and were now returning him.

"This is the secret to the success of Captain Wilkie Dogears," Massayo whispered to her, as if reading her mind. "Those put in a helpless situation by this man known as the Polite Pirate know that their surrender will not be disastrous. Count the crates that cross over those boarding planks in the next hour. It will not be half of *Golden Augur*'s booty, and Wilkie will leave the carrack enough supplies to get to Freeport, surely, for no goldfish commander wants to put in to a Behrenese port, or anywhere else along the coast that is whispered to be patrolled by Chezru Chieftain Brynn's hungry dragon."

"Have you ever seen that dragon?" Quauh asked, turning to regard the tall man.

"No, not I, and I am glad for that! But ask our minstrels and I am sure you will get a different answer. Almost all the folk of the desert kingdom have seen the great beast—or perhaps they were all instructed to say that they have seen it whenever asked by outsiders, to keep us away."

"Or at least, to keep you in line," Quauh offered to heighten the joke, which Massayo clearly appreciated.

"You should ask them on a quiet day," he said. "Perhaps they have songs to play of Brynn's great dragon."

"Perhaps I shall." She continued watching the scene unfolding on the carrack's deck, particularly the conversation between the captains, which seemed to have taken a jovial turn!

"Will we be boarding her, too?" she asked a short while later.

"Does that concern you?"

Quauh considered that for a bit, glad that Massayo had taken note of the potentially troubling possibilities for her. She might be recognized up close, after all, and what would that mean for her should she ever again fall into the hands of the Tonoloya Armada?

"No," she answered anyway, and honestly, she was surprised to realize.

"Yes, we are going over there," Massayo told her. He pointed

to a small pennant that had just been run up *Port Mandu*'s aft
halyard line, barely visible.

"What is that?"

"*Golden Augur* has benefited from impressment, it would
seem," Massayo explained. "Captain Wilkie uses that pennant
to tell me this."

"You intend to take those slaves from the carrack?"

"We are in need of crew, even now, and will need more soon
enough."

"So you will press them into your service instead?"

Massayo laughed, shook his head, and walked away. "Go
and assist Chimeg," he ordered.

Quauh found the To-gai-ru woman along the port wall of
Massayo's cabin, shielded from anyone watching from the captured
carrack. She was kneeling beside the seated Toomsuba, one hand
working the flesh about an arrow the large man had caught in
his shoulder during the exchange, her other hand holding a long
feather, perhaps from a goose. On the ground beside them was
a second arrow, red with Toomsuba's blood.

"Keep the skin stretched wide," Chimeg instructed her when
she moved beside them.

Quauh placed her thumb on one side of the arrow, her index
finger on the other, and increased her pressure as Chimeg let go.

"Yes, like that," Chimeg said. She inverted the feather before
her mouth and blew on the end of the hollow shaft, then slipped
that shaft in beside the arrow. She closed her eyes and let her
fingers "see" for her as she worked the quill about. Nodding,

she left it there, sticking up just beside the arrow shaft, and produced a second feather.

"Shift your fingers to the other side of the arrow," she instructed, and as soon as Quauh had them correctly set, widening the wound on the far side of the shaft, Chimeg went to work again.

She retracted her hand and smiled at Quauh, then gently grasped the arrow as close as she could to Toomsuba's skin, and easily slid it out.

Quauh's jaw hung slack as she stared at the arrow, its barbs sheathed by the hollow shafts of the feathers.

Toomsuba sighed in relief. "It does not hurt so much," he said.

"You have so much fat, I am not surprised," Chimeg teased.

"It is all muscle. Should I throw you up to your crow perch to prove it?"

Chimeg winked at him and motioned to Columbine, who was patiently waiting his turn.

"I will show you how," Chimeg told Quauh. "I will take the arrow from Columbine, and then you will repay your debt to Benny by removing the arrow from his belly."

"Benny?" she asked with more concern than she would have expected.

"He got hit in the first volley."

"I didn't know."

"He's Benny. He didn't want anyone to know, and certainly he was not about to surrender the wheel in the middle of a fight!" Chimeg said. "He saved you. It is only fitting that you save him."

"It is so simple," Quauh marveled. She had never heard of any technique like this before. Simply using feathers to defang barbed

332

arrows for extraction? It was so brilliant in its simplicity! "Like making a clavichord with a gourd," she whispered under her breath.

Again, the woman scolded herself for her arrogance. She had come to the east, like all her people, thinking the conquered lands full of sidhe. Not populated by fellow humans, but with sidhe. Primitive, barbaric, monstrous sidhe.

How wrong they had been. How wrong she had been!

When her turn came to extract the arrow, she hesitated and held up the stump of her right arm. "I am, I was, right-handed."

"You can do it," Chimeg assured her.

Quauh took a deep breath and took the first feather in her left hand, leaning in close to study the wound.

"Let your fingers see the barb," Chimeg instructed.

Only moments later, two feathers lining the arrow, Quauh easily slid the barbed head out of Benny's body. With her relief came the enormity of it all—and not just of this simple procedure. All of it, all the weight of her remarkable few weeks hit her in that moment. She hadn't been shaking when she treated Benny, calling on the same sense of purpose and duty that had made her a fine sailor and fine captain, but she was shaking indeed when she handed the extracted arrow over to Chimeg, whispering, "Thank you," repeatedly.

She meant that for all of them. She had been rescued from bloodthirsty pirates, rescued from certain indenture to the Behrenese, but most of all, Quauh was beginning to realize, she had been rescued from herself, and from a limited and arrogant view of the wide, wide world.

Soon after, Massayo called Chimeg and Quauh back to their

stations. Across the way, the boarding planks went up and *Port Mandu* was pushed away from *Golden Augur* with long poles, clearing the way for Massayo to sidle his sloop up and board.

Quauh accompanied him as he crossed the boarding plank. He was dressed in a splendid gold jacket of a commissioned Tonoloyan captain, and there she was, right behind him. She studied the stares coming back at her from the Xoconai sailors and officers, and even the civilians—people of great wealth and power, she knew. She didn't recognize any of them and was fairly sure that none recognized her, thankfully, but would the commanders they reported to back in Entel have to know the particulars of who she was to put it all together?

"Filthy pirates," she heard one finely dressed woman remark as Massayo walked past.

The captain pulled up short. "Filthy?" he echoed. "It is not dirt, dear lady, just the color of my skin." His shining smile disappeared in a flash, an ominous, almost wild, look coming over him. "My skin," he said again in a more even and threatening tone, "which is the same as the color of my mother's skin, and if you call my dear mother filthy again, I will bind you with a long rope, drop you from my prow, and pull you the length of my ship beneath the hull, which I assure you is thick with sharp barnacles."

"Good captain," the Xoconai commander said, "this is an amicable meeting of gentlefolk."

"Good captain," Massayo returned, "I remind you that you are defeated. Even gentlefolk are known to practice the art of keelhauling, yes? As they are known to enslave . . . I'm sorry, as you might more politely put it, to *impress* into service?"

Glancing from one to the other, Quauh noted one of the sailors of the carrack, a thin but muscular dark-skinned man with kinky hair. He was holding one of the ropes but dropped one hand from it and subtly pointed his index finger down, then his pinkie, then shook the hand to make it look like a headshake from a horned bull.

Massayo took note, she knew, when the sailor pointed at the Xoconai captain, and then, dropping his hand to his side, extended his pinkie a split second before opening the hand fully.

"How many?" Massayo asked.

"How many what?"

"Men and women who are here not by choice, but because you think them lesser and so determine their station to be one of serving you?"

"I?" the captain returned innocently. "I was given those . . ."

"Given? You were given other humans as if they were cattle?"

"Filthy barbarian," the fancy woman to the side muttered under her breath.

Never taking his stare from the Xoconai captain, Massayo reached out, grabbed the impertinent snob by the collar, and jerked her toward him, before shoving back and pitching her in a tumble over the rail. She dropped between the two ships into the water.

A couple of nearby Xoconai started for the rail, a movement that was halted when an arrow stabbed into the rail right where the woman had gone over. All eyes went up to the archer, Chimeg, standing on the edge of *Pinquickle*'s spar, another arrow nocked and ready.

Quauh shifted uncomfortably, and even thought to challenge Massayo by going over the rail herself to save the woman—who wouldn't be up for long, certainly, with her long and many-layered dress pulling her down.

"How many?" Massayo asked evenly.

"Seven."

"Get them. They are with me now."

The Xoconai captain stared hard at him.

"Get them, and have your crew go and save that ridiculous woman," Massayo said.

The captain nodded. A Xoconai man and woman dove over the rail, while others went to collect *Golden Augur*'s slaves.

"You have wounded," Massayo said. "Bring them to my ship now."

"We have two dead," the captain replied through his clenched jaw.

"Then perhaps you should not have fired upon us."

"You ask me to surrender Xoconai wounded. What will you do with them?"

"I will heal them, you idiot."

"We can heal our own."

Massayo mocked him with a snort and pointed across the deck, where a distressed, grimacing sailor was seated against the port rail, grabbing at his thigh. An arrow was stuck there, buried deeply into his flesh, with a woman gingerly grasping it and trying to work it back out. Blood flowed and spurted all about the wound.

"If she pulls it back, she will likely tear his veins and he will die in a deep puddle of his own blood," Quauh interjected, speaking in the tongue of the Xoconai.

Massayo gave her a suspicious look, but she held up her hand, begging his trust.

"If she pushes the arrow through, the damage will be extensive, perhaps fatal, and will cost the man at least his leg," she told *Golden Augur*'s captain.

"Who are you?"

"No one who matters."

The Xoconai captain looked around, his eyes falling on Massayo's golden jacket before snapping back to Quauh.

"You are from the *Uey*," he stated.

"No, the *Kikikuli*," she answered, recalling the name of a ship that had been declared lost on the very day she had arrived in Entel for the first time. The *Kikikuli* had been presented to the new arrivals as an example of the dangers of the eastern sea. The Xoconai did not know what had happened to that ship, only that she had never returned from a short voyage to Freeport, a journey that barely had them out of sight of land. Perhaps it was pirates or a powrie barrelboat, perhaps a rogue wave, perhaps a monster from these unknown waters.

The captain sucked in his breath, his eyes wide. "What happened?"

"A dragon," she lied. "A great flying beast breathing walls of fire upon us."

All about them, Xoconai sailors and civilians alike shifted nervously. Quauh glanced at Massayo. Because of his limited command of the language, he couldn't understand the whole of the conversation, she believed, but his wry smile told her that he approved of what she was doing, whatever it might be.

"I will trade for you," the Xoconai captain offered. "I will bring you home."

In the common language of the lands, so that all nearby could understand her, Quauh flatly replied, "I am already home, good captain. Now please, give us your wounded so that we can heal them and return them to you at once."

"Abellican magic," he replied derisively, and dismissively, in the Xoconai tongue.

Quauh slowly shook her head. "Simple human cleverness."

A short while later, the very drunk—so drunk that they had no idea of what had happened to them after they had been blindfolded—Xoconai patients were escorted back to *Golden Augur*, along with some extra linen to repair the carrack's shredded sails, well enough, at least, for the ship to limp back to Freeport in the north.

Massayo and Quauh stood side by side at the rail of their ship as the planks were lifted and the ships pushed apart.

"A dragon, you say, with breath of fire?" Massayo quipped, and it took Quauh a moment to realize that he was speaking in perfect Xoconai.

"I would have traded you to him, if I thought you so desired, even before your conversation," Massayo assured her, and walked away.

Quauh stood there smiling, truly content.

Truly at home.

CHAPTER 16

SANCTUARY ISLAND

P ort *Mandu* and *Pinquickle's Folly* approached the southern
harbor of Freeport side by side, brazenly flying their red
'n' blacks. For Captain Wilkie, it was the red face of a bulldog,
gaudy earrings dangling from its front-folded ears. For Massayo,
a dark red skull adorned with a bright red powrie beret, set on
the black background.

Quauh watched the two captains, standing at their respective
prows, high and solitary on their forecastles, as if they were the
figureheads set upon these increasingly notorious buccaneers.

Massayo was thoroughly enjoying this moment, Quauh could
see, particularly from the way he was leaning on the bullhead.
The successful merchant, stripped of his wealth, his business,
his station, and enslaved to the most menial and brutal work
of all, had risen once more.

Captain Massayo.

He had his ship, his command, and he wanted them all to
see it.

Quauh leaned over the rail a bit to look past him as the wide harbor came more clearly into view. Quauh and the *Uey* had stopped through to Freeport twice before, but both times settling in the quieter and much smaller eastern harbor of the island, as was customary for Xoconai warships. Now, with her first clear view of the southern harbor, the former captain understood why. Never had she seen so many ships in one place, not even in the great port of Anxelzin in the west. Scores and scores of every vessel imaginable: Behrenese biremes and triremes; heavy square-rigged carracks and brigs and large barques, fleet lateen-rigged sloops and schooners, and others she did not know, including a design that she first thought a brig, but with a pronounced, overhanging bow and stern, and a long bowsprit that made the graceful vessel appear as if it was moving even while anchored. She stared at it for a long while, awestruck by its grace and beauty. She looked for a name but found none, and upon a closer inspection as they glided past, she realized that this one was in for serious repair, or more likely an unfinished build.

As they drew closer to the inner harbor, she noted some Xoconai merchant ships, as well, mostly clustered on the western side of the wide bay, near the long wharfs. Quauh was surprised to see Massayo and Wilkie exchanging waves, then calling to their helmsmen to head that way.

She relayed the order, half to port, to Benny, who was snickering as he complied. Then, a moment later, as they came up on the ships moored farthest out, she called to Toomsuba and his team to go to half sail.

Pinquickle's Folly glided in easily under the expert handling, and it truly was just that, of Benny McBenoyt, even outpacing

Wilkie's boat. Quauh was about to call to Toomsuba to correct that, but her attention was seized quite suddenly as the sloop eased up behind a carrack with tattered sails and large lettering across the back of her quarterdeck: *Golden Augur*.

Now she understood the grins and waves between the two captains, and she couldn't believe the pluck of Massayo and Wilkie.

"Bring her alongside, close and slow!" Massayo called to Quauh, though loudly enough for all on the deck to hear. "And prepare a proper salute!"

Quauh stared at him intently, not quite sure of what he was about here. He motioned with his fingers, beckoning, but not to her, she realized after her initial surprise, but to some people standing behind him over by the starboard rail. The seven Massayo had rescued from *Golden Augur* solemnly and seriously walked across the deck and up to the port rail beside the captain. Massayo brought one in particular, a young man, perhaps even still a boy, to his side.

Quauh had watched this one from the time they had taken him from the Xoconai ship. He was so young, and seemed so broken. The other six had expressed their gratitude to Massayo and his crew with tears and strained smiles and great sighs of relief. But not this young man, this teenager. Had he even lifted his gaze from the deck in the weeks since the battle?

She watched now as Massayo put his arm about the young man's shoulders, physically straightened him, and began talking to him. Her curiosity getting the best of her, Quauh moved up to join them.

"What is your name?" Massayo asked the young man. When he mumbled an indecipherable reply, another of the new crew started to answer. But Massayo held up his hand to silence the woman.

"Your name?" he asked the young man again.

Another mumble—Quauh thought she heard the first syllable as "da."

"Stand tall!" Massayo told them all, and to the broken young man, he added, "Speak it louder. Mean it. Be proud of it."

"Dabego," the young man said.

"You are Dabego?"

The young man nodded.

Massayo pointed out over the rail. "Tell them," he implored Dabego and the other six. "Look them in the eye as we pass, all of you, and tell them your names! Not whatever name they tried to call you, but *your* names, given to you by the only people who earned the right to name you. Tell them! But first, you know the salute?"

That question brought smiles, even from Dabego, who looked up, nodding.

Quauh didn't understand.

Pinquickle's Folly glided past *Golden Augur*, the captain and crew of the damaged Xoconai ship throwing hard stares.

Massayo clicked to attention and crisply snapped his hand up to his forehead in salute—his *left* hand, not his right, as did the seven former slaves standing beside him. Even this didn't signify much to Quauh—she had seen it once before and had just assumed that the Durubazzi saluted with a different hand.

She noted, though, that as the salute ended, the hands didn't snap back down to the sides, but rather, turned, palms facing faces, ring finger and pinkie curling, middle and index fingers spreading as the hand slid down, running a V over the left eye of each respective saluting person.

When one Durubazzi sailor had done that to her on the previous occasion, it had seemed a subtle, almost unnoticeable thing, but now, watching all eight do it . . .

"I am Captain Massayo Mantili of *Pinquickle's Folly*!"

He looked down the line, and beginning with the farthest one from Massayo, each of the new crew members spoke their names loudly and clearly.

Until it came to Dabego, whose voice was thin.

"Tell them," Massayo quietly implored him. "Tell them who you are, and do it in a way so these unwelcome invaders know that they may make you bend, but they will never take from you who you are."

"Dabego," the young man said more firmly.

"They'll never break you. You are Dabego. You are Durubazzi. You are proud. You are stronger—stronger than their whips and warships."

"Dabego!" the young man yelled out to the captain across the way.

"Stronger than they'll ever understand," Massayo continued quietly to Dabego. "You are stronger than your flesh."

"I am Dabego!" the young man cried out. "You can whip me, you can wound me, you can kill me, aye, but no, you will *never* again own me! Never!"

The words, the movements of the eight Durubazzi lined at the rail, the set of their shoulders, all struck Quauh more profoundly than she had expected, indeed, more so than she would have believed possible. It wasn't just the words, or the salute, but the posture of these people that so captured her. This was a demand for dignity, but not from the captain and crew of *Golden Augur*—indeed, the Xoconai on the other boat simply stared across at the display with a notable dispassion.

But this wasn't about them. The onlooking Xoconai crew and captain didn't know that, but now, surprisingly, Quauh did. This wasn't a demand for dignity so much as it was a reminder of dignity.

But it wasn't supposed to be like this! Not from these people in the east, and surely not from those hailing from so far south. That wasn't what she had been taught these last fifteen years since the conquest. These were sidhe . . . but no, they truly were not!

Quauh wondered how she would behave in such a situation. Would she have even had the decency to let these slavers off so easily? Or would she have taken all their servants, perhaps the civilian Xoconai, then put *Golden Augur* to the bottom with her crew aboard?

And now? Massayo had been robbed of everything and placed into hard-labor servitude, sold like the mining equipment he had been forced to use. She looked at him as he and the others came down from the prow to the main deck. She could see the pain there, true hurt, and the simmering anger. It had taken so much from him to act as he had—but the things he had done, or not done, were for the benefit of them all, she understood. If he had exacted revenge on the Xoconai of *Golden Augur*, the reputations of Massayo Mantili and Wilkie Dogears would have been savaged, of course, and no ship would surrender to them again, making their games on the high seas so much more deadly for all.

But still . . . the pain, the indignity.

Led by Massayo, the Durubazzi were finding themselves once more as they had been before the advent of Quixi Tonoloya, before the Xoconai had come to their shores and upended their way of life and, in so many tragic cases, their very sense of self and self-worth.

As that notion truly filled her thought, Quauh found herself horrified and ashamed.

She had been part of that terrible oppression. The *Uey* had been served at some points by indentured servants—no, those words were too kind, she knew, and she scrubbed them from her thoughts. The men and women given her under her command, people of Honce, mostly, were slaves. She had treated them well, comparatively, and had even thought highly of herself for her "mercy."

But no, it was not laudable, and not merciful.

The notion stung her heart profoundly. It made her wonder how she could have possibly been so full of self-delusion. In this moment, this terrible, glorious moment, Quauh saw clearly.

She pushed past thoughts of remorse and self-loathing, and instead decided then and there who she was, who she would insist that she be.

Whatever the cost.

Quauh moved to the taffrail to watch as Captain Wilkie's ship glided in right behind Massayo's, passing very near to *Golden Augur.*

Her suspicions were confirmed—both crews nodded with respect, a mutual salute of sorts, signifying a gracious victory for Wilkie and a nod of thanks from the captain of *Golden Augur* for the mercy he and his had been shown.

Quauh wasn't sure how she felt about that.

This was all too complicated for her. She had known of the false hierarchy, of course, but seeing it so up close made it all so very real to her.

And all so very wrong to her.

Pinquickle's Folly executed a slow turn, moving back to the west along the lane between the moored vessels, then back to deeper waters far back from the docks. Massayo was with Benny at the wheel then, directing him, and very clearly looking to moor up as near to the western end of the harbor as possible.

She wasn't sure what he was up to, only that he was up to something.

He motioned to her to join him on the quarterdeck as soon as the ship was secured.

"You and I will go ashore on the first dinghy in," the captain explained. "Chimeg and Benny, too, if they want some time in Freeport this day."

"Not Toomsuba?" Quauh was surprised by that, as she had come to think of the four Massayo had named along with Toomsuba to be the core five of *Pinquickle's* crew.

"Toomsuba will not step foot onto Freeport," Massayo

explained. "He hates the place and considers it a conquered land, even though no one holds any real power there beyond the Seat of Free Men—and they're too busy arguing with each other about the rules of the Mirianic to give any real care to what happens on the island."

"The Seat of Free Men," Quauh echoed with a wry grin and a shake of her head. "We Xoconai refer to that council as the Buttholds of Buccaneers."

"You'd probably do well to not stroll about Freeport saying such things."

"Of course not. But why is Toomsuba so hostile to them?"

"Freeport was once the center of the nation formed by all the islanders, and now few of those people of the various island tribes can even be found on her shores. The Behrenese conquered Freeport centuries ago, the Bearmen of Honce conquered it soon after. So the Behrenese conquered it again from the Bearmen, and back and forth for two hundred years. You can probably guess who on the island took the biggest casualties in those centuries of strife."

It wasn't a difficult problem for Quauh to solve.

"The islanders, of course. And thus, the oldest culture on this end of the Mirianic was all but wiped out of Freeport," Massayo explained. "Now it is a shared place without hierarchy. Anyone is welcome and can do as they please, as long as they're not violating the freedom of another. Whatever you want, it is here. Gambling, liquor, all sorts of mushroom and pipe weed, companionship—everything can be had for a price. It is a strange truth, though. Everyone who comes here loves the place dearly, and so they do not wish to be banned. There is little crime in Freeport, even without the oversight of armed authorities."

"Blissful anarchy?"

Massayo just shrugged and laughed. "The Xoconai do not like such chaos, I have come to know. They would like nothing more than to conquer Freeport and make it their own, yes?"

"I cannot deny it," Quauh replied truthfully. "But they do not want war with Behren."

"Chezru Chieftain Brynn would burn their ships up and down the coast and cut off their supply of precious gold."

"We officers—" Quauh caught herself. "The officers of the Tonoloya Armada are not permitted ashore here, or only very rarely and with specific instructions and purpose."

"Perhaps Freeport can become the place where the various cultures of the land truly learn to appreciate each other," said Massayo.

Quauh found that hard to fathom, as much as she, surprisingly, wanted to believe. She was struggling with the reality of her own shocking evolution these last few weeks, but even that gave her little hope that many of her former colleagues would similarly awaken to the notion that they were not the only humans walking these lands. The profits, the gold, the magic, the power derived from the east depended upon them thinking of those they conquered—from the plateau overlooking Otontotomi in the west all the way to the shores of the Mantis Arm and the beaches of Entel, and now in the land of Durubazzi as well—as less than human, as sidhe, and whatever moment of enlightenment might have been found those fifteen years ago in the treaty formed on a faraway mountain, the spirit of it had not held. Not at all.

Massayo clapped his hands. "Come," he told her. "Let us get to the shore and conclude our day's business." He took a step toward the dinghy, which was being lowered over the side, but he paused and looked back at his first mate. "Make sure that Columbine, Aushin, and the other two powries are off the boat when we are."

"You think they'd steal from you? Columbine has been acting as your bosun."

"I think anyone on *Pinquickle's Folly* would steal from me if they had the chance to do it without consequence."

"I wouldn't."

Massayo laughed. "Give it time, O honorable first mate," he quipped. "You'll learn better."

Benny and the other four powries, Massayo and Quauh climbed out of the dinghy onto the Freeport docks a short while later, with Chimeg preferring to stay on the ship.

"Go and play," Massayo told the dwarfs. "But be back here when the shadows are long on the water and the western sky shows the orange and pink. We have a long night ahead of us."

With a tip of berets, the powries did not have to be asked twice to party.

"Are you going to tell me?" Quauh asked.

"The business immediately before us is equally important to you, my new friend. Focus on that for now."

He set off at a brisk pace, Quauh scurrying to keep up.

Before they ever left the docks, Quauh could see how different this city was from the ones she had known back in the west, or here in the east in Honce. She had suspected that from her time in the harbor, of course, but what really shocked her now was how different Freeport was from the Behrenese towns she had recently visited.

Particularly Djinnit. That place had been wide and spacious and full of music drifting through the market squares. It was alive and colorful, full of song and dance, full of bargaining and jovial arguing. It was a place of intensity, of life in the moment.

Everything, she came to see soon enough, that Freeport was not. Her streets were tight and crowded, low on light, with balconies overhead nearly touching those across the street. Half the people walking—people of all cultures, even the Xoconai—could not mark a straight line. Every nook smelled of piss and vomit, every voice seemed raised in distress or anger, with gambling replacing bargaining and shouting replacing song.

Quauh became very conscious of her truncated limb here, for it seemed like every corner held a person missing a limb and begging for coin—mostly sailors who had gotten caught between a line and a rail in a sudden gust, or who had lost an infested leg to the axe or saw.

"There is more to Freeport than what you see here," Massayo quietly told her, obviously sensing her discomfort.

"I have never seen such downtrodden," she admitted.

"Life at sea is difficult and dangerous, and many are wounded, or succumb to the rum. Where else might they go if not here?" He paused to put a handful of coins into the trembling hands of one young beggar, whose light skin was splotchy with rash and open wounds. When the poor boy smiled in response, Quauh noted that his gums were bloody.

Scurvy, she knew.

Not ten steps farther along, the doors of a tavern across the street blew open and a powrie came flying out, airborne until he landed facedown on the cobblestones. He bounced right up, or tried to, but staggered to the side, belched loudly, vomited abundantly, and fell over, snoring before he crashed against the stone.

At the opened doorway, several folks, including a young Xoconai woman, laughed wildly.

"Why would anyone come here?" Quauh wondered aloud.

"To live," Massayo answered, his voice surprising her, for she hadn't really been asking. "To live, free to do as they please, without some fool or another pretending to hold power over them."

"To indulge until they fall down?"

"If they so choose. To drink, to forget, to live in the moment and not the past nor the future, neither of which seem worth considering, likely. To swive and feel the touch of another. To feel, for just a moment, a bit, a flicker of hope in a bleak world when the bounce of the dice might actually offer a chance at a better existence."

"You seem to know Freeport quite well."

"It was my salvation for a full season the first time I escaped my bondage," Massayo replied. "Here, I fell to the bottom of despair's pit, you might think, but the pit allowed me to hold

the pride I could not recall under the whips of goldfish masters. When they learned who I was and dragged me back to
Durubazzi, I managed to escape only because I did not care if
they killed me. I took risks no sane person ever would. I would
have come back here, except that through sheer luck, I found
my way to Captain Wilkie."

"You love him like a brother."

"More a father, but yes."

"But you deceive him?"

Massayo stopped and turned sharply on her. "Take care your
words in the ears of Freeport. I act as Captain Wilkie showed
me how to act. To survive. Do you think he will be angry with
me when I reveal my plans?"

"Plans?"

"You will understand them soon. But enough," Massayo
insisted. "We are here for a purpose, and that purpose is your
arm."

As he spoke, he turned down a tighter lane and moved
swiftly to the left-hand side, stopping before a small shop with
storefront signage that read: *OOT O BOUNDS.*

"Oot?" Quauh said, her face crinkling. "What language?"

"The common tongue of Honce."

"Oot?"

Massayo grinned at her. "Say it like Chimeg."

Quauh considered that for a moment, hearing the To-gai-ru's
distinct accent, where she sounded out the letter combinations
with sharpness and bold diction. In the higher foothills of the
Belt-and-Buckle just west of Entel, the farmers kept a hairy breed

of cattle fitted for the higher and colder fields. About the lands, they were known as highland cows, but ask one of the farmers and the answer would sound much more like "heeland coos."

Chimeg's accent was somewhat like that.

"Oot," Quauh said quietly. "Out?" She gave a little laugh and looked to Massayo. "Out of Bounds."

The captain nodded. "A sailor's saying for anything that doesn't quite fit, you see. Everything on the ships is made to standards and specifics, to make it much easier to do repairs when you come to port, yes?"

Quauh nodded. She didn't know the saying, but she certainly understood the concept of common standards for the various contraptions on the ships. What good would a cringle be if it was too small for a too-thick rope to pass through it?

"My friend in here is someone who specializes in items that are out of bounds."

"Are fabricated limbs so uncommon?"

"They can be," Massayo replied wryly, and led the way inside.

The shop was littered with a mishmash of items, implements of all manner: many different tools, boxes of bolts, planers, knives of all sorts pegged up on one wall, brushes and small barrels. A large net hung from the ceiling, many different sizes and materials of ropes hanging haphazardly from it. There was a counter, though it was hard to see under the piles and piles of a million different things set all about, including before it, to either side, and even a small chest atop it. Behind it stood a man of about fifty years, with long hair—red, brown, and speckled with gray—tied back in a ponytail. He had an unkempt gray beard and was continually blowing shavings from it as he fiddled, whittling the end of a wooden pole with an enormous knife.

"Pray don't cut off your finger," Massayo said, startling the fellow, who did indeed nick his finger, pulling his hand away fast and giving a good shake as he turned an angry look at the captain.

That anger melted almost immediately, replaced by an ear-to-ear grin. "Massayo Mantili! Or—have I heard?—Captain Massayo?"

"Whispers seep through every crack," Massayo replied.

"They do," the man replied, his expression turning quite curious as he regarded Massayo's Xoconai companion with obvious surprise—and not a little trepidation, Quauh noted. "But not everything has been whispered, so it would seem."

"This is Qu—" Massayo started, but he cut himself off. "What was your name again, lass?"

"Qu-Quixi," she stammered.

"Quixi?" the man asked. "Your name is Eastern?"

"No, no, it also means sunrise," she bluffed, but his quiet chuckles told her that she wasn't fooling him at all.

"Talmadge of the Wilderlands, this is my friend," Massayo said. Then, clearly flummoxed, he added, "Quixi."

"And your jacket, Massayo," Talmadge added. "That is a captain's coat, is it not?"

"I am a captain."

"A Tonoloya Armada captain's coat."

"Is it?" Massayo replied, holding his arm up a bit and looking at it with feigned surprise. "Why, I found it on a beach, tattered, and had to spend good coin to have it resewn and refitted, for it would seem that the one who wore it before me was much smaller than I."

Quauh's gaze went from Talmadge's grin to Massayo, just in time to realize that the captain had looked at her when he had spoken that last part. She tried not to show her discomfort—why would he give any hint such as that?

"No matter," said Talmadge. "So, what might I do for you this—" He stopped and leaned over the counter, looking at the tied sleeve of Quauh's right arm. "Ah, I see."

He motioned Quauh over and moved very deliberately, looking to her assenting nods before continuing every bit. He untied the sleeve and studied the wound.

"A good and clean cut," he said.

Quauh grimaced at the words, the awful memory of the descending powrie axe coming clear once more.

"Your pardon, good lady," Talmadge said, and Quauh worked hard and fast to get that sour expression off her face. "The clean cut makes the supporting brace much easier," he explained. "Have you considered what you would like to have there?" He looked up to Quauh and to Massayo as he asked.

"Even with the one hand, she serves me well on *Pinquickle's Folly*," Massayo explained. "Her understanding of the sea is far beyond her years of experience. She is one of us."

"Quixi is?" Talmadge asked slyly.

Quauh almost blurted out her real name then, but she looked to Massayo, who shook his head. "For your own sake, yes, Quixi is."

"Well enough, and pleased to meet you," Talmadge said, and now he extended his left hand to shake Quauh's, and warmly.

He led the pair over to the far wall, moving behind a rack to an area covered with a tarp. "As you can see," he said, and pulled aside the tarp, revealing a wall full of potential arm caps. There were dozens of options: everything from thin hooks and carved metal hands to extended gaffs and the long blade of a knife. Even a small crossbow was on that wall, its butt appearing very strange indeed, but the body of it leaving no doubt as to what it was.

Quauh fell back a step, overwhelmed.

"A hook is the most common choice," Massayo said to her, obviously seeing her distress.

Talmadge held up his hand. "I should have shown you this first," he said, and rushed around the corner of the wall, where he reached down into a small cubby and pulled out a leather-and-metal item.

"This is the cap," he explained, exhibiting the leather sleeve of it—one that had a couple of nasty-looking metal spikes lining the interior of its inseam. "Attaching it will be painful, I'll not lie, but once it's in place, you will only have to remove it to clean it and ensure that your remaining length of arm is not infested or weeping. And this part . . ." He fumbled with the item, turning it up so she could see the metal front of it, turning the tip toward her to show a hollow, a ring of sorts, capping it. "This means you won't have to choose only one cap."

He pulled one of the metal hand imitations from the wall

and slid its wrist piece into the ring, then pressed and gave a slight turn, then held the whole of the end cap up, fake hand secure.

"You see? If you are out and about, as with today, and wish to avoid the stares, you just wear this. Your dress uniform, if you will. When you need utility, you can change it."

He pressed on the hand again and twisted, separating it, then put it back in place on the wall and took a hook. The same movement, press and twist, and the hook was set securely in place on the arm cap.

"Bravo, mate," said Massayo. "When did you come to this?"

"I have spent years trying to get it just right," Talmadge answered. "The screw-lock inside had to be strong enough and flexible enough for me to have confidence that it would hold and survive long enough against the stress and the salt. But I think I have it."

"You have great passion for this task," Quauh remarked. She didn't add the word "strangely" to her response, but it was clear enough in her tone.

"The only woman I ever truly loved would have benefited greatly from such an invention," Talmadge solemnly replied. "She lost her legs to the bite of a monster."

"I am so sorry."

"Do not be. She would not want any pity, and she lived a life quite rich and wonderful even after the tragedy. She was helped to a great degree through magic, a gift from a most wonderful witch who danced in the mountains. I don't have magic, but I have come to understand such things as these, and so I owe it to my dear beloved's memory to help others who are so afflicted, where I may."

"And how many have you helped?" Massayo prompted.

"You've seen many with hooks and hands fashioned in Oot o Bounds."

"With this new design, I mean."

Talmadge shook his head. "It is very recently created, and will no doubt need my tending now and again as it wears. Most who come to me are folk of very little means, of course, and this . . ."

"Ah, it is expensive, then," Massayo said.

Talmadge held up his hands helplessly. "To create the cap alone takes a week of my time, and many pieces of silver to the blacksmith I contract."

"So you show it to me, to Captain Massayo, because you think me a rich man now?"

"I show it to you because I had to show it to someone," Talmadge replied with a laugh.

"How much for the cap? I assume the individual pieces are priced . . ."

"I give it to you—to her," Talmadge said. "We have been friends for years, Massayo, and we both know that I owe you much. Pay me with information. Tell me any problems you find with it, or of any good uses, so that I might better perfect the design. And then, of course, if you see fit, my friend Massayo, a bit of coin would help me to service your fellow seamen."

Massayo flashed that huge and toothy white smile and laughed.

"Let me clean everything and check the fittings," Talmadge

offered. "Certainly, it will have to be properly resized to fit so thin an arm." He pulled a string set with equally spaced knots from his pocket and held it up before Quauh. "May I?"

She lifted her arm, but Talmadge waved her over to a cluttered desk, where he brushed several books and items from the top and spread out a parchment. With a bar of some gray material, he made a rough drawing of Quauh's damaged arm. Then he took his measurements of the lengths and diameters, from the top of the stub to the top of the forearm, just below the elbow.

"It's good that they saved the elbow," Talmadge told her.

"Will it work?" Massayo asked.

Talmadge half shrugged, half nodded. "I have to adjust it quite a bit. I'll need to go back to my blacksmith friend."

"How long?"

"His schedule is unpredictable. How long are you in port?"

"Perhaps to the end of the season, perhaps a few days. It is Captain Wilkie's choice. He might wish to make one more run south before the winds turn."

"Ah yes, he is eager now that he knows he has a proper sister ship, and one with a most interesting weapon."

Quauh gasped, and Massayo straightened and looked down at Talmadge suspiciously.

"A Xoconai carrack limped in earlier this week, her crew speaking to any who would hear of a most unusual encounter."

"Indeed?" Massayo said, seeming oblivious and unconcerned.

"Are you going to make me ask around?"

"Isn't that what you do?"

Quauh looked from one to the other, both grinning, both knowing.

"It worked?" Talmadge asked.

"It worked."

Talmadge laughed heartily. "Captain Massayo Mantili, indeed!"

Only then did Quauh understand that Talmadge had been in on Massayo's secret designs for a long time. She'd heard the pride in Massayo's voice when he confirmed that the weapon had worked.

Too much pride, she thought. It was a clever weapon, but it was limited and unwieldy—and it had to be mostly aimed, side to side and with elevation, by the movements of the ship!

But still, yes, it was clever, and Massayo's toy, which she understood now to be his creation, was worth that smile, particularly since the bullhead had put some measure of fear into the crew of *Golden Augur.*

Captain Massayo Mantili had done well.

Perhaps too well, she feared.

"I can have it ready by the end of the season," Talmadge said, looking directly at Quauh. "Perhaps earlier, maybe three weeks instead of the five when you'll have to go south. But if you give me the full five, perhaps I can add some other options to go with it. I have some ideas."

"So be it," Massayo agreed. "I need her to be of best service to my ship. She is my first mate."

"A goldfish first mate," Talmadge said, shaking his head. "Ever do you surprise."

"I am no goldfish," said Quauh, her voice even and firm, expressing full confidence in the claim.

"First Mate . . . Quixi, then," Talmadge said with a grin. "You were wise to accept the demotion."

Quauh's jaw dropped open in surprise.

"When the crew finally tires of the puffery of Captain Massayo, make sure to retrieve the coat before you help them throw him overboard, eh? I'm sure I can put it back to its original size."

Quauh didn't quite know how to take that—until Massayo gave a hearty laugh and pulled Talmadge in for a great hug. "Join us, friend," she heard Massayo whisper to the craftsman.

"Someday," Talmadge replied, but unconvincingly, and Quauh understood that Massayo had extended that invitation many, many times.

CHAPTER 17

UNMARQUED

"Where is he?" Captain Wilkie demanded. He had come aboard *Pinquickle's Folly* unexpectedly near to midnight, demanding to see Massayo at once.

"Certainly I would tell you if I knew, captain," Quauh replied.

Wilkie lifted a hand to rub an eye, showing a piece of parchment in his grasp. He was a bit drunk, Quauh noted, but whatever was bothering him was doing much to sober him.

"He went off with Toomsuba in the dinghy," Chimeg said from above, sitting on the lowest yard of the mainmast. "He'll not be long, surely, at this hour."

"Rouse your crew," Wilkie told Quauh. "Get her ready to sail. When you see *Port Mandu* weigh anchor, you follow, whether Captain Massayo has returned or not. And if he has not, then *Pinquickle* is yours until he finds his way back to her."

"Back to her where?" Chimeg asked before Quauh could.

"Inudada," Wilkie answered, and thrust the parchment into Quauh's hand. Before she even glanced at it, the captain moved back to the rail. His two awaiting crewmen helped him down into the dinghy and they pulled away with great urgency.

"Now!" Wilkie called back emphatically to Quauh.

Quauh rubbed the sleep from her eyes and looked up to Chimeg, who dropped down to the deck beside her. "A torch," she called to Aushin, who was up by the forecastle.

Before the light ever arrived, Quauh and Chimeg realized what Wilkie had given them, the heading bold and clear enough even in the waning moonlight.

Grand Augur Apichtli had revoked the Letters of Reprisal for *Port Mandu* and for *Pinquickle's Folly*.

It was a declaration of intent and of war on the two ships, Chezru Chieftain Brynn be damned.

Quauh understood that such a move by Apichtli held no real legal weight by Xoconai maritime code, for such an action would have to be undertaken by the powers back in the Tonoloya Basin, or at least in Ontontotomi. But that that hadn't mattered much to the crews of the *Dolphin* and Three Bits, had it?

"Rouse them all," Quauh told Chimeg, and to Aushin, added, "Get Columbine up here."

Her mind went to the task now at hand. She glanced once into the darkness, hoping against hope to see the dinghy returning. This was Massayo's ship, not hers, but she certainly understood Captain Wilkie's orders. She didn't much like the idea of sailing away without the captain, and she only grimaced harder when she remembered the other missing crewman.

Who would pull the bullhead in Toomsuba's absence?

Quauh put the thoughts aside. She had her duty. While the crew awakened around her, Columbine and Chimeg taking charge, she flopped down to sit and spread the parchment and smoothed it on the deck before her, then brought the torch over to read the details of the notice.

She immediately understood Captain Wilkie's urgency. The heading blared:

Be it known that the pirate Port Mandu
and her sister ship, Name Unknown,
are hereby UNMARQUED,
by order of Grand Augur Apichtli,
Prime Sovereign of Quixi Tonoloya

But how could this be? Quauh wondered. For the notice referenced the attack on the *Golden Augur.* The carrack could not have arrived into Freeport more than three days ahead of the buccaneers. How might they have gotten word to Apichtli, and then the Grand Augur making such a decision so quickly? And why? Why this time? The attack had been mild, *Golden Augur*'s wounded tended, no heavy reprisals against the Xoconai captain or crew.

It didn't really matter, Quauh realized. This was Captain Aketz acting on his own, pushing, pushing. She wasn't surprised, given all that she had learned of the man in her days of training and sailing here in the east. His ambition was no secret, nor was his consternation about the transport mirrors connecting Durubazzi and the island of Watouwa.

Because Aketz wasn't interested in efficiency, or in the functioning of the government of Mayorqua Tonoloya. He was interested in the reputation of Aketz. He knew that if just three more transport stations could be constructed between Watouwa and Entel, the pirates would become inconsequential, and the heroes of Mayorqua Tonoloya in the southern Mirianic would be mundunugu and macana warriors protecting those mirrors, not sea captains.

The man would risk open war with the kingdom of Behren before allowing his reputation to be so diminished.

Quauh shook even those thoughts from her head in that moment, however, realizing the most important matter of all: if these flyers were posted in Freeport City, then Aketz was very near, perhaps even watching them and ready to give chase.

They had to go. Immediately.

She folded the parchment and tucked it into her pocket, then jumped up with the torch in hand and began quietly whispering orders to ready the sails and weigh anchor, and instructing the crew to silence, as much as possible. She kept glancing at *Port Mandu*, her crew similarly at work, then out to the north, scanning the darkness for some sign of Massayo's and Toomsuba's return.

Soon after, *Port Mandu* raised a single sail and began a slow turn to glide out of Freeport Harbor. Columbine, Chimeg, and Benny came up to her.

"Should we weigh anchor and go?" Columbine asked.

Quauh winced. They really should, she knew, but how could she take Massayo's ship out from under him, particularly after all he was doing for her? And where was the man? Where had he gone, and why? Was it for her benefit, some meeting with that man, Talmadge?

She sighed as Chimeg prodded her.

"We can turn inside *Port Mandu* and catch them easily," Quauh replied. "Give it a bit longer."

"She's goin' full sail as soon as she's past the last line of moored boats," Benny warned.

"And we're small enough, fleet enough, and skilled enough to go full sail as soon as we weigh," Quauh snapped at him, rather harshly, her nerves getting the best of her.

"Aye, we are," Benny returned, staring hard.

"We owe too much to Captain Massayo—we all do," Quauh said. She looked to Chimeg and managed a smile. "And we wouldn't be the same without Toomsuba." Then, turning to Columbine, she asked, "Do you think you and your boys can pull the bullhead strap?"

"The five of us?"

"If it's the five of you, then who'll be on the wheel and rigging?" Chimeg asked.

"So we'll be out there without our primary weapon, being chased by the *Cipac*," Quauh said dryly. "Do you like those odds?"

"I'm not likin' them odds with or without the damned slingshot," Columbine said.

It was hard to disagree. Their only chance was to be away fast, in the night, and hope that Aketz wasn't watching.

"It's a big sea and lots of places to hide," Benny agreed. "Cap'n Massayo'll find us, don't ye worry, Cap'n Quauh."

The reference had the woman off-balance for just a moment, and with a nod, she steeled herself and was about to order the anchor up, but Chimeg interrupted, grabbing her by the shoulder and pointing beside her. Quauh breathed a sigh of relief when she turned to see the dinghy approaching.

"Set a detail to get them aboard at once," Quauh told Columbine. "And get that anchor up and those sails ready."

Toomsuba and Massayo came aboard soon after, the dinghy being pulled up the side even as the anchor pulled free and *Pinquickle's Folly* began her departure.

His face a mask of incredulity, Massayo rushed up to Quauh, who answered before he could blurt the obvious questions by handing over the parchment and saying but a single word: "Unmarqued."

They sailed through the night, running no lights, and didn't slow with the dawn. Inudada, the Drowned Isles, was their destination. Inudada was far to the south and east, a journey of more than twelve hundred miles, given all the lanes and lands they would have to avoid, and more than two weeks of sailing with favorable winds, which they didn't have in this season, and into deep waters, where they might well cross the path of a hurricane.

"We will need to resupply, and soon," Quauh told the captain.

"They've seen sails to the north," Massayo replied. "It is

Aketz, almost surely. Wilkie's afraid to stop, thinking we might not get back out."

"We should put out rain barrels and hope for a storm, then, and decide which of the crew we intend to eat," came the sarcastic reply.

Massayo started to reply as if the remark had been serious, before catching himself with a snort. "Get us near to Wilkie's starboard rail and push us ahead enough so that we can launch the dinghy and get scooped by him as he passes. You and I will go and meet with the good captain to better make our plans."

"Unless *Port Mandu* has supplies enough for both ships, our plans will be made for us," said Quauh.

She moved past the bullhead to the forecastle and ran a green-and-white pennant up the forward line, signaling a parley. The crew of the other ship knew the drill, clearly, for *Port Mandu* dropped a sail and slowed.

Pinquickle's Folly raced ahead and lowered the dinghy, and both ships were back to full sail soon after, not daring to slow.

Quauh turned down the offer of whiskey in Captain Wilkie's quarters, but Massayo took a glass, drained it, and held it out for a second.

"You've the taller mast. Is it the *Crocodile* behind us?" Massayo asked.

"Too far to see her flag, but she's no small boat and she's running fast," Wilkie answered. "He had to be in Freeport to get those flyers up so quickly, and now every ship friendly to the goldfish will be pointing his way at us."

"An early season, then. All the way to Inudada."

"Should we even stop there?" Wilkie asked. "Aketz will surround the isles and barter with our trustworthy colleagues to surrender us and be rewarded or be trapped in the Drowned Isles for a long, long while."

The sarcastic way he bit off "trustworthy" reminded Quauh of the truth of these new comrades with whom she had allied, and fostered serious doubts—which she quickly countered by reminding herself of Matlalihi and his treachery. Could anyone really be trusted?

"Would it be fair of us to go there with Aketz on our tail?" Massayo asked. "We could sail to Durubazzi, and even farther south along the southern continent's shore. Or to Behren to plead our case with Queen Brynn. Surely she cannot be happy with the goldfish suddenly overturning her Letters of Reprisal."

"Aketz is pushing her patience, no doubt, but do you really think the Chezru Chieftain will go to war over the fate of a couple of buccaneers?"

"Where will she be if all the buccaneers are gone and the goldfish wholly control the seas?"

"That is a long way off," Wilkie replied. "The urgency isn't yet there."

"So, we run, and we keep running, and maybe find scraps as a proper trader in the far southlands?"

Wilkie shrugged and took a sip of whiskey.

"If we do that, it is over, you understand," Massayo remarked. "For us and for all that we believe. If Aketz chases us off so easily, which of those we leave behind will he target next? Thorngirdle and whatever new pack he manages to put together? Kalle Narciss and *Rover*? One by one, he'll take them out."

"Ye propose that we all stand together now and do battle with him?" Wilkie asked with obvious skepticism. "Half are still moored in Freeport Harbor. Do ye think they're chasing the *Crocodile* to come to our aid?"

"They should be, for their own sakes!"

"But they're not."

Massayo had no answer, clearly, as he just brought his hands to his face and rubbed hard in pure frustration.

"I want to fight him. Aye, but I do," Wilkie said, and threw his glass against the wall. "The goldfish brought us all such loss. I'd like nothing more than to kill every damned goldfish that came over the western mountains."

Quauh shifted uncomfortably.

"Ye know what I mean," the captain apologized. "Not you."

"I am not your enemy, but I am Xoconai, or goldfish, as you call us," she said quietly. "There are many of us who wish it could be different, I believe. But most of my people have been taught to think of you as sidhe, not human, and certainly not equal to them. Even those who might not think you evil creatures serving a demon do not understand why you cannot simply accept this truth and behave."

"Behave?" Wilkie asked with a snort.

"I do not agree . . ."

He held up his hand, telling her that he needed no explanation, and again offering her some whiskey as he moved over to replace his glass.

"Well, we'll change no goldfish minds by letting Aketz chase us all away," Massayo put in. "Once he clears the seas of our kind, goldfish superiority will hold until and unless Brynn of Behren decides to go to war. And even if she does, if the goldfish find a way to minimize the effect of her dragon, or kill the beast, can she even hope to resist them?"

"I don't care," Wilkie said suddenly and far more intensely. "I don't care about Queen Brynn or whatever ye might call her, or about the buccaneers we leave behind, who did not sail out beside us that we might all take Aketz down and be done with this fool. This is about us, *Port Mandu* and *Pinquickle's Folly*. We run south or we fight, and if we fight, we lose and die, without doubt. But even with that fate staring into me eyes, I'd be a lying dog to tell that I want to run."

"But you'll not condemn our crews to death for your choice," Massayo added, lifting his glass in a toast, to which Wilkie lifted his as well.

"Suppose it's not without doubt?" Quauh asked, surprising both men. She walked over to the bar and poured herself a glass, then took a sip and nearly choked, but forced it down for the needed fortitude. She had been quietly mulling some ideas since they began their run from Freeport, using her understanding of the sea, of the Xoconai politics and Captain Aketz's motivations for this obviously risky play, and of possible ways she and her new companions could escape this seemingly unbreakable trap.

"Captain Aketz is boldly defying Chezru Chieftain Brynn out of desperation," she explained, and she was almost certain that she was correct here. "Grand Augur Apichtli didn't order that warrant against us. He probably doesn't even know about it."

"No one can challenge Aketz and *Crocodile*," said Wilkie. "What's he got to be desperate about?"

Quauh took another sip, a longer one. "Because the world is changing and he knows that his place in the new order will be greatly diminished."

The two captains eyed her curiously for the few heartbeats it took her to continue. This was the moment, she understood, from which she could never recover. This wasn't a robbery of a merchant ship, or a fight with some Xoconai, no, but a betrayal on an entirely different level.

This was the moment Quauh had to choose the course of her life.

"When the *Uey'Lapialli* sailed with her hold flush with Durubazzi gold, we did not load that cargo from the shores of Durubazzi."

"Watouwa," Wilkie said. "Thorngirdle says ye got it loaded at Watouwa."

Quauh nodded and swallowed hard. "The gold didn't go from Durubazzi to Watouwa by ship."

Now the captains looked at each other with obvious confusion.

"You know of the transport mirrors that dot the lands of Honce and into the west?"

Wilkie's mouth dropped open, but Massayo only shrugged.

"We move armies through them—their magic is how Honce was tamed and is now controlled."

"Ye built one on Watouwa?" Wilkie asked.

"And in the jungle of Durubazzi," Quauh confirmed. "We thought we had you all fooled and could begin bringing the gold to Entel unbothered by the buccaneers. We only did it that one time, that one disastrous sail. They wouldn't risk it again. Not after the treasures lost with the *Uey*."

"Then what is Captain Aketz afraid of? We are back where we were."

Quauh shook her head. "The range of the mirrors is impressive, but it is limited. The proper islands must be located and secured, but once that is completed, Grand Augur Apichtli will build more mirrors to frog-hop the gold magically from the mines to Entel."

"Frog-hop?" Massayo echoed with a snort.

"And the cargo ships won't be needed for yer gold," Wilkie said.

"And thus will Captain Aketz become a star that fast burns to darkness," said Quauh. "That scares him more than the edge of buccaneer steel ever could."

"So you're thinking that Aketz will be weakened soon enough for us to risk a fight with him?" Wilkie asked. "Ye said to suppose that the outcome of us fighting him wasn't without doubt."

"We know his advantages, and there may be ways for us to take them away," Quauh explained.

"To what end, if it will all soon enough be irrelevant?" asked Massayo.

Quauh smiled. "Two fish with one spear," she said. "If you

look at the way he destroyed the *Swordfish* and the *Dancing Dolphin*, his most devastating weapon was . . . light. A wave of magical light that prepared those ships to hungrily receive the flames. So the first question we should be asking as we prepare the battlefield is how we can defeat a wave of magical light, and perhaps even turn it back on him."

"The *Crocodile* could put us both to the bottom without that new weapon," Wilkie reminded her.

"Then the second question to answer is how we might turn our initial surprise most fully against him," Quauh said. "Consider all that we know about his wave of light and its consequences."

"It sounds like you've sorted this all out," Massayo remarked.

"I have some ideas, but I'll not pretend it will be easy, or that any of it will work."

"And if it doesn't, we all die."

"But our victory is not without doubt. Is that enough, captains?"

Wilkie and Massayo looked hard at each other, lifted their glasses in a toast, then turned back to Quauh and told her to continue.

Later that day, back on their own ships, the captains confirmed that it was indeed Captain Aketz chasing them when Wilkie's lookout made out the distinctive front of the far distant warship. They saw other ships about, Xoconai merchants, mostly, and legitimate traders, and understood that these witnesses would likely relay any information about them to the hunter.

They continued their run throughout the day. Then, as *Cipac* closed enough to be seen from the deck without a spyglass, the pirate captains nodded to each other from their respective decks and split apart, Wilkie turning west for Dinfawa and the protected shoreline of Behren, and Massayo holding the faster *Pinquickle* straight to the south.

"He'll chase *Port Mandu*," Quauh told Massayo as they stood at the sloop's taffrail and eyed the sails of *Cipac* to the far north. "He needs the bigger prize."

"Let's hope Wilkie makes Dinfawa, then."

"He will," Quauh replied confidently.

When the next dawn broke, there was no sign of *Cipac* from the crow's nest of *Pinquickle's Folly*, but Massayo didn't slow. They made a small island early that afternoon for a quick resupply, then set off again, straight south, toward the largest island in these southern waters.

A week later, they were moored in a secret cove on the rocky, cliff-strewn western end of Azucar, and there they waited.

If Wilkie had found any reinforcements for them, this would be the meeting place.

The day passed, then another.

"We have to go," Quauh told Massayo.

He nodded. He knew the timetable. "How many?" he asked.

"Not many, and they will not be looking for us, or for any who might present a threat. They are well-hidden, relying on secrecy."

Massayo nodded but looked again to the entrance of the cove, obviously hoping to see some familiar sails coming in.

"I will lead the expedition. You stay with your ship," Quauh said.

"You're the only one who knows the way. How many will you need?"

"Give me Chimeg to scout, Toomsuba to carry, and the five powries to finish what must be done," a grim Quauh answered.

"I know that this is asking a lot of you."

The remark caught the first mate off guard and rocked her to the point where her knees wobbled. She steadied herself and took a deep breath. "Not so much," she answered, and Massayo's smile told her that he saw the obvious lie for what it was, and that he appreciated it, indeed.

The band of eight landed on the shore soon after. Chimeg knew the way off the beach and so led the team up the cliffs to a high point. There, Quauh looked down at the distant town and the harbor where she had docked the *Uey* for the load of gold, needing that perspective to guide her to the correct direction.

Chimeg took the lead as the sun began to sink into the west, moving with all speed in the direction Quauh had indicated. They were in a deep fern jungle by dusk, the dim light slowing them.

When that turned to darkness, they regrouped and waited for the rising moon, while Quauh tried again to find her bearings.

"It should be that way," she whispered to Chimeg and the others.

"Are ye even sure it's still here?" Columbine asked, his voice alarmingly loud.

Chimeg told them to wait, then slipped off into the night. A long while passed before she returned.

"They have no sentries. A small camp at the base of . . ." She paused, grinned in the moonlight, and looked directly at Quauh. "A pyramid."

"With golden mirrors atop it," Quauh said.

Chimeg nodded and led the way. As they neared the camp, they came upon a Xoconai macana warrior sitting against a tree, and Quauh understood that what the archer really meant by "no sentries" was no *living* sentries.

The first mate turned away as Chimeg roughly tugged her arrow out of the woman's heart. She used that bloody arrow to first point out a second dead sentry, facedown in the grass, then to indicate a pair of tents beside a low-burning cook fire.

Quauh steadied herself and started forward, but Toomsuba pulled her back. "You stay here and keep watch," the giant man said.

She appreciated that, mostly because there was no judgment evident in the man's tone, with the others all nodding.

"Watch that way," Benny agreed, pointing the way they had come.

Quauh complied, but she wasn't really watching anything, which was the point, as the other seven rushed in at the tents. She tried to block out the grunts and the few screams, and she still hadn't looked back at the camp when Benny returned to her, holding his wet beret in hand.

"Four sheets o' gold set in a half circle atop it," he said, and she nodded.

"That all we need?"

"Dismantle the pyramid and look for gemstones, crystals, metal rods—anything that looks like it might be of some value or magical in nature. But yes, we mostly need the golden mirrors—keep them strung together. Just fold them atop each—"

"We know how to rob a place, Sparkleface," the powrie said with an exaggerated wink, and off he ran.

"And there has to be a cart nearby," Quauh called after him. "They didn't carry them in."

Replacing the mule that had pulled the cart into the jungle, Toomsuba had little trouble pulling the small, two-wheeled cart they found hidden in the brush to the side of the now-dismantled pyramid. The four golden sheets were each nearly seven feet tall and almost two wide, and though very thin, they each weighed as much as Quauh!

They had found four large gems in the stone base, deep red sapphires, each set in a separate block of some gray metal.

The going became slow very soon, as they left the trail and tugged their laden cart over roots and uneven ground, and it only got worse as they approached the cliffs, where the soil was replaced by jagged stones. Before they ever got to the descent, they abandoned the cart altogether. Toomsuba hoisted the back end of the piled golden sheets with two powries at the front, McKorkle and Aushin, soon replaced by Benny and Perridoo.

They came to the cliffs overlooking the bay, where Columbine suggested they cut the wires strung through the four sheets, binding them like a quartet of small jibs, but Quauh would hear none of that.

"These are not mundane items," she explained. "They are magical and very potent."

"And the wires matter for that?" Columbine groused back at her.

"I don't know," she admitted, but she wouldn't give an inch on this matter.

Columbine nodded to the small cove below, where *Pinquickle's Folly* swayed in the gentle roll of the morning tide. "Goin' to take us half the mornin' to get down there."

"They aren't leavin' without us," Benny interjected. "'Specially not when we're coming in thick with gold, eh?"

That broke any tension and ended any debate, and down the troop trudged along the zigzagging trails, with only minor mishaps.

As they neared the bottom of the cliff and the waiting dinghy, they discovered that their sloop was not alone out in the cove: a pair of barrelboats sat beside her.

Massayo watched the approach of those powrie crews from the rail, waving them in, accompanied by none other than Captain Thorngirdle himself, who seemed less than pleased.

"A quarter o' the gold for meself!" they heard Thorngirdle insisting as they neared the sloop. "Bah, but ye was supposed to wait. Me and me boys pedaled all the night, day, and night again to get here, and that treasure's not just for yerselves!"

Quauh was first up on the deck, Columbine close behind. She looked to the prow, where the Durubazzi were finishing the work on the frame they would need.

"It went well?" Massayo asked her.

"I had hoped that we would have prisoners," she answered,

turning a grim look over at the powrie, who stood under a newly bloodied, shining beret.

Columbine shrugged and grinned in reply. "They looked like they wanted a fight."

"While they were sleeping?" Quauh growled at him.

"All the better," said the powrie. "Ye wanted the gold, ye got the gold, and no witnesses to tell tales, eh?"

Massayo offered Quauh a sympathetic look and quietly murmured, "It's an ugly world, my friend."

"Goin' to get uglier if ye're thinkin' that me and me boys didn't earn that gold," Thorngirdle promised.

"I'm thinking no such thing," Massayo replied. "You came in good faith, and so earned your cut, and you'll get it as soon as we're done with it, which, I expect, will be within the week."

"Done with it?"

"We're using it," Massayo replied. "For the benefit of all of us."

"What're ye buyin', then?"

"Nothing."

"Then what?"

"We're using it to rid the seas of Captain Aketz and his miserable frigate."

"Who ye bribing, then?"

"No bribe. No payoff. We're fighting."

"Fighting? The *Crocodile*?"

"And we mean to win," said Massayo. "And we're hoping that you and . . . Are you Two Bits once more?"

"Six Bits."

"Where are the other four?" Quauh asked.

"Ain't bought 'em yet. Give me two sheets o' the gold and I'll get 'em. But even with 'em, I ain't fighting *Crocodile* again. No, mate, me and me boys, what few lived, don't need to be taught twice."

"We need the gold to battle Aketz," Massayo said flatly. "Your share will be given after the fight."

"Aketz is goin' to honor yer word, is he?"

"Your confidence is truly inspiring," Massayo deadpanned.

"He'll put ye to the bottom," Thorngirdle scoffed, "and if the water's not too deep, then be sure he'll go and get the gold. Cap'n Wilkie promised me a quarter if I came out to help ye. I came out to help ye."

"Five bars instead of the sheet," Massayo offered, and he led their gazes to the booty as it was finally hauled up onto the deck. Thorngirdle went over to inspect it, and with help from one of his crew, managed to lift one corner of the top sheet.

"This sheet's seven, at least," he said.

"Aye, but it wouldn't even fit in your barrelboat, and even if it did, you'd have to melt it down to be rid of it. Five is fair, and you can have it now, and when our fight is done, you can change it back to me for one of the golden sheets. Deal?"

"Now?"

"I'll write you the note," Massayo said. "My gold is in the Countinghouse in Dinfawa. They know well my signature. Deal?"

"Deal," said Thorngirdle, but he was shaking his head. "Ye've five bars—more'n that likely—in Dinfawa's Countinghouse, and four sheets o' gold sittin' here. Go to the Drowned Isles and let yer crew make merry for a year. Why would ye want to tangle with *Crocodile?*"

"Because we are unmarqued, like the *Dancing Dolphin*," Quauh interjected. "You met up with Captain Wilkie in Dinfawa because *Cipac* chased him there, and will be in chase again as soon as he sails out."

"We can run and be gone forever," Massayo added. "And who will be next on the list of Captain Aketz? Thorngirdle's new Six Bits, perhaps? No, my friend, it is time to put this savage to the bottom. Captain Wilkie and I plan to do just that, but easier would it be by far if Captain Thorngirdle joined in . . ."

"Not a chance," Thorngirdle interrupted. "Done that once. Once was too many."

There was no debate in his tone or his scowl, a reminder to Massayo and Quauh of the skill and ferocity of their intended target. It took a lot to shake any powrie, and especially one as accomplished as Captain Thorngirdle, who had seen more sea battles than Quauh had seen years of life.

"Well, when we sink him, I expect that you will be equally pleased," Massayo said.

Thorngirdle didn't argue that.

Massayo went to his quarters to pen the note.

"Can't believe ye're still livin', Cap'n Sparkleface," the powrie said to Quauh while they waited. "Good enough for ye. I know Benny always liked ye, and Benny's a good sort."

"He is."

"Might ask him back when I get four more boats."

"It's always his choice, aye," said Quauh with a shrug, but she knew in her heart that Benny wouldn't go. She doubted that any of the five powries would leave Massayo's crew for life on a barrelboat, and that thought made her smile.

"You can help us defeat Captain Aketz," she said to Thorngirdle.

"I just told ye . . ."

"Not like that, not in the fight," she explained.

"Then what?"

"Would you have any flares?"

"Flares? 'Course. Just stocked. Two boxes on each boat."

"Give them to us."

Thorngirdle stared at her skeptically.

"All, if you can. Or as many as you can spare."

"Coordinatin' a light show, are ye?"

"Something like that. The flares would help us immensely, I assure you, and might just tip the battle in our favor. You would like to see the *Cipac* removed from these waters, wouldn't you?"

Thorngirdle stared at her hard for a few heartbeats, then gave a shrill whistle. One of his boys ran over to answer the call.

"Get the flares, all o' them, both boats, and bring 'em to me friend Sparkleface."

The powrie deckhand seemed confused for a moment, staring at Quauh incredulously before running off to carry out the order.

"Back to the ship, boys of *Port Mandu*!" Mister Calloway announced in the tavern in Dinfawa. "You're putting out with the sunrise!"

A lot of grumbles followed, and several crew members drained their glasses, one even calling for one last drink, but it was all a predetermined act.

Mr. Calloway was doing Captain Wilkie's work here, knowing full well that the hated Captain Aketz had eyes and ears in here, and word would get to him within the hour. The crew selected to be in the tavern at this time knew it, too, and so played their appointed roles.

For *Port Mandu* wasn't leaving with the sunrise. The ship had been quietly readied and was going as soon as the crew returned, even in the unfavorable tide.

"Where're ye goin'?" one fellow asked a sailor.

The woman, *Port Mandu*'s lookout, replied, "We're done for the season. Straight for Inudada and a long winter o' drinking for us."

That, too, was a lie, although the course they would take was exactly that which would indeed take them to the Drowned Isles, except that they weren't intending to go that far at all.

All they wanted was a five-hour head start on Aketz, the man they called Captain Fury, and his vicious *Crocodile*.

When they finally spotted *Cipac*'s sails far to the northwest two days later, they knew the ploy had worked and they had gotten the five-hour head start they would need.

CHAPTER 18

REFLECTIONS AND WHITE FIRE

"Sails, port forward!" the lookout of *Port Mandu* called down to Captain Wilkie. "It's *Pinquickle*!"

Wilkie looked at the sun high above and nodded, mumbling, "Right on time." To the lookout, he called, "How far's Massayo, and how far's the *Crocodile*?"

"*Pinquickle*'s sails are at the edge, so might be three leagues," the lookout replied. Then, a moment later, she called down, "Two for the *Crocodile*."

Wilkie wetted his finger and held it up, gauging the wind. He looked to his pennants for confirmation, satisfied that he had properly anticipated the speed and direction.

The winds were favorable now, strong from the east off the hot summer sands, which meant that the larger but less agile *Crocodile* was gaining maximally in the current conditions. Wilkie measured that expected gain against the time it would take him to rendezvous with Massayo, and with enough leeway to put him in the better wind position for the confrontation.

With his jib setup, Captain Wilkie was certain that he

could do more with less wind, certainly more than Aketz might achieve. He turned to his helmsman.

"Keep her steady for another hour, mate. Soon as she calls down from the nest that the *Pinquickle*'s turning north, we'll begin our leeward veer."

With that, he went to his cabin for a drink. He wanted a nap but didn't dare. He had plotted this out with little breathing room. A change in the winds, higher seas, or a mistake by Massayo would force *Port Mandu* to improvise quickly.

There was no room for failure.

Captain Wilkie Dogears laughed as he considered that, since he didn't think there was much of a chance of success even if they were perfect. He couldn't see the *Crocodile* from the deck, of course, since she was still more than six miles away.

He was glad of that.

He didn't want to see the *Crocodile*.

"Yes, yes, I understand that, but *will it work?*" Massayo asked Quauh as they watched the powries hooking the blocks and sheaves in place on the framework.

"I know little of Captain Aketz's new weapon, perhaps no more than you know, and less than Chimeg, who saw its power against the *Swordfish*," she admitted.

"Then all of this is just a guess?"

"How many times will you ask me?"

Massayo looked to the east, where *Port Mandu* was now

clearly visible, tacking and working her jibs hard to keep ahead of the *Cipac*, which was also quite clearly visible, and angling to intercept *Port Mandu*'s run.

"It is a logical guess," Quauh told him, understanding his concern now that the moment of truth, and very possibly of doom, was upon them.

"We have to do more than minimize the effect of that weapon," Massayo remarked.

"I know."

"And if we do not?"

"Then we break south, *Port Mandu* north, and we run, as we agreed," Quauh bluntly replied. "Very likely, Captain Aketz will chase Captain Wilkie."

"And destroy him."

"Almost certainly."

"And destroy us before he ever has to give chase to our friends?" Massayo pressed. "A single volley of those jaws and a hundred flaming arrows should make short work of this little sloop."

"Less certainly, but very possibly."

"Twenty to starboard, Benny," the captain called. "Give Wilkie a little more room to make his turn and gain the wind's favor."

"I told you that our victory was not without doubt," Quauh reminded.

"I know, I know, and you've been honest and loyal through it all. I'll not forget that." Massayo glanced to the northeast and the distant frigate and shuddered visibly. "I am just thinking that perhaps I should have retired in Behren. Too late for that, I suppose."

"Unless we win," said Quauh.

"More likely, unless Aketz decides to kill *Port Mandu* and we somehow survive the first rounds."

Quauh wanted to disagree. She looked forward, where the powries had hit a snag in the ropes as they were trying to feed it through from the golden sheets to the frame. She could only sigh.

Soon after, *Port Mandu* crossed before *Pinquickle's Folly,* who fell behind in her wake as they continued a bit more to the north before beginning their turn back to the east, with Captain Wilkie determining the best wind advantage he could salvage when he made the straight run at the *Crocodile.*

In all that time, Quauh stood by the mainmast, watching the work on the frame, staring at the bullhead, and recalculating her plans, over and over again. Would her father and her lahtli Ayot approve of her strategy here, of how she had reshaped this watery battlefield to afford her ships the best possible chance?

She nodded, finding her courage, which was sapped again almost immediately as she realized that while they might be impressed by the thoughtful strategy, that would be all they would approve of from Quauh the traitor.

If she failed, then her plan failed, and so be it.

If her plan didn't fail, a frigate, the pride of the Tonoloya Armada here in the east, would perish, along with hundreds of her fellow Xoconai.

How had it come to this?

"They led us into an ambush?" an incredulous First Mate Cayo said to Captain Aketz when they saw the two buccaneer vessels running in a line to the north.

"Or this is their desperate attempt to try to get as many away as they can," the captain replied. "They might want us to pick our target and give chase as the other one flees. Likely, Captain Wilkie has transferred to the sloop, thinking we'll again go after the ketch. If they split, we sink the sloop, and both captains with her. Then we'll see what fight the fools on *Port Mandu* have left in them."

"Idiots," Cayo said with a laugh. "These sidhe are such predictably stupid creatures."

The two watched as the larger ship, *Port Mandu*, began her next turn, to port, and continued to port until she was directly lined up with *Cipac*'s bowsprit.

"Are they truly thinking to fight us?" Cayo asked.

"Watch for the sloop," Aketz warned. "Do they think to cripple us, slow us enough with a fight, for their leaders to flee on the smaller craft?"

"What do I do?"

"Ready your wave of light to dry her," the captain reasoned. "We will light her up and run past her to pursue the sloop. We'll need no magic to put that pathetic tub to the bottom."

Cayo called to the other augurs, who took their places around the golden mirrors and the crystal on *Cipac*'s forecastle. They began chanting as soon as they were assembled, and the crystal ball began to glow.

"Let them build the power of Scathmizzane," Cayo explained to Captain Aketz.

"Ready our jaws," Aketz called to his bosun. "Assemble the archers."

"One shot," he told Cayo. "We hit them and run by them."

The augur nodded, but even as he did, both he and Aketz gasped in surprise to see the charging ketch drop to battle sail, and then the sloop, which they had figured to be running straight back behind the visual barrier of the larger ship, appearing beside her, full sail, and running past her, turning back in to replace *Port Mandu*'s line.

Coming straight at *Cipac*!

"The fools are going to try to ram us with the sloop!" Captain Aketz reasoned. "Go to your weapon, Cayo, and send forth the wave!"

"They are launching their wave early," Chimeg called down when the bright light appeared at the prow of the warship and began snaking out toward the buccaneers.

"They think we have been put in front to ram them and cripple them," Massayo replied, and he stared at Quauh as he did, for she had predicted exactly this. "How did you know?" he asked her.

"Because that is what I would do," she answered. "You minimize the sacrifice to get out of an unwinnable situation. Were we to sail hard into the *Cipac*, they would never be able to repair and give chase fast enough to hope to catch *Port Mandu* before she reaches the southern haven."

"Maybe we should have done that, then," said the captain.

Quauh smirked at that, not sure she disagreed. She tried to hold faith in her plan—she had orchestrated this fight, from the split of the two ships ten days before all the way to this moment, and hopefully to the end of the battle.

"If it comes to that, perhaps we still can," she replied.

That seemed to startle the captain, who stared down at her with obvious concern.

Quauh understood more than Captain Massayo wanted to let on with that expression. He would have supported a plan to send the smaller *Pinquickle* in to ram the *Cipac*, but he surely wouldn't have stayed aboard!

So be it, she thought, and she decided not to judge him too harshly.

"The screen?" Massayo asked.

"Wait until the last moment," she answered. "We cannot let them decipher our intent or they'll surely turn and make it all much more tentative." She turned and looked over her shoulder to Toomsuba, who had just finished stretching the bullhead band all the way back and setting it down low for maximum elevation of the shot and maximum range. She motioned him up front to the rope on the starboard side of the frame they had built, with McKorkle and Perridoo holding the one to port.

Her gaze drifted up the mainmast to Chimeg, who had moved into position, standing against the mast extension, her anklet securing her against the gemstones in the strap.

Be perfect in your range estimations, Quauh thought as she looked at the grim-faced To-gai-ru archer, who had watched her friends die from this very weapon and enemy. Quauh didn't bother calling that up to Chimeg, though. She had never met a more competent person in her life.

Chimeg had to be perfect in her sighting, so Chimeg would be perfect. It was that simple.

The ships charged toward each other, the wave of brilliant light extending farther and farther from *Cipac*, closing in on the fast-sailing sloop.

Quauh moved to the back of the forecastle, to the side of the bullhead. Massayo stood on the main deck just below her, moving about nervously. She ignored him—she had to!—and kept her focus on that wave.

"Come on," she urged quietly, speaking to the ship and the wind, and to Chimeg high above.

They had to get in range before that wave reached them, but they had to stay out of the range of *Cipac*'s jaws and archers when they executed the plan. The bullhead could outdistance those side-mounted catapults, certainly, as well as the archers, particularly since the wind was at *Pinquickle Folly*'s back, but the margin for error remained slim and the cost of failure remained complete.

"*Crocodile* at three hundred, the light wave at two!" Chimeg called, at last, and Quauh relaxed just a bit. This magnificent bullhead Massayo had created could throw two hundred yards with some accuracy. A land catapult could exceed that, certainly, but those on the Tonoloya Armada warships couldn't go far beyond a hundred fifty with any hope of hitting anything. She wasn't sure about these side-mounted weapons, which were unique to the *Cipac*, but Quauh doubted they could even reach that.

"The light will be on us before we get in range!" Massayo called up from the deck.

Quauh nodded. "That was the plan."

"If it gets around your mirror . . . ," Massayo warned.

Quauh didn't answer.

"Two fifty for the *Crocodile*!" Chimeg called.

"Powries! Toomsuba! The ropes!" Quauh ordered, for the wave of light was barely thirty yards ahead now and closing fast.

The two powries port and the huge man starboard began hauling immediately, watching each other as they had practiced to make sure that one end of the golden shield didn't go up faster than the other, jamming the lines with a bad angle.

The first sheet of gold unfolded from the stack and climbed within the frame, then the second right behind, then the third and the fourth, putting a six-foot-high, seven-foot-wide wall of magical Xoconai gold across the prow at the base of the bowsprit.

As soon as the shield went up, the haulers secured their ropes fast, then went rushing back to get over the forecastle rail and behind the low wall.

Quauh held her ground but shielded her face and mostly her eyes with a hood as the magical light reached *Pinquickle's Folly*.

Most of it was reflected back, causing a thicker and brighter glow between the closing ships, but more than a bit bled around the mirrors, and she felt the sting of the heat, and could almost hear the wood of the sloop's prow drying.

She growled against the pain and told herself repeatedly that this was the best she could have hoped for.

The shouts and groans up by the prow alerted Captain Aketz to the problem. He rushed up the ladder, and he too cried out as his gaze met the brilliance of the shine of the approaching sloop and the sheer intensity of the light growing between the ships— growing and now flowing over the front of *Cipac*. Drying the beams, the planks, the lines, as with their enemy, and stinging the augurs profoundly.

"That's their play?" Aketz called out, shielding his eyes and his face, but snickering. "They think to defeat us with a mirror?" he laughed, trying to buoy those around him, but he recognized that there was some element of danger here. The buccaneers were conditioning his ship to burn more readily, as he was doing to their lead boat. His first instinct was that this would do no more harm than bring them back to an even field with the pirates, as it was before Cayo and that magical device he had installed. On that even field, Aketz would have no trouble handling a sloop and a ketch, certainly.

But he understood that he might take a serious beating if the enemy could get some fires onto *Cipac*. The victory could come at a great cost.

The light continued to grow, the glow intensifying and the wave coming forth more slowly, it seemed, from their prow, as if the magical light itself was a tangible thing.

The augurs stuttered, and raised their hands to block the pain, and tried to continue their chanting.

The ships were barely two hundred yards apart.

Less than two hundred.

"Captain!" First Mate Cayo pleaded.

"Cease, then!" the angry Aketz yelled back. "They are dried to burn! Ready the catapults! Archers, lift your bows!"

"Protect the payload!" Massayo yelled, for the forecastle was thick with light. "Quauh!"

Quauh stood at the trigger. She understood Massayo's urgency—if the light reached the three crates loaded into the bullhead's throwing pocket, it would be the end of them all.

"Come on," she urged. She could no longer see the *Crocodile*, for the light was simply too intense. "Come on, Chimeg," she whispered.

"One fifty!" the lookout yelled.

That was exactly what Quauh had hoped for, and she tugged that lever for all her life, and wisely fell back, dropping from the forecastle and squeezing her eyes shut as she curled into a ball behind the shielding wall.

For the boxes, specifically weakened, broke apart from the power of the throw, spewing forth their contents, scores and scores of powrie flares, above the golden shield *Pinquickle's Folly* had raised.

Some flew through enough of the intense magical light to ignite before they ever left the sloop, becoming white-hot as they flared, while most of them arced up into the air as spinning gray metal, floating out across the distance to the enemy ship and dipping again into the intense glow as they descended, fourscore little magnesite fireballs swarming the prow, the forecastle, the forward sails of the *Cipac*.

They embedded themselves in magically dried beams and planks, set afire parched rigging, ignited the sails, ignited the archers and crew at the large ship's forecastle!

"She's burning!" Chimeg yelled.

"Hard to port, Benny!" Quauh ordered, and the sloop bent in a left-hand turn almost immediately.

Their work was done here, at least for now, and what a beautiful and terrible job they had done, Quauh noted as the sloop bent out of the magical light and she could better view the warship, her nose roaring in flames, her augurs and crew screaming in pain as the magnesite flares melted through them, and her deck popping with explosions whenever any of those flaming bits of metal got splashed by the spray, or by a crewman foolishly trying to douse a flare.

Captain Aketz watched the rain of fire sweep over the front of his ship, lighting everything, wood and rope and sailcloth, and a dozen crewmen, including three of his five augurs.

First Mate Cayo was at the back of the forecastle, looking down at the captain, when a flare punched through a keg of water sitting beside them.

Cayo was there.

The sudden flash of the keg blowing apart blinded Aketz for a moment, the thunder of the blast shaking him nearly from his feet. He blinked open his eyes, noting one woman with a curved plank from the barrel driven through her belly, splintered shards stabbing her face and shoulders.

The captain turned back to call for his powerful augur.

But Cayo wasn't there.

Nor was the rail anywhere around where Cayo had been standing.

Aketz stumbled and blinked repeatedly. Where had his first mate gone?

He had to let the thought go, for the *Cipac* was still moving forward and the magical weapon was down, but the light remained, now flowing deeper onto the ship, drying it out, aiding the fires.

"Port! All you can to port!" he called frantically to his helmsman, and the wounded frigate began her awkward turn, her foremast burning, her mainsail behind it flapping wildly on her starboard side.

Captain Aketz rushed about, calling his crew to stations, trying to assess the damage and figure out how they might minimize it. He heard a splash and turned to see a thick rope lying on the deck, its end smoking.

They had lost their forward port anchor.

Finally, they came out of the glow.

"Drop the mizzen sails!" one crewman yelled, and Aketz recognized his bosun's voice.

"Water to the mizzen!" another cried.

"Smother the fires where you can. Let 'em burn where you can't!" the bosun instructed. "Check those side-mounted slingers!"

"Archers hold ready!" Aketz added when he caught sight of the sloop, moving out of the way but replaced by *Port Mandu*, coming on at battle sail.

"Oh, you think you've won, fool Wilkie?" Aketz muttered under his breath. Yes, his ship was wounded and would take a long time to get back under sail, but if *Port Mandu* came into range, he still had a large catapult on his quarterdeck, untouched by flames, and two ballistae that could outgun anything the ketch could offer.

He looked to the magical glob of light hanging over the rolling ocean, taking heart that it was diminishing by the heartbeat. These pirates couldn't hit him with flares again to any great effect.

"Starboard jaw's broken!" one man yelled from the front.

"Port jaw's intact," another said.

Captain Aketz nodded, his mind whirling as he considered all that he and his crew must do not only to get out of this, but to win the day.

"Get a gunnery crew on that forward jaw," he barked. "And another to repair the starboard jaw!" He turned about and ran for the stern, yelling to the gunners on the main catapult to load her thick and be ready to throw.

As soon as he said it, Aketz understood the problem here, for the *Cipac* was rolling and turning to the commands of the sea, not her wheel. He ordered the remaining forward anchor dropped, along with both off the stern.

They could not maneuver, but from a stable platform, those two lesser ships would be easy prey, from whatever angle they chose to engage.

"She's turning!" the lookout called down.

Aketz ran to the starboard rail. The magical glow was almost gone and no longer impeding his view, and far to starboard now, he noted the sloop coming for him once more.

"Come on, dogs," he muttered, then told the man with him to go to the quarterdeck catapult. "When she gets within one fifty, let fly," he instructed.

The woman ran off and Aketz turned his gaze to the larger buccaneer ship, which had turned to starboard as he had turned to port and now was out there, some three hundred yards away, he thought, sailing easily to circle the wounded *Cipac*.

Captain Wilkie was measuring the *Cipac*'s wounds, he knew.

Aketz did the same. They were considerable, he had to admit, but the ship wasn't bleeding much anymore, the crack crew working brilliantly to contain the damage.

"Round incoming starboard!" the lookout yelled.

Aketz spun back to regard the sloop, and the large ball flying in at his ship. He almost yelled for his gunners on the quarterdeck to return fire, but realized that the little sloop was still well over two hundred yards away.

"How?" he asked, and stood straight, and stayed right there as a volley of heavy stones splashed into the water, cracked hard against *Cipac*'s starboard broadside, and bounced across the deck and masts, blasting the life from more than a few of his crew.

Luck alone stopped Aketz from being pummeled.

Bad luck, he thought fleetingly, but he shook it away. He had no idea how that little ship was carrying a weapon capable of reaching them from this distance, but whatever it might be, he understood that the sloop wasn't capable of carrying enough rounds to do more than minor damage.

The sloop turned again and began running parallel to *Cipac*, circling left to right around the stern, while *Port Mandu* circled right to left around *Cipac*'s prow.

"Barracuda waiting for the crocodile to die," Aketz remarked. He started as he noted several of his crew near him, all staring at him nervously.

"We're not going to die," he told them with a wicked smile. "We're just going to find a way to make them think we are."

The Xoconai crew, warriors all, nodded grimly. "If any of those pirate dogs come within range, I want a hundred arrows sweeping their deck."

"Aye, captain," every voice around answered.

"I cannot find Cayo, Captain Aketz," a man, an augur—the last remaining priest on *Cipac*—said to him then.

"And you will not," Aketz assured him. He looked back to the blasted, scorched corner of the forecastle, and almost laughed at the absurdity of it all when he noted a single shoe, Cayo's shoe, sitting there, smoke wafting from it.

"We can run now," Massayo told Wilkie when the two ships came together some three hundred yards off the wounded *Crocodile*'s port rail. "They'll be a week and more rigging it up enough just to limp home."

"And then what?" Wilkie replied.

"And now what?" Massayo returned. "We have the range, but nowhere near enough shot to take her down. He's still got a hundred archers if he's got one."

"Aye, she ain't sinking," Wilkie admitted with a shake of his head. But he did offer a wide smile to Massayo, and mostly to Quauh, who had formulated this wild plan. "But we hit her good, eh?"

"Maybe we hit her a couple more times with the bullhead, then ask Aketz to surrender," Massayo offered.

"He will not," said Quauh. "Never."

"Well, your plan worked brilliantly," Wilkie said to her. "Got another?"

Quauh could only shrug. "We can run, safely," she offered.

Wilkie considered that for a moment, then went across his deck. "Run up a flag demanding surrender," he told his first mate. To others, he called for the tripod and megaphone to be set, aiming for their wounded enemy.

He waited for the responding flag and wasn't surprised by its red color, a flat refusal to even parley, let alone surrender.

"Ye can't win, Captain Fury!" Wilkie called out.

"Not today," came the reply. "But soon."

"We'll let ye go without further troubles if ye remove yer curse on our Letters of Reprisal and let it be as it was!" said Wilkie.

"You played your hand," came the response. "The pot is yours. And I will take it back from your hull on the bottom o' the Mirianic!" Captain Aketz promised.

Wilkie walked away from the bullhorn and waved for it to be broken down. Over at the rail across from Massayo, he said,

"We've a couple of flares. We'll put one over her when the moon's set and the night is dark so you can line up the throw. Put one on her deck in the dark of night and might that Captain Fury there will rethink his stubborn ways."

Massayo winked and smiled in reply, and *Pinquickle's Folly* lifted her sails and began to circle once more.

"He won't rethink anything," Quauh assured Massayo as they pulled away form *Port Mandu*. "You will have to sink them or kill Captain Aketz to get any kind of offer."

"Then maybe we'll put the throw right under his quarterdeck and spin the fool about in his bunk," Massayo replied with that toothy, wicked grin.

Quauh returned the smile but knew the boast for what it was. At the range they needed to maintain, in the dark of night with the seas rolling about them, they'd be lucky to hit the frigate at all, let alone target their shot to any specific point.

He turned to face his working crew, a fat and stubby finger banging against his pursed lips, then silently mouthing, "Quiet, quiet."

Slowly, the legs turned.

He turned back to his mirrored spyglass, looking forward into the angled mirror that looked up at a second angled mirror looking down, showing him what was forward of his boat.

He started in surprise when the view lit up before him, a flare, arcing beautifully on the other side of the large ship, backlighting it like the moon rising behind a dead tree.

Fitting, he thought, and he smiled to realize how close they were.

Captain Thorngirdle turned and called, "Now, me boys! Push it with all ye got!"

Ten powrie pedalers leaned forward and began pumping their legs with all their strength, all of them growling and driving hard.

The flare came to life forward of *Cipac*, rising high in the night sky.

"Throw! Fire!" yelled Aketz, and the working front side-mounted catapult let fly, and the crew at the rear turned their cranks to get the bigger catapult in line, and Xoconai archers bent their bows and sent missiles into the darkness.

Captain Aketz rushed to the forward rail and leaned out, staring, following the ball of glowing pitch that soared ahead.

And then splashed into the ocean, very near the ketch, but causing no damage.

"Come on!" he screamed back to his aft gunners, wanting to strike that pirate down there and then.

His bosun beside him shook his head, though. "They have to put it over our own masts," he explained. "Too high an angle. We'd just waste the load."

"Then ready the forward thrower, and get that second one fixed, damn you!"

"Aye," the bosun replied, and moved away.

Aketz turned his attention to the flare, which now arced

gracefully high above and came down, illuminating the frigate's starboard rail.

And blinding him to what might be beyond it, he knew.

"Throw that aft load starboard!" he called. "Archers, full volley starboard!"

Barely had he finished the orders when he heard a great splash just forward of his ship, and the sly captain grinned at his cleverness.

The flare from the ketch had been only to allow the sloop to move in to fire its strange weapon.

"Ballistae to starboard!" he yelled. "Throw! Throw!"

They couldn't see the sloop, for it was outside the glow of the flare, but it was out there, and Aketz meant to make life very uncomfortable for the buccaneer rats. He slapped his hand on the rail, calling for a bullhorn so he might taunt them for their miss. How many loads could that small ship carry, after all?

The jolt came behind him, near the stern on the port side, and hit with such force that many crewmen were thrown from their feet, one tumbling over the port rail. The frigate groaned in protest, her stern pushed to the limit of the anchor lines and more.

Captain Aketz's thoughts spun. In other years, he might have thought that a whale had rammed them, but out here in the east, he understood the dangerous truth of it.

"Lights to starboard!" he yelled, turning and moving that way.

Out of the corner of his eye, he caught a flicker in the flare light, and he spun back just in time to see a second barrelboat streaming in for the starboard prow.

"Powrie!" he yelled, reflexively moving back from the rail and jabbing his finger in the direction of the closing hunter.

He should have held the rail instead, for he found himself unceremoniously dropped on his butt when that second barrel-boat speared the *Cipac*.

"Back, back and keep backing!" Thorngirdle ordered his boys, who reversed their pedaling with growls of determination, pulling the tapered spear-like ram free of the frigate. Normally they would have stayed there, embedded, and come out to board and fight, but they were twelve and the crew of the large ship nearer to two hundred.

Stick and run, was the plan. Back into the darkness.

Working the rudder far aft, the powrie kept them perfectly straight as they moved away form the warship.

They heard the arrows tap-tapping their topside hull, like a heavy rain, and waited in silence for a larger throw from a ballista, or maybe those devilish chains that had jammed the rudder and propeller on one of their boats in their last fight with this frigate and doomed both ship and crew to a horrible and irretrievable death.

They breathed easier with each passing minute, and finally were far enough away for Captain Thorngirdle to order a turn, all the way about, so *One o' Two* could pedal off into the night.

He could only hope his second boat had found the same good fortune.

"It was a good try," Quauh said to Massayo after their shot missed the distant *Cipac. Better this one miss than the one full of flares from the initial encounter,* she thought, but did not add.

The returning fire had been more dangerous than their bullhead attack, obviously, with the deck of *Pinquickle's Folly* sporting a dozen new feathers, all on the back of Xoconai arrows. A ballista bolt had skipped through the water right past the fleeing sloop's starboard rail. Only good fortune had prevented a damaging hit on her stern.

"It was a foolish try," Massayo admitted, nodding at the first mate, who had counseled him against it. He ended with a sigh of dispirited resignation, for he so badly wanted to be rid of the *Crocodile* and her vicious captain.

But now he had to resign himself to the truth of the fight. For all their successes the previous day—the frigate would likely need to replace her foremast—and for all their advantages in maneuvering now, there was little more they could do against the formidable battle station. They could move about just beyond the range of the *Crocodile*'s archers and catapults, yes, but from that distance, their chances of inflicting any real damage on the large ship was small, and they would fast run out of loads to throw. And as good as the bullhead was performing, Aketz could adjust his two ballistae to return fire.

And that clever captain would likely come up with a few other tricks to add to Massayo's misery.

Every passing hour, it was becoming more and more likely

that *Port Mandu* and *Pinquickle's Folly* would be taking an early exit to the south this year, possibly never to return.

Given Massayo's grander plans, already insanely expensive and already well under way, that pain was all the more acute.

"Keep us moving, and not predictably," he instructed Quauh. "Set watches along all rails and tell them to remain alert. It would not be a surprise to see Captain Aketz sending out small boats of archers to strike us in the night. I am off to get some rest. The deck is yours."

"Aye, captain," she answered.

Massayo didn't intend to sleep, but he was out very soon after rolling into his hammock, sheer exhaustion overwhelming the many questions and concerns that followed him to his bed.

He was awakened suddenly, jostled by Quauh, and opened his eyes to find her staring down at him.

"To the deck, captain," she said. "At once."

"Trouble?"

"It would seem so, but not for us."

Massayo rolled to the side and put his long legs to the floor. It took him a moment to steady himself, a moment in which he realized that the sun was up. He stumbled out of his cabin, yawning, and noted that most of his crew, Quauh included, were at the port rail, and also that his ship was barely moving and that *Port Mandu* was right before her.

"What?" he asked, walking up near Quauh and noting the distant frigate.

"She's low and she's listing," Quauh explained. "She took a lot of water, it seems, and is likely taking more."

Massayo peered more intently and shifted to get a better view.

Unmistakably so, he realized, the *Crocodile* seemed lower in the water, and, after he ruled out a roll from a swell, he saw that she was listing to starboard at perhaps fifteen to twenty degrees.

"Did we hit her?" he asked. "Perhaps the stone splashed right before her waterline and still got to her hull."

"If we had, it would have been on her port side," Quauh reminded him. "Whatever happened, she's wounded. Perhaps the flare fires got belowdecks."

Massayo didn't answer other than to shake his head slightly. That didn't seem plausible.

"Wilkie?" he asked.

"As befuddled as we are," Quauh answered, "they spent their night watching for small attack boats, as we were, and saw the same surprise as we when the sun showed us our enemy."

Massayo called for his spyglass, then studied the frigate more closely. "Even if he somehow gets his mainsail up this very morning, he's not going to get that ship to port anytime soon. And if he's still taking water, and I think he is, that crew will not see land again."

"Unless we rescue them," Quauh remarked.

That surprised Massayo for just a moment, until he considered the source. Quauh was a decent one, to be sure. Decent to any and all. The impracticality of such a move was hard to get past, of course, given that the *Crocodile* had more than four times the crew, warriors all, than *Pinquickle's Folly* and *Port Mandu* combined.

"We've got company coming to starboard!" Chimeg called down from the lookout nest.

Three long strides across the deck took any concern from Massayo, for he came in view of a pair of powrie barrelboats, slowly approaching *Port Mandu*. Captain Thorngirdle sat on the top of one, leaning back rather comfortably, it seemed, against the vertical brace beam.

"Put a couple o' holes in her last night while yerselves were throwin' flares and such," the powrie called. "Sea's bleeding into her, bow and stern, don't ye doubt."

"Ye hear that, Captain Massayo?" Captain Wilkie called from his rail.

"I did, indeed."

"Run up your green-and-white," said Wilkie. "I think our Captain Fury friend might be interested in talking. You will speak for *Port Mandu*, and . . ." He looked to Thorngirdle.

The powrie snorted. "Don't got much to say. Said it all already with the pointy end. Get the goldfish off the ship soon enough and me boys and I will gladly go and see if she's got anything worth salvaging."

"Run up the pennant," Massayo instructed Quauh. "Toomsuba, put a load of chains and grape in the pocket and stretch the bullhead to ready. Battle sail," he added to Columbine. "If they show their pennant, bring us in slowly."

He lifted his spyglass and considered the wounded frigate then, and also Thorngirdle's words. There was something on the *Crocodile* he wouldn't mind salvaging.

Two somethings, actually.

The responding pennant went up *Cipac's* line, and *Pinquickle's Folly* began her approach. They got to a hundred yards, noting that the Xoconai captain had set up his large bullhorn, and turned broadside to the frigate, starboard to starboard, with enough sea between them to afford them a good chance of safely fleeing.

"We are here to discuss terms," Massayo called. "You are sinking, clearly. You have lost. We could stand back and let the sea take you, then hunt any dinghies you launch and easily destroy them. We both know this, so . . ."

"The terms start with our guaranteed safety and an escort to a safe harbor," Captain Aketz called back. "Do not think you have won, pirate. We can bail and stay up, and we have enough supplies to outlast you. If you help tow us in, I will offer a probation to you and to Captain Wilkie. You can sail these waters as *honest* traders. Only as such."

Massayo turned a skeptical look to Quauh.

"He's sinking," she quietly answered that expression. "He knows that he cannot survive without our tow."

"Do you think he would hold to the deal?"

She nodded without hesitation. "He is vicious, but he is a captain in the Tonoloya Armada. His word must be good." She paused, and Massayo saw her curiosity clearly. "Are you thinking of accepting?"

"It's more than I expected," he admitted.

"And Captain Wilkie? And Captain Thorngirdle?" Quauh asked.

"Never," came a voice from above, that of Chimeg, who had moved down to the main yard and was watching the two with a sour look.

"Still, a good start," Massayo told her, and she snorted and climbed back up the mast.

"We will tow the *Croc*—the *Cipac*, into Azucar," Massayo called back. "It is not so far a sail. But only on the word of Captain Aketz that he will lift the order of unmarque from all of us, and that he will retire to the west, where he and his people properly belong."

Aketz started to protest, but Massayo yelled long and loud into the bullhorn until the man relented and let him finish.

"And before any of this, I will see two hundred bows, a thousand arrows, two ballistae, and the arms of your catapults thrown into the sea."

Captain Aketz sputtered and snorted like a raging hog for several moments. "Are you mad?" he yelled. "Do you see the flag you now insult? I've a deck lined with the best archers on these waters and two ballistae and a catapult ready to take you from the water right now!"

High above the deck, Chimeg stood against the rail, listening to the shouting, but hardly hearing the words, her gaze locked on the vicious Captain Fury, the man who had tortured her friends and tied poor Jocasta to the prow of the *Swordfish* and let the tide slam it, and her, into jagged rocks.

Aketz continued his tirade into the huge bullhorn, scolding Massayo, retracting his initial offer, and making a second one, far less enticing. He promised to hunt the sloop, the ketch, and the powries until they were all properly keeled or hanged or fed to sharks if Massayo didn't agree right then to tow them in.

And he kept going, the ravings of a man who thought himself impervious, who was verbally spitting on them as if they were his lessers, as if they were sidhe.

Hardly aware of her actions, Chimeg reversed the magnetism in her ankle bracelet and threw herself out in a swing to *Pinquickle's Folly*'s stern, then came swinging back in and used the magic to shift her momentum and throw her out above Massayo and Quauh and the others, out beyond the sloop's starboard rail.

Her bow came up, an arrow nocked, and what a marvelous target the wide end of the bullhorn made!

The missile skipped into the megaphone and was funneled right to Captain Fury's opened mouth, catching him in mid-roar and driving through the back of his mouth and his brain stem.

He uttered no sound, but just dropped to the deck.

In that moment of shock, the first to react were Toomsuba and the four powries, lifting the sails, while Benny worked to get them away.

"What did you do?" Massayo called up from the deck, while Quauh was telling the crew to find cover.

"Gave the dog a better death than he deserved," Chimeg muttered. She continued to swing, setting another arrow to her bowstring, ready to respond to any who fired at the fleeing sloop.

Surprisingly few missiles came forth, however. A couple of archers put arrows into the sloop, while many more let fly at

Chimeg. Only one of the ballistae fired, the long spear crashing through the wall of the quarterdeck cabin and hanging there, half-in and half-out.

"Now what?" Massayo asked Quauh, crouching beside her at the rail.

"I do not know," she answered honestly.

"What would you do if you were first mate on the *Cipac*?"

She considered the question for a long while, holding her answer until they were far enough away for her and Massayo to stand and head for the quarterdeck. The captain paused and opened the door to his cabin before going up the ladder.

"Right into the side of my desk," he groused. "My favorite desk."

He joined Quauh at the taffrail, the two staring back at the immobile frigate.

"Well?" Massayo prompted.

Quauh pointed to the *Cipac*'s green-and-white, now being pulled down the line. "I'd take the green-and-white down," she said. "As they are. Then I would survey my crew and replace it with a flag that was only white."

"Surrender?"

"They are sinking. Two hundred Xoconai will drown or be adrift in small boats—and any of those boats approached by us will have to surrender or be sent to the bottom."

"I hope you are right," Massayo said. He directed Quauh's gaze up to Chimeg, standing once more against the mainmast high above.

"And what do I do with her?" he asked.

"She broke a sacred truce," Quauh replied. "Even by your buccaneer code, that must be recognized."

"She watched that beast torture and murder her best friend," Massayo reminded.

"And?"

"And what do I do?" an aggravated and frustrated Massayo snapped at her.

"You say that *Cipac* shot first, but Chimeg shot better," Quauh replied, quite casually.

Quauh was still mulling over that conversation when *Pinquickle's Folly* approached *Port Mandu*, hardly believing that she had spoken such sea-code blasphemy.

But she found, upon reflection, that she stood by the actions taken by the bucccaneers.

"That went well, eh?" Captain Wilkie snorted as the sloop came up alongside.

"Captain Fury is no more," Massayo replied. He looked up and pointed up at Chimeg. "Right into the bullhorn and right into his big mouth."

Thorngirdle slapped his thigh and gave a hearty laugh, while Wilkie just guffawed and shook his head.

"It's their move, and if they don't make a move, we just let them sink," Massayo said.

"There's their move," Quauh informed him, turning him

and the other captains back to the frigate, where a new pennant was being pulled up the line.

Massayo lifted his spyglass, then chuckled, shook his head, and stared at Quauh.

"It is the right thing for the first mate to do," the woman explained. "He didn't lose the ship, and the captain who did lies dead on her deck. They'll put up the green-and-white again shortly. You go to over to *Port Mandu*, captain, and take all but the powries and Toomsuba with you. And especially take Chimeg. I will go and deliver our terms."

"And what might they be?" Thorngirdle demanded.

"They throw their bows and arrows into the sea and we will tow them in, just outside of Azucar. There, we'll let them ferry all their crew ashore and we'll let the sea take the *Cipac*."

"When the goldfish leave her, me an' me boys're going aboard," Thorngirdle said.

"We'll split whatever treasure we find evenly, four ways," Captain Wilkie decided. "One for me, one for Massayo, and one for each of your boats."

"Fair's fair," Thorngirdle agreed.

"I want her ballistae, and maybe that back catapult," Wilkie went on. "And her cloth."

"Coming out o' yer cut," said the powrie captain, and Wilkie nodded.

"I want her jaws," Massayo announced.

Thorngirdle snorted. "Them front guns? Ha! They'll weigh the front o' yer dinghy tub right under!"

"I know, but I want them."

Captain Wilkie stared at the man after that surprising request.

"You'll carry them to Freeport for me?" Massayo asked him, and Wilkie nodded, but never blinked.

"Freeport or Inudada?" Wilkie asked.

"Freeport," Massayo answered. "We've time, and we'll beat word of the sinking of the *Crocodile*, or maybe we'll take that word with us."

Wilkie just stood staring for a few more heartbeats before nodding his agreement.

"South for us," said Thorngirdle. "Got four more boats to buy and fill." He leaned over the rail and looked across *Pinquickle*'s deck. "Ye hear that, ye bloody-capped lubbers? We can get ye back in a proper boat!"

The five all grinned widely at that, but one by one, they politely declined with a shake of their hairy heads.

"Bah! Ye fools!" Thorngirdle said, his light tone belying his snorting. "Yerself and yer boys stinged him, aye," he said to Massayo and Wilkie, "but don't ye e'er forget and don't ye let anyone else e'er forget that it was me and me boys who put the *Crocodile* down."

Quauh took it all in, her gaze landing on Massayo and there lingering.

He was up to something, as usual.

CHAPTER 19

TRIM HER IN GOLD

"We came back for you, because you earned it," Massayo told Quauh when they came in sight of Freeport's southern harbor weeks later. The evacuating and scuttling of the *Cipac* went well. They towed the ship to Azucar, anchored her off the northern coast, ferried the crew to the harbor, then let the ship die against the rocks—after getting all they could of value off her.

They sailed back to Dinfawa from there to withdraw their holdings from the Countinghouse, which Massayo did mostly in the dark of night with his co-conspirators, funneling the gold bars belowdecks and once more securing them under the planks of the hold.

Now they were back in the north, their last trip before their long sail to Inudada and a winter of respite in the safety and hedonistic paradise of the Drowned Isles.

Quauh gave the helm to Columbine to get them in and just took in the sights as they glided past the many, many moored ships. Ships of all types and flying under all the different flags of the region, including more than a few who wore the red 'n' black. She had so much more insight now into the meaning behind all those flags and the politics of the region, the value of the people—not sidhe, for even thinking such a thing was folly.

She felt as if she had learned more about the world in the months with the buccaneers than in the decades previous.

And maybe, she had learned more about herself.

That last part bothered her.

She was drawn from her contemplations by a most beautiful sight: that same vessel she had seen under repair or perhaps initial construction on their earlier visit to Freeport Harbor. More work had been done on the ship, and she seemed even more graceful somehow, with her rigging lines set on the long bowsprit and her floating quarterdeck catching the reflections of the waves on its freshly varnished sides.

Massayo seemed quite insistent in telling half the crew to go ashore late that afternoon, the musicians and the seven Durubazzi, who had been too busy with their duties to find the opportunity to leave the boat on their short visit a few weeks before. He implored them to go and walk as free men and women. To the surprise of Quauh and everyone else watching, Massayo even handed out a generous amount of silver coins to them all.

"Better clothes, better shoes, and whatever else makes this stopover worth your time," he told them, and he lifted his own shoe to show off the rubber sole. "But stick together, and if trouble finds you, you tell them you're with Wilkie and Massayo."

Toomsuba and Benny ferried them in with the dinghy, which took two trips.

"That coin's coming out o' yer own split, aye?" Columbine asked when the second dinghy had launched, leaving Columbine and his three powrie companions alone on *Pinquickle's Folly* with Massayo, Quauh, and Chimeg. "Figuring we're done for the season now and it's time to divvy Benny's gold, eh?"

"Quit worrying about the split, good Columbine," Massayo replied. "We have investments to make."

"Not sure I'm likin' the sound o' that," said the scraggly-bearded, broad-shouldered Perridoo. He put on an expression then to fit his red-glowing beret and wild red hair, which hung down his face to either side of a crooked nose that spoke of a lot of fights.

"You will be," Massayo promised. "We need to be getting most of this gold off-loaded quickly. We've a long row ahead and we can't be taking chances."

"Ye going to tell us where we're goin'?" Columbine demanded.

"I'm going to show you."

"And if we're not agreeing?"

"Then you're fools. Chimeg, up and on watch," he ordered. "Make sure none are too interested in our work here this night. Now, come, all of you. Belowdecks to retrieve the booty."

"How many bars?" Columbine asked.

"All but five."

That brought gasps and doubting looks from all the others, even Quauh.

"The five for Cap'n Thorngirdle?"

"Those were left in the Countinghouse for him to retrieve, and I suspect he's got them already."

"And where's the rest?" Columbine asked.

"The rest is here, all of it."

"Then ye gived Wilkie his two shares already," Columbine remarked slyly.

"I am investing it for him," Massayo insisted, leading them to the hatch.

They had all the gold ready for off-loading by the time Benny and Toomsuba returned from their last ferry to Freeport. Massayo met the rowboat and told the crew to tie it up, then gathered his most trusted inner circle and the four powries who had an interest, in his cabin.

"Chimeg and Toomsuba will remain on *Pinquickle*," he explained, and when Toomsuba wore a disappointed look, he added, "The boat will be weighed down with gold, and I fear that your great girth will put them under."

It was an obvious excuse, of course, but Toomsuba sighed, flexed his great and huge arms, and accepted it.

"Once we go out from *Pinquickle*, there is no talking. Not a sound. You all understand what we're carrying here and how it might interest everyone else moored in this harbor."

"It'd be a bit finer if we knew where we were going," Columbine complained.

"Aye, ye're askin' for a lot o' trust," added McKorkle.

"I am asking you now, all of you, if you wish to formally and under oath remain as part of my crew."

That brought a lot of curious looks.

"I am the captain of *Pinquickle's Folly*," Massayo stated flatly. "Does anyone here wish to challenge that?"

"If we did, we'd've gone with Thorngirdle back in Azucar," Columbine reminded.

"A fine scow, at best, so I ain't seein' much worth challenging," Perridoo snorted.

The powrie at his side began to laugh.

"Shut up, Ohshit," Benny warned.

"No?" Massayo asked.

"Yerself's the captain," Columbine agreed. "None of us're challenging that—and why would we? Ye led a couple o' good fights out there."

"Good. And my first mate is Quauh here," Massayo added. "She earned it over and over again, aye? She knows our enemies better than any of us. This was her jacket, the jacket of an armada captain."

"One who got her boat put to the bottom," Columbine reminded him.

"She hadn't a chance," Benny said. "Besides, she's good enough folk, and tough, too. Anyone here heard a word of complaint about her missing hand?"

"Benny is helmsman, Toomsuba commands the rigging crew, and Chimeg, the watch," Massayo explained. "And you, Columbine . . ."

The powrie narrowed his gaze.

Massayo looked to Quauh. "Been acting it, aye?"

"Aye, and well," she answered.

"I name Columbine as bosun of *Pinquickle's Folly*."

Columbine's expression softened immediately.

"Third in command, whose word carries power, and whose advice to me will be met with an open mind and a grateful smile."

"Ye hardly know me."

"But I see the loyalty these other three worthy sailors show to you," Massayo replied. "We are a team or we are all lost."

"If we're a team, then why's Massayo decidin' all about the gold, hey?" asked McKorkle.

"Fair point," the captain conceded. "So let us go and let us be silent, and I'll show you the investment I have planned. Any who disagree will get their cut, but then they're out of the crew, because I'll not sail with any who puts himself so far above his fellows. Fair enough?"

"Worth a look," Bosun Columbine decided.

They set off in the dinghy as soon as the gold was loaded, with Massayo directing from the prow, Columbine and Perridoo immediately behind him. On the middle bench, Benny and McKorkle each handled an oar, leaving Quauh with Aushin at the stern.

Quauh watched the captain carefully, noting how he kept glancing side to side, though whether to see if they were being watched or in search of something, she could not tell. She cracked a smile when she noted that their course would take them past that strange and graceful ship she had seen when she had first come into this harbor. No lights showed on her deck, but her silhouette against the green glow of the equatorial aurora could not be mistaken. The individual differences were somewhat subtle, but the overall design was very different from anything else in the harbor—indeed, from any vessel Quauh had ever seen.

Her excitement grew as they drew ever closer. She thought at first that Massayo was using this dark vessel to block the view of some other ship, but no, that was not the case, she realized even as the dinghy quietly pulled in under the flying stern of the ship. Two cords were hanging there from the floor of the elevated stern, a long and thick hemp line, which Massayo grabbed and used to tie off the dinghy, and a shorter one. He reached up and snatched that one, tugged on it twice, then paused, then tugged thrice.

Up above, Quauh heard the muffled ring of a bell with each pull.

She could barely see it in the dark, but a trapdoor opened directly above them and a hand came forth, guiding a rope ladder to Massayo.

"Up oars," he quietly instructed Benny and McKorkle, then he motioned for all to follow him.

Up the ladder he went, disappearing through the trapdoor and into the flying quarterdeck, then reached back down as the powries fed up the small sacks of gold bars.

Columbine, Perridoo, Benny, and McKorkle followed in short order. Quauh waved for Aushin to go next, but the powrie shook his head, pointed to her half arm, and invited her to go first. She did, and was a bit surprised, a bit shocked, momentarily outraged, but finally grateful when Aushin, the troublesome malcontent they had all labeled as Ohshit, put his hand against her backside and helped push her upward, steadying her as she used her one good hand to climb.

She came into a dark room, smelling the others all about her, hearing their breathing. She couldn't even make out their silhouettes, so dark was it, but she fumbled her way aside from the hatch and reached back to take Aushin's hand, pulling him up. No sooner had he cleared the hatch area than the creaking trapdoor was lifted over and back in place, and no sooner had the hatch been sealed than a single candlelight flared to life, revealing now nine people about the small unfurnished room, with the humans all sitting, for even the powries had to crouch a bit under the low ceiling.

Massayo introduced his crew to the two people Quauh did not know, a man and a woman from the great northern land of Alpinador. Both were sitting, but even so, she could tell that they were quite tall—the man probably taller than Massayo. Both were light-skinned, tattooed, and bejeweled. The right half of the man's face was light blue, and both of his light gray eyes were thickly circled in dark eye shadow, with his eyelids glazed in smoky gray. His head was shaved on the sides, but the center mop of hair was long and golden, trailing down behind and back over his shoulders like a scarf. Several silver rings pierced his left nostril, and he wore a heavy chain of silver about his muscular neck.

His vest was sleeveless, his bare arms chiseled with muscle, adorned with tattoos of symbols Quauh didn't recognize, with his wrists sporting a pair of black leather bracers that nearly engulfed the whole of his muscular forearms.

Everything about him spoke of action, of power, of intensity, and Quauh felt a little shiver along her spine just looking at him.

The woman was no less exotic, and strangely beautiful, Quauh thought. Her hair was thick and long, some of it braided, most of it loose and wavy. Streaks of purple had been dyed into the raven mane. Her eyes were completely encircled with the same eyeliner as her partner, along with dark eye shadow. But hers were crystal blue, such a startling contrast to the aura of darkness about her. When she smiled, her teeth showed brilliant whiteness, and showed, too, a pair of sharpened fangs.

Her flicking tongue played constantly with those canines, which Quauh found very distracting—and which she soon enough realized was intended to be distracting.

She wore earrings dangling bloodred jewels and had tears of blood tattooed under her right eye, running down her cheek. Her feet were bare, toenails painted red, and she wore pants sealed tight about her calf just below her knees. Her blousy white shirt was tied up just under her breasts, revealing a midriff angled with hard muscle. She kept the sleeves rolled up to her elbow, revealing many hoop bracelets of various metals on her left arm, and a tattoo of a red skull on her right forearm.

Quauh got the sense that she was calmer than the other, not on the edge of explosion, but also that she was likely more dangerous, and in more ways than murder.

"And this is Yrsa," Massayo told the crew, indicating the woman. "And her friend Skardey."

"Bloody caps?" Skardey said, and it was obvious that the

cursed name had been on his lips since the time the candle had been lit, at least. "You bring powries to Dame Yrsa's artwork?"

"I bring my crew," Massayo corrected.

The man started to argue, but Yrsa slapped him on the side of the head to shut him up.

"Massayo trusts powries?" she asked.

"If any of us could be trusted, would we really be pirates?" Massayo answered lightly.

The woman tilted her head so that her thick hair cascaded over one eye, which made her stare with the visible eye seem all the more intense.

"I trust them, mighty Yrsa," Massayo explained. "We have formed a bond, a gallery of misfits who take comfort in this new family."

"A goldfish?" Yrsa said with a laugh, and she crawled over to Quauh, moving very close, almost nose to nose, where she sniffed loudly. "Yes, a painted devil." She laughed and turned back to Massayo.

"A goldfish captain," Massayo replied. "Formerly. And now my first mate, and a treasure of knowledge."

Skardey snorted with obvious derision, but Yrsa's howl of laughter buried that sound and that sentiment.

"That is what I like about you, my friend," she said. "You always surprise me. You are not boring." She snapped her head around, startling Quauh, who was still very close. "Are you?"

Quauh didn't have any idea of how to respond to that, but she didn't shy away at all, matching stares and scowls until Yrsa's face at last softened into a toothy grin.

"You have all the gold?" she asked Massayo.

"All of it and more," he answered, nodding toward the sacks.

"More?" Columbine said, and he didn't seem pleased.

All eyes went to the bosun.

"Massayo knows that he gets what he pays for," Yrsa told the dwarf.

"Aye, and what's he payin' for?"

"A xebec."

"A what?"

"You are sitting in it," Massayo answered.

It took a moment for that to register with any of them, but when Quauh realized the truth of it, she gasped aloud, bringing Yrsa's face back around.

"Sittin' in it?" Columbine echoed.

"Ye took me gold and bought a boat?" Benny asked sourly.

"Not just a boat," Quauh heard herself saying before Massayo could respond, and before Yrsa, or more likely, Skardey, could leap up and pummel the powrie.

That brought a hush to all, and eight sets of eyes settled on Quauh.

"You purchased this boat?" Quauh asked Massayo. "This . . ." She looked to Yrsa.

"Xebec," the woman said, seeming pleased and proud, for Quauh hadn't hidden her feelings from them with her excited tone.

"Is she as swift as she looks?" she asked Yrsa, who smiled even wider.

"Faster!"

"And she'll turn inside a carrack," Quauh said.

Yrsa glanced back at Massayo. "Ah, my beautiful captain, you have found a treasure in this one." As she spoke, she dropped a hand familiarly on Quauh's shoulder.

Quauh noted Massayo's nod, but her eyes then went to that skull tattoo. She realized that it was covering a large and deep scar, as if a chunk of Yrsa's forearm had been gouged away.

No, not gouged, but bitten, as if by a shark.

"We saw you come in," Yrsa said. "The bullhead? There are whispers that you put it to use on a goldfish carrack."

"One shot for *Golden Augur*," Massayo replied.

"One good shot?"

"One shot to end the fight. We took her sails to shreds."

"So she aims well, then," Skardey said.

Massayo shook his head. "The design is incomplete and crude. We were in a hurry. We had good fortune with that shot, and more than that, we had . . . her." He nodded to Quauh.

"My first mate here used the roll and pitch to call the shot," Massayo explained.

"Yrsa will make your shooting easier on the xebec," Skardey insisted.

Quah noted then that Massayo was offering nothing of *Pinquickle's Folly*'s second fight. No reason to spread the word of the *Cipac*'s demise until they were far south.

"And what of the ballistae?" Massayo asked. "The second deck?"

"She's tight down there," Yrsa admitted. "But fortune shows

that you have found the crew to work it. The powrie deck, I name it."

"And what's that meanin'?" Columbine asked.

"Do you like launching payloads at enemy ships?" Massayo asked.

"Aye, 'course!"

"Then it means you and your boys are going to have a grand time," Massayo said.

"Twelve to a side," said Yrsa. "Twenty-four throwers."

That brought some whispered conversations, but Quauh didn't listen in, too intent on Massayo. He was buying a very different kind of ship here than the usual pirate shore-running vessels. If she was understanding correctly, this was a warship, and one quite formidable.

"How long?" Massayo asked the Alpinadoran shipbuilders.

"She still needs her rigging and sails," said Skardey.

"We will be out of Freeport in the spring," Yrsa promised. "Before the spring if the winter winds come late."

"Did you get enough of the *caoutchou*?"

"She is lined inside already," Yrsa assured him. "We will be coating the hull the next time we bring her into the cave. I will not have any watching."

"Ye're lining her with rubber?" Benny asked.

"She'll be tighter than the coin purse of a Behrenese street vendor," Aushin blurted.

"Good one, Ohshit," McKorkle congratulated the young powrie. Aushin bobbed his head with a smile, which melted fast into a sigh as he registered the nickname attached to the cheer. Even his own buddies were taking up Benny's insult.

"It will not take us long," Yrsa promised. "You will see the pale purple sails gathering the wind beyond the harbor of Inudada before the year's longest day."

"If we have the means," Skardey added.

Massayo lifted a nearby sack and dropped it down to thump on the floor. "You have the means."

"I am painting her black," Yrsa remarked, and she leaned forward toward Massayo. "I am rather fond of the color. And I do not want your *caoutchou* coating to be obvious. Black! Shiny black, like Massayo's sweaty chest in the island heat."

Massayo considered it for a moment and nodded. "Who am I to tell the artist how to paint?"

"Trim her in gold," Quauh blurted.

"Who are you to tell the artist how to paint?" Skardey growled at her, as Yrsa swung around once more to stare at her, very close.

"Trim her in gold," Quauh quietly bade the shipwright. "It will be beautiful, and fitting this vessel."

"And it'll drive the goldfish crazy," Benny added, deflecting Skardey's next growl his way.

"I like this goldfish," Yrsa said, relieving the tension. She held Quauh's stare for a long while, her tongue playing hungrily with her fangs. Never looking back at the captain, she said, "I need a name."

"A name to shine in gold lettering across the stern," said Quauh, and Yrsa verily trembled at the thought, and for a moment, Quauh thought the woman might just bite her or something.

Massayo laughed and sat back, crossing his arms.

"Ye should call it *Benny's Gold*," an obviously grumpy Columbine scoffed. "As ye stole the booty to buy the damned thing."

"Then *Quauh's Gold*," Benny interjected with a scowl. "Was her own before mine."

But Massayo didn't seem concerned about Columbine's sourness at all and was shaking his head. "We have this wonderful animal running the jungles in Durubazzi. It is not the biggest creature, but it can outrun any predator and dodge any diving bird. You rarely see them, other than a flicker of shadow as they flash past you—unless they have eaten, and eaten well. Ah, then they proudly display themselves, splayed across the sun-warmed rocks. They want you to know that they have eaten, even if from your garden. They want you to see them, to want to catch them, because they know, and know that you know, that you cannot."

"What are ye babblin' about?" Columbine demanded.

"He's talking about us, and meself's likin' what he's sayin'," said McKorkle.

"*Fat Rabbit*," said Massayo.

Yrsa beamed. "*Fat Rabbit*," she echoed, nodding her approval. "With sails of mauve."

"And trimmed in gold," said Quauh.

"And glistening black," Yrsa answered her, flashing her those eyes and fangs one more time.

Massayo pulled a small pack from his back and produced

a rolled parchment. He spread it on the floor before him, then reached into the nearest sack and brought out four bars of gold to hold it flat by the corners. Next came a quill and an inkwell, which he set just beneath the parchment. A contract, Quauh realized.

"Shouldn't we wait for Chimeg and Toomsuba?" Quauh asked.

Massayo motioned her closer and pointed to the bottom of the parchment, to his signature and two others, those of Chimeg and Toomsuba.

"My original crew," he explained. "Co-conspirators, if you will. Include your title, if you will," he explained, handing the quill to Quauh.

"I'm in," McKorkle loudly announced as the other powries began to murmur. He turned to the young dwarf beside him. "And I'll give ye two points o' me first cut if ye sign it Ohshit instead of Aushin!"

"Done and done," Ohshit replied.

"Wait!" groused Columbine. "We got good gold in our pockets to walk away."

"There is enough right there to serve as your cut, and that of another," Massayo said, pointing to the four bars holding the parchment.

"He made ye the bosun," Perridoo argued.

Columbine shook his head, then slapped his hands in frustration against his ruddy cheeks. "Benny?"

"I'm owin' Cap'n Massayo too much to walk away," Benny explained. "I'm in, and if this ship . . . if *Fat Rabbit*'s as fast and dartin' as they're sayin', then who but Benny McBenoyt's fit for her wheel, eh?"

"Come on, then, Columbine," said McKorkle. "It's the best gig we e'er got. Who's to catch us if she's all they're saying, and who's wantin' to catch us with Chimeg flying about up top and filling their faces with arrows, eh?"

"Aye, and with the powrie deck launching giant spears at any tryin'," Ohshit reminded Columbine, then declared, "We'll take the whole damned coast!"

Columbine looked from one to the other, then to Massayo. His expression shifted a dozen times, but finally he sighed and declared, "Bosun Columbine reportin' for duty, Cap'n Massayo. Let's drive them pretty-faced goldfish crazy."

Quauh laughed.

The cheer that followed from the five powries was certainly too loud for Massayo's secretive heart, Quauh knew, but despite that, the man was smiling wider than she had ever seen.

"Make her everything you promised and more, my dear artist Yrsa," Massayo said. "We raise her red 'n' black on Hot Solstice Day in the harbor of Port Seur in Inudada."

Skardey blew out the candle and pulled open the hatch, and the seven began debarking back to the dinghy.

Last on was last out, Quauh crawling past Yrsa to the open hatch.

"You knew," Yrsa whispered to her. "You are of the sea."

"The western sea."

"This is the best I've ever done, from a dream that came to me again and again as a girl in Narvikkfjord in Alpinador, where the winds blow strong and cold all the year. The vision has haunted me—I do not expect to ever build another. There is nothing more for me to give. And you knew, and I am glad."

"She's the most beautiful vessel I've ever seen," Quauh replied, and she meant it. And wanted to be sailing on it, aye, and first mate would do . . .

. . . for now.

That impulsive notion hit the Xoconai sailor hard, mostly because she couldn't deny the sudden ambition. There had been no going back for a while now, of course, but now Quauh understood without any doubt at all, without fearing the disappointment in her Lahtli Ayot's voice, or the scorn of her fellow Tonoloya Armada officers, or anyone else in all the world.

She knew who she was now, the woman carved by talent and expectations for most of her life, and by the great change and opening of her eyes that had come through the circumstances of the last few weeks.

But now she had something more. Her plan had saved the crews of *Port Mandu* and *Pinquickle's Folly*.

Her plan. Not Massayo's, or Wilkie's.

Her plan.

Her demands for decency had spared hundreds of *Cipac*'s crew.

She knew who she was now, and rather fancied it.

She moved to debark, but was surprised when Yrsa pulled her close for a hug that nearly broke her back, and she felt the woman, this powerful, intimidating, competent, beautiful artist, sobbing on her shoulder.

"Trim her in gold," Quauh whispered into her ear. "Anything less would be an insult to the beauty of *Fat Rabbit*."

Quauh closed her eyes and swayed with the roll of the sea beneath her, feeling very much like she was home.

At long last.

ACKNOWLEDGMENTS

First, I have to thank Diane for insisting to me that I keep writing DemonWars. She knows what this world means to me and won't let me walk away until I'm ready!

Next, to Paul Lucas, my agent, who has supported expanding and strengthening all of the DemonWars series for years now. Perhaps it was the tone of my voice whenever discussing DemonWars—I don't know. But whatever the reason, these two understood how much I need to keep this world alive.

Enter Joe Monti, longtime convention friend, and now editor of Saga Books. Joe has always kept up on my work, and always had good words about DemonWars, even though he wasn't publishing them. When it became time to find a new home for these books, Joe made it easy. His enthusiasm and understanding of the world is what any author hopes for when signing those contracts.

So, a big thank you to Joe and the team at Saga for staying on top of every detail and working hard to make this new series the best it can be. And a special call-out to Valerie Shae, as thorough and tough a copyeditor as I've ever seen, and also one who respects the style of her victim . . . err, author.